# THE Heir

# GRACE BURROWES

sourcebooks
casablanca

Published by Sourcebooks Casablanca, an imprint of Sourcebooks,
Inc.
P.O. Box 4410, Naperville, Illinois 60567-4410
(630) 961-3900
FAX: (630) 961-2168
www.sourcebooks.com

Printed and bound in the United States of America
RRD 10 9

Dedicated to
The late Norman H. Lampman, the first person
Who honestly helped me with my writing,
And to loving families everywhere, of any description,
Most especially to the family who loves *me*.

# One

GAYLE WINDHAM, EARL OF WESTHAVEN, WAS ENJOYING a leisurely measure of those things that pleased him most: solitude, peace, and quiet.

The best plans were the simplest, he reflected as he poured himself a single finger of brandy, and his brother's suggestion that Westhaven hide in plain sight had proven brilliant. The unmarried heir to a dukedom had a nigh impossible task if he wanted to elude the predatory mamas and determined debutantes of polite society. He was in demand everywhere, and for form's sake, he had to be seen everywhere.

*But not this summer.* He smiled with relish. This summer, this stinking, infernally hot summer, he was going to remain right where he was, in the blessedly empty confines of London itself. Not for him the endless round of house parties and boating parties and social gatherings in the country.

His father had too free a hand in those environs, and Westhaven knew better than to give the duke any unnecessary advantage.

The Duke of Moreland was a devious, determined, unscrupulous old rogue. His goal in life was to see to it his heir married and produced sons, and Westhaven had made it a matter of pride to outwit the old man. There had already been one forced engagement, which the lady's family had thwarted at the last minute. One was more than enough. Westhaven was a dutiful son, conscientious in his responsibilities, a brother who could be relied upon, an heir more than willing to tend to the properties and investments as his father's power of attorney. He would not, however, be forced to marry some simpering little puppet to breed sons on her like a rutting hound.

And already, the pleasure of days and nights uncluttered by meaningless entertainments was bringing a certain cheer to Westhaven's normally reserved demeanor. He found himself noticing things, like the way his townhouse bore the fragrance of roses and honeysuckle, or how an empty grate was graced with a bouquet of flowers just for the pleasure of his eye. His solitary meals tasted more appealing; he slept better on his lavender-scented sheets. He heard his neighbor playing the piano late at night, and he caught the sound of laughter drifting up from his kitchen early in the morning.

*I would have made an exemplary monk*, he thought as he regarded the bowl of roses on the cold andirons. But then, monks had little solitude, and no recreational access to the fairer sex.

A modest exponent thereof silently entered the library, bobbed her little curtsy, and went about refilling the water in the several vases of flowers gracing the room. He watched her as she moved around without a sound, and wondered when she'd joined his household. She was a pretty little thing, with graceful ways and a sense of competence about her.

The chambermaid paused to water the flowers in the hearth, reaching over the fireplace screen to carefully top up the wide bowl of roses sitting on the empty grate. *Who would think to put flowers in a cold fireplace?* Westhaven wondered idly, but then he realized the chambermaid was taking rather too long to complete her task.

"Is something amiss?" he asked, not meaning to sound irritated but concluding he must have, for the girl flinched and cowered. She didn't, however, straighten up, make another curtsy, and leave him to his brandy.

"Is something amiss?" He spoke more slowly, knowing menials were not always of great understanding. The girl whimpered, an odd sound, not speech but an indication of distress. And she remained right where she was, bent over the hearth screen, her pitcher of water in her hand.

Westhaven set down his brandy and rose from his wing chair, the better to investigate the problem. The girl was making that odd sound continuously, which pleased him not at all. It wasn't as if he'd *ever* trifled with the help, for God's sake.

When he came near the hearth, the chambermaid positively cringed away from him, another irritant, but her movement allowed Westhaven to see the difficulty: The buttons on the front of her bodice were

caught in the mesh of the hearth screen. She wasn't tall
enough to set down her pitcher, leaving her only one
hand with which to free herself. That hand, however,
she needed for balance.

"Hush," Westhaven said more gently. He did have
five sisters, after all, and a mother; he understood
females were prone to dramatics. "I'll have you free
in no time, if you'll just hold still and turn loose of
this pitcher."

He had to pry the girl's fingers from the handle
of the pitcher, so overset was she, but still she said
nothing, just warbled her distress like a trapped animal.

"No need to take on so," he soothed as he reached
around her so he could slide his fingers along the
screen. "We'll have you free in a moment, and next
time you'll know to move the screen before you try to
water the flowers." It took an infernally long time, but
he had one button forced back through the screen and
was working on the other when the girl's whimpering
escalated to a moan.

"Hush," he murmured again. "I won't hurt you,
and I almost have your buttons free. Just hold still—"

The first blow landed across his shoulders, a searing
flash of pain that left his fine linen shirt and his skin
torn. The second followed rapidly, as he tightened his
arms protectively around the maid, and at the third,
which landed smartly on the back of his head, everything went black.

∾⚬∾

Westhaven moaned, causing both women to startle
then stare at him.

"St. Peter in a whorehouse," Westhaven muttered, bracing himself on his forearms and shaking his head. Slowly, he levered up to all fours then sat back on his heels, giving his head another shake.

He raised a ferocious scowl to survey the room, caught sight of the chambermaid, and then the other woman. His mind stumbled around for the proper associations. She worked for him but was entirely too young for her post. Mrs.... Every housekeeper was a Mrs....

Sidwell? He glared at her in concentration. Sommers... no. Seaton.

"Come here," he rasped at her. She was a sturdy thing, on the tall side, and always moving through the house at forced march. Cautiously, she approached him.

"Mrs. Seaton." He scowled at her thunderously. "I require your assistance."

She nodded, for once not looking quite so much like a general on campaign, and knelt beside him. He slid an arm around her shoulders, paused to let the pain of that simple movement ricochet around in his body, and slowly rose.

"My chambers," he growled, leaning on her heavily while his head cleared. She made no attempts at conversation, thank the gods, but paused to open the door to his room, and then again to carefully lower him to the settee flanking the hearth in his sitting room.

She turned to the chambermaid, who had followed them up the stairs. "Morgan, fetch the medical supplies, some hot water, and clean linens, and hurry."

Morgan nodded and disappeared, leaving the door slightly ajar.

"Silly twit," the earl muttered. "Does she think I'm in any condition to cause you mischief?"

"She does not, but there is no need to forego the proprieties."

"My privacy necessitates it," the earl bit out. "Moreover…" He paused, closed his eyes, and let out a slow breath. "As you tried to kill me, I don't think you're in a position to make demands, madam."

"I did not try to kill you," his housekeeper corrected him. "I attempted to protect your employee from what I thought were improper advances on the part of a guest."

He shot her a sardonic, incredulous look, but she was standing firm, arms crossed over her chest, eyes flashing with conviction.

"I sent word I would be returning from Morelands today," he said. "And the knocker isn't up. You misjudged."

"The post has not arrived for the past two days, your lordship. The heat seems to have disrupted a number of normal functions, and as to that, your brother does not observe the niceties when he is of a mind to see you."

"You thought *my brother* would bother a chambermaid?"

"He is friendly, my lord." Mrs. Seaton's bosom heaved with her point. "And Morgan is easily taken advantage of." Morgan reappeared, bobbing another curtsy at the earl then depositing the requested medical supplies on the low table before the settee.

"Thank you, Morgan." Mrs. Seaton looked right at the maid when she spoke, and her words were formed deliberately. "A tea tray, now, and maybe a muffin or some cookies to go with it."

A *muffin*? Westhaven felt his lips wanting to quirk. She was going to treat a bashed skull with tea and crumpets?

"If you would sit on the table, my lord?" Mrs. Seaton wasn't facing *him* as she spoke. "I can tend to your back and your... scalp."

Damn it all to hell, he needed her help just to rise, shift his weight, and sit on the coffee table. Each movement sent white-hot pain lancing through his skull and across his shoulders. For all that, he barely felt it as Mrs. Seaton deftly unbuttoned his shirt, tugged it free of his waistband, and eased it away.

"This is ruined, I'm afraid."

"Shirts can be replaced," the earl said. "My father rather has plans for me, however, so let's get me patched up."

"You were coshed with a fireplace poker," Mrs. Seaton said, bending over him to sift through the hair above his nape. "These wounds will require careful cleaning."

She wadded up his shirt and folded it to hold against the scalp wound.

"Passive voice," the earl said through clenched teeth, "will not protect you, Mrs. Seaton, since you did the coshing. Jesus and the apostles, that hurts." Her hand came up to hold his forehead even as she continued to press the linen of his ruined shirt against the bleeding wound.

"The bleeding is slowing down," she said, "and the wounds on your back are not as messy."

"Happily for me," her patient muttered. Her hand bracing his forehead had eased the pain considerably, and there was something else, too. A scent, flowery but also fresh, a hint of mint and rosemary that sent a cool remembrance of summer pleasures through his awareness.

A soft hand settled on his bare shoulder, but then she was tormenting him again, this time with disinfectant that brought the fires of hell raging across his back.

"Almost done," she said quietly some moments later, but Westhaven barely heard her through the roaring in his ears. When his mind cleared, he realized he was leaning into her, his face pressed against the soft curve of her waist, his shoulders hunched against the length of her thigh.

"That's the worst of it," she said, her hand again resting on his shoulder. "I am sorry, you know." She sounded genuinely contrite now—now that he was suffering mortal agonies and the loss of his dignity, as well.

"I'll mend."

"Would you like some laudanum?" Mrs. Seaton lowered herself to kneel before him, her expression concerned. "It's not encouraged for head injuries."

"I have been uncomfortable before. I'll manage," the earl said. "But you will have to get me into a dressing gown and fetch my correspondence from the library."

"A dressing gown?" Her finely arched sable eyebrows flew up. "I'll fetch a footman, perhaps, or Mr. Stenson."

"Can't." Westhaven tried to maneuver himself back onto the settee. "Stenson stayed at Morelands, as His

Grace's man had some time off, and no footmen or butler either, as it's the men's half-day." Faced with that logic, Mrs. Seaton wrapped her arm around the earl's waist and assisted him to change his seat.

"A dressing gown it is, then." She capitulated easily, leaving him staring at her retreating figure as she went to fetch his garment.

&

How hard could it be to drape a dressing gown over a set of bare, masculine shoulders? Except seeing the earl, Anna had to refine on her question: A set of unbelievably well-muscled, broad, bare shoulders, God help her.

Anna had, of course, noticed her employer on occasion in the weeks she'd been in his household. He was a handsome man, several inches over six feet, green-eyed, with dark chestnut hair and features that bore the patrician stamp of aristocratic breeding. She put his age at just past thirty but had formed no opinion of him as a person. He came and went at all hours, seldom invading the lowest floor, closeting himself for long periods in his library with his man of business or other gentlemen.

He liked order, privacy, and regular meals. He ate prodigious amounts of food but never drank to excess. He went to his club on Wednesdays and Fridays, his mistress on Tuesday and Thursday afternoons. He had volumes of Byron and Blake in his library, and read them late at night. He had a sweet tooth and a fondness for his horse. He was tired more often than not, as his father had put the ducal finances in severe disarray before tossing his heir the reins, and righting that situation took much of the earl's time.

Westhaven appeared to have an exasperated sort of affection for his lone surviving brother, Valentine, and grieved still for the two brothers who had died.

He had no friends but knew everybody.

And he was being pressured to take a wife, hence this stubborn unwillingness to leave Town in the worst heat wave in memory.

These thoughts flitted through Anna's mind in the few moments it took her to rummage in the earl's wardrobe and find a silk dressing gown of dark blue. She'd bandaged his back, but if the scalp wound should reopen and start bleeding, the color of the fabric would hide any stain.

"Will this do, my lord?" She held up the dressing gown when she returned to his sitting room, and frowned at him. "You are pale, *methinks*. Can you stand?"

"Boots off first, *methinks*," he replied, hefting one large foot onto the coffee table. Anna's lips pressed together in displeasure, but she deposited the dressing gown on the settee and pushed the coffee table over at an angle. She tugged at his boots, surprised to find they weren't painted onto him, as most gentlemen's riding boots were.

"Better." He wiggled his bare toes when she'd peeled off his socks. "If you would assist me?" He held out an arm, indicating his desire to rise. Anna braced him and slowly levered him up. When he was on his feet, they stood linked like that for a long moment before Anna reached over and retrieved the dressing gown. She worked awkwardly, sliding it up one arm, then the other, before getting it draped across his shoulders.

"Can you stand unassisted?" she asked, still not liking his pallor.

"I can." But she saw him swallow against the pain. "My breeches, Mrs. Seaton."

She wasn't inclined to quibble when he looked ready to keel over at any minute, but as she deftly unfastened the fall of his trousers, she realized he intended for her to *undress* him. Did a man ask a woman he was going to charge with attempted murder to help him out of his clothes?

"Sometime before I reach my eternal reward, if it wouldn't be too great an imposition."

In his expression, Anna perceived he wasn't bothered by their enforced proximity anywhere near as much as she was, and so she unceremoniously shoved his waistband down over his hips.

Dear God, *the man wasn't wearing any smalls.* Blushing furiously, she wasn't prepared for him to thrust an arm across her shoulders and balance on her as he carefully lifted first one foot then the other free of his clothing. Again, he lost momentum as pain caught up with him, and for the space of two slow, deep breaths, he leaned on her heavily, his dressing gown gaping open over his nudity, his labored breathing soughing against her cheek.

"Steady," she murmured, reaching for the ends of the belt looping at his waist. She tucked his dressing gown closed and knotted it securely, but not before she'd seen...

She would never, *ever* stop blushing. Not ever, if she lived to be as old as Granny Fran, who sat in the kitchen telling stories that went back to old German George.

"To bed, I think," the earl said, his voice sounding strained.

She nodded, anchored her arm around his middle, and in small steps, walked him into the next room and up to the steps surrounding his great, canopied bed.

"Rest a minute," he bit out, leaning on her mightily. She left him propped against the foot of the bed and folded down his covers.

"On your stomach will likely be less uncomfortable, my lord." He nodded, his gaze fixed on the bed with grim determination. Anna took up her position at his side, and by careful steps, soon had him standing at the head of the bed. She turned so their backs were to the bed and sat with him on the mattress.

He paused again, his arm around her shoulders, catching his breath.

"My correspondence," he reminded her.

She gave him a dubious scowl but nodded. "Don't move, your lordship. You don't want to fall and hit your head again."

❧

She took her leave at the stirring pace Westhaven associated with her, leaving him to admire the view again and consider her advice—were he to die, his brother Valentine would not forgive him. Carefully, he toed the chamber pot from under the bed, made use of it, replaced the lid as quietly as he could by hooking the handle with his toes, then pushed it back out of sight.

God, he thought as he gave his cock a little shake, his housekeeper had seen the ducal family jewels…

He should have been wroth with indignation, to be subjected to her perusal, but all he felt was amusement and a vague gratitude she would provide him the care he needed. She could have sent for a physician, of course, but Westhaven hated doctors, and his housekeeper must have known it.

Reaching across the bed carefully, he rearranged pillows so he could rest on his side. That movement so pained his back, that when his housekeeper returned, he was still sitting on the bed.

He arched an eyebrow. "Tea?"

"It can't hurt," she replied, "and I brought iced lemonade, as well, as the warehouse just stocked your icehouse this morning."

"Lemonade, then."

His rooms were at the back of the house, heavily shaded and high-ceilinged. They remained particularly comfortable, probably because the clerestory windows had been left open, the better to draw the heat up and out.

Mrs. Seaton handed him a tall, sweating glass, which he sipped cautiously. She'd sugared it generously, so he took a larger sip.

"You aren't having any?" he asked, watching as she moved around the room.

"You are my employer." She went to the night table and retrieved a pitcher, giving the little bouquet in the window a drink. "Your roses are thirsty."

"So is it you who has turned my house into a flower shop?" Westhaven asked as he finished his drink.

"I have. You have a very pretty house, my lord. Flowers show it to advantage."

"You will waken me if I fall asleep for more than an hour or so?" he asked, unable to reach the nightstand to place his glass on the tray. She took the glass from his hand and met his eyes.

"I will check on you each hour until daybreak, my lord, but as you had neither tea nor supper, I think you had best try a little food before you lie down."

He eyed the tray whereupon Mrs. Seaton had set a plate sporting a big, sugary muffin that looked to be full of berries.

"Half of that." He nodded warily. "And sit if you please." He thumped the mattress. "I cannot abide a fluttering female."

"You sound like your father sometimes, you know," she said as she sliced the muffin in half and took her place beside him. "Imperious."

"Ridiculous, you mean," he said as he glanced skeptically again at the muffin then tried a bite.

"He is not ridiculous, but some of his machinations are."

"My housekeeper is a diplomat"—the earl sent her a sardonic smile—"who makes passably edible muffins. Might as well eat the whole thing rather than waste half."

"Would you like some butter on this half?"

"A touch. How is it you know of my father's machinations?"

"There is always gossip below stairs." She shrugged, but then must have realized she was perilously close to overstepping. She paused as she slathered butter on his muffin. "It is said he spies on you at your regular appointments."

"What is ridiculous," the earl retorted, "is to think the old rascal is tricking the young ladies who waylay me at every social function, Mrs. Seaton. Those lambs go willingly to slaughter in hopes of becoming my duchess. I won't have it." And as for spies in his mistress's house, Westhaven thought darkly... Ye gods. "Despite my father's scheming, I will choose my own duchess, thank you very much. Did you bring up only one of these things?" He waved his last bite of muffin at her.

"On the off chance that they were passably edible, I brought up two. A touch more butter?" She withdrew the second muffin from the linen lining a little basket at the side of the tray.

He caught her eye, saw the humor in it, and found his own lips quirking.

"Just a touch. And perhaps a spot more lemonade."

"You aren't going to have me brought up on charges, are you?" She posed the question casually then frowned, as if it had come out of her mouth all unintended.

"Oh, that's a splendid notion," the earl said as he accepted the second muffin. "Tell the whole world the Moreland heir was subdued by his housekeeper who thought he was trying to molest a chambermaid in his own home."

"Well, you were. And it wasn't well done of you, my lord."

"Mrs. Seaton." He glared down his nose at her. "I do not accost women under my protection. Her buttons were caught in the mesh of the screen, and she could not free herself. Nothing more."

"Her buttons…?" Her hand went to her mouth, and in her expression, Westhaven could see his explanation put a very different light on her conclusions. "My lord, I beg your pardon."

"I'll mend, Mrs. Seaton." He almost smiled at her distress. "Next time, a simple 'My lord, what are you about?' might spare us both a great lot of indignity." He handed her his glass. "I will have my revenge, though."

"You will?"

"I will. I make a terrible patient."

❧

Anna was dozing off after dark when she heard the earl call her from the other room.

"My lord?"

"In here, and I will not shout in my own home for the attention of my own staff."

Oh, he was going to make a perfectly insufferable duke, she fumed as she got to her feet and crossed to his bedroom. "What can I do for you?" she asked as pleasantly as she could.

"I am loathe to attempt the use of pen and ink while recumbent," he said, peering at her over wire-rimmed spectacles. "If you'd please fetch the lap desk and attend me?"

"Of course." Anna disappeared into the sitting room to retrieve the lap desk, but returned to the bed only to realize there was no chair for her to sit upon.

"The end of the bed will do." The earl gestured impatiently. Anna permitted herself to toss him a peevish look—a very peevish look, given the impropriety—but scuffed out of her slippers and climbed on the bed to sit cross-legged, her back against a bedpost.

"You are literate?" the earl asked, inspecting her again over his glasses.

"In French, English, and Latin, with a smattering of German, Gaelic, Welsh, and Italian."

His eyebrows rose momentarily at her tart reply, but he gave her a minute to get settled then began to slowly recite a memorandum to one of his land stewards, commending the man for progress made toward a sizeable crop of hay and suggesting irrigation ditches become a priority while the corn was maturing.

Another letter dealt with port sent to Morelands at the duke's request.

Yet another went to the widow of a man who'd held the living at one of the estate villages, expressing sorrow for her loss. And so it went, until a sizeable stack of correspondence was completed and the hour approaching midnight.

"Are you tired, Mrs. Seaton?" the earl asked as Anna paused to trim the pen.

"Serving as amanuensis is not that taxing, my lord," she said, and it hadn't been. His voice was beautiful, a mellifluous baritone that lost its habitual hauteur when he was concentrating on communication, leaving crisp consonants and round, plummy vowels redolent of education and good, prosperous breeding.

"Would that my man of business were so gracious," the earl said. "If you are not fatigued, then perhaps I can trouble you to fetch some libation from the kitchen. Speaking at such length tires the voice, or I wouldn't ask it."

"Is there anything else I could get you from the kitchen?" she asked, setting the desk on the night table.

"Perhaps one of those muffins," he allowed. "My digestion is tentative, but the last one stayed down easily enough."

"The last two," she said over her shoulder.

⌒⌒

He let her have the last word—or two—and also let himself enjoy the sight of her retreating backside again. He'd put her age well below thirty. The Corsican's years of mischief had left a record crop of widows in many lands, perhaps including his housekeeper.

And more than just young, he was seeing for the first time that she was pretty. Oh, she didn't emphasize it, no sane woman in service would. But to the earl's discerning eye, her drab gowns hid a marvelous figure, one enforced proximity had made all too apparent to him. Her hair was a lustrous shade of dark brown, shot with red and gold highlights, and her eyes a soft, luminous gray. The cast of her features was slightly exotic—Eastern, Mediterranean, or even Gypsy. She was the antithesis of his mistress, a petite, blond, blue-eyed woman who circulated easily on the fringes of polite society.

He wondered on a frown why he'd chosen a diminutive woman for his intimate attentions, as tall women fit him better. But then, finding a mistress of any description was no easy feat. Given his station, the earl was unwilling to frequent brothels. He was equally loathe to take his chances on the willing widows, knowing they would trap him in marriage just as quickly as their younger counterparts would.

So that left him with Elise, at least when she was in Town.

Still frowning, he picked up an epistle from his brother, who was standing guard at Morelands while the duke and duchess enjoyed a two-week holiday there. Valentine was happiest in the country, playing his piano at all hours and riding the countryside.

The man was no fribble, though, and he'd appended a little postscript to his report: "The land you rent on Tambray is being ploughed, if not planted, by Renfrew in your absence. One wonders to whom the harvest will fall."

Elise's rented house was on Tambray Street, and Baron Renfrew was one of those fun-loving, randy young lords the ladies doted on. Well, let Elise have her fun, the earl mused, as his arrangement with her was practical. When they were both in Town, he expected her to be available to him by appointment; otherwise, she was free to disport where she pleased, as was he.

If he had the time—and the inclination—which, lately anyway, he did not.

"Your drink, my lord." Mrs. Seaton placed a tray on the foot of the bed and held a glass out for him.

He glanced at the tray then regarded her thoughtfully. "I believe it might be more comfortable on the balcony, Mrs. Seaton."

"As you wish, my lord." She set the glass back on the tray, opened the French doors, and shifted to stand beside his bed. Carefully, he levered himself over to the side of the bed and waited for her to sit beside him and slip an arm around his waist.

"What is that scent?" he asked, pausing when she would have risen.

"I make my own," she said, glancing over at him. "Mostly lavender, with a few other notes. It turned out particularly well this year, I think."

He leaned in and sniffed at her, assessing.

"Lavender and something sweet," he decided, ignoring the presumptuousness of his gesture. "Lilies?"

"Perhaps." Mrs. Seaton was blushing, her gaze on her lap. "The details will shift, depending on one's sense of smell, and also with the ambient scents."

"You mean with what I'm wearing? Hadn't thought of that. Hmm."

He gave her another little sniff then squared his shoulders to rise. To his unending disgust, he had to steady himself momentarily on his housekeeper's shoulder. "Proceed," he said when his head had stopped swimming. They were soon out in the silky summer darkness of his balcony.

"Honeysuckle," he said, apropos of nothing but the night air.

"There is some of that," Mrs. Seaton said as they closed in on a padded wicker chaise. His balcony overlooked the back gardens, and a soft breeze was stirring the scents from the flowers below.

"Sit with me," the earl said as he settled onto the chaise. Mrs. Seaton paused in her retreat, and something in her posture alerted him to his overuse of the imperative. "Please," he added, unable to keep a hint of amusement from his tone.

"You were not born to service," the earl surmised as his housekeeper took a seat on a wicker rocking chair.

"Minor gentry," she concurred. "Very minor."

"Brothers and sisters?"

"A younger sister and an older brother. Your lemonade, my lord?"

"Please," he replied, recalling he'd sent her down two flights in the dark of night to fetch it.

But it was a moonless night and dark as pitch on the balcony, so when Mrs. Seaton retrieved the drink, she reached for his fingers with her free hand and wrapped his grip around the glass.

"You are warm," she said, a frown in her voice. She reached out again, no doubt expecting to put the back of her hand against his forehead but instead connecting with his cheek. "I beg your pardon." She snatched back her hand. "Do you think you are becoming fevered?"

"I am not," he replied tersely, setting down his drink. He reached for her hand and brought it to his forehead. "No warmer than the circumstances dictate."

He felt—or thought he felt—her fingers smooth back his hair before she resumed her seat. The gesture was no doubt intended as maternal, and it was likely Elise's protracted absence that had him experiencing it as something much less innocent.

"How is your head, my lord?"

"Hurts like blue blazes. My back is on fire, and I won't be wrestling my chestnut geldings any time soon, either. You pack quite a wallop, considering the worst I could have done in broad daylight was perhaps grope the girl."

This recitation inspired his housekeeper to a very quiet yawn.

"Is my company that tiresome, Mrs. Seaton?" He wasn't offended, but neither had he intended his tone to come out sounding so wistful.

"My day is long in your service, my lord. We do a big market on Wednesday, and Cook and I spend much of the day laying it in, as the men aren't underfoot to bother us."

"So you are tired," he concluded. "Go rest, Mrs. Seaton. The settee in my sitting room will do, and I'll call when I need your assistance." She rose but hesitated, as if filling her sails for a lecture about propriety and decency and other virtues known mostly to domestics.

"Go, Mrs. Seaton," he urged. "I treasure my solitude, and I have much to think about. I will not fall asleep out here, and you need to at least nap. Were you anybody but my housekeeper, you'd know the Earl of Westhaven has no need to bother his help."

That must have appeased her or spiked her guns, for she departed, leaving Westhaven to sip his tea and enjoy his thoughts.

Her scent, he reflected, blended beautifully with the summer night air. It made a man want to nibble on her, to see if she tasted of lavender, roses, and honeysuckle. He cast back, trying to recall when he'd hired the pretty, younger-than-she-should-be, more-protective-than-she-needed-to-be, Mrs. Seaton. Early spring, perhaps, when he'd made the decision to leave the ducal townhouse, lest he strangle his dear papa and the endless parade of shirttail cousins his mama trooped past him for consideration as his broodmare.

The whole business was demeaning. He understood his parents, having lost two sons, were desperate for progeny from their two remaining legitimate sons. He understood Val affected a preference for men—at least he claimed it was an affectation—rather than suffer the duke's importuning. He understood Devlin would be years recovering from Waterloo and the Peninsular War.

He did not understand though, how—given that the ducal responsibilities took every spare hour and minute—he was going to find the time to locate a woman he could tolerate not just in his bed but as the mother of his children and his companion at the breakfast table.

❧

"Westhaven!" Elise flew across her sitting room, arms outstretched to envelope him in an enthusiastic hug. "Did you miss me?" She squeezed him to her ample bosom and kissed his cheek. "I have expired for lack of you, Westhaven." She kept her hands wrapped around his arm, pressing her breast to his bicep as she did. "A month is too long, isn't it? I'm sure you were very naughty in my absence, but I'm here now, and you needn't go baying at the moon for lack of me."

She was tugging at his clothing, her mouth chattering on, and Westhaven knew a moment's impatience. Desire was a bodily craving, like fatigue or hunger or physical restlessness. He tended to it, usually twice a week, sometimes more, and lately less. It had been mildly alarming to find Elise's departure for a month-long house party had inconvenienced him not one bit.

But she was back, and it had been a month, and his clothes were rapidly accumulating in a pile on the floor.

"Elise," he said, stilling her hands, "you know I don't like to be untidy."

"But you do like to be naked," Elise quipped, bending to scoop up his shirt, waistcoat, and cravat. She dumped them over the back of a chair and pushed him onto her fainting couch, the better to extricate him from his boots. "And I like to get you naked." Like a small, blond fury, Elise finished peeling him out of his clothes, showing an enthusiasm he didn't usually find in her.

"You've added flesh," she observed when she'd thrown his breeches onto the chair, as well. "You aren't as skinny, Westhaven. Oh, and look, you are glad to see me."

His cock was glad to see her, anyway. Glad enough that when she pushed him onto his back on her silly red bed, he could concede a month of celibacy had been enough.

"Let me taste you." Elise was still in her dressing gown, but she climbed onto the bed and knelt at his hip.

Now this was something new. Elise liked having him for a protector, liked thinking the heir to a dukedom had chosen her for his pleasures. She did not, however, particularly like him or like sex. These factors bothered him a little, but no more than they bothered her. In many ways, it was easier if she wasn't personally attached to him, nor he to her.

Her tongue lapped at his cock, the sensations tantalizing and more arousing than the rest of Elise's repertoire of foreplay put together. Elise, however, had been reluctant to indulge him thus previously, so with her, he usually contented himself with more pedestrian sexual play. The lapse of time since they'd last been together, and the enthusiastic efforts of her mouth, combined to undermine his usual self-discipline.

"I'll come in your mouth, Elise," he warned her several minutes later. "When you suck on my cock, it tempts me—"

"You'll do no such thing." Elise glanced up at him sharply, alarm flitting across her face. She opened her dressing gown and lay down on the mattress beside him. "You can't have all the fun, Westhaven."

She obligingly spread her legs, so he rolled and settled himself over her.

"I take care of you, Elise," he said, nuzzling at her neck. She wasn't much of one for kissing on the mouth, but she tolerated attention to her breasts fairly well.

"You do," she agreed, arching up against him. "Though you take your damned time about it." The words were teasing, but something in her tone was petulant, ungracious, so he dispensed with further preliminaries and found the entrance to her body with his cock.

"I will assume"—he began to rock his way to a fuller penetration—"you have simply missed your pleasures, Elise."

"I have," she said, wrapping her legs around his flanks and locking her ankles at the small of his back. "Now fuck my feeble brains out and cease jabbering."

His cock liked that idea just fine, but in the part of him that always watched, always considered, something about Elise felt just the slightest degree *off*. Her enthusiasm didn't seemed feigned, exactly, but neither was it… warm.

"Harder," she urged, flexing her hips to meet his thrusts. "I want it rough today, Westhaven."

*Rough?* Where in the hell did that come from? He obligingly thrust harder and felt his own arousal ratchet up. Elise's heels dug into his spine, though, and the distraction allowed him to hold back his orgasm as he listened for hers to approach.

"Oh, God…" Elise was flailing her hips at him desperately, her passion a welcome and uncharacteristic display. "God damn you, Westhaven…"

She bucked against him harder, until he felt his own climax bearing down on him. He held off until he was sure Elise had found her pleasure in full then arched his back to withdraw.

Elise held him all the more tightly, her legs vised around his waist.

With a sudden wrench, he broke her scissor hold and lunged back.

"What in God's name are you doing?" he roared. He sat back on his heels, panting with frustrated lust, while Elise stared up at him, eyes dazed with passion and anger.

"Why?" she yelled back. "Why for once couldn't you just come like most men and not be so goddamned careful? You can't just fuck, Westhaven. You have to be a damned duke even in this!"

"What on earth are you going on about?" He

speared her with an incredulous look. "You know my terms, Elise, and…"

He watched her face, and realization dawned.

"Oh, Elise." He climbed to the side of the bed and sat with his back to her, lungs heaving. "You let Renfrew plant his bastard in your belly and hoped to pass it off as mine." He didn't need to see her eyes to know he'd come across yet another ducal ploy to trap him into marriage. Renfrew was tall, green-eyed, brown-haired, and randy as a goat.

"His Grace promised…" Elise wailed quietly. "His man said if I conceived, the duke would see us wed."

Westhaven shook his head in exasperation, "Elise, the duke would not have seen us wed when I told him the child was Renfrew's."

"And how would he have known that?"

"I am not stupid, Elise, and I have never spent my seed inside you. My father would believe me in that much, at least," he said as he rose.

"Where are you going?" She sat up, closing the dressing gown around her as if he might peek at her nakedness.

"I am going to take a cold bath, I suppose." He began to sort through his clothes. "Would you prefer diamonds, emeralds, or rubies?"

"All of the above," she replied, crossing her arms over her chest. "You were a damned lot of work, Westhaven."

"Was I really?" He was momentarily nonplussed by the thought but then resumed dressing. "How so?"

"This is just sex." Elise waved her hand at the bedroom in general. "But still, it's sex with another *person*."

"You don't think I know you are a person? I didn't see to your pleasure?" he asked, more curious than he wanted to let on.

"You." She glared at him with reluctant affection. "You probably had a list in your pocket as you set out today: Replace right hind shoe on gelding; draft terms for running the universe; visit Elise; meet cronies at the club. Except you don't have cronies. And when you get here," she ranted on, "kiss her cheek, and carefully disrobe. After folding each article of clothing precisely *so*, twiddle her bubbies, twiddle her couche, insert cock, and stir briskly for five minutes. Oh"—she threw up her hands—"just forget I opened my mouth."

"Twiddle, Elise?" Westhaven said, sitting next to her on the bed. "I perceive you are disappointed in me, but twiddle is a bit harsh. And given your sentiments, perhaps it's best you aren't going to be my duchess, hmm?"

"Yes." She nodded. "I would likely have killed you, Westhaven, though you aren't a bad fellow underneath it all."

"A ringing endorsement." He rose then turned and studied her. "What will you do, Elise? Renfrew is pockets to let, for all that he's a good time."

"I don't know, but I'd appreciate it if you'd give me some time to figure it out."

"Take all the time you need." He hugged her, a simple, affectionate gesture that seemed somehow appropriate. "I believe I'll swear off mistresses for the nonce, and the lease here is paid up through the year, so you might as well put the place to use."

"Most generous. Now be gone with you." Elise shoved him away from her. "I'm swearing off titles. I'll find myself a rich, climbing cit and get the blighter to marry me, bastard and all."

"Seriously, Elise." He paused to force her to meet his eyes. "I'll provide if there's a child. You will allow it." He put every ounce of ducal authority into his expression, and she visibly shrank from his gaze.

"I will." She nodded, swallowing.

"Then good-bye." He bowed, as if they'd just shared a waltz, and kissed her cheek.

Westhaven left his mistress's pretty little house, thinking he should have been angry with Elise and most especially with his father. The duke, though, had simply covered a logical base: If Westhaven were already swiving a woman, it made sense that woman was the most likely to conceive his child.

But Elise, as a mother? Good God… His Grace must be getting senile.

Mentally, Westhaven found himself adding to his list of tasks to complete: Send parting gift to Elise, diamonds, emeralds, and rubies, if possible; replace Elise; draft epistle to His Grace, decrying his suborning of bastardy.

And had Val not sent him an alert, would Westhaven have seen through Elise's ploy?

He should just damned marry, he thought as he gained the steps to his townhouse. But if finding a mistress had been difficult, finding a woman worthy to be his duchess *and his wife* was going be almost impossible.

"The prodigal returns," a voice sang out in his front hallway.

"Valentine?" Westhaven found himself smiling at his younger brother, who lounged in the doorway to the library. "You left our sire unsupervised? Our sisters unprotected?"

"I'm up only for the weekend." Val shoved away from the door and extended a hand. "I got to fretting about you, and His Grace is under the supervision of Her Grace, which should be adequate for a few days."

"Fretting about me?"

"I overheard Renfrew bragging." Val turned to lead his brother into the library. "Then it occurred to me my note was perhaps not clear enough."

"Elise and I have come to an amicable if somewhat costly parting. I will call upon Renfrew in the near future to suggest, quite discreetly, that should he see fit to precede me into holy matrimony, a token of my good wishes would be forthcoming."

Val whistled. "Elise was playing a desperate game. The girl has cheek."

"She and Renfrew would understand each other," Westhaven said, "and I've been looking for a way to unload Monk's Crossing. It takes two weeks each year just to put in an appearance there, and it isn't as if we're lacking for properties."

"Why not sell what isn't entailed? You wear yourself out, Gayle, trying to keep track of it all and staying on top of His Grace's queer starts."

"I have sold several properties that were only marginally producing, and I should be doing a better job of keeping you informed of such developments, as you are, dear Brother, the spare of record."

"Yes," Val said, holding up a hand, "as in, 'spare

me.' I'll pay attention if you insist, but please do not intimate to His Grace I give a hearty goddamn for any of it."

"Ah." Westhaven smiled, going to the sideboard to pour them each a finger of brandy. "Except you do. How are the manufactories coming?"

"I don't think of them as manufactories, but we're managing."

"Business is good?" Westhaven asked, hoping he wasn't offending his brother.

"Business in the years immediately following decades of war is going to be unpredictable," Val said, accepting his drink. "People want pleasure and beauty and relief from their cares, and music provides that. But there is also a widespread lack of coin."

"In some strata," Westhaven agreed. "But organizations, like schools and churches and village assemblies are not quite as susceptible to that lack of coin, and they all buy pianos."

"So they do." Val saluted his brother with his glass. "I hadn't thought of that, because I myself have never performed in such venues, but you are right. This confirms, of course, my bone-deep conviction you are better suited to the dukedom than I."

"Because I have one minimally useful idea?" Westhaven asked, going to the bell pull.

"Because you think about things, endlessly, and in depth. I used to think you were slow."

"I am slow, compared to the rest of the family, but I have my uses."

"You don't honestly believe that. You are not as outgoing as our siblings, perhaps, but we lack your ability to concentrate on a problem until the damned thing lies in tiny pieces at our mental feet."

Westhaven set aside his drink. "Perhaps, but we needn't stand here throwing flowers at each other, when we could be stuffing ourselves with muffins and lemonade."

"Traveling does give one a thirst, and it is hotter than blazes, even at Morelands. Speaking of flowers, though, your establishment has benefited from the warmer weather." He nodded at the flowers around the room.

"My housekeeper," Westhaven said, going to the door to order tea. "Mrs. Seaton is…"

"Yes?" Westhaven saw Val was watching him closely, as only a sibling alert to the subtleties might.

"One can keep a house tidy," Westhaven said, "and one can make it… homey. She does both."

He'd noticed it, after his mishap with the fireplace poker earlier in the week. If he looked closely, the details were evident: The windows weren't just clean, they sparkled. The woodwork gleamed and smelled of lemon oil and beeswax; the carpets all looked freshly sanded and beaten; the whole house was free of dust and clutter. And more subtly, air moved through the rooms on softly fragrant currents.

"She must be feeding you properly, as well," Val noted. "You've lost some of that perpetually lean and hungry look."

"That is a function of simply having my own home for the past few months. His Grace wears on one, and our sisters, while dear, destroy a man's peace regularly."

"His Grace sets a very childish example." Val put his empty glass back on the sideboard. "I think you do well being both brother and earl, and you did better getting the damned power of attorney from him and corralling his ridiculous impulses where they can do little harm. That was particularly well done of you, Westhaven."

"At too high a price."

"But you didn't end up marrying the lady," Val pointed out, "so all's well."

"All will not be well until I have presented His Grace with several legitimate grandsons, and even then, he'll probably still want more." He went to the French doors overlooking his terrace as he spoke.

"He'll die eventually," Val said. "Almost did last winter, in fact."

"He was brought down more by the quacks who bled him incessantly than by lung fever itself." Westhaven glanced over his shoulder at his brother and scowled. "If I am ever seriously ill, Valentine, you must promise to keep the damned quacks and butchers away from me. A comely nurse and the occasional medicinal tot, but otherwise, leave it in the hands of the Almighty." He swiveled his gaze back to the terrace and watched as Mrs. Seaton appeared, baskets and shears in hand while she marched to the cutting garden along one low stone wall.

"You put me on the spot." Val smiled. "Do you honestly think I wouldn't do everything in my power to keep you alive, despite your wishes to the contrary?"

"Then pray for my continued good health." Mrs. Seaton was bareheaded today, her dark mane pulled back into a thick knot at her nape. By firelight, he knew, there were red highlights in that hair.

Lemonade arrived, complete with fat muffins, fresh bread with butter, sliced meats and cheese, sliced fruit, and a petite bouquet of violets on the tray. Nestled in a little folded square of linen were four pieces of marzipan, glazed to resemble fruit.

"This is tea at your house of late?" Val arched an eyebrow. "No wonder you look a bit more the thing. I will move in directly, provided you promise to tune the piano."

"You should, you know," Westhaven said. He was putting together a plate, but his words had come out far less casually than he'd planned. "I know you don't like staying at the ducal manse, and I have more than enough room here."

"Wouldn't want to impose," Val said, reaching for his own share of the bounty, "but that's generous of you."

"Not generous. The truth is... I could use the company. I miss your music, in fact. There's a neighbor, or somebody, who plays late at night, but it isn't you, for all that I enjoy it. I thought I'd have a harder time keeping track of His Grace were I to set up my own place, but I've been surprised at how little effort he makes to elude my scrutiny."

The door opened without the obligatory knock, and Mrs. Seaton marched into the room.

"I beg your pardon, your lordship, Lord Valentine." She stopped, her basket of flowers bouncing against her skirts. "My lord, I thought you'd be at your appointment until this evening."

*Twiddling my mistress's bubbies*, Westhaven thought with a lift of an eyebrow.

"Mrs. Seaton." Val rose, smiling as if he knew he was viewing the source of his brother's happier household and healthier appearance. "My compliments on the offerings to be had here for tea, and the house itself looks marvelous."

"Mrs. Seaton." The earl rose more slowly, the display of manners hardly necessary for a housekeeper.

"My lords." She curtsied but came up frowning at Westhaven. "Forgive me if I note you rise slowly. Are you well?"

The earl glanced at his brother repressively.

"My brother is not in good health?" Val asked, grinning. "Do tell."

"I merely suffered a little bump on the head," the earl said, "and Mrs. Seaton spared me the attentions of the physicians."

Mrs. Seaton was still frowning, but the earl went on, forestalling her reply. "You may tend to your flowers, Mrs. Seaton, and I echo my brother's compliments: Tea is most pleasant."

"I'll dice you for the marzipan," Val said to the earl.

"No need," Mrs. Seaton offered over her shoulder. "We keep a goodly supply in the kitchen, as his lordship favors it. There are cream cakes and chocolates, as well, but those are usually served with the evening meal." She busied herself with substituting fresh flowers for the wilted specimens as the fragrance of roses, lavender, and honeysuckle wafted around the room.

Val eyed his brother. "Perhaps I will avail myself of your hospitality after all, Westhaven."

"I would be honored," Westhaven said absently, though he noted the speculation in his brother's eyes. Mrs. Seaton was humming a little Handel; Westhaven was almost sure it was from the *Messiah*. She turned to go but flashed them a smile and a little curtsy on her way.

"Oh, Mrs. Seaton?" The earl stopped her two steps shy of the door.

"My lord?"

"You may tell the kitchen my brother and I will be dining in tonight, informally, and will continue to do so until further notice."

"Lord Valentine will be visiting?"

"He will; the blue bedroom will do." Westhaven turned back to the tray, still counting four pieces of marzipan.

"Might I suggest the green bedroom?" Mrs. Seaton rejoined. "It has higher ceilings and is at the back of the house, which would be both cooler and quieter. Then too, it has a balcony."

The earl considered castigating her for contradicting him, but she'd been polite enough about it, and the back bedrooms were worlds more comfortable, though smaller.

"As you suggest." The earl waved her on her way.

"That is a very different sort of housekeeper you have there," Val said, when the library door had closed behind her.

"I know." Westhaven made a sandwich and checked again to make sure his brother hadn't pilfered the marzipan. "She's a little cheeky, to be honest, but does her job with particular enthusiasm. She puts me in mind of Her Grace."

"How so?" Val asked, making a sandwich, as well.

"Has an indomitable quality about her," Westhaven said between bites. "She bashed me with a poker when she thought I was a caller molesting a housemaid. Put out my lights, thank you very much."

"Heavens." Val paused in his chewing. "You didn't summon the watch?"

"The appearances were deceiving, and she doesn't know I'd never trifle with a housemaid."

"And if you were of a mind to before," Val said, eyeing the marzipan, "you'd sure as hell think twice about it now."

"And what of you?" Westhaven paused to regard his brother. Val shared the Windham height and green eyes, but his eyes were a darker green, while Westhaven's shade was closer to jade, and Val's hair was sable, nearly black.

"What of me?" Val buttered a fat muffin.

"Are you bothering any housemaids, lately?"

"Doing an errand for Viscount Fairly earlier in the season, I met an interesting woman out in Little Weldon," Val said, "but no, I am more concerned with misleading His Grace than in having my ashes hauled."

"Don't mislead him too well," Westhaven cautioned. "There are those who are not tolerant of left-handed preferences."

"Well, of course there are," Val said, "and they're just the ones wondering what it would be like to be a little adventurous themselves. But fear not, Westhaven. I mince and lisp and titter and flirt, but my breeches stay buttoned."

"It appears," Westhaven said, frowning as he reached for the marzipan, "mine will be staying buttoned, as well."

He bit into a plump, soft confection shaped like a ripe melon and stifled a snort of incredulity. His breeches would be staying buttoned, and the only thing he'd be twiddling would be his… thumbs.

# Two

THREE RULES, ANNA REMINDED HERSELF WHEN SHE reached the privacy of her own little sitting room. There were three rules to succeeding with any deception, and old Mr. Glickmann had drilled them into her:

Dress the part.

Believe your own lies.

Have more than you show—including an alternative plan.

Today, she was remiss on all three counts, God help her. A housekeeper wore caps, for pity's sake. Great homely caps, and gloves out of doors, and there she went, sailing into the library, bareheaded, barehanded, for the earl and his brother to see.

Believe your own lies—that meant living the deception as if it were real, never breaking role, and with the earl she'd broken role badly ever since she'd brained him with a poker. He had to have seen her, arms around Morgan, even as he lay bleeding on the floor. And then, curse her arrogant mouth, she'd as good as informed him she was raised as a bluestocking—fluent in three languages, Mother of God! Housekeepers read mostly their Bible, and that only slowly.

Have more than you show, including second and even third plans. On that count, she was an unmitigated disaster. She had a small stash of funds, thanks to her wages here, and Mr. Glickmann's final generosity, but funds were not a plan. Funds did not guarantee a new identity nor safe passage to foreign soil, if that's what it took.

"So what has you in such a dither?" Nanny Fran toddled into the kitchen, her button eyes alight with curiosity.

"We're to have company," Anna replied, forcing herself to sit down and meet Nanny Fran's eyes. "His lordship's brother will be staying with us, and as it's the first company since I've started here, I'm a little flustered."

"Right." Nanny Fran smiled at her knowingly. "Lord Val's a good sort, more easygoing than Westhaven. But these two"—she shook her head— "they weren't the ones who gave me trouble. Lord Bart was a rascal and spoiled, for all he wasn't mean; Lord Vic was just as bad, and didn't he get up to mischief, and nobody but Westhaven the wiser?"

"No carrying tales, Nanny." Anna rose, unwilling to start Nanny gossiping. "I'm off to warn Cook we'll have company, and their lordships will be dining informally at home for the foreseeable future. Have you seen Morgan?"

"She's in the stillroom," Nanny supplied, coming to her feet in careful increments. "Smells like lemons today, and limes."

Anna did find Morgan in what had become the stillroom, a portion of the large laundry that took up part of the house's understory. The girl was humming tunelessly and grinding something to powder with her mortar and pestle.

"Morgan?" Anna touched Morgan's shoulder, pleased to find she hadn't startled her. "What are you making? Nanny said it smelled like lemon and lime."

Morgan held out a large ceramic bowl with dried flowers crushed into a colorful mixture. Anna dipped her face to inhale the scent, closing her eyes and smiling.

"That is lovely. What's in it?"

Morgan lined up a number of bottles, pointing to each in turn, then took a pencil and scrap of paper from her apron pocket, and wrote, "Needs something. Too bland."

Anna cocked her head and considered the pronouncement. Morgan's nose was sophisticated but unconventional.

"Whose room is it for?"

Morgan made a supercilious face and arched a haughty eyebrow.

"The earl's," Anna concluded. "It does need something, something subtly exotic and even decadent." Morgan grinned and nodded. She reached for a small vial and held it up for Anna's consideration.

"*Mouget du bois*?" Anna raised her own eyebrow. "That's feminine, Morgan."

Morgan shook her head, confident in her decision. She added a few drops, stirred the bowl's contents gently with one finger, then covered them with a fitted ceramic lid.

"I'm glad you're done here for now," Anna said. "His lordship's brother will be staying with us for a time and will have need of the guest bedroom at the back of the house. Can you prepare it for him?"

Morgan nodded and tapped the left side of her collarbone, where a lady's watch pin might hang.

"You have time, because the gentlemen will be dining here this evening. Give him plenty of scented wash water and a crock of ice to start with tonight. He'll need flowers too, of course, and the sheets should be turned, as the ones on the bed have likely lost all their fragrance. Air the room, as well, and I'd leave the top windows open, the better to catch a zephyr."

Morgan smiled again and breezed past Anna, who followed her out but paused in the kitchen to talk to Cook.

"You'll be cooking for two gentlemen tonight," Anna said with a smile.

"His lordship's having company?" Cook asked, looking up from the bread dough she was turning on a floured board.

"Lord Valentine, his brother. He's a year or two younger than Westhaven but looks to be every bit as fit and busy as the earl."

"Good appetites, then." Cook nodded, pleased. "The earl's interest in his tucker has picked up here in recent months, I can tell you. Shall we do it a bit fancy tonight?"

"Not fancy, I don't think." Anna frowned in thought. "It's too hot for anything heavy, and the dining room can be stuffy. Why not a meal for the back terrace, something a little closer to a picnic but substantial enough for men?"

"Cold fare, maybe." Cook frowned as she put the dough in a bowl and covered it with a clean towel. "Chicken, with that basil you planted, and we've early tomatoes coming in. I can slice up some fruit and put it on ice…" Cook trailed off, her imagination putting together what was needed with what was on hand.

Anna's next stop was the head footman, whose job it would be to set up the terrace for dining. Anna set out scented torches, candles, linen, and cutlery suited to an al fresco meal, then quickly put together a little bouquet for a low centerpiece.

"Mrs. Seaton?" A male voice in the small confines of the butler's pantry gave her a start.

"Lord Valentine?" She turned to find him standing immediately behind her.

"My apologies." He smiled down at her, a perfectly charming expression. "I called, but the din in the kitchen probably drowned me out. Would it be possible at some point this evening to request a bath?"

"Of course. Your brother bathes before retiring most nights, unless he's going to be from home until late. There is time before dinner, but your room is only now being readied. We can send a bath up to the front guest room, if you'd like."

"That would be marvelous." He remained in the oversized closet with her, his smile fading. "You take good care of him, Mrs. Seaton, and it shows, though it must have been quite some blow to his hard head if it slowed him down even marginally."

Anna frowned at his retreating back and realized Westhaven had discussed the week's earlier mishap with Lord Val. Well, damn the man anyway.

And that reminded her, his lordship had sneaked out that morning without letting her tend him. He would scar at this rate and prolong his convalescence. Grabbing her medical supplies, Anna went in search of her quarry, hoping to find him where he usually was at this pleasant hour of the early evening, out on his balcony.

He lounged on his wicker chaise in lordly splendor, his waistcoat slung over the back of the chair, cravat folded tidily over that, his shirt open at the throat, and his cuffs rolled back.

"Your lordship?" Anna waited for his permission to step from his bedroom, feeling absurd for doing it and abruptly self-conscious.

"Mrs. Seaton," he drawled, glancing up at her. "You've come to poke at my injured self. Does nothing deter you from the conscientious prosecution of your duties?"

"Craven evasion," she replied, stepping out onto the balcony. "As when my patient disappears at first light, not to be seen until tea time, and then only in the company of his protective little brother."

"Val is protective of me?" Westhaven scowled as he eased forward to the end of the chaise, then dragged his shirt over his head and turned his back to her. "I suppose he is at that, though he knows I'd bite his head off were he to imply I need protection. Jesus Christ, that still stings."

"We all need protection from time to time," she said, dabbing gently at his back with arnica. "Your bruises are truly magnificent, my lord. They will heal more quickly if you don't duck out of a morning—and skip your breakfast."

"It's too hot to ride later in the day, at least at the pace I prefer." He winced again as she went at the second large laceration.

"You shouldn't be out riding hell-bent, your lordship. Your injuries do not need the abuse, and I can see where you've pulled this cut open along this edge." She drew a chiding finger along the bottom seam of a laceration. "What if you were unseated, and no one else about in the dawn's early light?"

"So you would come along to protect me?" he challenged lazily. She began to redress his back.

"Somebody should," she muttered, focused on the purple, green, and mottled brown skin surrounding the two mean gashes on his back.

The earl frowned in thought. "In truth, I am in need of somebody to protect. I fired my mistress today."

"My lord!" She was abruptly scowling at him nineteen to the dozen, as much disapproval as she dared show, short of jeopardizing her position outright.

"There is always gossip," he quoted her sardonically, "below stairs."

She pursed her lips. "Gossip and blatant disclosure are not the same thing. Though in this heat, why anyone would…"

She broke off, mortified at what had been about to come out of her mouth.

"Oh, none of that, Mrs. Seaton." The earl's smile became devilish. "In this heat?"

"Never mind, my lord." She wetted her cloth

with arnica again and gently tucked his head against
her waist. "This one is looking surprisingly tidy.
Hold still."

"I have a thick skull," he said from her waist. And
now that she was done with his back, came the part he
always tolerated almost docilely. She sifted her fingers
carefully through his hair and braced him this way,
his crown snug against her body, the better to tend
his scalp.

And if his hair was the silkiest thing she'd ever had
the pleasure to drift her fingers over, well, that was
hardly the earl's fault, was it?

❧

He should have brought himself off when he didn't
complete matters at Elise's. Why else would he be
baiting his housekeeper, a virtuous and supremely
competent woman? She was done with her arnica and
back to exploring the area around the scalp wound
with careful fingers.

"I don't understand why you haven't more swelling
here." She feathered his hair away from the scalp
wound. "Head wounds are notoriously difficult, but
you seem to be coming along wonderfully."

"So we can dispense with this nonsense?" He
reluctantly sat back and waved his hand at her linen
and tincture.

"Another two days, I think." She put the cap
back on the bottle. "Why is it so difficult for you to
submit to basic care, my lord? Do you relish being stiff
and scarred?"

"I do not particularly care what the appearance of

my back is, Mrs. Seaton. Ever since my brother took several years to die of consumption, I have had an abiding disgust of all things medical."

"I'm sorry." She looked instantly appalled. "I had no idea, my lord."

"Most people don't," Westhaven said. "If you've never seen anyone go that way, you don't fully comprehend the horror of it. And all the while, there were medical vultures circling, bleeding, poking at him, prescribing useless nostrums. He tolerated it, because it created a fiction of hope that comforted my parents even as it tortured him."

He fell silent then stood and went to the railing to stare out at the lush evening sunlight falling over his back gardens.

"And then late this winter, my stubborn father had to go riding to hounds in a weeklong downpour, only to come home with a raging lung fever. The leeches went at him, his personal physicians doing nothing more than drinking his brandy and letting his blood. When he was too weak to argue with me, those idiots were thrown out, but they came damned close to costing me my father."

"I'm sorry," she said again, turning to stand beside him, laying a hand on his back. He heard her sharp intake of breath as she realized her error—his shirt was still off. He didn't move off, though, but waited to see how she'd manage. Her hand was comforting, and without him willing it, his own slid along her waist and drew her against his side.

She remained facing the gardens, her expression impassive, her breath moving in a measured rhythm, her hand resting on his back as if it had arrived there despite her complete indifference to him as a person. Slowly, he relaxed, sensing her innate decency had, for just a few moments, trumped her notions of propriety, class distinction, and personal rectitude.

She offered comfort, he decided. Just comfort, for him, upon his recounting some very dark moments and his frustration and helplessness in those moments.

But what about for her?

He turned her to face him, brought her slowly against his body, and rested his cheek against her temple.

Just that, but it changed the tenor of the moment from gestures of comfort to the embrace of a man and a woman. His arms draped over her shoulders while hers looped at his naked waist, even as he told himself to end this folly *immediately*, or she'd have grounds for believing he trifled with the help after all.

She didn't end it. She stood in the loose circle of his arms, letting him positively wallow in the clean summery scent of her, the soft curves fitting him in all the right places. He urged her with patient strokes of his hands on her back to rest more fully against him, to give him her weight. He wasn't even aroused, he realized, he was just... consoled.

When he finally did step back, he placed a single finger softly against her lips to stop her from the admonitory and apologetic stammers no doubt damming up behind her conscience.

"None of that." He shook his head, his expression solemn. "This wasn't on my list either, Anna Seaton."

She didn't tarry to find out if he would say more, but shook her head in dismay, no curtsy, no resounding whack to his cheek, no offer of resignation. She left him, heir to the dukedom, standing half dressed, bruised, and alone on his private balcony.

❧

"His lordship begs the favor of yer comp'ny, mum," John Footman informed the housekeeper. Except, Anna knew, the man's name really was John, and his father and grandfather before him had also both, for a time, been footmen in the ducal household.

"He's in the library?" Anna asked, putting her mending aside with a sigh.

"He is," John replied, "and in a proper taking over summat."

"Best I step lively." Anna smiled at the young man, who looked worried for her. She squared her mental shoulders and adopted a businesslike—but certainly not anxious—gait. It had been a week since she'd clobbered the earl with a poker, a few days since that awkward scene on his balcony. She'd tended his bruises for the last time this morning, and he'd been nothing more than his usual acerbic, imperious self.

She knocked with a sense of trepidation nonetheless.

"Come." The word was barked.

"Mrs. Seaton." He waved her over to his desk. "Take a chair; I need your skills."

She took a seat and reluctantly agreed with the footman. His lordship was in a taking, or a snit, or an upset over something. The faint frown that often marked his features was a scowl, and his manner peremptory to the point of rudeness.

"My man of business is unable to attend me, and

the correspondence will not wait. There's paper, pen, and ink." He nodded at the edge of the desk. "Here, take my seat, and I'll dictate. The first letter goes to Messrs. Meechum and Holly, as follows…"

Good morning to you, too, Anna thought, dipping her pen. An hour and a half and six lengthy letters later, Anna's hand was cramping.

"The next letter, which can be a memorandum, is to go to Morelands. A messenger will be up from Morelands either later today or tomorrow, but the matter is not urgent." The earl let out a breath, and Anna took the opportunity to stand.

"My lord," she interrupted, getting a personal rendition of the earl's scowl for her cheek. "My hand needs a rest, and you could probably use some lemonade for your voice. Shall we take a break?"

He glanced at the clock, ready to argue, but the time must have surprised him.

"A short break," he allowed.

"I'll see about your drink," Anna said. When she got to the hallway, she shook her poor hand vigorously. It wasn't so much that the earl expected her to take lightning-fast dictation, it was more the case that he never, ever needed a pause himself. He gave her time to carefully record his every word, and not one tick of the clock more.

Sighing, she made her way to the kitchen, loaded up a tray, then added a second glass of lemonade for herself and returned to the library. She had been away from her post for twelve minutes but returned to find the earl reading a handwritten note and looking more thoughtful than angry.

"One more note, Mrs. Seaton," he said, rummaging in the desk drawers, "and then I will have something to drink."

He retrieved a scrap of paper from the back of a drawer, glaring at it in triumph when his fingers closed over it. "I knew it was in here." As he was back in his rightful place behind the desk, Anna repositioned the blotter, paper, pen, and ink on her side of the desk and sat down.

"To Drs. Hamilton, Pugh, and Garner, You will attend Miss Sue-Sue Tolliver at your earliest convenience, on the invitation of her father, Marion Tolliver. Bills for services rendered will be sent to the undersigned. Westhaven, etc."

Puzzled, Anna dutifully recorded the earl's words, sanded the little epistle, and set it aside to dry.

"I see you have modified your interpretation of the rules of decorum in deference to the heat," the earl noted, helping himself to a glass of lemonade. "Good God!" He held the glass away from him after a single sip. "It isn't sweetened."

"You helped yourself to my glass," Anna said, suppressing a smile. She passed him the second glass, from which he took a cautious swallow. She was left to drink from the same glass he'd first appropriated or go back to the kitchen to fetch herself a clean glass.

Looking up, she saw the earl watching her with a kind of bemused curiosity, as if he understood her dilemma. She took a hefty swallow of lemonade—and it did have sugar in it, though just a dash—and set her glass on the blotter.

"Tolliver is your man of business, isn't he?" she asked, the association just occurring to her.

"He is. He sent word around he was unavoidably detained and would not attend me this morning, which is unusual for him. I put one of the footmen on it and just received Tolliver's explanation: His youngest is coming down with the chicken pox."

"And you sent not one but three physicians for a case of chicken pox?" Anna marveled.

"Those three," the earl replied in all seriousness, "were recommended by an acquaintance who is himself a physician. Garner and Pugh were instrumental in saving His Grace's life this winter."

"So you trust them."

"As much as I trust any physician," the earl countered, "which is to say no farther than I could throw them, even with my shoulders injured."

"So if we ever need a physician for you, we should consult Garner, Pugh, or Hamilton?"

"My first choice would be David Worthington, Viscount Fairly, who recommended the other three, but you had better hope I die of whatever ails me, as I will take any quackery quite amiss, Mrs. Seaton." The earl speared her with a particularly ferocious glare in support of his point.

"May I ask an unrelated question, my lord?" Anna sipped her drink rather than glare right back at him. He was in a mood this morning to try the patience of a saint.

"You may." He put his empty glass on the tray and sat back in his chair.

"Is this how you work with Mr. Tolliver?" she asked. "Dictating correspondence word-for-word?"

"Sometimes," the earl replied, frowning. "He's been with me several years, though, and more often than not, I simply scratch a few notes, and he drafts the final missive for my signature."

"Can we try that approach? It sounds like my grandfather's way of doing business, and so far, your correspondence has been perfectly mundane."

"We can try it, but I am reminded of another matter I wanted to raise with you, and I will warn you in advance I won't have you sniffing your indignation at me for it."

"Sniffing my indignation?"

The earl nodded once, decisively. "Just so. I told you the other night I have parted company with my current *chere amie*. I inform you of this, Mrs. Seaton, not because I want to offend your sensibilities, but because I suspect the duke will next turn his sights on my own household."

"What does His Grace have to do with your... personal associations?"

"Precisely my question," the earl agreed, but he went on to explain in terse, blunt language how his father had manipulated his mistress, and how Elise had altered the plan in its significant details. "My father will likely try to find a spy on my own staff to inform him of when and with whom I contract another liaison. You will foil his efforts, should you learn of them."

"My lord, if you wanted to elude your father's scrutiny, then why would you hire half your footmen from his household and give him exclusive access to your valet for weeks on end?"

The earl looked nonplussed as he considered the logic of her observation.

"I made those arrangements before I comprehended the lengths to which my father is prepared to go. And I did so without knowing he already had spies in Elise's household, as well."

Anna said nothing and resumed her seat across the desk from the earl. He shuffled the stack, put two or three missives aside, then passed pen and paper to Anna.

"To Barstow," he began, "a polite expression of noninterest at this time, perhaps in future, et cetera. To Williams and Williams, a stern reminder that payment is due on the first, per our arrangements, and sword-rattling to the effect that contractual remedies will be invoked." He passed over the first two and went on in that vein until Anna had her orders for the next dozen or so letters.

"And while you obligingly tend to spinning that straw into gold"—the earl smiled without warning—"I will fire off the next salvo to His Grace."

For the next hour, they worked in companionable silence, with Anna finding it surprisingly easy to address the tasks set before her. She'd spent many, many hours in this role with her grandfather and had enjoyed the sense of partnership and trust such a position evoked.

"Well, what have we here?" Lord Valentine strode into the library, smiling broadly at its occupants. "Have I interrupted a lofty session of planning menus?"

"Hardly." The earl smiled at his brother. "Tolliver's absence has necessitated I prevail on Mrs. Seaton's good offices. What has you up so early?"

"It's eleven of the clock," Val replied. "Hardly early when one expects to practice at least four hours at his pianoforte." He stopped and grimaced. "If, that is, you won't mind. I can always go back to the Pleasure House if you do."

"Valentine." The earl glanced warningly at Mrs. Seaton.

"I've already told your housekeeper I am possessed of a healthy affection for pianos of easy virtue." Val turned his smile on Anna. "She was shocked insensible, of course."

"I was no such thing, your lordship."

"A man can take poetic license," Val said, putting a pair of Westhaven's glasses on his nose. "If you will excuse me, I will be off to labor in the vineyard to which I am best suited."

A little silence followed his departure, with the earl frowning pensively at the library door. Anna went back to the last of her assigned letters, and a few minutes later, heard the sound of scales tinkling through the lower floors of the house.

"Will he really play for four hours?" she asked.

"He will play forever," the earl said, "but he will practice for at least four hours each day. He spent more time at the keyboard by the age of twenty-five than a master at any craft will spend at his trade in his lifetime."

"He is besotted," Anna said, smiling. "You really don't mind the noise?"

"It is the sound of my only living little brother being happy," the earl said, tossing down his pen and going to stand in the open French doors. "It could never be noise." The earl frowned at her over his shoulder. "What? I can see you want to ask me something. I've worked you hard enough you deserve a shot or two."

"What makes you happy?" she asked, stacking the completed replies neatly, not meeting his eyes.

"An heir to a dukedom need not be happy. He need only be dutiful and in adequate reproductive health."

"So you are dutiful, but that evades the question. Your father manages to be both duke and happy, at least much of the time. So what, future Duke of Moreland, makes you happy?"

"A good night's sleep," the earl said, surprising them both. "Little pieces of marzipan showing up at unlikely spots in my day. A pile of correspondence that has been completed before luncheon, thank ye gods."

"You still need to read my efforts," Anna reminded him, pleased at his backhanded compliment, but troubled, somehow, that a good night's sleep was the pinnacle of his concept of pleasure.

The earl waggled his fingers at her. "So pass them over, and I will find at least three misspellings, lest you get airs above your station."

"You will find no misspellings, nor errors of punctuation or grammar." Anna passed the stack to him. "With your leave, I will go see about luncheon. Would you like to be served on the terrace, my lord, and will Lord Valentine be joining you?"

"I would like to eat on the terrace," the earl said, "and I doubt my brother will tear himself away from the piano, when he just sat down to his finger exercises. Send in a tray to him when you hear him shift from drills to etudes and repertoire."

"Yes, my lord." Anna bobbed a curtsy, but his lordship was already nose down into the correspondence, his brow knit in his characteristic frown.

"Oh, Mrs. Seaton?" The earl did not look up.

"My lord?"

"What does a child suffering chicken pox need for her comfort and recuperation?"

"Ice," Anna said, going on to name a litany of comfort nursing accoutrements.

"You can see to that?" he asked, looking up and eyeing his gardens. "The ice and so forth? Have it sent 'round to Tolliver's?"

"I can," Anna replied, cocking her head to consider her employer. "Regularly, until the child recovers."

"How long will that take?"

"The first few days are the worst, but by the fifth day, the fever has often abated. The itching can take longer, though. In this heat, I do not envy the child or her parents."

"A miserable thought," the earl agreed, "in comparison to which, dealing with my paltry letters is hardly any hardship at all, hmm? There will be more marzipan at lunch?"

"If your brother hasn't plundered our stores," Anna said, taking her leave.

She didn't see the earl smile at the door nor see that the smile didn't fade until he forced himself to resume perusing her drafts of correspondence. She wrote well, he thought, putting his ideas into words with far more graciousness and subtlety than old Tolliver could command. And so the chore of tending to correspondence, which had threatened to consume his entire day, was already behind him, leaving him free to… Wonder what gave him pleasure.

❧

"I'd put John to setting the table," Cook said, "but he went off to get us some more ice from the warehouse, and Morgan has gone to fetch the eggs, since his lordship didn't take his ride this morning, and McCutcheon hasn't seen to the hens yet."

So I, Anna thought, will spend the next half hour setting up a table where his lordship will likely sit for all of twenty minutes, dining in solitary splendor on food he doesn't even taste, because he must finish reading *The Times* while at table.

His crabby mood had rubbed off on her, she thought as she spread a linen cloth over a wrought-iron table. Well, that wouldn't do. Mentally, she began making her list of things to send over to Tolliver's for the little girl, Sue-Sue.

"You look utterly lost in thought," the earl pronounced, causing Anna to jump and almost drop the basket of cutlery she was holding.

"I was," she said, blushing for no earthly reason. "I have yet to see to your request to send some supplies around to Tolliver and was considering the particulars."

"How is it you know how to care for a case of chicken pox?" The earl grabbed the opposite ends of the tablecloth and drew them exactly straight.

"It's a common childhood illness," Anna said, setting the basket of cutlery on the table. "I came down with it myself when I was six." The earl reached into the basket and fished out the makings of a place setting. Anna watched in consternation as he arranged his cutlery on the table, setting each piece of silverware precisely one inch from the edge of the table.

"Don't you want a linen for your place setting?" Anna asked, unfolding one from the basket and passing it to him.

"Well, of course. Food always tastes better when eaten off a plate that sits on both a linen and a tablecloth."

"No need to be snippy, my lord." Anna quirked an eyebrow at him. "We can feed you off a wooden trencher if that's your preference."

"My apologies." The earl shot her a fulminating look as he collected the silverware and waited for Anna to spread the underlinen. "I am out of sorts today for having missed my morning ride."

He was once again arranging his silverware a precise distance from the edge of the table while Anna watched. He would have made an excellent footman, she concluded. He was careful, conscientious, and incapable of smiling.

"In this heat, I did not want to tax my horse," the earl said, rummaging in the basket for salt and the pepper. He found them and eyed the table speculatively.

"Here." Anna set a small bowl of daisies and violets on the table. "Maybe that will give you some ideas."

"A table for one can so easily become asymmetric."

"Dreadful effect on the palate." Anna rolled her eyes. "And where, I ask you, will we hide his lordship's marzipan?"

"Careful, Mrs. Seaton. If he should come out here and overhear your disrespect, I wouldn't give two pence for your position."

"If he is so humorless and intolerant as all that," Anna said, "then he can find somebody else to feed him sweets on the terrace of a summer's day."

The earl's gaze cooled at that retort, and Anna wondered at her recent penchant for overstepping. He'd been annoying her all morning, though, from the moment she'd been dragooned into the library. It was no mystery to her why Tolliver would rather be dealing with a sick child than his lordship.

"Am I really so bad as all that?" the earl asked, his expression distracted. He set aside the pepper but hefted the salt in one hand.

"You are..." Anna glanced up from folding the linen napkin she'd retrieved from her basket.

The earl met her gaze and waited.

"Troubled, I think," she said finally. "It comes out as imperiousness."

"Troubled," the earl said with a snort. "Well, that covers a world of possibilities." He reached into the basket and withdrew a large glazed plate, positioning it exactly in the center of his place setting. "I tried to compose a letter to my father this morning, while you beavered away on my *mundane* business, and somehow, Mrs. Seaton, I could not come up with words to adequately convey to my father the extent to which I want him to just *leave me the hell alone.*"

He finished that statement through clenched teeth, alarming Anna with the animosity in his tone, but he wasn't finished.

"I have come to the point," the earl went on, "where I comprehend why my older brothers would consider the Peninsular War preferable to the daily idiocy that comes with being Percival Windham's heir. I honestly believe that could he but figure a way to pull it off, my father would lock me naked in a room with the woman of his choice, there to remain until I got her pregnant with twin boys. And I am not just frustrated"—the earl's tone took on a sharper edge—"I am ready to do him an injury, because I don't think anything less will make an impression. Two unwilling people are going to wed and have a child because my father got up to tricks."

"Your father did not force those two people into one another's company all unawares and blameless, my lord, but why not appeal to your mother? By reputation, she is the one who can control him."

The earl shook his head. "Her Grace is much diminished by the loss of my brother Victor. I do not want to importune her, and she will believe His Grace only meant well."

Anna smiled ruefully. "And she wants grandchildren, too, of course."

"Why, of course." The earl gestured impatiently. "She had eight children and still has six. There will be grandchildren, and if for some reason the six of us are completely remiss, I have two half siblings, whose children she will graciously spoil, as well."

"Good heavens," Anna murmured. "So your father has sired ten children, and yet he plagues you?"

"He does. Except for the one daughter of Victor's, none of us have seen fit to reproduce. There was a rumor Bart had left us something to remember him by, but he likely started the rumor himself just to aggravate my father."

"So find a wife," Anna suggested. "Or at least a fiancée, and back your dear papa off. The right lady will cry off when you ask it of her, particularly if you are honest with your scheme from the start."

"See?" The earl raised his voice, though just a bit. "Honest with my *scheme*? Do you know how like my father that makes me sound?"

"And is this all that plagues you, my lord? Your father has no doubt been a nuisance for as long as you've been his heir, if not longer."

The earl glanced sharply at his housekeeper, then his lips quirked, turned back down, and then slowly curved back up.

"Why are you smiling?" she asked, his smiles being as rare as hen's teeth.

"I found your little parlor maid in the hay loft," the earl said, setting out his water glass and wine glass precisely one inch from the plate. "She discovered our mouser's new litter, and she was enthralled with the cat's purr. She could feel it, I think, and understood it meant the cat was happy."

"She would," Anna said, wondering how this topic was related to providing the duke his heirs. "She loves animals, but here in Town, she has little truck with them."

"You know Morgan that well?" the earl asked, his tone casual.

"We are related," she replied, telling herself it was a version of the truth. A prevaricating version.

"So you took pity on her," the earl surmised, "and hired her into my household. Has she always been deaf?"

"I do not know the particulars of her malady, my lord," she said, lifting the basket to her hip. "All I care for is her willingness to do an honest day's work for an honest day's pay. Shall we serve you tea or lemonade with your luncheon?"

"Lemonade," Westhaven said. "But for God's sake don't forget to sugar it."

She bobbed a curtsy so low as to be mocking. "Any excuse to sweeten your disposition, my lord."

He watched her go, finding another smile on his face, albeit a little one. His housekeeper liked having the last word, which was fine with him—usually. But as their conversation had turned to the question of her *relation*, she had dodged him and begun to dissemble. It was evident in her eyes and in the slight defensiveness of her posture.

A person, even one in service to an earl, was entitled to privacy. But a person with secrets could be exploited by, say, an unscrupulous duke. And for that reason—for *that* reason—the earl would be keeping a very close eye on Anna Seaton.

# *Three*

"BEG PARDON, MUM." JOHN FOOTMAN BOBBED A BOW. "His lordship's asking fer ya, and I'd step lively."

"He's in the library?" Anna asked with a sigh. She'd spent three of the last four mornings in the library with his lordship, but not, thank the gods, today.

"In his chambers, mum." John was blushing now, even as he stared holes in the molding. Anna grimaced, knowing she'd sent a bath up to the earl's chambers directly after luncheon, which was unusual enough.

"Best see what he wants." Anna rose from the kitchen table, got a commiserating look from Cook, and made her way up two flights of stairs.

"My lord?" She knocked twice, heard some sort of lordly growl from the other side, and entered the earl's sitting room.

The earl was dressed, she noted with relief, but barely. His shirt was unbuttoned, as were his cuffs, he was barefoot, and the garters were not yet closed on his knee breeches.

He did not glance up when she entered the room but was fishing around on a bureau among brushes and combs. "My hair touches my collar, at the back." He waved two fingers impatiently behind his right ear. "As my valet continues to attend His Grace, you will please address the situation."

"You want me to trim your hair?" Anna asked, torn between indignation and amusement.

"If you please," he said, locating a pair of grooming scissors and handing them to her handles first. He obligingly turned his back, which left Anna circling him to address his face.

"It will be easier, my lord, if you will sit, as even your collar is above my eye level."

"Very well." He dragged a stool to the center of the room and sat his lordly arse upon it.

"And since you don't want to have stray hairs on that lovely white linen," Anna went on, "I would dispense with the shirt, were I you."

"Always happy to *dispense* with clothing at the request of a woman." The earl whipped his shirt over his head.

"Do you want your hair cut, my lord?" Anna tested the sharpness of the scissor blades against her thumb. "Or perhaps not?"

"Cut," his lordship replied, giving her a slow perusal. "I gather from your vexed expression there is something for which I must apologize. I confess to a mood both distracted and resentful."

"When somebody does you a decent turn," she said as she began to comb out his damp hair, "you do not respond with sarcasm and innuendo, my lord." She took particular care at the back of his head, where she knew he was yet healing from the drubbing she'd given him.

"You have a deft touch. Much more considerate than my valet."

"Your valet is a self-important little toady," Anna said, working around to the side of his head, "and that is not an apology."

"Well, I am sorry," the earl said, grabbing her hand by the wrist to still the comb. "I have an appointment at Carlton House this afternoon, and I most petulantly and assuredly do not want to go."

"Carlton House?" Anna lowered her hand, but the earl did not release her. "What an important fellow you are, to have business with the Regent himself."

He turned her hand over and studied the lines of her palm for a moment.

He smoothed his thumb over her palm. "Prinny will likely stick his head in the door briefly, tell us how much he appreciates our contributions to this great land, and then resume his afternoon's entertainments."

"But you cannot refuse to go," Anna said, taking a guess, "for it is a great honor, and so on."

"It is a tiresome damned pain in my arse," the earl groused. "You have no wedding ring, Mrs. Seaton, nor does your finger look to have ever been graced by one."

"Since I have no husband at present," Anna said, retrieving her hand, "a ring is understandably absent also."

"Who was this grandfather," the earl asked, "the one who taught you how to do Tolliver's job while smelling a great deal better than Tolliver?"

"My paternal grandfather raised me, more or less from childhood on," Anna said, knowing the truth would serve up to a point. "He was a florist and a perfumer and a very good man."

"Hence the flowers throughout my humble abode. Don't take off too much," he directed. "I prefer not to look newly shorn."

"You have no time for this," Anna said, hazarding another guess as she snipped carefully to trim up the curling hair at his nape. She'd snip, snip then brush the trimmings from his bare shoulders. It went like that, snip, snip, brush until she leaned up and blew gently on his nape instead, then resumed snipping.

When she leaned in again, she caught the scent of his woodsy, spicy cologne. The fragrance and putting her mouth just a few inches from his exposed nape left her insides with an odd, fluttery disconcerted feeling. She lingered behind him, hoping her blush was subsiding as she finished her task. "There." This time she brushed her fingers over his neck several more times. "I believe you are presentable, or your hair is."

"The rest of me is yet underdressed." He held out his hand for the scissors. "Now where is my damned shirt?"

She handed him his damned shirt and would have turned to go, except his cravat had also sprouted wings and flown off to an obscure location on the door of his wardrobe, followed by his cuff links, and stickpin, and so forth. When he started muttering that neck-cloths were altogether inane in the blistering heat, she gently pushed his fingers aside and put both hands on his shoulders.

"Steady on." She looked him right in the eye. "It's only a silly committee, and you need only leave a bank draft then be about your day. How elegant do you want to look?"

"I want to look as plain as I can without being a Quaker," the earl said. "My father loves this sort of thing, back-slapping, trading stories, and haggling politics."

Anna finished a simple, elegant knot and took the stickpin from the earl's hand. "Once again, you find yourself doing that which you do not enjoy, because it is your duty. Quizzing glass?"

"No. I do put a pair of spectacles on a fob."

"How many fobs, and do you carry a watch?" Anna found a pair of spectacles on the escritoire and waited while the earl sorted through his collection of fobs. He presented her with one simple gold chain.

"I do not carry a time piece to Carlton House," he explained, "for it serves only to reinforce how many hours I am wasting on the Regent's business." Anna bent to thread the chain through the buttonhole of his waistcoat and tucked the glasses into his watch pocket, giving the earl's tummy a little pat when the chain was hanging just so across his middle.

"Will I do?" the earl asked, smiling at her proprietary gesture.

"Not without a coat, you won't, though in this heat, no one would censor you for simply carrying it until you arrived at your destination."

"Coat." The earl scowled, looking perplexed.

"On the clothespress," Anna said, shaking her head in amusement.

"So it is." The earl nodded, but his eyes were on Anna. "It appears you've put me to rights, Anna Seaton, my thanks."

He bent and kissed her cheek, a gesture so startling in its spontaneity and simple affection, she could only stand speechless as the earl whisked his coat across his arm and strode from his room. The door slammed shut behind him as he yelled for Lord Valentine to meet him in the mews immediately or suffer a walk in the afternoon's heat.

Dumbstruck, Anna sat on the stool the earl had used for his trimming. He had a backward sort of charm to him, Anna thought, her fingers drifting over her cheek. After four days of barking orders, hurling thunderbolts, and scribbling lists at her in Tolliver's absence, he thanked her with a lovely little kiss.

She should have chided him—might have, if he'd held still long enough—but he'd caught her unawares, just as when he'd frowned at her hand and seen she had no wedding ring.

Her pleasure at the earl's kiss evaporating, Anna looked at her left hand. Why hadn't she thought of this detail, for pity's sake? Dress the part, she reminded herself.

She hung up some discarded ensembles of court-worthy attire, straightened up both the escritoire and the earl's bureau, which looked as if a strong wind had blown all into disarray. When she opened his wardrobe, she unashamedly leaned in and took a big whiff of the expensive, masculine scent of him while running her hand along the sleeve of a finely tailored dark green riding jacket.

He was a handsome man, but he was also a very astute man, one who would continue to spot details and put together facts, until he began to see through her to the lies and deceptions. Before then, of course, she would be gone.

❧

When he finally returned to his townhouse that evening, the earl handed his hat, gloves, and cane to a footman then made his way through the dark house to the kitchens, wanting nothing so much as a tall, cold glass of sweetened lemonade. He could summon a servant to fetch it but was too restless and keyed up to wait.

"My lord?" Mrs. Seaton sat at the long wooden table in the kitchen, shelling peas into a wooden bowl, but stood as he entered the room.

"Don't get up. I'm only here to filch myself some cold lemonade."

"Lord Valentine sent word you'd both be missing dinner." She went to the dry sink and retrieved the pitcher. The earl rummaged in the cupboards and found two glasses, which he set down on the table. Anna glanced at him curiously but filled both, then brought the sugar bowl to the table.

Westhaven watched her as she stirred sugar into his glass, his eyebrows rising in consternation.

"I take that much sugar?"

Anna put the lid back on the sugar bowl. "Either that, or you curse and make odd faces and scowl thunderously at all and sundry." She pushed his glass over to him, and took a sip out of hers.

"You don't put any in yours?" he asked, taking a satisfying swallow of his own. God above, he'd been craving this exact cold, sweet, bracing libation.

"I've learned not to use much," Anna said, sipping again. "Sugar is dear."

"Here." He held up his glass. "If you enjoy it, then you should have it."

Anna leaned back against the sink and eyed him. "And where is that sentiment in application to yourself?"

He blinked and cocked his head. "It's too late in the day for philosophical digressions."

"Have you even eaten, my lord?"

"It appears I have not."

"Well, that much of the world's injustices I can remedy," she said as she rinsed their glasses. "If you'd like to go change out of those clothes, I can bring you up a tray in a few minutes."

"If you would just get me out of this damned cravat?" He went to stand near her at the sink, waiting while she dried her hands on a towel then nudged his chin up.

"The cravat is still spotless," she informed him, wiggling at the clasp on the stickpin, "though your beautiful shirt is a trifle dusty and wilted. Hold *still*." She wiggled a little more but still couldn't undo the tiny mechanism. "Let's sit you back down at the table, my lord."

He obligingly sat on the long bench at the table, chin up.

"That's it," she said, freeing the stickpin and peering at it. "You should have a jeweler look at this." She set it on the table as her fingers went to the knot of his neckcloth. "There." She loosened the knot until the ends were trailing around his neck, and a load of weariness abruptly intensified low down, in his gut, where sheer exhaustion could weight a man into immobility. He leaned in, his temple against her waist in a gesture reminiscent of when she tended his scalp wound.

"Lord Westhaven?" Her hand came down to rest on his nape, then withdrew, then settled on him again. He knew he should move but didn't until she stroked a hand over the back of his head. God in heaven, what was he about? And with his housekeeper, no less. He pushed to his feet and met her eyes.

"Apologies, Mrs. Seaton. A tray would be appreciated."

Anna watched him go, thinking she'd never seen him looking quite so worn and drawn. His day had been trying, it seemed, but it struck her that more than the challenge of a single meeting at Carlton House, what likely bothered him was the prospect of years of such meetings.

When she knocked on his door, there was no immediate response, so she knocked again and heard a muffled command of some sort. She balanced the tray and pushed open the door, only to find the earl was not in his sitting room.

"In here," the earl called from the bedroom. He was in a silk dressing gown and some kind of loose pajama pants, standing at the French doors to his balcony.

"Shall I put it outside?"

"Please." He opened the door and took half a step back, allowing Anna just enough room to pass before him. "Will you join me?" He followed her out and closed the door behind him.

"I can sit for a few minutes," Anna replied, eyeing the closed door meaningfully.

If he picked up on her displeasure, he ignored it. Anna suspected he was too preoccupied with the thought of sustenance to understand her concern, though, so she tried to dismiss it, as well.

He was just in want of company at the end of a trying day.

He took the tray and set it on a low table then dragged the chaise next to it. "How is it you always know exactly what to put on a tray and how to arrange it, so a man finds his appetite perfectly satisfied?"

"When you are raised by a man who loves flowers," Anna said, "you develop an eye for what is pleasing and for how to please him."

"Was he an old martinet, your grandfather?" the earl asked, fashioning himself a sandwich.

"Absolutely not," Anna said, taking the other wicker seat. "He was the most gracious, loving, happy man it will ever be my pleasure to know."

"Somehow, I cannot see anyone describing me as gracious, loving, and happy." He frowned at his sandwich as if in puzzlement.

"You are loving," Anna replied staunchly, though she hadn't exactly planned for those words to leave her mouth.

"Now that is beyond surprising." The earl eyed her in the deepening shadows. "How do you conclude such a thing, Mrs. Seaton?"

"You have endless patience with your family, my lord," she began. "You escort your sisters everywhere; you dance attendance on them and their hordes of friends at every proper function; you harry and hound the duke so his wild starts are not the ruination of his duchy. You force yourself to tend to mountains of business which you do not enjoy, so your family may be safe and secure all their days."

"That is business," the earl said, looking nonplussed that his first sandwich had disappeared, until Anna handed him a second. "The head of the family tends to business."

"Did your sainted brother Bart ever tend to business?" Anna asked, stirring the sugar up from the bottom of the earl's drink.

"My sainted brother Bart, as you call him, did not live to be more than nine-and-twenty," the earl pointed out, "and at that age, the heir to a duke is expected to carouse, gamble, race his bloodstock, and enjoy life."

"And what age are you, your lordship?"

He sat back and took a sip of his drink. "Were you a man, I could tell you to go to hell, you know."

"Were I a man," Anna said, "I would have already told you the same thing."

"Oh?" He smiled, not exactly sweetly. "At which particular moment?"

"When you fail to offer a civil greeting upon seeing a person first thing in the day. When you can't be bothered to look a person in the eye when you offer your rare word of thanks or encouragement. When you take out your moods and frustrations on others around you, like a child with no sense of how to go on."

"Ye gods." The earl held up a staying hand. "Pax! You make me sound like the incarnation of my father."

"If the dainty little glass slipper fits, my lord..." Anna shot back, glad for the gathering shadows.

"You are fearless," the earl said, his tone almost humorous.

"I don't mean to scold you"—Anna shook her head, courage faltering—"because you are a truly decent man, but lately, my lord…"

"Lately?"

"You are out of sorts. I have mentioned this before."

"And how do you know, Anna Seaton, I am not always a bear with a sore paw? Some people are given to unpleasant demeanors, and it is just their nature."

Anna shook her head. "Not you. You are serious but not grim; you are proud but not arrogant; you care a great deal for the people you love but have only limited means of expressing it."

"You have made a study of me," the earl said, sounding as if he were relieved her conclusions were so flattering—if not quite accurate. "And where in my litany of virtues do you put my unwillingness to marry?"

Anna shrugged. "Perhaps you are simply not yet ready to limit your attentions to one woman."

"You think fidelity a hallmark of titled marriages, Mrs. Seaton?" The earl snorted and took a sip of his drink.

So I'm back to Mrs. Seaton, Anna thought, knowing the topic had gotten sensitive.

"You want what your parents have, my lord," Anna said, rising.

"Children who refuse to marry—assuming they remain extant?" the earl shot back.

"Your parents love each other," Anna said, taking in the back gardens below as moonlight cast them in silvery beauty. "They love each other as friends and lovers and partners and parents." She turned, finding him on his feet directly behind her. "That is why you will not settle for some little widgeon picked out by your well-meaning papa."

The earl took a step closer to her. "And what if I am in need, Anna Seaton, not of this great love you surmise between my parents but simply of some uncomplicated, lusty passion between two willing adults?"

He took the last step between them, and Anna's middle simply vanished. Where her vital organs used to reside, there was a great, gaping vacuum, a fluttery nothingness that grew larger and more dumbstruck as the earl's hands settled with breathtaking gentleness on her shoulders. He slid his palms down her arms, grasping her hands, and easing her toward him.

"Passion between two willing adults?" Anna repeated, her voice coming out whispery, not the incredulous retort she'd meant it to be.

The earl responded by taking her hands and wrapping them around his waist then enfolding Anna against his body.

She had been here before, she thought distractedly, held in his arms, the night breezes playing in the branches above them, the scent of flowers intoxicatingly sweet in the darkness. And as before, he caressed her back in slow, soothing circles that urged her more fully against him.

"I cannot allow this." Anna breathed in his scent and rested her cheek against the cool silk of his dressing gown. He shifted, easing the material aside, and her face touched his bare chest. She did not even try to resist the pleasure of his clean, male skin beneath her cheek.

"You cannot," he whispered, but it didn't sound like he was agreeing with her. "You should not," he clarified, "but perhaps, Anna Seaton, you can allow just a kiss, stolen on a soft summer evening."

Oh dear lord, she thought, wanting to hide her face against the warmth of his chest. He thought to kiss her. *He was kissing her*, delicate little nibbles that stole a march along her temple then her jaw. Oh, he knew what he was about, too, for his lips were soft and warm and coaxing, urging her to turn her head just so and tip her chin thus...

He settled his mouth over hers with a sigh, the joining of their lips making Anna more aware of every aspect of the moment—the crickets singing, the distant clop of hooves one street over, the soughing of the scented breeze, and the thumping of her heart like a kettledrum against her chest.

"Just a kiss, Anna..." he reminded her, her name on his lips a caress Anna felt to her soul. Her sturdy country-girl's bones melted, leaving her weight resting against him in shameless wonder. When his tongue slipped along the seam of her lips, her knees turned weak, and a whimper of pleasure welled. Soft, sweet, lemony tart and seductive, he stole into her mouth, giving her time to absorb each lush caress of lips and breath and tongue.

And then, as if his mouth weren't enough of a sin, his hands slid down her back in a slow, warm press that ended with him cupping her derriere, pulling her into his greater height and into the hard ridge of male flesh that rose between them. She didn't flinch back. She went up on her toes and pressed herself more fully against him, her hands finding their way inside his dressing gown to knead the muscles of his back.

She wrapped herself around him, clinging in complete abandon as her tongue gradually learned from his, and her conscience gave up, along with her common sense. She tasted him, learned the contours of his mouth and lips then tentatively brushed a slow, curious hand over his chest.

*Ye gods…*

"Easy." He eased his mouth away but held her against his body, his chin on her temple. Anna forced her hands to go still as well, but she could not make herself step back.

"I'll tender my resignation first thing tomorrow," she said dully, her face pressed to his sternum.

"I won't accept it," the earl replied, stroking her back in slow sweeps.

"I'll leave anyway." She knew he could feel the blush on her face.

"I'll find you," the earl assured her, pressing one last kiss to her hair.

"This is intolerable."

"Anna," he chided, "it is just a kiss and entirely my fault. I am not myself of late, as you've noted. You must forgive me and accept my assurances I would never force an unwilling female."

She stayed in his arms, trying to puzzle out what he was going on about. Ah, God, it felt too good to be held, to be touched with such consideration and deliberation. She was wicked, shameless, lost and getting more lost still.

"Say you will forgive me," the earl rumbled, his hands going quiet. "Men require frequent forgiveness, Anna. This is known to all."

"You don't sound sorry," she muttered, still against his chest.

"A besetting sin of my gender," and Anna could tell he was teasing—mostly.

"You aren't truly sorry." She found the strength to shove away from him but turned out to regard the night rather than face him. "But you have regret over this."

"I regret," he said directly above and behind her ear, "that I may have offended you. I regret just as much that we are not now tossing back my lavender-scented sheets in preparation for that passion between consenting adults I mentioned earlier."

"There will be no more of that," Anna said, inhaling sharply. "No more mentioning, no more kissing, no more talk of sheets and whatnot."

"As you wish," he said, still standing far too close behind her. He was careful not to touch her, but Anna could tell he was inhaling her scent, because she was doing the same with his.

"What I wish is of no moment," she said, "like the happiness of a future duke. No moment whatsoever."

He did step back at that, to her relief. Mostly, her relief.

"You have accepted my apology?" he asked, his voice cooling.

"I have."

"And you won't be resigning or disappearing without notice?"

"I will not."

"Your word, Anna?" he pressed, reverting to tones of authority.

"My word, *your lordship*."

He flinched at that, which was a minor gratification.

A silence, unhappy for her, God knew what for him, stretched between them.

"Were you to disappear, I would worry about you, you know," he said softly. He trailed his fingers down over her wrist to lace with hers and squeeze briefly.

She nodded, as there was nothing to say to such folly. Not one thing.

❧

In the moonlight, he saw her face in profile, eyes closed, head back. His last comment seemed to strike her with the same brutal intensity as her use of his title had hit him, for she stiffened as if she'd taken an arrow in the back before dropping his hand and fleeing.

When he was sure she'd left his rooms, the earl went inside and locked his bedroom door then returned to the darkness of the balcony. He shucked his trousers, unfolded the napkin from the dinner tray, and lay back on the chaise. As his eyes fell closed, his dressing gown fell open, and he let memories of Anna Seaton fill his imagination.

In the soft, sweet darkness, he drew out his own pleasure, recalling each instant of that kiss, each *pleasure*. The clean, brisk scent of her, the softness of her lips, the way she startled minutely when his hands had settled on her shoulders. When he finally did allow himself satisfaction, the sensations were more gratifying and intense than anything he'd experienced with Elise.

It was enough, he assured himself. He was content for one night to have kissed her and pleasured himself resoundingly. If she truly insisted he keep his distance, he would respect that, but he would make damned sure her decision was based on as much persuasive information as he could put before her.

As the night settled peacefully into his bones, he closed his eyes and started making a list.

~

Anna was up early enough the next morning to see to her errand, one she executed faithfully on the first of each month—rain, shine, snow, or heat. She sat down with pen, plain paper, and ink, and printed, in the most nondescript hand she could muster, the same three words she had been writing each month for almost two years: All is well. She sanded that page and let it dry while she wrote the address of an obscure Yorkshire posting inn on an envelope. Just as she was tucking her missive into its envelope, booted footsteps warned her she would soon not have the kitchen to herself.

"Up early, aren't you, Mrs. Seaton?" the earl greeted her.

"As are you, my lord," she replied casually, sliding the letter into her reticule.

"I am off to let Pericles stretch his legs, but I find myself in need of sustenance."

"Would you like a muffin, my lord? I can fix you something more substantial, or you can take the muffin with you."

"A muffin will do nicely, or perhaps two." He

narrowed his eyes at her. "You aren't going to be shy with me, are you, Mrs. Seaton?"

"Shy?" And just like that, she blushed, damn him. "Why ever would I...? Oh, shy. Of course not. A small, insignificant, forgivable indiscretion on the part of one's employer is hardly cause to become discomposed."

"Glad you aren't the type to take on, but I would not accost you where someone might come upon us," the earl said, pouring himself a measure of lemonade.

"My lord," she shot back, "you will not accost me *anywhere*."

"If you insist. Some lemonade before you go out?"

"You are attempting to be charming," Anna accused. "Part of your remorse over your misbehavior last evening."

"That must be it." He nodded. "Have some lemonade anyway. You will go marching about in the heat and find yourself parched in no time."

"It isn't that hot yet," Anna countered, accepting a glass of lemonade, "And a lady doesn't march."

"Here's to ladies who don't march." The earl saluted with his drink. "Now, about those muffins? Pericles is waiting."

"Mustn't inconvenience dear Pericles," Anna muttered loudly enough for the earl to hear her, but his high-handedness did not inspire blushes, so it was an improvement of sorts. She opened the bread box—where anybody would have known to look for the muffins—and selected the two largest. The earl was sitting on the wooden table and let Anna walk up to him to hand over the goodies.

"There's my girl." He smiled at her. "See? I don't bite, though I've been known to nibble. So what is in this batch?"

"Cinnamon and a little nutmeg, with a caramel sort of glaze throughout," Anna said. "You must have slept fairly well."

Now that she was close enough to scrutinize him, Anna saw that the earl's energy seemed to have been restored to him. He was in much better shape than he had been the previous evening, and—oh dear—the man was actually smiling, and at her.

"I did sleep well." The earl bit into a muffin. "And he is dear, you know. Pericles, that is. And this"—he looked her right in the eye—"is a superb muffin."

"Thank you, my lord." She couldn't help but smile at him when he was making such a concerted effort not to annoy her.

"Perhaps you'd like a bite?" He tore off a piece and held it out to her, and abruptly, he was being very annoying indeed.

"I'll just have one of my own."

"They are that good, aren't they?" the earl said, popping the bite into his maw. "Where do you go this early in the morning, Mrs. Seaton?"

"I have some errands," she said, pulling a crocheted summer glove over her left hand.

"Ah." The earl nodded sagely. "I have a mother and five sisters, plus scads of female cousins. I have heard of these errands. They are the province of women and seem to involve getting a dizzying amount done in a short time or spending hours on one simple task."

"They can," she allowed, watching two sizeable

muffins meet their end in mere minutes. The earl rose and gave her another lordly smile.

"I'll leave you to your errands. I am fortified sufficiently for mine to last at least until breakfast. Good day to you, Mrs. Seaton."

"Good day, my lord." Anna retrieved her reticule from the table and made for the hallway, relieved to have put her first encounter of the day with his lordship behind her.

"Mrs. Seaton?" His lordship was frowning at the table, but when he looked up at her, his expression became perfectly blank—but for the mischief in his eyes.

"My lord?" Anna cocked her head and wanted to stomp her foot. The earl in a playful mood was more bothersome than the earl in a grouchy mood, but at least he wasn't kissing her.

He held up her right glove, twirling it by a finger, and he wasn't going to give it back, she knew, unless she *marched* up to him and retrieved it.

"Thank you," she said, teeth not quite clenched. She walked over to him, and held out her hand, but wasn't at all prepared for him to take her hand in his, bring it to his lips, then slap the glove down lightly into her palm.

"You are welcome." He snagged a third muffin from the bread box and went out the back door, whistling some complicated theme by Herr Mozart that Lord Valentine had been practicing for hours earlier in the week.

Leaving Anna staring at the glove—the gauntlet?—the earl had just tossed down into her hand.

"Good morning, Brother!"

Westhaven turned in the saddle to see Valentine drawing his horse alongside Pericles.

"Dare I hope that you, like I, are coming home after a night on the town?" Val asked.

"Hardly." The earl smiled at his brother as they turned up the alley toward the mews. "I've been exercising this fine lad and taking the morning air. I also ran into Dev, who seems to be thriving."

"He is becoming a much healthier creature, our brother," Val said, grinning. "He has this great, strapping 'cook/housekeeper' living with him. Keeps his appetites appeased, or so he says. But before we reach the confines of your domicile, you should be warned old Quimbey was at the Pleasure House last night, and he said His Grace is going to be calling on you to discuss the fact that your equipage was seen in the vicinity of Fairly's brother yesterday."

"So you might ply his piano the whole night through," Westhaven said, frowning mightily at his brother. Val grinned back at him and shook his head, and Westhaven felt some of his pleasure in the day evaporating in the hot morning air. "Then what is our story?"

"You have parted from Elise, as is known to all, so we hardly need concoct a story, do we?"

"Valentine." Westhaven frowned. "You know what His Grace will conclude."

"Yes, he will," Val said as he dismounted. "And the louder I protest to the contrary, the more firmly he'd believe it."

Westhaven swung down and patted Pericles's neck. "Next time, you're walking to any assignation you have with any piece of furniture housed in a brothel."

They remained silent until they were in the kitchen, having used the back terrace to enter the house. Val went immediately to the bread box and fished out a muffin. "You want one?"

"I've already had three. Some lemonade, or tea?"

"Mix them," Val said, getting butter from the larder. "Half of each. There's cold tea in the dry sink."

"My little brother, ever the eccentric. Will you join me for breakfast?" Westhaven prepared his brother's drink as directed then poured a measure of lemonade for himself.

"Too tired." Val shook his head. "I kept an eye on things at the Pleasure House until the wee hours then found myself fascinated with a theme that closely resembles the opening to Mozart's symphony in G minor. When His Grace comes to call, I will be abed, sleeping off my night of sin with Herr Mozart. You will please inform Papa of this, and with a straight face."

His Grace presented himself in due course, with appropriate pomp and circumstance, while Val slept on in ignorant bliss above stairs. The footman minding the door, cousin to John, knew enough to announce such an important personage, and did so, interrupting the earl and Mr. Tolliver as they were wrapping up a productive morning.

"Show His Grace in," the earl said, excusing Tolliver and deciding not to deal with his father in a parlor, when the library was likely cooler and had no windows facing the street. Volume seemed to work as well as brilliance when negotiating with his father, but sheer ruthlessness worked best of all.

"Your Grace." The earl rose and bowed deferentially. "A pleasure as always, though unexpected. I hope you fare well?"

"Unexpected." His Grace snorted, but he was in a good mood, his blue eyes gleeful. "I'll tell you what's unexpected is finding you at a bordello. Bit beneath you, don't you think? And at two of the clock on a broiling afternoon! Ah, youth."

"And how is Her Grace?" the earl asked, going to the sideboard. "Brandy, whiskey?"

"Don't mind if I have a tot," the duke said. "Damned hot out, and that's a fact. Your mother thrives as always in my excellent and devoted care. Your dear sisters are off to Morelands with her, and I was hoping to find your brother here so I might dispatch him there, as well."

The earl handed the duke his drink, declining to drink spirits himself at such an early hour.

The duke sipped regally at his liquor. "I suppose if Valentine were about, I'd be hearing his infernal racket. Not bad." He lifted his glass. "Not half bad, after all."

Mrs. Seaton's words returned to the earl as he watched his father sipping casually at some of the best whiskey ever distilled: You fail to offer a civil greeting upon seeing a person first thing in the day… You can't be bothered to look a person in the eye when you offer your rare word of thanks or encouragement…

And it hit him like a blow to the chest that as much

as he didn't want to be the next Duke of Moreland, he very especially did not want to turn into another version of *this* Duke of Moreland.

"If I see Val," Westhaven said, "I will tell him the ladies are seeking his company at Morelands."

"Hah." The duke set aside his empty glass. "His mother and sisters, you mean. They're about the only ladies he has truck with these days."

"Not so," the earl said. "He is much in demand as an escort and considered very good company by many."

The duke heaved a martyr's sigh. "Your brother is a mincing fop, but word is you at least had him in hand at Fairly's whorehouse. Have to ask, how you'd do it?"

Now that was rare, for the duke to ask a question to which he sought an answer. Westhaven considered his reply carefully.

"I had heard Fairly has an excellent new Broadwood on the premises, which, in fact, he does." A truth, as far as it went.

"So all I have to do," the duke said with sudden inspiration, "is find some well-bred filly of a musical nature, and we can get him leg-shackled?"

"It might be worth considering, but I'd be subtle about it, ask him to escort Her Grace to musicales, for example. He won't come to the bridle if he sees your hand in things."

"Damned stubborn," His Grace pronounced. "Just like his mama. A bit more to wet the whistle, if you please." Westhaven brought the decanter to where his father sat on the leather couch, and poured half a measure into the glass. On closer inspection, the heat was taking a toll on His Grace. His ruddy complexion looked more florid than usual, and his breathing seemed a trifle labored.

"Speaking of stubbornness," the earl said when he'd put the decanter back on the sideboard, "I no longer have an association with the fair Elise."

"What?" His Grace frowned. "You've lost your taste for the little blonde?"

"I wouldn't say I've lost my taste for the little blonde, so much as I've never had a taste for my privacy being invaded nor fancied the Moreland title going to somebody who lacks a drop of Windham blood."

"What are you blathering on about, Westhaven? I rather liked your Elise. Seemed a practical woman, if you know what I mean."

"Meaning she took your bribe, or your dare," the earl concluded. "Then she turned around and offered her favors elsewhere, to at least one other tall, green-eyed lordling that I know of, and perhaps several others, as well."

"She's a bit of a strumpet, Westhaven, though passably discreet. What would you expect?" The duke finished his drink with a satisfied smack of his lips.

"She's Renfrew's intended, if your baiting inspired her to get with child, Your Grace," the earl replied. "You put her up to trying to get a child, and the only way she could do that was to pass somebody else's off as mine."

"Good God, Westhaven." The duke rose, looking pained. "You aren't telling me you can't bed a damned woman, are you?"

"Were that the case, I would not tell you, as such

matters are *supposed* to be private. What I am telling you is if you attempt to manipulate one more woman into my bed, I will not marry. Back off, Your Grace, or you will wish you had."

"Are you threatening your own father, Westhaven?" The duke thumped his glass down, hard.

"I am assuring him," the earl replied softly, "if he attempts even once more to violate my privacy, I will make him regret it for all of his remaining days."

"Violate your...? Oh, for the love of God, boy." The duke turned to go, hand on the door latch. "I did not come here to argue with you, for once. I came to tell you it was well done, getting your brother to Fairly's, reminding him what... Never mind. I came with only good intentions, and here you are threatening me. What would your dear mama think of such disrespect? Of course I am concerned; you are past thirty, and you have neither bride nor heir nor promise thereof. You think you can live forever, but you and your brother are proof that even when a man has decades to raise up his sons, sometimes the task is yet incomplete and badly done. You aren't without sense, Westhaven, and you at least show some regard for the Moreland consequence. All I want is to see the succession secured before I die, and to see your mother has some grandchildren to spoil and love. Good day."

He made a grand, door-slamming exit and left his son eyeing the decanter longingly. When a soft knock came a few minutes later, the earl was still so lost in thought, he barely heard it.

"Come in."

"My lord?" Mrs. Seaton, looking prim, cool, and

tidy, strode into the room and gave him her signature brisk curtsy. "The luncheon hour approaches. Shall we serve you on the terrace, in the dining parlor, or would you like a tray in here?"

"I seem to have lost my appetite, Mrs. Seaton." The earl rose from his desk and walked around to sit on the front of it. "His Grace came to call, and our visit degenerated into its usual haranguing and shouting."

"One could hear this," Mrs. Seaton said, her expression sympathetic. "At least on His Grace's part."

"I was congratulated on dragging my little brother to a brothel, for God's sake. The old man would have fit in wonderfully in days of yore, when bride and groom were expected to bed each other before cheering onlookers."

"My lord, His Grace means well."

"He will tell you he does," the earl agreed. "Just being a conscientious steward of the Moreland succession. But in truth, it's his own consequence he wants to protect. If I fail to reproduce to his satisfaction, then he will be embarrassed, plain and simple. It's not enough that he sired five sons, three of whom still live, but he must see a dynasty at his feet before he departs this earth."

Mrs. Seaton remained quiet, and the earl recalled he'd sung this lament in her hearing before.

"Is my brother asleep?"

"He is, but he asked to be awakened not later than two of the clock. He wants to put in his four hours before repairing again to Viscount Fairly's establishment."

"I do believe my brother is studying to become a madam."

Again, his housekeeper did not see fit to make any reply.

"I'll take a tray out back," the earl said, "but you needn't go to all the usual bother... setting the table, arranging the flowers, and so forth. A tray will do, as long as there's plenty of sweetened lemonade to go with the meal."

"Of course, my lord." She bobbed her curtsy, but he snaked out a hand to encircle her wrist before she could go.

"Are you unhappy with me?" he asked, eyeing her closely. "Bad enough His Grace finds fault with me at every turn, Mrs. Seaton. I am trying very hard not to annoy my staff as much as my father annoys me."

"I do not think on your worst day you could be half so annoying to us as that man is to you. Your patience with him is admired."

"By whom?"

"Your staff," she replied. "And your housekeeper."

"The admiration of my housekeeper," the earl said, "is a consummation devoutly to be wished."

He brought her wrist to his lips and kissed the soft skin below the base of her thumb, lingering long enough that he felt the steady beat of her pulse.

She scowled at him, whirled, and left without a curtsy.

So much, the earl thought as he watched her retreat, for the admiration of his housekeeper.

# *Four*

"I NEVER DID ASK IF YOU SUCCESSFULLY COMPLETED your errands this morning." Westhaven put aside his copy of *The Times* as Anna set his lunch tray before him.

"I did. Will there be anything else, my lord?"

He regarded her standing with her hands folded, her expression neutral amid the flowers and walks of his back garden.

"Anna," he began, but he saw his use of her name made her bristle. "Please sit, and I do mean will you please."

She sat, perched like an errant schoolgirl on the very edge of her chair, back straight, eyes front.

"You are scolding me without saying a word," the earl said on a sigh. "It was just a kiss, Anna, and I had the impression you rather enjoyed it, too."

She looked down, while a blush crept up the side of her neck.

"That's the problem, isn't it?" he said with sudden, happy insight. "You could accept my apology and treat me with cheerful condescension, but you *enjoyed* our kiss."

"My lord," she said, addressing the hands she fisted in her lap, "can you not accept that were I to encourage your... mischief, I would be courting my own ruin?"

"Ruin?" He said with a snort. "Elise will be enjoying an entire estate for the rest of her days as a token of ruin at my hands—among others—if ruin you believe it to be. I did not take her virginity, either, *Mrs. Seaton*, and I am not a man who casually discards others."

She was silent then raised her eyes, a mulish expression on her face.

"I will not seek another position as a function of what has gone between us so far, but you must stop."

"Stop what, Anna?"

"You should not use my name, my lord," she said, rising. "I have not given you leave to do so."

He rose, as well, as if she were a lady deserving of his manners. "May I ask your permission to use your given name, at least when we are private?"

He'd shocked her, he saw with some satisfaction. She'd thought him too autocratic to ask, and he was again reminded of his father's ways. But she was looking at him now, really looking, and he pressed his advantage.

"I find it impossible to think of you as Mrs. Seaton. In this house, there is no other who treats me as you do, *Anna*. You are kind but honest, and sympathetic without being patronizing. You are the closest thing I have here to an ally, and I would ask this small boon of you."

He watched as she closed her eyes and waged some internal struggle, but in the anguish on her face, he suspected victory in this skirmish was to be his. She'd grant him his request, precisely because he had made it a request, putting a small measure of power exclusively into her hands.

She nodded assent but looked miserable over it.

"And you," he said, letting concern—not guilt, surely—show in his gaze, "you must consider me an ally, as well, Anna."

She speared him with a stormy look. "An ally who would compromise my reputation, knowing without it I am but a pauper or worse."

"I do not seek to bring you ruin," he corrected her. "And I would never force my will on you."

Anna stood, and he thought her eyes were suspiciously bright. "Perhaps, my lord, you just did."

He stared after her for long moments, wrestling with her final accusation but coming to no tidy answers. He could offer Anna Seaton an option, a choice other than decades of stepping and fetching and serving. He desired her and enjoyed her company out of bed, a peculiar realization though not unwelcome. But his seduction would be complicated by her reticence, her infernal notions of decency.

For now, he could steal some delectable kisses—and perhaps more than kisses—while she found the resolve to refuse him altogether and send him packing.

He was lingering over his lemonade when Val wandered out looking sleepy and rumpled, shirt open at the throat and cuffs turned back.

"Ye gods, it is too hot to sleep." He reached over and drained the last of his brother's drink. "You do like it sweet."

"Helps with my disposition. And as I did indeed have to deal with His Grace this morning, I feel entitled."

"How bad was he?" Val asked as he sat and crossed his long legs at the ankle.

"Bad enough. Wanted to chat about the scene at Fairly's but left yelling about grandchildren and disrespect."

"Sounds about like your usual with him," Val said as John Footman brought out a second tray, this one bearing something closer to breakfast.

"Mrs. S said to tell you this one is sweetened, my lord." John set one glass before the earl. "And this one, less so," he said as he placed the other before Val.

"I think she puts mint in it," Val said after a long swallow.

"Mrs. Seaton?" the earl asked, sipping at his own drink. "Probably. She delights in all matters domestic."

"And she did not appear to be delighting in you, when she was out here earlier."

"Valentine." The earl stared hard at his brother. "Were you spying on me?"

Val pointed straight up, to where the balcony of his bedroom overlooked the terrace. "I sleep on that balcony most nights," he explained, "and you were not whispering. I, however, was sleeping and caught the tail end of an interesting exchange."

The earl had the grace to study his drink at some silent length.

"Well?" He met his younger brother's eyes, awaiting castigation.

"She is a decent woman, Westhaven, and if you trifle with her, she won't be decent any longer, ever again. What is a fleeting pleasure for you changes her life irrevocably, and you can never, ever change it back. I am not sure you want that on your appallingly overactive conscience, as much as I applaud your improvement in taste."

The earl swirled his drink and realized with a sinking feeling Val had gotten his graceful, talented hands on a truth.

"Maybe," Val went on, "you should just marry the woman, hmm? You get on with her, you respect her, and if you marry her, she becomes a duchess. She could do worse, and it would appease Their Graces."

"She would not like the duchess part."

"You could make it worth her while," Val said, his tone full of studied nonchalance.

"Listen to you. You would encourage me into the arms of a pox-ridden gin whore if it would result in His Grace getting a few grandsons."

"No, I would not, or you wouldn't have gotten that little postscript from me regarding Elise's summer recreation, would you?"

The earl rose and regarded his brother. "You are a pestilential irritant of biblical proportions. If I do not turn out to be an exact replica of His Grace, it will be in part due to your aggravating influence."

Val was grinning around a mouthful of muffin, but he nonetheless managed to reply intelligibly to his brother's retreating back. "Love you, too."

❧

Anna wasn't fooled. Since their confrontation over the lunch table earlier in the week, the earl had kept a distance, but it was a thoughtful distance. She'd caught him eyeing her as she watered the bouquets in his library, or rising to his feet when she entered a room. It was unnerving, like being stalked by a hungry tiger.

And as the week wore on, the heat became worse, with violent displays of lightning and thunder at night but no cooling rains to bring relief. The entire household was drinking cold tea, lemonade, and cold cider by the gallon, and livery was worn only at the front door. Everybody's cuffs were turned back, collars were loosened, and petticoats were discarded.

Anna heard the front door slam and knew the earl had returned after a long afternoon in the City, transacting business of some sort. She assembled a tray and waited to hear which door above would slam next. She had to cock her head, because Valentine was playing his pianoforte. The music wasn't loud, but rather dense with feeling, and not happy feeling at that.

"He misses our brothers," the earl said from the kitchen doorway. "More than I realized, as, perhaps, do I."

The music shifted and became dark, despairing, all the more convincingly so for being quiet. This wasn't the passionate, bewildered grief of first loss; it was the grinding, desolate ache that followed. Anna's own losses and grief rose up and threatened to swamp her, even as the earl moved into the kitchen and eyed the tray on the counter.

His eyes shifted back up just in time for Anna to be caught wiping a tear from the corner of her eye.

"Come." He took her hand and led her to the table, sitting her down, passing her his handkerchief, fetching the tray, then taking the place beside her, hip to hip.

They listened for long moments, the cool of the kitchen cocooning them both in the beauty and pain of the music, and then Val's playing shifted again, still sad but with a piercingly sweet lift of acceptance and peace to it. Death, his music seemed to say, was not the end, not when there was love.

"Your brother is a genius."

The earl leaned back to rest his shoulder blades along the wall behind them. "A genius who likely only plays like this late at night among whores and strangers. He's still a little lost with it." He slipped his fingers through Anna's and gently closed his hand. "As, I suppose, am I."

"It has been less than a year?"

"It has. Victor asked that we observe only six months of full mourning, but my mother is still grieving deeply. I should have offered Valentine a bunk months ago."

"He probably would not have come," Anna said, turning their hands over to study his brown knuckles. "I think your brother needs a certain amount of solitude."

"In that, he and I and Devlin are all alike."

"Devlin is your half brother?" Ducal bastards were apparently an accepted reality, at least in the Windham family.

"He is." Westhaven nodded, giving her back her hand. "Tea or cider or lemonade?"

"Any will do," Anna said, noting that Val's music

was lighter now, still tender but sweetly wistful, the grief nowhere evident.

"Lemonade, then." The earl sugared his, added a spoonful to Anna's, and set it down before her. "You might as well drink it here with me, and I'll tell you of my illustrious family." He sat again, but more than their hips touched this time, as his whole side lay along hers, and Anna felt heat and weariness in his long frame. One by one, the earl described his siblings, both deceased and extant, legitimate and not.

"You speak of each of them with such affection," Anna said. "It isn't always so with siblings."

"If I credit my parents with one thing," the earl said, running his finger around the rim of his glass, "it is with making our family a real family. They didn't send us boys off to school until we were fourteen or so, and then just so we could meet our form before we went to university. We were frightfully well educated, too, so there was no feeling inadequate before our peers. We did things all together, though it took a parade of coaches to move us hither and thither, but Dev and Maggie often went with us, particularly in the summer."

"They are received, then?"

"Everywhere. Her Grace made it obvious that a virile young lord's premarital indiscretions were not to be censored, and the die was cast. It helps that Devlin is charming, handsome, and independently wealthy, and Maggie is as pretty and well mannered as her sisters."

"That would tend to encourage a few doors to open."

"And what of you, Anna Seaton?" The earl cocked his head to regard her. "You have a brother and a sister, and you had a grandpapa. Did you all get along?"

"We did not," Anna said, rising and taking her glass to the sink. "My parents died when I was young. My brother grew up with a lack of parental supervision, though my grandfather tried to provide guidance. My parents, I'm told, loved each other sincerely. Grandpapa took us into his home immediately when they died, but as my brother is ten years my senior, he was considerably less malleable. There was a lot of shouting."

"As there is between my father and me." The earl smiled at her when she sat back down across from him.

"Your mother doesn't shout at him, does she?"

"No." The earl looked intrigued with that observation. "She just gets this pained, disappointed look and calls him Percival or Your Grace instead of Percy."

"My grandfather had that look polished to a shine." Anna grimaced. "It crushed me the few times I merited it."

"So you were a good girl, Anna Seaton?" The earl was smiling at her with a particular light in his eyes, one Anna didn't understand, though it wasn't especially threatening.

"Headstrong, but yes, I was a good girl." She rose again, and this time took his glass with her. "And I am."

"Are you busy Tuesday next?" he asked, rising to lean against the wall, arms crossed over his chest as he watched her rinse out their glasses.

"Not especially," Anna replied. "We do our big market on Wednesday, which is also half-day for the men."

"Then can I requisition your time, if it's decent weather?"

"For?" She eyed him warily, unable to sense his mood.

"I have recently committed into another's keeping a Windham property known as Monk's Crossing," he explained. "My father and I agree each of my sisters ought to be dowered with some modestly profitable, pleasant property, preferably close to London. Having transferred ownership of one, I am looking at procuring another. The girls socialized little this year, due to Victor's death, but at least two of them have possibilities that might come to something in the next year. I'd like to have their dower properties in presentable condition."

"So what are we doing, Tuesday next?" Anna asked, folding her arms across her chest.

"I am going to inspect a potential dower property out in Surrey, a couple hours from Town, and for sale at a suspiciously reasonable price. I would like you to accompany me to assess its appeal to feminine sensibilities."

"Whatever does that mean?"

The earl pushed off the wall and waved a hand. "There are things about a house I just don't take in, being male. You women understand subtleties, like where windows will give effective ventilation, what rooms will be cold in winter, or which fireplaces are unfortunately situated. You can assess the functionality of a kitchen at a glance, whereas I can barely find the bread box."

He moved to stand before her, looking down at her. "I can assess if a property is priced properly in relation to its size, location, and appointments, but you can assess if a house can be made into a home."

"I will go then." Anna nodded. It was a task to which she was suited, and probably only a morning's work. "But you must consider which sister will end up with this property and think about her, so you can tell me her likes and dislikes."

"Fair enough. We can discuss those particulars on the way there."

He left, moving in the direction of the music room, where Val was once again between pieces, or moods. Anna watched him go, unable to help but appreciate the lean play of muscle along his flanks.

One had to wonder how the ladies of polite society had ever managed, when all the Windham brothers had assembled in one place, particularly in evening finery or riding attire or shirt sleeves...

# *Five*

"THE ESTATE IS CALLED WILLOW BEND," THE EARL began as they tooled out of the mews in the gray predawn light. "We should be there in less than two hours, even giving Pericles a few chances to rest."

"Have you seen it before?" Anna asked, enjoying the breeze on her face as the horse gained the street and broke to the trot.

"I have seen only sketches, hence the necessity for this trip. I should warn you I am inclined to buy it based on proximity alone. There is only so much land for sale around London, and the city grows outward each year."

The miles fell away as they talked, occasionally challenging each other, more often just sharing viewpoints and observations. When they were well out of town, the earl pulled up his gig to let the horse rest.

"Shall we walk? Pericles will stand there until Domesday or he eats every blade of grass at his feet." The earl handed her down then released the checkrein so the horse could graze for a few minutes.

"He takes his victuals seriously," Anna said.

"To any Windham male, victuals are of significant import."

"Good thing I brought a very full hamper, then, isn't it?" The earl offered her his arm, and she took it, realizing they had never in the months she'd worked for him simply walked side by side like this.

"It's a lovely morning," Anna said, taking refuge in the weather. "After all the noise and wind, I was expecting we would get at least some rain last night."

"A few drops. Val sleeps on his balcony these days and said that's all he felt."

"And where was he off to this morning?"

"To see our little niece, Rose," the earl replied, pausing before a wooden stile. "Had I been able, I'd have moved this appointment to join him, but there are several people interested in Willow Bend."

"Or so the land agent told you."

"Repeatedly and emphatically. Had I coordinated more closely with Val, though, he could have at least escorted us for much of the distance. Welbourne is not far from Willow Bend."

"Do you like children?" The stile was level at the top, so Anna settled on it, the better to watch his smile disappear at the question when he took a seat beside her.

"Babies rather intimidate me, as one can drop them, and they break, but yes, I like children. I am not particularly charming, as Val is, but children don't mind that. They want honest regard, much like a good horse does."

"But Rose was not much taken with you?"

"More to the point, Rose's mother, to whom His Grace would have seen me wed, was not much taken with me, and in the way of children, Rose comprehended that as clearly as I did."

They fell silent, sitting side by side, until Anna felt the earl's hand steal over hers to rest there.

"Today, I am going to call you Anna, and you are going to permit me to do so, please? We will be congenial with each other and forget I am the earl and you are my housekeeper. We will enjoy a pleasant morning in the country, Anna, with none of your frowning and scolding. This is agreeable to you?"

"We will share a lovely morning in the country," Anna agreed, wanting nothing so much as to start that morning by letting her head rest against his shoulder. It was a wicked impulse and would give him all the wrong ideas.

"And seal our agreement"—the earl shifted to stand before her—"with a kiss."

He gave her time to wiggle off the hook, to hop down off the stile and dash past him, to deliver a little lecture even, but she sat, still as a mouse, while he framed her face with his bare hands and brought his lips to hers. He propped one booted foot on the stile and leaned over her as his mouth settled fully over hers.

While Anna's common sense tried to riot, the earl was in no hurry, exploring the fullness of her lips with his own, then easing away to run his nose along her hairline, then cruising back over her mouth on the way to kissing the side of her neck.

Her common sense gave a last, despairing whimper and went silent, because Anna liked that, that business of him nuzzling and kissing at her neck, at the soft flesh below her ear, at the place where her neck met her shoulder. He must have liked it, too, as he spent long minutes learning the various flavors of her nape and throat, the spots that were ticklish and the spots he could soothe with his tongue and lips.

She swayed into him, wrapping a hand around the back of his neck for support, wishing she'd thought—as he had—to take off her gloves. Oh, she knew nothing of the details of being wicked, nothing at all except that with him, she liked it. She liked the way she felt more alive wherever he touched, liked the way her insides melted at the scent and taste of him. Liked the feel of his long, muscular body so close to hers.

Anna felt a hairpin plink against her cheek and made herself draw back.

"Oh dear." She stared up at him, dumbstruck by the heat in his green eyes. "Dear, dear, dear."

The earl looked down and traced a finger along the slope of her breast to pluck the hairpin from her dress. He held it out to her, smiling as if he were presenting her with a flower.

"I may be feeling winded," he said, offering her his arm, "but by now Pericles should be well rested."

Anna took his arm, glancing over at him cautiously. The sensation of his finger sliding down her breast had been enough to make her heart kick against her ribs. God in heaven, he knew how to touch a woman, but it didn't seem to wind him at all, contrary to his words.

"You are quiet, Anna," he remarked as they climbed aboard and gained the road.

"I am overwhelmed," she said. "I think I must be a very wicked woman, my... What do I call you?"

The earl urged Pericles to the trot. "Today, you call me whatever pleases you, but why do you say you are wicked?"

"I should be remonstrating you, making you behave, chiding you for your lapses," Anna informed him, warming to her topic. "Our lapses. But my self-restraint has departed for the Orient, I suppose, and all I want…"

"All you want?" The earl kept his eyes on the empty road.

"Is to forget every pretense of common sense." Anna completed the thought, and now—now that he was all cool composure beside her—she was uncomfortable with herself. "To share more lapses with you."

"I would like that, Anna," he replied simply. "If it would please you to lapse with me, then I would enjoy it, too."

"It can't lead to anything," Anna said miserably, "except more and worse mischief."

The earl glanced over at her but had to keep some focus on the road. "Why not just enjoy these hours as we choose to spend them? I will not take liberties you deny me, Anna, not today, not ever. But for today, I will enjoy your company to the fullest extent you allow, and I will do so without regard to whether today leads to something or merely rests in memory as a pleasurable few hours spent in your company."

Anna fell silent, considering his words. If Westhaven's brother Victor could have had such a morning, able to breathe without coughing, would he have fretted over a few kisses leading to nothing, or would he have seized the hours as a gift? Knowing he could well have been riding to his death in the next battle, would Lord Bartholomew have demurred, or would he have stashed a bottle of wine in the hamper?

"And now," Anna said after a time, "you are quiet."

"It is a pretty morning." He smiled at her, including her in that prettiness. "I am in good company, and we are about a pleasant errand. Just to be away from Town, away from Tolliver's infernal correspondence, and away from Stenson's grasping fingers is reason to rejoice."

"I could not abide the touch of someone I did not like," Anna said, grimacing.

"So I do my best to stay out of his reach and to bellow like the duke when he transgresses," Westhaven said. "He is getting better, but tell me, Anna, did you just indirectly admit to liking me?"

She drew in a swift breath and saw from his expression that while he was teasing, he was also... fishing.

"Of course I like you. I like you entirely too well, and it is badly done of you to make me admit it."

"Well, let's go from bad to worse, then, and you can tell me precisely why you like me."

"You are serious?"

"I am. If you want, I will return the favor, though we have only several hours, and my list might take much longer than that."

*He is flirting with me*, Anna thought, incredulous. In his high-handed, serious way, the Earl of Westhaven had just paid her a flirtatious compliment. A lightness spread out from her middle, something of warmth and humor and guilty pleasure in it.

"All right." Anna nodded briskly. "I like that you are shy and honorable in the ways that count. I like that you are kind to Morgan, and to your animals, and old Nanny Fran. You are as patient with His Grace as a human can be, and you adore your brother. You are fierce, too, though, and can be decisive when needs must. You are also, I think, a romantic, and this is no mean feat for a man who spends half his days with commercial documents. Mostly, I like that you are *good*; you look after those who depend on you, you have gratitude for your blessings, and you don't think enough of yourself."

Beside her, the earl was again silent.

"Shall I go on?" Anna asked, feeling a sudden awkwardness.

"You could not possibly pay me any greater series of compliments than you just have," he said. "The man you describe is a paragon, a fellow I'd very much like to meet."

"See?" Anna nudged him with her shoulder. "You do not think enough of yourself. But I can also tell you the parts of you that irritate me—if that will make you feel better?"

"I irritate you?" The earl's eyebrows rose. "This should be interesting. You gave me the good news first, fortifying me for more burdensome truths, so let fly."

"You are proud," Anna began, her tone thoughtful. "You don't think your papa can manage anything correctly, and you won't ask your brothers nor mother nor sisters even, for help with things directly affecting them. I wonder, in fact, if you have anybody you would call a friend."

"Ouch. A very definite ouch, Anna. Go on."

"You have forgotten how to play," Anna said, "how to frolic, though I cannot fault you for a lack of appreciation for what's around you. You appreciate; you just don't seem to… indulge yourself."

"I see. And in what should I indulge myself?"

"That is for you to determine," she replied. "Marzipan has gone over well, I think, and sweets in general. You have indulged your love of music by having Val underfoot. As to what else brings you pleasure, you would be the best judge of that."

The earl turned down a shady lane lined with towering oaks and an understory of rhododendrons in vigorous bloom.

"It was you," he said. "Before Val moved in, I thought it was a neighbor playing the piano late in the evenings, but it was you. Were you playing *for me*?"

Anna glanced off to the park beyond the trees and nodded.

"It seemed somebody should. Nanny Fran said you have a marvelous singing voice, and you play well yourself, but you'd stopped playing or singing when Bart died."

"Life did not change for the better for anyone when Bart died."

They pulled up to a pretty Tudor manor house, complete with fresh thatch on the roof and gleaming mullioned windows. Pericles blew out a horsy breath that sounded suspiciously like a sigh, but the earl did not climb down.

"Before Bart left," the earl said, fiddling with the reins, "he told me he wouldn't go if I forbade it. That was the word he used… forbid. He asked my permission, and knowing his temper and his penchant for dramatics, I had misgivings about his joining up, but I did not stop him. I could see that battling the duke day after day was killing them both. Bart was getting wilder, angrier, and the duke was becoming so bewildered by his cherished heir it was painful to watch."

"If you had to do it again, would you still give your permission?"

"I would." The earl nodded after a moment. "But first I would have told my brother I loved him, and then, just maybe, he would not have had to go."

"He knew," Anna said. "Just as you know he loved you, but he was coping as well as he could in a situation where every option came with significant costs."

A considering silence stretched between them, while Anna marveled that the man beside her was so given to introspection and so adept at hiding even that.

"Let's put away this difficult topic," the earl suggested, "and look over the property, shall we?" Because the place was uninhabited, it fell to them to lead Pericles to a roomy stall in the carriage house cum stable and see him tucked in with hay and water.

They made their way to the back terrace of the house, where the earl set down the wicker hamper he'd carried from the gig, and bent to loosen a particular brick from the back stoop. He produced a key from under the brick, opened the back door, and gestured for Anna to precede him.

"I like what I see," Anna said, folding her shawl on the kitchen counter. She turned to put her gloves on top of the shawl, only to find the earl had been standing immediately behind her.

"As do I," he said, looking directly down at her. His eyes were steady, even searching. Looking into those eyes, Anna admitted she'd been deceiving herself. She was a good girl, but at least part of her was here to be wicked with him—maybe just a little wicked by his standards but more wicked than Anna had ever wanted to be before.

He made no move to touch her, though, and so she frowned until insight struck: He was waiting for her to touch him, to do as she pleased.

He merely stood there, hands at his sides, watching her, until she closed the distance between them, slid both hands around his waist, and rested her forehead against his collarbone.

"Is this all you want, Anna?" He brought his arms around her and urged her to lean into him. "Merely an embrace? I'll understand it, if you do."

"It isn't merely an embrace," she replied, loving the feel of his lean muscles and long bones against her body. "It is *your* embrace, and your scent, and the cadence of your breathing, and the warmth of your hands. To me, there is nothing mere about it. "

She remained in his arms, feeling the way his hands learned the planes and angles of her back, feeling his mind absorb and consider her words.

"Let's explore the house," he suggested, "then poke around the grounds and outbuildings before it gets too hot."

She nodded, feeling a hint of wariness.

"Anna." He smiled faintly as he stepped back. "I am

not going to maul you, ever. And I did bring you out here for the purpose of evaluating this property, not becoming my next mistress."

"Your next…?"

"Badly put." The earl took her hand. "Forget I said it."

She let him tow her along out of the kitchen and through the various pantries, cellars, laundries, and servants' quarters on the ground floor. Not until he led her up the stairs to the main floor and she was standing beside him in the library did Anna find the words she needed.

"This was the former owner's pride and joy," the earl said, "and I must admit, for a country library, it is a magnificent room." The ceilings were twelve feet at least, with windows that ran the entire height of the room on two walls. Two massive fieldstone fireplaces sat one on each outside wall, both with raised hearths and richly carved chestnut mantels.

"It's such a pretty wood," the earl remarked, stroking a hand across one mantel. "Warmer to the eye than oak, and lighter in weight, but almost as strong." Anna watched that hand caressing the grain of the carved surface and felt an internal shiver.

"I would never be a man's mistress, you know." She sat on the hearth and regarded him. Somewhere in their travels through the house, he had taken off his jacket and waistcoat, and turned back his cuffs. He had dispensed with a neckcloth altogether in deference to the heat, but the informality of his attire only made him handsome in a different way.

"Why not?" The earl didn't seem surprised nor

offended, he just sat himself beside her on the cool, hard stones and shot her a sidewise glance.

"It isn't my precious virtue, if that's what you're thinking." Anna wrapped her arms around her knees.

"The thought had crossed my mind you might set store by a chaste reputation."

"Of course I do." She laid her cheek on her knees and regarded him with a frown. "Though only up to a point. Being a mistress has no appeal, though, because of the money."

"You eschew good coin?" the earl said, and though his tone was casual, Anna detected a hint of pique in it.

"I most assuredly do not, but how can a man accept intimacies from a woman who is paid to pretend she cares for his attentions? It seems to me an insupportable farce and as degrading to the man as the woman."

"Degrading how?" He was amused now, or at least diverted.

"If a woman will allow you liberties only if you pay her," Anna explained, "then it's your coin she treasures, not your kisses or caresses or whatnot."

He was trying not to smile now. "Most men care only for the whatnot, Anna. They trouble themselves little about what they parted with or put up with to procure it."

"Then most men are easily manipulated and to be pitied. One begins to suspect holy matrimony was devised for the protection of men, and not the fairer sex after all."

"So you have no more regard for being a wife than you do being a mistress?"

"It depends entirely on whose wife we're talking

about." Anna rose and went to look out the windows. "This room is so pretty and light and inviting. I could particularly see curling up on one of these window seats with Sir Walter Scott or some John Donne."

"Let's assess some more of the house," the earl said, lacing his fingers with hers. As they wended their way from room to room, Anna noted that the earl, away from his townhouse at least, was a toucher. She'd seen the same tendency when he was with his brother. He laid a hand on Val's sleeve, straightened Val's collar, patted his back, and otherwise treated his brother with affection. It was the same with Nanny Fran, whom he kissed on the cheek, hugged, and allowed to treat him with similar familiarity.

With Anna, he took her hand, offered his arm, put his hand on the small of her back, brushed aside her hair, and otherwise kept up a steady campaign of casual touches.

Casual to him, Anna thought, knowing she was being sillier than any woman of five and twenty had a right to be. To her, these little gestures were sweet and attractive, that is, they fascinated her and made her want to stand too close to him.

Outside, he assisted her over stiles and fences, picked her a daisy and positioned it behind her ear, stole a little kiss under the rose arbor, and tucked her against his side while they explored the garden walks.

"Were you like this with Elise?" Anna asked when they'd found a wooden bench in some shade near the roses.

"Good God, Anna." The earl looked over at her

in consternation. "A man does not discuss his mistress with decent women."

"I am not asking about Elise. I am asking about you."

"When I saw Elise in social settings," the earl replied, eyes on the house across the gardens, "we were cordial. I occasionally danced with her, but she did not enjoy my partnering, as I am too tall."

"You are too...?" Anna scowled at that. "You are not too tall."

"Perhaps you can prove that point by dancing with me sometime?"

She cocked her head at him and decided he was teasing. "So when you met socially, you behaved as acquaintances. What about when you were simply whiling away a morning?"

"When I did not run into Elise at an evening gathering of polite society, I saw her by appointment, in the afternoon," the earl said, resting an arm along the back of the bench with a sigh.

"By *appointment, only*?" Anna's surprise seemed to perplex him.

"You know my week included visits to her," the earl replied mildly. "Regular visits allowed her to schedule the rest of her affairs, so to speak."

"The rest of her affairs? And is this all you wanted? An hour of her attention twice a week, scheduled in advance so as to only minimally inconvenience her?"

"Well, more or less," the earl admitted, clearly puzzled by Anna's indignation.

"And *that* is how you go about *passion*? I suppose you left her free to pursue any other pair of broad shoulders she pleased when you were not bothering her?"

"In retrospect, one can admit there were a few subtle indicators the situation was not ideal, but we are not discussing this further, Anna Seaton. And for your information, that is not how I prefer to go about passion." He folded her hand between both of his and fell silent. Topic closed.

"You deserve more than to be tolerated for a few hours a week in exchange for parting with your coin. Any good man does."

"Your sentiments are appreciated," the earl said, amusement back in his tone. "Shall we see what we can find in that hamper you brought? The thing weighed a ton, which is good, as my appetite is making itself known."

Topic closed, subject *changed*.

"We'll need the blanket from the gig, I think," Anna said, willing to drop the discussion of his former mistress. "I saw no dining table nor much in the way of chairs inside."

"I gather the matched sets and so forth were auctioned this spring," the earl said, tugging Anna to her feet. "What do you think of the place so far?"

"It's pretty, peaceful, and not too far from Town. So far I love it, but who are your neighbors?"

"Now that is not something I would have considered, except that you raise it, and to a widow, such a thing would matter. I will make inquiries, though I know my niece dwells less than three miles farther up the road we came in on."

"Her aunt would like that, I'm sure, being close to Rose," Anna said as they walked back into the kitchen.

"Rose wouldn't mind, either. She gets on with everybody, even His Grace."

"You see him only as a father. As a grandpapa, he may be different."

They retrieved the blankets—two of them—and strolled through the lawns toward the spot for which the property was named, a grassy little knoll over-looking a wide, slow stream. Weeping willows grew on both banks, their branches trailing into the slow-moving water and giving the little space a private, magical quality.

"Perfect for wading," Anna said. "Will you be scandalized?"

"Not if you don't mind my disrobing to swim," the earl replied evenly.

"Naughty man. I bet you and your brothers did your share of that, growing up at Morelands."

"We did." The earl unfolded a blanket and flapped it out onto a shady patch of ground. "Morelands has grown, generation by generation, to the point where it's tens of thousands of acres, complete with ponds, streams, and even a waterfall. I learned to hunt, fish, swim, ride, and more just rambling around with my brothers."

"It sounds idyllic."

"So where did you grow up, Anna?" The earl sat down on the blanket. "You aren't going to loom over me, are you?"

Anna folded to the blanket beside him, realizing how vague her notion of the day had been. A few kisses, a tour of the property, and back to the realities of their lives at the townhouse. She hadn't considered they would talk and talk and talk, nor that she would enjoy that as much as the kissing.

"Hand me the hamper," she ordered. "I will make us up plates. There is lemonade and wine, both."

"Heaven forefend! Wine on a weekday before noon, Mrs. Seaton?"

"I love a good cold white," Anna admitted, "and a hearty red."

"I hope you put some of what you love in that hamper. This is a long way to come for bannocks."

"Not burned bannocks, please," she said, pawing carefully through the hamper. When she finished, Westhaven was presented with sliced strawberries, cheese, buttered slices of bread, cold chicken, and two pieces of marzipan.

"And what have we here?" The earl peered into the hamper and extracted a tall bottle. "Champagne?"

"What?" Anna looked up. "I didn't put that in there."

"I detect the subtle hand of Nanny Fran. A glass, if you please."

Anna obligingly held the glass while the earl popped the cork. She shamelessly sipped the fizzy overflow and held the glass out to him. He drank without taking the glass into his own hand and smiled at her.

"That will do," he declared. "For a hot summer day, it will do splendidly."

"Then you can pour me a glass, as well."

"As you wish," he replied, accommodating her order and filling a glass for himself, too. To Anna's surprise, before either drinking or diving into his meal, the earl paused to wrench off his boots and stockings.

"I have it on good authority extreme heat is dangerous

and one shouldn't wear clothes unnecessarily, or so my footmen tell me when I catch them only half liveried." He sipped at his wine, hiding what had to be a smile.

"I did not precisely tell them that, though it's probably good advice."

"So are you wearing drawers and petticoats?" the earl asked, waggling his eyebrows.

"No more champagne for you, if only two sips make you lost to all propriety."

"You're not wearing them," he concluded, making himself a sandwich. "Sensible of you, as it seems even more oppressively hot today than yesterday."

"It is warming up. It also looks to be clouding up."

"More false hope." He glanced at the sky. "I can't recall a summer quite so brutal and early as this one. Seems we hardly had a real spring."

"It's better in the North. You get beastly winters there, but also a real spring, a tolerable summer, and a truly wonderful autumn."

"So you were raised in the North."

"I was. Right now, I miss it."

"I miss Scotland right now, or Stockholm. But this food is superb and the company even better. More champagne?"

"I shouldn't." Her eyes strayed to the bottle, sweating in its linen napkin. "It is such a pleasant drink."

The earl topped off both of their glasses. "This is a day for pleasant, not a day for shoulds and should nots, though I am thinking I should buy the place."

"It is lovely. The only thing that gives me pause are the oaks along the lane. They will carpet the place with leaves come fall."

"And the gardeners will rake them." The earl shrugged. "Then the children can jump in the piles of leaves and scatter them all about again."

"A sound plan. Are you going to eat those strawberries?"

The earl paused, considered his plate, and picked up a perfect red, juicy berry.

"I'll share." He held it out to her but withdrew it when Anna extended her hand. Sensing his intent, she sat back but held still as he brought it to her mouth. She bit down, then found as the sweet fruit flavor burst across her tongue that her champagne glass was pressed to her lips, as well.

"I really did not pack that champagne," she said when she'd savored the wine.

"I did," the earl confessed. "Nanny Fran is sworn to secrecy as my accomplice."

"She adores you." Anna smiled. "She has more stories about 'her boys' than you would recognize."

"I know." The earl lounged back, resting on his elbows. "When Bart died and she'd launch into a reminiscence, I used to have to leave the room, so angry was I at her. Now I look for the chance to get her going."

"Grief changes. I recall as a child sitting for hours in my mother's wardrobe after she died; that was where I could still smell her."

"I recall you lost both parents quite young."

"I was raised by my father's father. He loved us as much as any parent could, probably more, because he'd lost his only son."

"I am sorry, Anna. I've talked about losing two brothers, both during my adulthood, and I never considered that you have losses of your own." He did not raise the issue of the departed Mr. Seaton, for which Anna was profoundly grateful.

"It was a long time ago," Anna said. "My parents did not suffer. Their carriage careened down a muddy embankment, and their necks were broken. The poor horse, by contrast, had to wait hours to be shot."

"Dear God." The earl shuddered. "Were you in that carriage, as well?"

"I was not, though I often used to wish I had been."

"Anna…" His tone was concerned, and she found it needful in that moment to study her empty wine glass.

"I have become maudlin by virtue of imbibing."

"Hush," Westhaven chided, crawling across the blanket. He wrapped her in his arms then wrestled her down to lie beside him, her head on his shoulder. She cuddled into him, feeling abruptly cold except where his body lay along hers.

"Val had a bout of the weeps the other day." The earl sighed. "I forget he is so sensitive, because he hides with that great black beast of his and tries so hard not to trouble others. When Bart died, Val went for days without leaving the piano, and only Her Grace's insistence that he be indulged preserved him from the wrath of the duke."

"Your family has not had an easy time of it. One would think rank and riches would assure happiness, but by the Windham example, they do not."

"Nor do they condemn one to misery," the earl pointed out, his hand making circles on her back. "I, for one, do not relish the thought of being poor."

"There is poor, and there is poor. In some ways,

I have more freedom than you do, and freedom is a form of great wealth."

"It is," Westhaven agreed, "but I don't see where you have it in such abundance."

"Oh, but I do." Anna sat up and put her chin on her drawn-up knees. "I can leave your employ tomorrow and hare off to Bath, there to keep house for any beldame who will have me. I can answer an advertisement to be a bride for an American tobacco farmer or go live with the natives in the American west. I can join a Scottish convent or journey to darkest Africa as a missionary to the heathen."

"And I, poor fellow"—the earl smiled up at her—"have none of those options."

"You do not," Anna agreed, grinning at him over her shoulder. "You are stuck with Tolliver and Stenson and His Grace, and barely recalling what pleasure is when your housekeeper remembers to sweeten your lemonade."

The earl folded his hands behind his head. "There is a pleasure you could allow me, Anna." He kept using her name, she thought, using it like a caress, a reminder that he knew the taste of her.

"There are many pleasures I could allow you," she said, caution in her tone, "few that I will."

"So I'm to earn your favors?" He merely smiled. "Then, allow me this: The heat and our rambling are threatening the integrity of your coiffure. Let me brush your hair."

"Brush my…?" Anna blinked and gave him a puzzled look.

"I used to brush Her Grace's hair when I was small,

then my sisters'. I've taken a turn or two with Rose, but she demands a certain dispatch only her step-papa and mama seem to have perfected."

"You want to brush my hair," Anna said, as if to herself. "That is an unusual request."

"But not too unusual. It requires no removal of clothing nor touching of the hands nor lascivious glances."

"All right," Anna said, more perplexed than alarmed, but then, she was in the company of a man who scheduled his passions. She fished inside the hamper and withdrew her reticule, producing a small bone-handled brush.

"Pretty little thing," the earl remarked, thumbing the bristles. "Now"—he sat up—"sit you here." He thumped the blanket beside him, and Anna scooted, only to find that the earl had shifted so she sat between his bent knees.

"Is this decent?" she murmured.

"Have another glass of wine," the earl suggested. "It will feel frustratingly decent."

They fell silent, and Anna felt the earl's fingers easing through her hair to find her hairpins. He slid them free carefully and began piling them to one side. When the bun at the nape of Anna's neck was loosened, he let her thick plait tumble down her back.

"I like this part," he said. "When you free up a braid, and a single shiny rope becomes skeins and curls and riots of silky, soft hair. How do you keep it so fragrant?"

She felt him lean in for a sniff, and her heart nearly skipped a beat.

"I make a shampoo scented with roses." And

ye gods, it had been a struggle to utter that single coherent sentence. His hands were lacing through her unbound hair to massage her scalp and the back of her neck. His touch was perfect—deliberate, knowing, and competent without using too much strength. He trailed her hair down her back, leaving little trickles of pleasure to skitter along her spine, and then she felt him gathering the mass of it, to move it to one side.

"It's beautiful," he murmured, his words breathed near her ear. "I'm going to forbid you to wear those hideous caps of yours when we return to Town."

His thumb brushed along her nape, and then something softer, followed by a puff of breath.

*God, yes*, Anna thought, letting her chin drop forward. Westhaven scooted closer, the better to kiss her neck, and Anna tilted her head, the better to allow it.

"Ah, Anna," he whispered before pressing his lips to her cheek and letting them drift to her throat. His mouth was open on her skin, as if he'd consume her or sink his teeth into her flesh. Then he paused and scooped her against his chest, dropping one knee and angling her legs across his thigh.

Anna blinked up at him, her back supported by his one upraised knee.

"None of that," he scolded. "I can see you preparing to think, Anna Seaton, and this is not a moment for thinking."

Before she could blink again, his mouth came down on hers in a voluptuously ravenous kiss. His tongue was in her mouth, plundering and demanding and promising. Oh, God, the things his kiss was promising.

His hand slipped down her arm to close around her fingers where they lay limp in her lap. He brought up her hand and put it around his neck, giving her a place to hold on as he gathered her more closely against him. His scent was all around her, and Anna felt heat, not the sweltering summer's heat but something clean and fiery and new singing through her veins. With it came desire—desire for him and desire for closeness with him. She clung and kissed him back, imitating the thrust and drag of his tongue with her own.

And then his lips were gone, leaving his forehead pressed to hers, his breath fanning against her cheek.

"God, Anna." He took a slow inhale then breathed out. "Almighty, everlasting God."

"What?" She felt suddenly unsure, wondering if she'd done something wrong.

"Lie back," he said, easing her to her back and stretching out on his side beside her. He laced his fingers through hers and squeezed. "I just need to catch my breath."

But he didn't catch his breath, instead he frowned down at her, as if trying to puzzle out some frustrating mystery.

"Anna." His frown deepened. "I want to make love with you."

"Isn't that what that was, lovemaking?"

"Let me be blunt: I want to fornicate with you. Urgently."

"Urgently," Anna repeated, still perplexed.

"Here." He took her hand in his and rolled to his back, putting her palm over his very evident erection. "I want you."

She didn't pull away as she should have but gently shaped him along his length.

"This does not feel very comfortable," she said, knowing exactly what was beneath her fingers. She should be repulsed, but with him, she was fascinated.

"If you keep that up," the earl cautioned, "the urgency will only become greater."

She did keep it up but rolled to her side to peer at his face.

"And then what?" Anna asked, wanting badly to undo his breeches, knowing she could never manage it.

"I am not a rapist," the earl said, closing his eyes. "But I will want badly to spend. Very badly." Anna passed a long, thoughtful moment, stroking at him lazily. His hips began to undulate minutely as she mentally rooted around and tried to find the reasons why she should get up and walk straight into the nice, cold stream.

"What does that mean?" Anna said, using her nails to scratch along the rigid length of him through the fabric.

"Oh, for God's sake." He closed his eyes then pushed her hands away. She thought he was going plunge into the stream, or at least get up and stomp away, but instead, he undid the fall of his breeches and shoved them down over his hips then hiked up his shirt to his ribs.

"Please, love." He took her hand and wrapped it around his erection. "Just bring me off and have done with it."

To her shock, his hand was moving hers, stroking it along this very odd part of him, while Anna watched, shamelessly inspecting something she hadn't seen by the light of day at this range ever before. His skin was soft, smooth, and slightly pink, particularly around the head of his penis. The actual length of him, though, was surprisingly thick, rigid, and hot.

"Like that," he rasped. "Jesus, *yes*, just like that."

His hips moved in counterpoint to the way she was stroking him, and his fingers closed more tightly around hers. This had to be hurting him, she thought distractedly, as his back was arched, his jaw clenched, and the muscles of his neck taut.

"God, Anna, don't stop," he warned just when she would have said something. "That feels too good... Jesus Christ." His breath soughed out on a long, groaning sigh as a milky liquid spurted rhythmically over their fingers and onto the bare flesh of his stomach.

His hand went still over hers, but he kept their fingers laced.

"Dear, sweet, merciful God." He sighed, opening his eyes. "I did not plan for this to happen, Anna. Have we a napkin to hand?"

Dumbly, she handed him one, her eyes fixed on his softening penis.

"Can I let go now?"

"You may," he replied, frowning at her. He swiped at himself with the napkin and then tossed it aside.

"Does it hurt?" Anna nodded at him, and he regarded her carefully.

"You haven't done this before."

"I didn't know one *could*," she said, not taking her eyes off his groin. "Or two could. It looked uncomfortable for you."

"Arousal has an element of discomfort to it, until satisfied, and then it is pleasurable beyond description." He did not move to tuck himself up, and she did not stop looking.

"One would not necessarily reach that conclusion, watching you," Anna said. "But you are not... aroused now?"

"No." His smile was sweet, pleased. "If you keep looking at me like that, I will be again soon."

"May I touch you?"

"Just be gentle, but indulge your curiosity however you please."

Anna didn't want to ask any more questions, feeling she'd revealed quite enough ignorance to a man who was utterly blasé about something so odd she could barely comprehend it.

So she let her fingers ask the questions, traveling along the softening length of him, lifting him this way and that, manipulating his foreskin and exploring his testicles, all with a frown of deepest puzzlement on her face, while he obligingly kept his eyes closed and gave every appearance of a man dozing off.

"You are..."—she waved a hand over his genitals—"becoming unrelaxed again."

He opened his eyes and smiled. "You are a treasure. Let me hold you."

When Anna hesitated, he tugged her down to his side, tucking her under his arm, her head on his shoulder. He lifted his hips to tug up his breeches but left the falls open and himself half exposed.

"If I touched you again," Anna asked, "would you do that a second time?"

"With you? At least three times, eventually. A man does need some time to recover, though. Anna…?"

"Hmm?" Her hand was resting over his cock, but just that, not moving him nor attempting any further exploration.

"Thank you." The earl's eyes drifted shut. "There's a great deal more to be said, of course, and soon, but for now, thank you."

Anna didn't know what to say to that, for she felt like thanking him, too. She had shared something with him, something wicked and dear and dangerous, and yet it was as he'd said. Her clothes were on and her physical virtue uncompromised. He had given her knowledge, of his body and of him, but he had not demanded comparable knowledge of her.

Maybe he would, Anna thought. Maybe that was the "great deal more" yet to be discussed. She hoped not, because as much as she might want to, she could not afford to allow him those liberties, not if she valued her freedom.

# Six

"Come." The earl held out a hand and grabbed the hamper, putting the blankets on top. "We need to talk, and the library will be less gloomy than the kitchen."

They'd had to sprint for the kitchen when a summer squall had caught them napping on their blankets, and the rapid shift from pleasantly dozing to a dead run still had Anna disoriented. She put her hand in his but found she dreaded this talking he wanted. Words could land with the force of a blow, and she was going to hurt herself with what must be said, and very likely anger him, as well.

When they arrived at the library, he pulled the cushions from the window seats and fashioned a nest on the floor with those and the blankets. Retrieving the champagne bottle from the hamper and cracking one window, he settled cross-legged on the blanket and watched her as Anna moved restlessly around the room.

"Have some." He held up the bottle. "We can swill from the bottle like heathens if it won't offend you." She joined him and took a pull from the bottle.

"You are sworn to secrecy," she warned him. "Mrs. Seaton does not tipple."

"Neither does Westhaven." He followed her example. "Heir to a bloody duke, you know."

In that moment, she lost a piece of her heart to him. His hair was curling damply against his neck, his clothing was in disarray, and he was sitting cross-legged on the floor of an empty room, swilling champagne. In that posture, in his dishevelment, with grave humor dancing in his green eyes, the Earl of Westhaven was impossibly dear to her.

"I like that look in your eye, Anna," he said. "It bodes well for a man housebound with little to do."

"You are lusty," she said, not a little surprised.

"Not particularly," the earl said, passing her the bottle. "Or not any more than others of my age and station. But I am lusty as hell with you, dear lady."

His expression softened, the humor shifting to a tenderness she hadn't seen in him before.

She put aside the bottle. "That look does not bode well for a mere housekeeper who wants to preserve her paltry little reputation."

He reached into the hamper to retrieve her hairbrush, untying a hair ribbon from its handle. "We traveled in an open carriage, Anna, and when this rain blows over, I'll have you directly back to Town. You never even let me get a hand on your delicate ankles."

"That isn't the magnitude of the problem, and you know it."

"I can see we are going to have a substantial discussion. At least let me put your hair to rights so you can't glare at me while we do."

"I do not reproach you for what happened outside," Anna said, scooting around to present him her back.

"Good." The earl kissed her neck. "I want to reproach myself, but at present, I just feel too damned pleased with life, you know? Perhaps in a day or two I will get around to being ashamed, but, Anna, I would not bet on it."

She could hear the uncharacteristic smile in his voice, and thought: I put that smile there, just by sharing with him a few minutes of self-indulgence.

"I am not ashamed, either." Anna tried on the lie. "Well, only a little, but this direction could easily become shameful, and I would not want that. For you or for me, as we are not shameful people."

"You will not be my mistress," Westhaven said, sifting his hands through her hair in long, gentle sweeps. "And you did not sound too keen on being a wife."

Anna closed her eyes. "I said it depended on whose wife, but no, in the general case, taking a husband does not appeal."

"Why not?" He started with the brush in the same slow, steady movements. "Taking a husband has some advantages, you know."

"Name one."

"He brings you pleasure," the earl said, his voice dropping. "Or he damned well should. He provides for your comfort, gives you babies. He grows old with you, providing companionship and friendship; he shares your burdens and lightens your sorrows. Good sort of fellow to have around, a husband."

"Hah." Anna wanted to peer over her shoulder at him, but his hold on her hair prevented it.

"He *owns* you and the produce of your body," she retorted. "He has the right to demand intimate access to you at any time or place of his choosing, and strike you and injure you should you refuse him, or simply because he considers you in need of a beating. He can virtually sell your children, and you have nothing to say to it. He need not be loyal or faithful, and still you must admit him to your body, regardless of his bodily or moral appeal, or lack thereof. A very dangerous and unpleasant thing, a husband."

The earl was silent behind her, winding her hair into a long braid.

"Were your parents happy?" he asked at length.

"I believe they were, and my grandparents were."

"As are mine, as were mine," the earl said, fishing her hair ribbon out of his pocket and tying off her braid. "Can you not trust yourself, Anna, to choose the kind of husband I describe rather than that night-mare you recount?"

"The choice of a woman's husband is often not hers, and the way a man presents himself when courting is not how he will necessarily behave when his wife is fat with his third child a few years later."

"A housekeeper sees things from a curious and unpleasant perspective." He hunched forward to wrap his arms around her shoulders. "But, Anna, what about the example of our parents? The duke and duchess when they open an evening with the waltz still command every eye. They dance well, so well they move as one, and they function that way in life, too. My father adores my mother, and she sees only the best in him."

"They are happy," Anna said, "but what is your point? They are also very lucky, as you and I both know."

"You will not be my mistress," the earl said again, "and you are very leery of becoming a wife, but what, Anna, would you think of becoming a duchess?"

He said the words close to her ear, the heat and scent of him surrounding her, and she couldn't stop the shudder that passed through her at his question.

"Most women," she said as evenly as she could, "would not object to becoming a duchess, but look at your parents' example. Had I to become your father's duchess, I would likely do the man an injury."

"And what if you were to become my duchess?" the earl whispered, settling his lips on the juncture of her shoulder and neck. "Would that be such a dangerous and unpleasant thing?"

She absorbed the question and understood that he was asking a hypothetical question, not offering a proposal. In that moment, her heart broke. It flew into a thousand hurting pieces, right there in her chest. Her breath wouldn't come, her lungs felt heavy with pain, and an ache radiated out from her middle as if old age were overcoming her in the space of an instant.

And even if it had been a proposal, she was in no position to accept.

"Anna, love?" He nuzzled at her. "Do you think I would be such a loathsome, overbearing lout?"

"You would not," she said, swallowing around the lump in her throat. "Whomever you took to wife would be very, very blessed."

"So you will have me?" He drew her back against him, resting an arm across her collarbones.

"Have *you*?" Anna sat up and slewed around. "You are proposing to *me*?"

"I am proposing to you," he said. "If you'll have me as your husband, I would like you to be my duchess."

"Oh, God help us," Anna said under her breath, rising abruptly, and going to a long window.

He rose slowly. "That is not an expression of acceptance."

"You do me great honor," Anna said mechanically, "but I cannot accept your generous offer, my lord."

"No my lording," he chided. "Not after the way we've been behaving, Anna."

"It will have to be my lording, and Mrs. Seatoning, as well, until I can find another post."

"I never took you for a coward, Anna," he said, but there was more disappointment than anger in his voice.

"Were I free to accept you," she said, turning to face him, "I would still be hesitant." She left the *my lord* off, not wishing to anger him needlessly, but it was there in her tone, and he no doubt heard it.

"What would cause your hesitation?"

"I'm not duchess material, and we hardly know each other."

"You are as much duchess material as I am duke material," he countered, "and few titled couples know each other as well as we already do, Anna Seaton. You know I like marzipan and music and my horse. I know you like flowers, beauty, cleanliness, and pretty scents."

"You know you like kissing me, and I…"

"Yes?"

"I like kissing you, as well," she admitted on a brittle smile.

"Give me some time, Anna," he said, the aristocrat stooping to bargain, not the importuning suitor. "You think you'd not make a suitable duchess, and you think we don't know each other well. Give me the opportunity to convince you of your errors."

"You want me for a mistress," she said, "but I will not take your coin."

"I am *asking*," he said with great patience, "the opportunity to gain a place in your affections, Anna. Nothing more."

Was he asking for an affair? She should refuse him even that, but it was all too tempting.

"I will think about it, though I believe it best if I pursue another position. And no matter what, you mustn't be seen to embarrass me with your attentions."

"I will draft you a glowing character," the earl said, his eyes hooded, "but you must agree to give me at least the summer to change your mind."

"Write the character." Anna nodded, heart shattering all over again. "Give it to Lord Valentine for safekeeping, and I will promise not to seek other employment this summer, unless you give me cause."

"I would not disrespect you, and I would never get a bastard on any woman, Anna." The earl leveled a look of such frustration at her that Anna cringed.

"Were you to get a bastard on me, we would be forced to wed. I cannot see either of us inviting such circumstances."

His expression changed, becoming thoughtful.

"So if I were to get you pregnant, you would marry me?"

Anna realized too late the trap she had set for herself and sat on the window seat with a sigh. "I would," she admitted, "which only indicates how unwilling I will be to permit the occasion to arise."

He sat down beside her and took her hand, and she sensed his mind beginning to sift and sort through the information she'd disclosed and the information she'd withheld.

He drew a pattern over her knuckles. "I am not your enemy, and I never will be."

She nodded, not arguing. He slipped an arm around her shoulders and hugged her to his side.

"You are not my enemy," Anna said, letting him tuck her against him. "And you cannot be my husband nor my keeper."

"I will be your very discreet suitor for the summer, and then we will see where we are. We are agreed on this." He voice was purposeful, as if he'd finished exploring the challenge before him and was ready to vanquish it.

"We are agreed," Anna said, knowing his best efforts would in a few weeks time put them no closer to his goals than they were in that moment. But she needed those weeks, needed them to plan and organize and regroup.

And in the alternative, she needed the time to grieve and to hoard up for herself the bittersweet procession of moments like this, when he held her and comforted her and reminded her of all she could not have.

They stayed like that, sitting side by side for a long time, the only sound the rain pelting against the windows. After a time, Westhaven got up and looked around the room.

"I will go check on Pericles. I am thinking I should also lay a fire in here, as the rain does not appear to be moving off."

"Lay a fire? We have hours of light yet," Anna said, though in truth they'd had more than a nap outside by the stream, and the afternoon was well advanced. "We could make it back to Town were we to leave in the next couple of hours."

He pursed his lips, obviously unwilling to argue. Anna let him go, knowing it would ruin his gig were they to try to get it back to Town in this downpour. He came back soaked to the skin but reporting the horse was contentedly munching hay and watching the rain from his stall.

They spent the next hour retrieving more blankets and the medical bag kept in the gig, then, as the rain had not let up, filling up the wood boxes in the library. The earl split logs from a supply on the back porch, and Anna toted them into the house. They continued in that fashion, until the wood boxes built beside the library hearths were full and the earl had left a tidy pile of logs split for the next time somebody needed a fire.

He returned to the library where Anna had laid a fire but not lit it.

"I should not be chilled," he mused. "I've just hefted an ax for the first time in several years, but I find I am a trifle cold."

Unusual, Anna thought, as she herself was not cold, and she hadn't split wood, but then, the earl had gotten wet tending to his horse and Anna was quite dry. She'd found flint and steel in the wood box, thank heavens, or the earl would have had to get another soaking just as his clothing was drying.

"I'll light your fire," Anna said, missing entirely the smile her comment engendered on the earl's face.

"And I will forage for a piece of marzipan."

"There should be plenty," Anna said from the hearth, "and some lemonade, though it isn't likely very cold."

He found the marzipan, taking two pieces, and then the lemonade.

"So where should we sleep?" he asked, glancing around the room as he chomped on his candy.

"At home, I hope."

The earl gave her a quelling look. "I did not plan this weather."

"No, you did not, but if we stay here alone overnight, my reputation will be in tatters."

"And you still would not marry me?"

"England is a big place. A tattered reputation in London can easily be mended in Manchester."

"You would flee?"

"I would have to."

"I would not allow that, Anna." The earl frowned at her as he spoke. "If you come to harm as a result of this situation, you will permit me to provide for you."

"As you did for Elise?" Anna said, sitting on a stone hearth. "I think not."

"I'm going to check on the horse again," he said, "and bring in the last of the supplies from the gig, just in case the rain doesn't stop soon." Anna let him go, knowing his retreat was in part an effort to cool the irritation he must be feeling with her and the situation.

❧

Westhaven did check on the horse and stepped out under the stables' overhang to relieve himself, undoing his breeches and taking his cock in hand. His throat was scratchy from all their talking, and hefting the ax had set up an ache in his muscles that was equally unwelcome. Anna was getting twitchy about being stranded with him, and his temper was growing short. Not his best moment.

But then he looked down at himself and smiled, recalling the day's earlier pleasures. Anna Seaton had a wanton streak that was going to win the day for them both. He shook himself off, gave himself a few affectionate strokes, then buttoned up. He was going to convince his housekeeper to trade her silly caps for a tiara, and he was going to use her passions against her shamelessly if he had to.

He tossed Pericles a small mountain of hay, topped off the water bucket from the cistern, and retrieved the provisions from the gig. On the way back to the house, he began to plan the seduction of his future wife, pausing to pluck her a single rose just as the sky opened up with a renewed downpour.

They dined on leftovers from the hamper, shared the lemonade, and talked by the fire as the light began to wane. He rubbed her back, held her hand, and avoided discussing the need to spend the night in the deserted house.

Anna rose from the cushions and stretched. "I suppose it's time to admit we'll be sleeping here tonight—the question is where specifically?"

Thank you, God, the earl thought. His Anna was being practical, though she wasn't pleased with their situation.

"The master bedroom comes to mind," the earl suggested. "The bed there was probably built where it stands and conveys with the house. The room was clean enough, but it will be cold without a fire."

"We can haul enough wood up there to get the room warmed up," Anna said. "Since the other option is this floor. With only a few blankets between us, we're probably better off sharing that bed."

"We are," he agreed, finding that for all they were before a fire, he still just couldn't quite banish a sense of chill in his bones. "And as splitting wood seems to have left me a little stiff, the bed appeals."

"To bed then," Anna said resignedly as she began to gather an armload of logs from the wood box. It took several trips to move wood, blankets, and provisions to the bedroom. By the time they were finished, the entire house was growing gloomy with the approaching night.

Westhaven left the room to fetch a bucket of wash water from the kitchen, while Anna scouted the bed drawers for the linens sewn to fit the bed.

"Your water," the earl said when he returned moments later. "I see your treasure hunt was successful."

"The bed is made up." Anna smiled at him. "We have soap and towels, though only our two blankets."

"That should suffice." The earl yawned as he knelt

by the open drawer. "How about if you take the nightshirt, and I take the dressing gown?"

"As you wish, but a few minutes privacy would be appreciated, and…"

"And?" He was just pulling off his boots again, but in the dim firelight, at the end of the day, it struck him as a particularly intimate thing for her to watch.

"You will not touch me tonight? You will not expect me to touch you?"

"Touch as in, your knee bumps my shin, or touch as in what happened this afternoon?" the earl asked, peering into his boot.

"What happened this afternoon. I'll try not to kick at you, either."

"I will not make demands of you," the earl said, leveling a look at her, "but I will want to." He set aside his boots and rose, leaving her the privacy she requested to wash, change into the nightshirt, and dive beneath the chilly sheets of the bed.

When Westhaven returned, he looked over at the bed and saw Anna was feigning sleep. He had every intention of keeping his word to her, of behaving himself once he climbed into that bed. He was more tired than he had a right to be, considering he'd done little more than tool along in the gig, stroll around the property, and talk with Anna.

But he was exhausted, and he'd taken some sort of chill in the rain, and he could barely keep his eyes open. Still, he wasn't going to waste an opportunity to torment his intended duchess, so he stripped out of his shirt, his breeches, stockings, and smalls, and took

the bucket to the hearth, the better to illuminate him
for Anna's peeping eyes.

Truth to tell, it felt good to be naked and in the
same room with her. He found a towel and the soap
on the hearth, where Anna had left them, and slowly
began to wash himself from toes to fingertips. When
he'd made a thorough job of it, he blew out their two
candles, tossed the dressing gown to the foot of the
bed, and climbed in beside Anna.

∽∾

In the darkness hours later, Anna awoke to feel his
hand on her flesh, making a slow journey over her
hip to her buttock and back again. The creaking and
shifting of the old bed suggested he was moving more
than his hand, and his breathing—slow, but audible—
supported the theory.

*He's pleasuring himself again.* Were all men so
afflicted with lust? she wondered, even as that single,
repetitive stroke of his hand left a trail of warmth
across her flesh. If she rolled over, began kissing him
or simply let him hold her, what other means would
he find to torment her?

His breathing hitched, sighed, and hitched again,
and then his hand went still. Anna felt him moving
around and then subsiding down under the covers.
That same hand curled around her middle, and her
back was enveloped in the heat of his chest. He kissed
her cheek then fitted himself behind her, leaving her
bewildered but oddly pleased, as well.

She could not permit him the liberties he so clearly
wanted, but this cuddling and drowsing together, it

was more of a gift than he could ever know. While the storm pelted down from the heavens, Anna slept a dreamless, contented sleep in the arms of the man she could not marry.

❧

Had Westhaven kept his dressing gown on, Anna might have been much slower to diagnose his ailment. As it was, they slept late, the day making a desultory arrival amid a steady rain that left the sky gray and the house gloomy. Anna's first sensation was of heat, too much heat. Of course it was summer, but with the change in weather, the house itself was downright chilly.

Westhaven, she realized, was still spooned around her, and the heat was radiating from his body. She shifted away, and he rolled to his back.

He reached for the water glass. "I feel like I came off Pericles at the first jump, and the whole flight rode over me. And it is deucedly hot in this bed." He rose, wrestling the blankets aside, and sat for a moment on the edge of the mattress as if finding his equilibrium.

"No," he went on. "I feel worse than that, no reflection on present company, of course." Without thinking, Anna rolled over to respond and saw him rise, naked as the day he was born, and make for the chamber pot.

"Good morning to you, too," she muttered, flouncing back to her side, unwilling to be as casual as he about his nudity. He came back to the bed, took a sip of his water, and frowned.

"I am inclined to purchase this property," he

reflected, "but this bed will have to go. I have never risen feeling less rested."

Anna rolled to her other side, a retort on her lips regarding earls who did not keep their hands to themselves, but she stopped and fell silent. Westhaven was sitting up, leaning against the pillows, his water glass cradled in his lap.

"Oh, my Lord," Anna whispered, pushing her braid over her shoulder.

"No my lording," Westhaven groused. "I am quite simply not in the mood for it."

"No," Anna said, scrambling to her knees. "My Lord, as in Lord above." She reached out and ran a hand over his torso, causing him to look down at his own body.

"You were peeking last night," he said. "It isn't as if you haven't seen me unclothed, Anna Seaton."

"It isn't that," Anna said, drawing her hand back then brushing it over his stomach. "Oh, Lord."

"Oh, Lord, what?"

"You." She sat back, her head moving from side to side in disbelief. "You're coming down with the chicken pox." A stunned beat of silence followed, then the earl's snort of displeasure.

"I most certainly am not," he informed her. "Only children get the chicken pox, and I am not a child."

"You never had them as a child," Anna said, meeting his eyes, "or you wouldn't have them now."

The earl glared at his torso, which was sprinkled with small red dots. Not that many, but enough that they both knew they weren't there the night before. He inspected his arms, which sported a few more.

"This is Tolliver's fault," he declared. "I'll see him transported for this, and Sue-Sue with him."

"We need to get you home," Anna said, slogging her way to the edge of the bed. "In children, chicken pox are uncomfortable but usually not serious. In an adult, they can be much more difficult."

"You are going to make a sick man travel for hours in this damned rain?" The earl speared her with a look then glared at his stomach again. "Bloody hell."

"We have few medicinals here, and you will feel worse before you get better, possibly much worse. Best we get you home now."

"And if the damned gig should slide down a muddy embankment, Anna?" he retorted. "It wouldn't matter if the chicken pox got me, or a broken neck."

She turned her back on him for that and went to the window, assessing the weather. He had a point, though he'd made it as meanly as possible. The rain was pelting down in torrents, as it had been for much of the night.

"I'm sorry," the earl said, pushing himself to the edge of the bed. "Being ill unnerves me."

"Our situation is unnerving. Is there a village nearby large enough to sport a physician or apothecary?"

The earl grabbed the dressing gown and shrugged into it, even those movements looking painful. "Nearby is a relative term. About a mile the other side of Welbourne there is something large enough to boast a church, but not in the direction of London."

"Welbourne is where your niece lives."

"Anna, no." He rose off the mattress stiffly and paused, grimacing. "I am not imposing on Amery and his wife. You will recall the lady and I were briefly and miserably betrothed. They are the last people I want to see me unwell."

"I would rather they see you unwell, Westhaven, then see you laid out for burial."

"Are you implying I am too arrogant to accept assistance?"

"Stubborn." Anna crossed her arms. "And afraid to admit you are truly ill."

"Perhaps it is you who are anxious, Anna. Surely the chicken pox aren't so serious as all that?" He sat back down on the bed but held her eyes.

Her chin came up a half inch. "Who just said he's never risen feeling so uncomfortable?"

"Unrefreshed," the earl corrected her, considering his bodily state. He felt like pure, utter hell. His worst hangover at university did not compare with this, the flu did not, the broken arm he'd suffered at thirteen did not. He felt as if every muscle in his body had been pulled, every bone broken, every organ traumatized, and he had to piss again with a sort of hot, whiney insistence that suggested illness even to him.

"Welbourne it is," he said on a sigh. "Just to borrow a proper coach and a sturdy team. I won't have Amery gloating over this, nor his viscountess."

Getting even the three miles to Welbourne was an ordeal for them both and for the horse. In the hour it had taken them to dress, load, and hitch the gig, Westhaven's condition worsened. He sat beside Anna, half leaning on her, using what little strength he still claimed just to remain upright on the seat.

They didn't speak, the earl preoccupied with remaining conscious, Anna doing her best to help the horse pick his way along at a shuffling walk. When she saw the gateposts for Welbourne, Anna nearly cried, so great was her relief. Even through the layers of damp clothing between them, she could feel the earl's fever rising and sense the effort the journey was costing him.

The stables were closed up tight, but Anna didn't even turn into the yard. She steered Pericles up to the manor house and pulled him to a halt.

"Westhaven." She jostled him stoutly. "We're here. Sit up until I can get down and help you to alight."

He complied silently and nearly fell on Anna as she tried to assist him from the gig. Getting up the front steps saw them almost overbalancing twice, and Anna was panting with exertion by the time they gained the front porch.

The front door opened before Anna could knock. "For the love of God, get him in here."

Anna's burden was relieved as Westhaven's free arm was looped across a pair of broad shoulders belonging to a blond man dressed only to his waistcoat and shirt-sleeves. The man was fortunately as tall as Westhaven and far more equal to the task than Anna.

"You," the fellow barked at a footman. "Have Pericles put up and see he's offered a warm mash. You." He fixed fierce blue eyes on Anna. "Sit down before you fall down."

Taken aback, Anna could only follow as Westhaven was half-carried to a parlor and there deposited on a settee.

"He is coming down with chicken pox," Anna said, finding her voice at last. "He thought to come here

only to borrow a closed vehicle that he might return
to Town."

"Douglas Allen." The man offered her a bow.
"Viscount Amery, at your service." He jerked the
bellpull and surveyed the man dripping on his
couch. "Westhaven?"

"Amery?"

The earl's voice was a croak, but one that conveyed
a spark of pride.

"If you insist on attempting to travel on in your
condition," Amery said, "I will send a note forthwith
to His Grace, and *tattle* on you. I will also hold you up
to Rose as a *bad example*, and worse, my viscountess
will *worry*. As she is the sole sustenance of my heir, I
am loathe to worry her, do I make myself clear?"

"Ye gods…" Westhaven muttered, peering at his
host. "You are serious."

Amery quirked an eyebrow. "As serious as the
chicken pox, complicated by a lung fever, and further
compounded by Windham pride and arrogance."

"Douglas?" A tall woman with dark auburn hair
entered the parlor, her pretty features showing curiosity and then concern.

"Guinevere." The man slid a shameless arm around
the lady's waist. "Look you, on yonder couch, 'tis your
former betrothed, come to give us all the chicken pox."

"Oh, Westhaven." The woman stepped forward,
but Anna had the presence of mind to rise from her
seat and step between Lady Amery and the earl.

"My lady." Anna bobbed a curtsy. "His lordship
informed me you have an infant in the house, so had
best not be coming too close to the earl."

"She's right." Amery frowned. "I know I've had the chicken pox."

"As have I," Guinevere said, but she returned to her husband's side. "And so has Rose. Douglas, you can't let him travel like this."

"Using the third person," the earl rasped from the couch, "when a man is present and conscious, is rude and irritating."

"But fun," Amery said, coming to peruse his visitor. He put the back of his hand to the earl's forehead and knelt to consider him at closer range. Though both men were of an age, the viscount's gestures were curiously paternal. "You are burning up, which I needn't tell you. I know you hold physicians in no esteem whatsoever, but will you let me send for Fairly?"

"You will not notify the duke?" Westhaven met his host's eyes.

"Not yet, if you stay here like a good boy and get better before my Christian charity is outstripped by my honesty," Amery said, sending his wife a glance.

"Send for Fairly," the earl replied, "but only him, and not those damned quacks who think they attend His Grace."

"I would not so insult Fairly," the viscount said, rising. "Not even to aggravate you."

While the viscount wrested permission to summon the doctor from the earl, Lady Amery conferred with the footman then turned to Anna.

"I'm sorry," Lady Amery said, smiling. "You have me at a loss, Miss...?"

"Mrs. Seaton," Anna replied, curtsying again. "Mrs.

Anna Seaton. I keep house for his lordship in Town and accompanied him to Willow Bend, a property three miles east of here, which he thinks to purchase."

"Pretty place," Amery murmured, "but first things first."

"The back bedroom will serve as a sick room and is being made up now," Guinevere said. "You and the earl could both probably use hot baths and some sustenance, and I'm sure we can find you something dry to change into, as you and I appear to be of a height."

"Come, Westhaven." The viscount tugged the earl to his feet. "We'll ply you with foul potions and mutter incantations by your bedside until you are recovered for the sake of your sanity. You should probably see Rose now, or she will just sneak into your room when you are feeling even worse and read her stories to you."

It should have made him shudder, Westhaven thought as Amery tugged and carried and insulted him up to the bedroom. To be here with the man who had stopped his wedding to Gwen, and to be so ill and virtually helpless before him and Gwen. It should have been among his worst nightmares.

But as Douglas got him out of his wet clothes and shoved him into a steaming, scented bath, then fussed him into swilling some god-awful tea, Westhaven realized that what he felt was safe.

❧

"He'll want to notify his brother," Anna said, sipping her hot tea with profound gratitude.

"We'll send him a message with the one going to

Fairly," Gwen replied, handing Anna a plate with a hot buttered scone on it.

"Send it in code."

"I beg your pardon?" Gwen set down her cup and waited for an explanation.

"It's the duke," Anna said. "His Grace has spies everywhere, and if you leave a note to the effect that Westhaven is seriously ill, where somebody can read it, the duke will be on your doorstep, wreaking havoc and giving orders in no time."

"He most assuredly will not." Douglas spoke from the door of the parlor, and there was something like amusement in his expression. "This is one household where His Grace's mischief gets him nowhere. May I have a spot of tea, my love?" He lowered his long frame beside his wife, draping an arm across the back of the couch.

"How is Westhaven?" Gwen asked, fixing her husband a cup of tea.

"Sleeping, but uncomfortable. I thought you must be mistaken, Mrs. Seaton, as he has no evidence of chicken pox on his face, but your diagnosis is borne out by inspection of the rest of him."

"I had a rather severe case as a child," Anna said. "I'm available for nursing duty."

"I can assist," the viscount said, "and I will do so gleefully. But you, my love, should likely avoid the sickroom."

"I will," Gwen said, "for the sake of the baby, and because having you see him in distress is likely enough penance even for Westhaven. He doesn't need me gloating, too."

Anna sipped her tea, watching the smiles and glances and casual touches passing between these two.

"Westhaven said it was a miserable betrothal."

"For all three of us," Gwen said. "But quickly ended. You did the right thing, bringing him here. He is family, and we don't really hold the betrothal against him, any more than we delight in his illness."

"His sickness is serious," Anna said, "in adults, anyway. And he is… fretful about illness generally. I honestly would not let the doctors near him if it's avoidable."

"The man is too proud by half," Douglas remarked, topping off his own tea cup. His wife watched, amused, but said nothing.

"It isn't pride, my lord," Anna said. "He is afraid."

"Afraid." Douglas pursed him lips thoughtfully. "Because of his brother Victor?"

"Not precisely." Anna tried to organize her thoughts—her feelings—into coherent order. "He is the spare, and dying would be a dereliction of his duty. For all he does not enjoy his obligations, he would not visit them on Lord Valentine, nor the grief on his remaining family. Then, too, he has seen more incompetent doctoring than most, both with his brother, and early this spring, with His Grace."

"Hadn't thought of that," Douglas said, flicking another glance at his wife. "Guinevere?"

"Send for David," Gwen said. "He'll know how to handle the earl and how to treat the chicken pox, too."

"We speak of the Viscount Fairly," Douglas explained. "A family connection of Gwen's, and friend of mine. He is a skilled physician, and we trust him, as, apparently, does Westhaven."

"He does," Anna said. "And in Fairly's absence, he would tolerate the attendance of…"—she struggled to recall the names—"Pugh, Hamilton, and there was a third name, but it escapes me."

"Fairly will know," Douglas assured her. "But how is it, Mrs. Seaton, you and the earl come to be on our doorstep at this hour? Surely Westhaven was not fool enough to venture from Town in this downpour?"

Gwen abruptly looked fascinated with her tea cup, while Anna felt like a butterfly, pinned to a specimen board by the viscount's steady blue eyes.

"We traveled out to Willow Bend yesterday," Anna said, knowing this man would not tolerate untruths. "And then the rain caught us unawares. I convinced the earl to come here this morning only when he realized he had fallen ill."

"Nonsense," Amery replied, crossing his legs at the knee. It should have been a fussy gesture on a man. On him it was… elegant. "Westhaven, being a man of sense and discretion, had you on our doorstep well before dark last evening, didn't he, Guinevere?"

"He did." Gwen nodded, swirling her tea placidly. "He was particularly quiet at dinner, though Rose was in transports to see him."

The viscount sent Anna an indecipherable look. "The child has no sense with those she loves. None at all. Takes after her dear mama. More tea, Mrs. Seaton?"

He poured for her, his wife smiling tolerantly as he did, and Anna felt the love between them almost as strongly as she felt her own gratitude toward them. Someday, she thought, I want to love a man so thoroughly that even when he pours tea for my guests, it is merely one more reason to be pleased with him and with my life because he is in it.

~

"Fairly can't attend you." Douglas waved a missive at Westhaven. "He doesn't know if he's had the chicken pox or not."

"Christ. How can you not know if you've turned as spotted as a leopard and felt like something a leopard killed last week?"

"He was raised by his mother in Scotland until he was six and cannot consult with that lady regarding his early health. He has no recollection of having had the illness, either, so he is being cautious." Douglas sat on the end of the bed and surveyed the patient.

"Why are you staring?" Westhaven asked irritably. "Is my face breaking out?"

"No, though I might enjoy seeing that. Fairly writes in some detail we are to provide you comfort nursing and to particularly manage any tendency you have to fevers and discourage you strongly from being bled. And you are not to scratch."

"I don't itch," the earl said, "I *ache*." And he wondered, when she wasn't with him, how the viscount and his wife were treating Anna. Douglas was a stickler, at least with regard to manners and decorum, for all he'd been willing to break some rules to prevent Gwen's marriage to the earl—a lot of rules, come to that.

"Shall I beat you at cribbage?" Douglas offered. "Or perhaps you'd like me to send in Rose?"

"She was here earlier. She lent him to me." He held up a little brown stuffed bear.

"Mr. Bear." Douglas nodded. "He presided over my own sickroom when I ended up with the flu down in Sussex. Good fellow, Mr. Bear. Not much of one for handing out useful advice, however."

"We have Rose for that." Westhaven almost smiled. "She told me to obey her mother, and I would get better."

"Disobeying Guinevere would be rather like trying to disobey a force of nature. One does so at one's mortal peril. She is a formidable woman."

"She would have made a formidable duchess," Westhaven said then realized what had come out of his mouth. "Sorry."

"She would"—Douglas merely nodded—"but her taste in husbands is impeccable, and it is my ring she wears."

"Does it bother you?" Westhaven held up the bear and stared into his button eyes. "My being here?"

"Don't flatter yourself, Westhaven." Douglas rose and crossed the room to an escritoire, extracting a deck of cards and a cribbage board. "Gwen has explained to me you offered for her only because you assumed she was free to refuse you. She has since said you would have tried very hard to make the marriage happy, and I believe her. Cut for the deal." Douglas slapped the board and the deck down on the bed.

"That's it, then?" Westhaven turned up a two, and Douglas pitched his draw down in disgust. "I would have made her happy, no harm done?"

"If Guinevere sees no reason to dwell in the past, then why should I, as my future with Rose, little John, and Guinevere is an embarrassment of happiness?"

"My crib," Westhaven intoned, pondering Douglas's words. What was it like to face a future that could be described with a straight face as an embarrassment of happiness?

Douglas trounced him, going about the game with the same seriousness of purpose that he brought to every endeavor. By the time the board was put away, Westhaven's eyes were growing heavy, and Douglas was angling in the direction of a strategic retreat. A knock on the door heralded Anna's turn at the earl's bedside and allowed Douglas to leave in search of his wife.

"I see you have a friend." Anna nodded at the bear.

"A guardian bear, Rose claims." The earl again brought the bear up to face him and frowned thoughtfully. "He seems a solid sort, if a bit reserved."

"Rather like the viscount."

"Douglas?" The earl smiled at her characterization. "Don't underestimate him, as my father and I did. He appears to be a proper little Puritan, tending his acres and adoring his wife, but Heathgate, Greymoor, and Fairly all listen when Douglas deigns to address a topic."

"He does seem to adore his viscountess, but I believe he is just a protective sort of man in general."

"Protective?" The earl considered the word, but his brain was becoming as creaky as the rest of him. "Perhaps. He certainly dotes on Rose and would cheerfully strangle any who sought to do her harm."

"He has a problem with his memory, though," Anna said, opening a bottle of lotion and sniffing at it. "His wife is similarly afflicted."

"They are? That's news to me, as both of them exhibit frightening mental acuity."

Anna put the lid back on the bottle. "If anybody asks them, they will recall we joined them for an early dinner last night, and you were somewhat subdued, but Rose was quite glad to see you."

Westhaven's eyebrows shot up then crashed down.

"Gwen told you this?" he asked, surprise warring with gratitude.

"No," Anna said, her voice echoing with disbelief. "It was Amery's idea."

"Perhaps she married the better man after all."

# Seven

"MY, MY, MY." DOUGLAS FROWNED AS HE CLOSED THE door to the sick room. "Is this the state Mrs. Seaton left you in, susceptible to any draft and breeze?"

"It is not." The earl sighed, trying to recall where he'd last put the chamber pot. "I was hot, and that nightshirt of yours itches like the very devil."

"Behind the screen," the viscount suggested. "A close stool and a chamber pot. I'll leave if you like, or assist."

"Neither." Westhaven made his way across the room, Douglas watching impassively.

"I thought you'd gained some flesh," Douglas remarked. "A closer inspection suggests I was right. You were getting too thin."

"I was." The earl yawned behind the privacy screen. "But, Anna... Mrs. Seaton has taken me in hand and seen to my meals. Part of the problem was an uninspired cook."

"And your housekeeper inspired her?"

"Anna... Mrs. Seaton interviewed the duchess's cook, who takes pride in knowing the preferences of each member of the family. The menus became interesting." The earl emerged from behind the screen, eyed the bed, and gathered his energy. "And she fussed at me did I not eat, told me I was offending my kitchen staff."

"Up you go." Douglas took him unceremoniously by one spotted arm and boosted him up the step to the bed. "Hold still." He dropped the nightshirt over the earl and peered at him. "You are ill," Douglas concluded on a sigh. "Best get back in bed, and behave yourself. Tonight will likely be the worst, and tomorrow night, but after that, you should be on the mend."

"Douglas?" Westhaven sat on the edge of the bed, and to his surprise, Amery sat beside him.

"Hmm?"

"When you were courting Gwen," Westhaven said, finding the bear among his pillows, "did you...?"

"Did I what?" Douglas prompted. "Mrs. Seaton will be returning with your next infusion, and hopefully some food, so you'd best spit it out, as she's guarding you rather carefully."

"She is?"

"She left your side to eat, but otherwise, unless I'm here, she is," Douglas replied. "You had a question?"

"When you were courting Gwen," the earl tried again. "Was there an almost constant...? I mean, did you find your thoughts turning always to...?"

"I swived her every chance I got," Douglas interjected. "And if I couldn't be inside her, I held her or held her hand or just looked at her like a starving man looks at a banquet he can't eat. The situation was particularly disturbing, because I had come to a point in my life where any kind of passion was beyond me, including the carnal."

"Why do you tell me this? It cannot be easy to part with such a confidence; not for you, and not to me."

"I am meddling," Douglas confessed, his blue eyes warming with humor. "I have my wife's permission, so it isn't quite as difficult as if I were acting without her knowledge."

"Meddling?"

"Encouraging your situation with Mrs. Seaton," Douglas clarified. "I believe you would suit."

"As do I. She is not of like mind."

"Then you must change her mind. If that means a very slow recovery, then so be it. You are the Moreland heir, after all, and no chances must be taken with your health."

The earl smiled crookedly. "A slow recovery... by God. I never stood a chance against you, did I?"

"One hoped not." Douglas rose. "Though you assuredly scared the hell out of me and put rather a wrench in my plans with Guinevere. You were never my enemy, nor hers. Rather, the duke was the common nuisance."

Douglas left the bedroom to admit Anna bearing a tray. She stayed with the patient when the viscount departed, and the next hour was spent nagging Westhaven to eat, making him as comfortable as she could, and letting him drift off to sleep until he woke in the small hours of the morning.

"Anna?" His voice was a croak.

"Here." She rose from the chair and sat on the bed at his hip.

"Feel like hell."

"Your fever is high," Anna said, the back of her hand on his forehead. "Now that you are awake, I can sponge you off, if you'd like. It will cool you down and probably soothe your skin, as well."

He nodded, and Anna brought bath sheets, a basin, and sponge to the bed. She got him arranged on top of the covers, his lower half covered by a blanket, the rest of him exposed and resting on layers of toweling.

"Fairly had a groom deliver this. It's witch hazel and some herbal infusions to help your skin heal." The cool sponge touched his skin, and Westhaven sighed. She brought it again and again down the length of his back, his arms, his shoulders, and sides, then shifted the blanket to bathe his legs and feet. She started the whole process over again and again, until he was nearly resting comfortably, his fever abating. By morning, Westhaven could honestly say he was at least no worse.

There was a discreet tap on the door, and then the viscount was with them, looking refreshed and ready for his day.

"Good morning, Mrs. Seaton, or might I call you Anna?" he asked. "And good morning, Westhaven." He laid his hand on the earl's forehead and frowned. "Better than I thought you might be."

He shooed off Anna to Gwen's company, leaving the men alone.

"How is it," Douglas asked his patient, "your fever responds only to her touch, hmm?"

"Shut up," the earl replied tiredly. "She put

something in the water, if you must know. I think it helps."

By the time Douglas had clean sheets on the bed and Westhaven extracted from his morning bath, the patient was once again growing drowsy. Douglas forced more willow bark tea down the hapless earl's gullet, tucked him in, and left him dozing peacefully beside his borrowed guardian bear.

∼

The next day was a mosaic of little activities and naps. Val sent out a note saying he'd visit shortly, Westhaven penned a note to His Grace, explaining that he was making a visit to Rose at Welbourne. Rose did visit her uncle, but Westhaven invariably found that fifteen minutes into any task or visit, he needed to either use the chamber pot or to nap or both.

The evening passed just as slowly, with Anna first beating him at cribbage then reading to him from a translation of Caesar's Gallic letters. He dozed in that twilight between sleeping and waking, aware of her voice but not the sense of her words. He did rise to wakefulness when she fell silent, but only to open his eyes and see Anna had paused, her own eyes closed, the book facedown on her lap. Sensing she was tired, he did not disturb her but let himself slip back into sleep.

The night was difficult for them both, with the earl again dozing between bouts of higher fever and Anna tending him as best she could. Sponge baths helped, but not as much as either of them wished.

"I think you would be more comfortable if we

doused you in cool water from head to toe," Anna said as the clock struck two.

"That would involve moving, and right now, Anna, it hurts to breathe."

"But if we can get your fever down it won't hurt as much."

"If you insist." The earl made the monumental effort to push himself to the edge of the bed, but he needed Anna's assistance to climb into the tub and lower himself to the water. In less than ten minutes, his teeth were chattering, though to the touch, the water was almost warm. Anna got him out of the tub and wrapped him in bath sheets to sit by the fire while she toweled his hair dry.

"So tomorrow night should be easier?"

"It should," Anna said. "In adults, this sickness can be much more severe than in children."

"Do you have children?" the earl asked from the depths of the towel around his head.

Her hands went still, but her voice was steady when she answered. "I do not. Do you?"

"None. But marry me, Anna, and you can have all the children you can carry." In fact, he would enjoy having children with her, he thought, feeling—in the midst of his other discomforts—his cock stir.

"I will not marry you," she said, going to stand behind him. He felt the first gentle tug of the brush through his hair. "But you should have children. You will be a very good father, and children will be good for you."

"How so?" He closed his eyes, the better to enjoy the feel of the brush stroking gently across his scalp.

"My father has hardly given me an example I want to emulate."

"That's just bluster." Anna waved a hand. "You paint him as a pompous, self-important, old-fashioned aristocrat, but he apparently went to tremendous lengths to attempt to secure access to his granddaughter."

"Ridiculous lengths," Westhaven said. "I would regale you with the details, but I hardly have the strength to keep my eyes open." He rose under his own power when Anna put down the brush, but grabbed her hand when he sat on the bed and brought it to his forehead. "I must trust you and Amery when you tell me I am following the predictable course for this illness, but I don't feel myself improving, particularly."

"Nor are you worsening, particularly."

"True." He closed his eyes and inhaled the rosy fragrance of her skin. "If I should worsen, you must promise me not to let His Grace inflict his cronies on me."

Anna leaned in and kissed his forehead.

"I will not let your father bother you. It has occurred to me that were you in need of someone to guard you from his mischief, Lord Amery and his wife are probably better equipped to do that than the Queen's own."

"Come to think of it, you are right. I will sleep better for the realization."

She tucked in the covers around him, laid a hand on his forehead, then smoothed back his hair. When his breathing evened out into sleep, she blew out the candles, banked the fire, and drew the extra blanket around her shoulders. As she curled down to rest her cheek against the bed, she felt the earl's hand stroking her hair in a slow, repetitive caress. The tenderness of the gesture soothed them both, and Anna soon followed him into slumber.

# *Eight*

"YOUR GRACE WILL NOT DISTURB A GUEST UNDER my roof."

Douglas's voice, raised but not quite shouting, came from the corridor as Anna blinked herself awake. Dear God, the duke was going to find her in here, sprawled beside…

She hopped off the bed, shaking the earl's shoulder firmly.

"My lord," she hissed, "wake up." He groaned and rolled, the covers slipping down his naked, spotted torso. "My *lord*!" He curled to his side, frowning.

"Gayle Tristan Montmorency Windham, *wake up*!"

"I am awake," he said, automatically shoving the blankets aside, "and feeling like hell. Make way, lest I embarrass myself."

"Your father is here," Anna informed him, thrusting his dressing gown at him.

"Stand aside, Amery." The duke's voice rang with authority and disdain. "You will not keep a man from his son's sick bed, or the magistrate will know the reason why."

"Hurry." The earl shoved his arms into his dressing gown, his father's voice galvanizing him. "Find the book," he ordered, and in a feat of desperate strength, shoved the tub across the room behind the privacy screen. Anna tossed the covers back over the bed, opened the drapes, and pulled two chairs up to the hearth.

"Your son is not an infant," Douglas said with equal disdain. "He does not need his papa checking up on him. You will please wait in the parlor like any civilized caller, even at this uncivilized hour."

"You insult your betters, Amery," the duke stormed, "and you would not know a father's affection if it landed on the back of your horse. *I will see my son.*" The door crashed open, causing Anna to look up from where she was tending the hearth. She rose slowly but kept hold of the poker.

"Westhaven." The duke marched up to his son, who was reading Caesar by the hearth. "What are you doing rusticating here, when you should be in the care of our personal physicians?"

"Do I look ill?" Westhaven stood and raised a lordly eyebrow at his father, who did not quite match his son in height. "Or any more ill than I usually appear, as fatigue is a constant companion when one has as much to see to as I do."

Douglas stifled a snort at that but quickly frowned as two rotund gentlemen pushed past him into the room, having obviously escaped the barrier of footmen at the foot of the stairs.

"We can examine him immediately, Your Grace," the shorter of the two said, opening a black satchel. "If the young lady would please leave us?"

"Out, girl," the duke barked at Anna.

"I don't answer to you, my lord," Anna barked right back. "If your son were sick, his health would be best served by allowing him rest, *Your Grace*. I suggest you take your minions and wait in the parlor, lest Lord Amery be the one to summon the magistrate to eject trespassers."

The duke glared at his host. "Amery, your help is insufferable."

"No, *Your Grace*," Westhaven bit out with the same disdain Anna had shown. "You are insufferable. I am here to visit my niece, and there is no call whatsoever for you to interfere. You have, as usual, caused a great deal of drama at the expense of others, for your own entertainment. Your absence would be appreciated."

"And how about mine?" Valentine Windham strolled into the room. "Westhaven, my apologies. I have no idea how His Grace has managed to track you here. Shall I engage in a physical display of disrespect toward our parent?"

"This I must see," said another masculine voice from the corridor.

A tall, dark-haired man with icy blue eyes sauntered in behind Lord Valentine.

"Greymoor." Douglas nodded, his eyes glinting with humor.

"Amery." The latest player on the stage nodded in return.

"What is he doing here?" the duke thundered, glaring at Greymoor. "And I suppose your rakehell brother is bringing up the rear?"

Greymoor offered a slight bow. "The marquis may join us shortly, but was up most of the night with a colicky infant, which this fellow," Greymoor cocked an eyebrow at the earl, "is most assuredly not."

"I insist that I be assured of his health, and immediately," the duke snapped. "Woman, you will leave this room, or I will physically see to it myself."

"Lay a hand on her," the earl interjected softly, "and you will see just how robust I can be, Papa." Unbidden, Douglas, Valentine, and Greymoor shifted to flank Anna and the earl by the hearth.

"I will not have this," the duke shouted. "A man has the right to be assured of the health of his heir!"

"*Grandpapa!*" Rose trumpeted from the doorway. "Shame on you! There is a no-shouting-in-the-house rule, just as there is a no-running-in-the-barn rule."

And clearly, her tone said, a grandpapa was expected to know and obey the rules.

"Rose," the duke said, his volume substantially decreased, "if you will excuse us, poppet, your uncles and I were just having a small disagreement."

Rose crossed her arms over her skinny chest. "You were the one yelling, Grandpapa, and you didn't apologize."

To the amazement of all, the duke nodded at his older son and at Lord Amery. "Gentlemen, my apologies for raising my voice to a level that disturbed my granddaughter."

"Apology accepted," Westhaven ground out.

"Now, poppet," the duke said with exaggerated patience, "will you excuse us?"

"Papa?" Rose turned to her step-father, who held out a hand to her.

"No need to go just yet, Rose," he said. She bounded over to him and was soon perched on his hip. The duke, looking frustrated beyond bearing, stomped out of the room, snapping his fingers to indicate his lackeys were to follow.

Greymoor closed the door and locked it. Val went to assist his brother into a chair, and Douglas tossed Rose onto the bed.

"Grandpapa was in a temper," Rose said, bouncing on the mattress. "His neck was red, and I think his physicians ought to examine him."

"Apoplexy isn't something I would wish on even him," Douglas said. "Rose, don't bounce so high, you'll hit the canopy." This inspired Rose to reach up and try to touch the canopy on every leap, while Val scowled at his brother.

"You really do not look well, Westhaven," he concluded. "How in the hell did His Grace get word you were ill in the first place?"

"I know not," the earl replied wearily.

"Spies," Greymoor said. "Might I have an introduction to the other lovely lady in the room before we get to that?"

"My apologies," Douglas said. "Mrs. Anna Seaton, may I make known to you Andrew Alexander, Lord Greymoor. Mrs. Seaton is visiting with us while Westhaven recuperates."

"What about me?" Rose flopped down on the bed. "You didn't bow to me, Cousin Andrew."

"You get off that bed and make a proper curtsy," Lord Andrew said, "and I will make you a proper bow." He scooped up Rose as she made an elaborate curtsy. "Magic misses you," Lord Andrew whispered. "He's telling George just how much right now."

"Oh, can I go visit Sir Magic before you leave?" Rose squealed, perfectly content to remain cuddled against her mother's cousin.

"Of course, but I think there are weighty matters to discuss first." He sat on the bed with Rose and tossed an expectant look at the earl. "Westhaven, what's wrong with you?"

"He has the chicken pox," Rose volunteered. "You know, where you get all spotty and itchy and cranky?"

"I noticed the cranky part." Greymoor nodded. "You must have a serious case, Westhaven, the symptoms have been in evidence for some time. I don't see the spots, though."

In reply, the earl hiked the sleeve of his dressing gown, exposing a spotty, hairy, muscular forearm.

"Poor blighter," Lord Andrew murmured. "Had 'em myself when I was seven."

"Seems we've all had them," Lord Valentine commented, "except for Fairly."

Westhaven sat down wearily. "I am told I'm recuperating despite the absence of a quack, but it seems we should send somebody downstairs to keep His Grace from further mischief."

"I'll go with you, Douglas," Greymoor said, "and referee your entertainment of the duke. Val, can you valet your brother?"

"Of course." Val rose and extended a hand to Anna. "Mrs. Seaton, as my brother appears to be recovering, you have my thanks." He drew her to her feet, smiling a particularly warm smile.

"Anna?" Westhaven caught her eye, and she turned a curious gaze on him. "My thanks, as well." She nodded and silently took her leave.

"Come, Rose." Greymoor snatched up his small cousin. "We have an assignation in the stable with two handsome knights."

Val closed the door behind the entourage and met his brother's eyes.

"I will raid Amery's wardrobe," Val said, "and then we will talk, brother."

The instant his brother was gone, Westhaven stepped behind the privacy screen, making the best use of the rare moment of solitude. God, how had his brother Victor survived the years of being an invalid, with no privacy, no hope, no possibility of recovery?

Looking as healthy as he possibly could, flanked by his brother, his host, and Lord Greymoor, Westhaven spent the next hour balancing the need to control his father with the respect due one's ducal sire. It was a long, largely unpleasant hour, made bearable only by Greymoor's willingness to occasionally distract the duke with insolent humor, and then, before His Grace got truly bilious, with talk of horses.

When the others had drifted off, leaving the duke alone with his heir and his spare, His Grace speared his son with a hard look.

"You two." The duke shook his head. "Don't think I am not appreciative of the interest you take in our Rose, but I know you're up to something, and I won't rest until I know what it is."

"Tell me," Westhaven asked, his tone bored, "does

Her Grace know you've gone haring off in this downpour to bother Amery with your odd starts?"

"Your mother should not be needlessly worried."

"And wasn't it just such weather that precipitated your near fatal bout of lung fever, Your Grace?"

"Hush, boy," the duke hissed. "Don't be making your mother to fret, I say. I'll never hear the end of it."

"Behave yourself, and we won't have to tattle on you, Your Grace. Don't behave yourself, and you will leave us no choice."

"Behave myself." The duke scowled. "Behave myself; this from a grown man who has no mistress, no wife, no fiancée... Behave myself. You behave yourself, Westhaven, and see to the succession."

He swept out with perfect ducal hauteur, leaving Val and his brother to roll their eyes behind His Grace's back. The silence, in the wake of the duke's ranting and posturing, was profoundly comforting.

"Sit," Val said. "Or would you prefer to return to your room?"

"I should go back upstairs," the earl replied. "But, Val? I think he's getting worse. More heedless, to come out here and invade Amery's home... Gwen and Douglas would have been within their rights to have him barred from their property."

"He is Rose's grandfather," Val said as they gained Westhaven's room. "But I agree. Since Victor died, and since his own illness, I think our papa has become almost obsessed with the need for heirs."

"I nominate you."

"And I nominate you," Val responded. "Shall we sit?"

"We shall. I find my energy greatly depleted;

though rest is helpful, the effect is temporary. When I lie down, I go out like the proverbial candle."

"I'll get your boots." Val pushed him into a wing chair, hauled off his brother's boots, and ordered them up some breakfast.

"So you spent three nights with Mrs. Seaton," Val said, apropos of nothing.

"I did," the earl admitted, closing his eyes. "I behaved, Valentine." Barely, but he did. "She is a decent woman, and I would not force my attentions on any female."

"Your attentions?" Val's eyebrows rose. "His Grace will be marching you both down the aisle posthaste if he learns of your folly."

"She won't be marched, and neither will I. He did that to me once before, Val, and I won't let it happen again."

"He did it to you, and he did it to Gwen, who had one hell of a lot more family at her back than Mrs. Seaton does. If he can outflank Heathgate, Amery, Greymoor, and Fairly, what chance would one little housekeeper stand against him?"

"You raise a disturbing point, Valentine"—the earl frowned—"though His Grace manipulated Gwen into accepting my proposal largely by threatening her family. If Mrs. Seaton has no family, then she is less vulnerable to His Grace's machinations."

"Talk to her, Westhaven." Val rose and went to answer a tap on the door. "Make her understand what risks she's dealing with, and just what a desperate duke will do to see his heir wed." He opened the door, admitting a footman pushing a breakfast trolley.

As the earl joined his brother for tea, toast, and a

few slices of orange, he considered that Val was right: If Anna Seaton had weaknesses or vulnerabilities, it was best she disclose them to the earl, for sooner or later, if the duke learned of them, he would be exploiting them.

And as much as Westhaven sensed they could make a good job of marriage to one another, the earl would not under any circumstances accept Anna Seaton served up as his wife, bound and gagged by the duke's infernal mischief.

❧

Westhaven healed, albeit slowly, and had to agree with Douglas that what was needed was mostly sleep. On the third day, the rain stopped, on the fourth, the earl slept through the night. On the fifth, he began to grouse about returning home and was marshaling his arguments in the solitude of his room when Rose cajoled him into a visit to the stables. He managed to groom his horse and entertain Rose with a few stories of her father.

But the outing, tame as it was, had been taxing and left him overdue for a stint in bed, much to his disgust. He parted company from Rose, sending her off to draw pictures of the stories he'd told her, and sank down on his bed.

He had a feeling something was off, not right somehow in a nagging way. He peeled out of his clothes and stretched out on the mattress, but still, the sense of something missing wouldn't leave him.

*Anna*, he realized as he slipped between the freshly laundered sheets. He'd gone all of two or three hours without seeing her, and her absence was tolling in the back of his mind. All the more reason, he thought, closing his eyes, to get back to Town where his routine would prevent prolonged periods of proximity such as they'd had at Welbourne.

Wanting to bed the woman—even offering to wed her—wasn't the same as wanting to live in her pocket, after all. A man would have to be besotted to allow feelings like that.

# *Nine*

A WEEK SPENT AT LORD AMERY'S HAD CREATED DEFINITE changes in the way Westhaven went on with the object of his unbesottedness. By necessity, while in Surrey he'd kept his hands to himself, and the enforced discipline had yielded some odd rewards.

Anna, for example, had touched him, and in ways a housekeeper would never have touched her employer. She'd bathed him, shaved him, brushed his hair, dressed and undressed him, and even dozed beside him on the big bed. As soon as his fever had abated, she'd left his most personal care to others, but the damage had been done.

Or, Westhaven thought as he tugged on his boot, the ground had been gained.

He had also had a chance to observe her over longer periods of time and watch more carefully how she interacted with others. The more he saw, however, the more puzzled he became. The little clues added up… and not to the conclusion that she was a mere housekeeper.

"What on earth has put that frown on your face?"

Devlin St. Just came strolling into the earl's townhouse bedchamber, dressed to ride and sporting a characteristic charming grin.

"I am considering a lady," the earl replied, scrounging under his bed for the second boot.

"And frowning. What seek you under the bed, Westhaven? The lady?"

"My damned boot," Westhaven said, extracting the missing footwear. "I sent Stenson off to Brighton with Val, to assure myself some privacy, but the result is I must look after my own effects." He pulled on the boot, sat back, and smiled. "To what do I owe the pleasure of a visit?"

"Val commissioned me to keep an eye on you," Dev said, plopping down on the end of the bed. "Said he was decoying Stenson, so the state of your health would not become common knowledge in the ducal household."

"I am still very obviously recovering from the chicken pox," the earl admitted. "At least, it's very obvious when I am unclothed; hence, Stenson was sent elsewhere."

"His Grace came by to interrogate me." Dev leaned back on his elbows. "Knowing nothing, I could, as usual, divulge nothing. He looked particularly choleric to me, Westhaven. Are you and he at outs?"

"I don't think he tolerates the heat well," Westhaven said, glancing around the room for his cravat. He'd ring for his housekeeper, who seemed to know where his clothing got off to better than he did, but with Dev on the bed, that wasn't an option.

"He'd tolerate the heat better if he unbent a little in

his attire," Dev said. "He was in full regalia at two in the afternoon on a sweltering day. I'm surprised Her Grace lets him go about like that."

"She chooses her battles," Westhaven said, spying a clean pair of cravats in his wardrobe. "Do me up, would you? Nothing fancy." He held up the linen, and Dev rose from the bed.

"So where are you off to? Chinny up." He whipped the linen into a simple, elegant, and perfectly symmetric knot in moments.

"The wharves, unfortunately," Westhaven said, now seeking his waistcoat.

"Why unfortunately?" Dev asked, watching his brother root around in the wardrobe.

"The stench in this heat is nigh unbearable," Westhaven replied, extracting a lightweight green and gold paisley waistcoat from the wardrobe.

"Hadn't thought of that. And here I thought being the heir was largely a matter of dancing with all the wallflowers and bellowing His Grace into submission every other Tuesday."

"Don't suppose you'd like to join me?" Westhaven asked, his goal now to locate a suitable pin for his cravat.

"I have lived these thirty and more years," Dev said, plucking a gold pin from the vanity, "without experiencing the olfactory pleasure of the wharves on an unbearably hot day. We must remedy my ignorance. Hold still."

He deftly dealt with the cravat and stood back to survey the results.

"You'll do." He nodded. "If you attempt to wear your coat before we arrive, I will disown you for lunacy."

"You can't disown me. You've been formally recognized."

"Then I'll tattle to Her Grace," Dev said, grabbing his own coat, "and tell her you've been ill."

"For God's sake, Dev." Westhaven stopped and glared. "Don't even joke about such a thing. Fairly reports that a serious bout of chicken pox in an adult male has been blamed for a loss of reproductive function in rare cases. His Grace will have me stripped and studied within an inch of my most private life."

"No, he will not. You'll not allow it, neither will I, neither will Val."

"I do not put the use of force past him," Westhaven said as they traversed the house. "You think he appears choleric, Val, and I think he's become less constrained by appearances."

"He's afraid of dying," Dev suggested, "and he wants his legacy assured. And, possibly, he wants to please Her Grace."

"Possibly," Westhaven allowed as they reached the stables. "But enough of that depressing topic. How fares your dear Bridget?"

"Alas." Dev rolled his eyes. "She has taken me into disfavor or taken another into greater favor."

"Well, which is it? One wants the dirty details."

"Unbeknownst to me"—Devlin rolled his sleeve down then right back up—"my Bridget had a potential Mr. Bridget waiting for her in Windsor. One cannot in good conscience thwart the course of true love. She lacked only for a modest dowry."

"You dowered your doxy, thus proving you are a Windham," Westhaven said. "Though you do not bear the name, you yet have His Grace's inability to deal badly with a woman you care for."

"Perhaps his only redeeming feature," Dev said. "Hullo, sweetheart." Morgan was walking out of the stables, a kitten in her hand. She offered them a perfunctory curtsy but went on her way, keeping her customary silence.

"Is she simple?"

"Not in the least." Westhaven mounted Pericles and waited while Dev used the mounting block in his turn. "She does not speak, or not clearly, and can hear only a little, or so Val says. But she works hard and is a favorite of the older staff. She arrived with my housekeeper several months ago."

"The one with you at Amery's?" Dev asked with studied nonchalance.

"The very one." Westhaven shot him a look that said he wasn't fooled by Dev's tone. "What exactly do you want to know that you weren't able to get out of Val?"

"Where did you find her? I am in the market for same."

"I lured her to my employ with my endless buckets of charm," Westhaven said dryly.

"You are charming," Dev said when they were trotting along. "You just can't afford to be flirtatious, as well."

Westhaven aimed a smile at his brother, grateful for the simple understanding and support. His was grateful, as well, for his brother's continued company throughout the rest of the afternoon, as Dev was well versed in the mechanics of bringing a cargo to or from Ireland, which was the particular focus of Westhaven's errand.

"I am beyond glad to have that particular situation resolved," Westhaven said as they trotted into his mews. "I didn't know you exported your stock to France."

"Now that the Corsican is properly half a world away, there is a raging demand for horses on the Continent. The French cavalry that galloped off to Moscow in '12 boasted something like forty thousand horses. As best we can calculate, within a year, there were less than two thousand suitable mounts. If it has four hooves and will take a bridle, I can find a buyer on the Continent."

"Enterprising of you. What are you doing for dinner?" Westhaven asked as they swung down from their saddles. "In fact, as you are without a housekeeper, what are you doing for the next little while?"

Devlin's expression closed, but not before the earl saw the shadows clouding his eyes. Dev had been to war and come home, thankfully, but as a veteran of every major battle on the Peninsula, the Hundred Days, and Waterloo itself, Dev had also left pieces of his soul all over the Continent.

"If you're thinking of a sortie to the Pleasure House," Devlin said, "I will decline."

"Not my cup of tea." Westhaven shook his head. "From what Val tells me, the place has lost a little of its brilliance. I wasn't suggesting we go carousing, in any case, but rather that you move in with me and Val."

"Generous of you," Dev said, pursing his lips in

thought. "I have at least three horses needing stabling and regular work if they're to be sold next spring as finished mounts."

"We've room," Westhaven said. "I'll confess to curiosity. Are your beasts so sought after you can live on the proceeds of those sales?"

"Not just those sales," Dev replied, though it was as personal a question as they'd ever exchanged. "But I'd appreciate having you look over my whole operation sometime, if you've a mind to. I am sure, with your more extensive commercial connections, you'll see efficiencies I've overlooked."

Westhaven glanced over, but Dev was accomplished at keeping his emotions to himself. There was nothing to suggest the idea was anything other than a casual fancy.

"I'd be happy to do that."

"You might make the same offer to Val, you know," Dev said as they dismounted. "He imports instruments from all over the Continent and has two different manufactories producing pianos, but he hasn't wanted to impose on you regarding some of the business questions."

"Val hasn't wanted to *impose on me*? And you, Dev? Have you also not wanted to impose on me?"

Dev met his eye squarely and nodded.

"We do not envy you your burdens. We would not add to them."

"I see," Westhaven muttered, scowling. "And is that all you have to offer me? Burdens? Were you not more knowledgeable than I regarding the harbor at Rosslare? The packet schedule to Calais?"

"Westhaven, we think to spare you, not add to your load."

"My lord?" Anna Seaton stood to one side, her silly cap covering her glorious hair, her demeanor tentative, and it was a measure of the earl's consternation with his brothers he hadn't noticed her on the terrace.

"Mrs. Seaton." Westhaven smiled at her. "May I make known to you my dear brother, Devlin St. Just. St. Just, my housekeeper, florist, and occasional nurse, Mrs. Anna Seaton."

"My lord." Anna bobbed a curtsy while St. Just bowed and offered a slight, not quite warm smile.

"I am hardly a lord, Mrs. Seaton, being born on the wrong side of the ducal blanket, but I am acknowledged, thanks to Her Grace."

"And I have offered him a place in my household," Westhaven said, meeting his brother's eye, "if he will have it."

A beat of silence went by, rife with undercurrents.

"He will have it," Dev said on a grin, "until you toss me out."

"Val's playing might take some getting used to," Westhaven cautioned, "but Mrs. Seaton takes the best of care of us, even in this god-awful heat."

"Speaking of Lord Valentine?" Anna chimed in.

"Yes?" Westhaven handed off Pericles to the groom and cocked an eyebrow. The cap was more atrocious than silly, he saw, and Anna seemed tense.

"He writes he will be back from Brighton tomorrow," Anna said, "and warns you might need to have some other task arranged for Mr. Stenson."

"I'll take over Stenson," Dev said. "My former

housekeeper had no skill with a needle, so Mr. Stenson can be set to looking after my wardrobe for at least the next few days."

"That will help. Was there something further, Anna?"

"I assume dinner will be for two, my lord, and on the terrace?"

"That will do, and some lemonade while we wait for our victuals, I think. Which bedroom shall we put my brother in?"

"There is only the one remaining at the back of the house, my lord. We have time to ready it before this evening."

He nodded, dismissing her but unable to take his eyes off her retreating figure until she was back through the garden gate. When he turned back to his brother, Westhaven found Dev eying him curiously.

"What?"

"Marry her," Dev said flatly. "She's too pretty to be a housekeeper and too well spoken to be a doxy. She won't be cowed by His Grace, and she'll keep you in fresh linens and good food all your days."

"Dev?" Westhaven cocked his head. "Are you serious?"

"I am. You have to marry, Westhaven. I would spare you that if I could, but there it is. This one will do admirably, and she's better bred than the average housekeeper, I can tell you that."

"How can you tell me that?"

"Her height for one thing," Dev said as they made for the house. "The peasantry are rarely tall, and they never have such good teeth. Her diction is flawless, not simply adequate. Her skin is that of lady, as are her manners. And look at her hands, man. It remains true you can tell a lady by her hands, and those are the hands of a lady."

Westhaven frowned, saying nothing. Those were the very observations he had made of Anna while they rusticated at Amery's. She was a lady, for all her wielding of dusters and wearing of caps.

"And yet she says her grandfather was in trade," Westhaven noted when they arrived to the kitchen. "He raised flowers commercially, and she bouquets the house with a vengeance. We're also boasting a very well-stocked pantry and a supply of marzipan for me. The sweet of your choice will be stocked, as well, as I won't take kindly to your pinching mine."

"Heaven forefend," Dev muttered as Westhaven procured a fistful of cookies.

"We are permitted to spoil our dinner, as well," Westhaven said. "Grab the pitcher, the sugar bowl, and two glasses."

Dev did as bid and followed his brother back onto the shady back terrace. Westhaven poured them both a tall glass of lemonade, adding liberal amounts of sugar to his own.

"I haven't had lemonade since I was a lad," Dev remarked when he'd chugged half of his. "It refreshes."

"Tastes better with extra sugar. Val adds cold tea to his. Try mine."

"As I have had the chicken pox," Dev said, sipping from Westhaven's glass. "Give me that sugar bowl."

They passed an amiable evening, chatting over dinner about the marriage prospects for their sisters, the house party at Morelands, and the state of British government in general.

When the earl was alone in the library at the end of the evening, he found himself wondering why he hadn't offered his brothers the use of the townhouse earlier. It would have allowed them both to be near their sisters without residing at the ducal mansion, and it would have provided some company.

Anna had been company out at Welbourne, but in the week since their return, she'd faded back into the role of invisible housekeeper. When he walked into a room, she left. When he sat down to a meal, she was nowhere to be found. When he retired to his rooms, she'd been through earlier, cleaning and tidying then disappearing.

The door clicked softly, and as if he'd conjured her with his thoughts, Anna padded in on bare feet, clad only in her night rail and wrapper.

❧

"Anna." He rose, and she watched as he took in her dishabille.

"My lord," she said and earned a thunderous scowl from him as he stalked over to her.

"What have I done, Anna, to earn your use of my title?"

"I cannot be sure we are private," she said then blinked at her tactical error. "And I do not believe such familiarity wise."

"Ah." He backed away, leaning on the desk, arms crossed. "Shall we discuss this change of heart on your part? You've been avoiding me since we got back to Town, and don't think to tell me otherwise."

"You are no longer ill," she said, raising her chin. "And you are capable of dressing yourself."

"Barely," he said with a snort. "So tell me, how am I to court you if you won't stay in the same room with me? How am I to persuade you to marry me if you maneuver always to have others present when I am about? You aren't playing fair, Anna."

She watched him warily, trying to formulate an answer that wouldn't aggravate him further. If she'd known he was in here, lurking in the solitude and darkness, she would have run in the opposite direction—she hoped.

"Come here." He gentled his tone and held out a hand.

"You will take liberties," Anna said, crossing her arms. "And you know I do not encourage your courting. I warned you your efforts would be for naught."

The difficulty, Anna silently admitted, was that she had made no efforts of her own, efforts to secure yet another position, another identity, another escape route. Like one of her grandfather's fat, wooly sheep, she'd just gone about her tasks, cutting flowers, airing sheets, and telling herself *soon* she would press his lordship for that character, *soon* she would explain the situation to Morgan, *soon* she would make inquiries at some different agencies.

A week had gone by, and she'd accomplished nothing, except another seven days of longing for a man she had no business desiring.

"You will make me work for it, won't you?" Westhaven said with a faint smile. He pushed away from the desk and approached her silently. "That's as it should be."

His arms closed around her, and Anna just bowed her head, knowing even more than his kisses and his wicked caresses, the comfort of his embrace had the power to paralyze her. He was warm, vital, and strong, and while it wasn't his aim to protect her, the illusion that he could was irresistible.

"Let me hold you," he whispered, "or I'll have a relapse of the chicken pox to inspire you to closer attendance of me."

"You can't have a relapse."

"Actually, I can," he murmured, his hands easing over her back, "but Fairly says it's quite rare. Relax, Anna, I just want to feel you in my arms, hmm?"

She couldn't remain tense, not with his big hands stroking so knowingly over her muscles and bones. He touched her the way he might touch a horse, listening with his hands for what her body would tell him without her mind's consent.

"You need to eat more," he said. "You've put weight on me but neglected yourself."

"You lost weight, being ill," Anna corrected him, her voice sleepier than she'd intended it. "And you have to stop this."

"Why is that?" She felt his lips against her temple, and leaned into him a little more heavily.

"Because, I like it too well, and then you'll be kissing me and your hands will be wandering and I will want to let them wander."

"Good," the earl said, humor in his voice and something else. Something not quite as relaxed as his hands might have suggested. "I do want to kiss you. Have for days, but you've been dodgy as a feral cat." His lips brushed her cheek, and Anna felt her meager defenses crumbling.

"You must not," she said, cuddling into his chest as if he could protect her from his own wayward intentions.

"I rather think I must," he argued softly. "I have never met a lady so in want of kissing." Those lips were moving along her jaw now, then teasing at her neck. Oh, the wretched, wretched man... Anna let her head fall to the side, vowing she would do better next time. She wouldn't let him get past the first embrace. But for now...

She was wicked. Her brother had told her she was headstrong, unnatural, and ungrateful, and all that added up to wickedness. She should not be misleading the earl like this, should not be giving him ideas, should not be *enjoying* giving him ideas. But he touched her, and all the loneliness and worry and fear went away, taking her honor and common sense with them, leaving her melting and trusting and entirely too willing.

"That's it," he coaxed, his teeth scraping gently at her skin. "Don't think, just let me bring you pleasure, bring us both pleasure."

"Westhaven..." she whispered, trying still to end this, to put him firmly in his place. He'd told her he would never force her; that he would stop if she asked it of him.

She could not ask it of *herself*, Anna thought despairingly as the earl's lips settled softly over hers.

She tried to hold back, to keep herself aloof from his caresses and his kisses, but she had no experience with sexual self-restraint. Her hands crept up to caress his neck and jaw, her body pressed into his with shameless disregard for anything save the need to be *closer*, and her mouth parted on a sigh.

"Oh, not this…" She broke the kiss when he began to rock his hips against her but stayed in his arms, her forehead resting on his sternum. "You are interested, and soon you will be indecent with me again."

"I would love to be indecent with you, Anna."

"I cannot allow it," she wailed. "You do not understand all of my circumstances, Westhaven. This is nothing but folly. We must stop."

"Soon," he assured her. "Your virtue is not at risk, Anna. Not tonight. Just let me pleasure you."

"You want to be indecent," she accused again, gripping his waist tightly.

"Unless you ask it of me, I will not remove my clothing," he replied, his voice steadier than hers.

"Do you promise? You won't even unfasten your trousers?" She lifted her face to regard him by the light of the fire.

"I will not unfasten my trousers," he replied, his gaze rock steady with maybe a touch of humor in his green eyes. "Let me hold you and kiss you and bring you pleasure."

If he kept his pants up, Anna reasoned, she wouldn't be so tempted to wantonness, wouldn't be tempted to touch him, to explore his intriguingly hard and yet delicately smooth male member with her fingers… and lips and tongue. If he kept his pants up, she could manage to keep her own wits about her.

She leaned up and kissed him, only to find herself lifted in his arms, turned, and deposited on the corner of his huge desk.

"Here." He dragged over a chair and a hassock, the better to support her dangling feet. "If you need to hold on to something, hold on to me."

Hold on, she did, as his lips settled over hers with unmistakable purpose. His tongue was in her mouth, thrusting in the same lazy rhythm as his hips were pushing against her sex. He wedged himself more tightly between her legs, and Anna felt something hot and needy wake up below the pit of her stomach. One of his arms stayed anchored around her back, but his free hand was wandering, stealing around her waist, leaving heat and wanting in its wake.

"Touch me, Anna." Westhaven's voice was a rough whisper, insistent and seductive. "Touch me however it pleases you."

It pleased her to slide her hands over his chest, but the fine linen of his shirt wasn't the goal she sought. Without taking her mouth from his, Anna tugged his shirttails free and slid a hand along his ribs, the feel of his warm skin bringing her some unnameable sense of relief.

"Don't stop," he urged, as she lifted his shirt free, all the way around his waist, and further gratified herself with the smooth, muscular planes of his back beneath her other hand. To touch him like this, skin to skin, at once soothed and aroused. She needed to touch him and couldn't get enough of his skin beneath her hands.

"Jesus," Westhaven hissed when Anna found his nipple. She paused, and he nipped at her neck, "Jesus, that feels good." He shifted the angle of his hips, and Anna gasped, the sensation resulting from his rigid flesh against her sex sending a bolt of pure, hot desire skittering through her vitals.

"I like it, too," he murmured, repeating the move but making no effort to open his falls. "Spread your legs, love. I'll make it feel even better."

When she grasped the meaning of his words, she complied, her own hands greedily learning the contour and sensitivities of his chest and neck and abdomen. She wanted to put her mouth on him, but his damned shirt…

"Shirt off," she got out before drawing his tongue strongly into her mouth. She was growing frantic, but for what, she could not have said. *For more*, she thought. Please, almighty God, for *more*. They broke apart for a mere instant while Westhaven whipped the shirt over his head then plunged himself tongue-deep back into their kiss.

His hands shifted from her back to bunch the soft billows of her night rail and wrapper up in her lap.

*Good*, Anna thought, wanting only to be closer to him. And when Westhaven wedged himself between her legs again, she could only pull him closer, hoping he would again find that spot, that one place where the weight and thrust of his rigid length brought her such startling pleasure.

"Use me," he growled. "Let yourself come." Anna could not puzzle out the sense of his words but rocked her hips against him, seeking the same fit they'd found earlier.

"I can't find…" she panted, trying to form words as Westhaven's hand slipped lower and lower.

"I can," he whispered, his fingers slipping over

her intimate folds. His touch was infernally knowing, light, and teasing, *maddening*. Then he shifted the angle of his hand, so his thumb was pressing, *right there*, and he gave her a hint of relief with the tip of his finger inside her body.

"Westhaven," she panted, "...dear God, what are you...?"

But his free hand had parted her night clothes enough to find a nipple and apply a gentle, pulsing pressure to it. That was all it took, just the start of attention to a breast, a bit of his finger, some pressure from his thumb, and her body seized in great, clutching spasms of pleasure.

She came silently, her body bucking against him for long fraught moments in complete abandon. When it was over, she hung limp and winded against him, shuddering as aftershocks wracked her, her cheek pressed over his heart.

༄

Westhaven wanted nothing more than to plunge his raging erection into her wet heat and thrust like a mad bull, but his instincts suggested the moment wasn't right. There had been too much ignorance in Anna's responses, too little ability to anticipate and manage her own reactions.

Too much *innocence*.

So he held her to his chest and stroked her hair, and tried to pay attention to her and not to the indignant clamoring of his impatient cock.

"I cannot fathom what just passed between us," she whispered.

"Has no one seen to your pleasure?" Westhaven

kissed her temple, unable to stifle the smile in his voice. She might not be a virgin fresh from the school-room, but it pleased him to think he was the first to bring this to her. A husband exercised his rights, but a lover pleasured.

"Pleasure," she echoed his thought, sounding inebriated. "Profound pleasure."

"I hope so," the earl rumbled. "It's been a while, hasn't it?" He brushed her hair back over her ear, and regarded her carefully. The disorientation on her face, coupled with the trusting, boneless weight of her in his arms caused a spike of profound *affection* for her to spread out from the center of his chest.

"I would like a little of the same for myself," he whispered, arms going more tightly around her. "You will oblige me?"

"Oblige?" Anna's brain had clearly slipped its leash, and Westhaven was hard put not to gloat.

"Let me come against you," the earl urged, his voice intimate with anticipated pleasure. "The couch will do." Hearing no objection, he hoisted her from the desk and laid her down on the long sofa.

"Lovely," he whispered, coming down on top of her.

*On top of her*, thank Christ, he was at long last on top of her.

He blanketed her there on the couch, for the first time laying his half-naked body over hers, though he was careful with his weight. His lips found hers, his hand strayed to her breast, and he thought he heard her sigh "lovely" as she lifted up her hips, trying to stroke herself against him again.

"Easy," he murmured, nipping at her earlobe. "I promised not to remove my own clothing unless at your request; you will have to oblige."

Or, he reasoned, he could come in his knickers like the schoolboy he'd once been. But Anna was tugging at his falls and gently extracting his cock from his clothing.

"Much better," he breathed, feeling himself grow more aroused now that he was free of his clothing.

He took his time, though it had been a long, frustrating week, apparently for them both. There was a hint of revenge in the languor with which he went about this loving. He kept his kisses slow and sweet, and he only gradually let her have the full weight of his hips, snugging his cock low against her belly. But Anna took a little revenge of her own, as her hands were free to roam his back, his chest, into his hair, over his features. He groaned quietly when she found his nipples then less quietly when she fastened her mouth on one and her fingers on the other.

"Oh, love, I can't... Jesus, Anna..."

She eased off but didn't desist completely, and then he felt her tilt her hips, the better to trap him against her. Her arms urged him to rest on her more fully.

"I like it," she whispered, kissing his cheek. "I like your weight on me, like you being around me, above me."

Encouraged by the rasp in her voice as much as her words, he began to thrust with more purpose, firmly putting aside the temptation to shift his hips and hilt himself in the wet heat of her. Her tongue found his nipple again, but this time he arched his back to make the angle easier for her.

"Your mouth, Anna," he rasped, "please... *God in heaven.*"

She wrapped her legs around his waist, suckled at him, and clamped her hand tightly on his buttocks as he thrust hard against her. When the warmth of his seed coursed onto her stomach, she held him all the more closely, until he levered up on his elbows and stared down at her in the firelight.

He lasted only a moment, suspended above her, before she slipped a hand around his nape and urged him back down against her. He capitulated to her silent request and was soon breathing in counterpoint with her, as naturally as if they'd made love every night for years. She traced patterns on his back, sifted her hands through his hair, and took his earlobe in her mouth for the occasional nip.

"One of us," the earl said, "is going to have to get up. I nominate you."

"Happy to serve," Anna murmured drowsily. "But can't fit it onto the schedule just at the moment."

"Suppose that leaves me." The earl sighed and heaved up, first onto straight arms then to his feet. His stood above her, brooding down at her half-naked, utterly relaxed sprawl so long she self-consciously moved to close her legs.

"Don't," he said, but it was a request, for all he didn't state it as such. "Please. You are lovely." But he moved away, sensing her defenses were weak, and she needed a moment. When he turned back to her, he'd pulled up his breeches but not buttoned them. To his shamelessly primitive delight, she'd not covered herself, not sat up, nor in any way disturbed the wanton pose in which he'd left her.

"Let me." The earl sat down at her hip and began to dab gently at her with his dampened handkerchief. He made a sensual game out of it, stroking the cool cloth over her stomach, up under her breasts, and down to her sex. When she shifted her dressing gown, likely thinking to afford herself some small modesty, he applied a gentle pressure to the inside of her thigh.

"Let me," he repeated. He held the cloth against her, and Anna closed her eyes, her blush evident even by firelight.

"Anna Seaton." He leaned down and brushed his lips over her heart. "The pleasures you and I could share…" He said no more, feeling strangely off balance by their encounter. He set aside the cloth, pushed the halves of her clothing even farther to the side, and climbed over her again.

He wasn't ready to bounce up and take himself upstairs to bed, wasn't ready to dive back into the last few pieces of correspondence, wasn't ready to pour himself a brandy and take it up to his balcony. Completely out of character for him, all he wanted to do was stay here with Anna, holding her and being held by her.

The feeling was mutual, he guessed, as Anna's arms went around his shoulders. She kissed his cheek, and with her hands, urged his head down to her shoulder. Westhaven obliged, keeping himself awake by force of will.

This situation with Anna was proving more complicated than he wanted it to be. With Elise, he would have been out the door by now. She had accommodated him, but in hindsight, Westhaven saw it was barely even that. Elise had never let her fingers drift over his scalp like this, making delicious circles on his skin. She would never have clutched at his buttocks, the better to hold him to her. Elise would never—probably not even if he'd asked it of her—put her mouth to his nipple.

And he would most assuredly not have asked it of her, not in a million years.

*You shouldn't have had to ask.* He could hear Anna's tart tones in his head, even as he knew the thought was also his own.

Anna was different, he conceded. Just how different, he hadn't accurately seen when he'd initially proposed. She held him at arm's length, or tried to, then capitulated with sweet abandon, leaving him disoriented, so great had been his pleasure.

"Love?" He raised up on his forearms and brushed her hair off her forehead. "How are you? You're too quiet, and you leave a fellow to fret."

"I am… beyond words." Anna smiled up at him. And he knew what thoughts were stirring in her busy brain: She should be vexed by this turn of events, troubled, dismayed, and she would be—soon. But not just yet, not with her body still languorous and pleased with itself, pleased with him.

He kissed her forehead. "I hope you're beyond words in a positive sense."

"I am." She sighed and stretched, bringing her pelvis up against his.

"None of that." He smiled and nuzzled at her neck, then slipped lower, going up on his knees to take a nipple into his mouth. Anna merely cradled his head against her and sighed again.

"Next time," he murmured, resting against her sternum, "I will know where to start. You have sensitive breasts, my dear. Inspiringly so."

"None of that."

"None of what?" He raised his face to regard her in puzzlement.

"None of that next-time talk," Anna clarified. "This was a lapse."

Westhaven hung above her, considering, even as he ignored the considering being done by his cock. "We need to discuss this, and for that, you will have to be decently covered."

"I will?"

His took his weight and warmth away from her and fortified himself with the disappointment in her voice.

"You will." He sat at her hip and began to straighten her clothing, but paused to brush his thumb over her pubic curls. "When this next time comes around, that we are not going talk about, I will put my mouth on you here." He closed his fingers over her sex. "You will enjoy it, but not half so much as I."

She looked surprised then intrigued as he closed her buttons and bows, and the earl concluded she was a virgin to oral sex as well as orgasms. Mr. Seaton, God rest his lazy, inconsiderate, bumbling, unimaginative, selfish soul, had much to answer for.

"Up you go." He tugged Anna to a sitting position then settled down beside her and wrapped an arm around her shoulders. Her head rested against his chest, and her hand stole onto his bare stomach.

He yawned sleepily. "I should put on a shirt if we're to have a meaningful discussion."

"You needn't," Anna assured him. "It won't take long at all to tell you this sort of thing has to stop."

"Going back on your word, Anna?" Westhaven leaned over to kiss her temple and to again inhale the fragrance of her hair.

"I agreed not to seek another position until the end of summer," she reminded him. The glow in Westhaven's body faded a tad with each clipped syllable. "I did not agree to become your light-skirt."

"Were you a virgin, you would still be considered chaste."

"But I wouldn't be for much longer if this keeps up."

Westhaven knew some genuine puzzlement. "I will not force you, Anna."

"You won't have to," she bit back. "I will spread my legs for you just as eagerly as I did tonight."

"With results just as pleasurable, one hopes, but we're talking past each other, Anna. Why won't you let yourself enjoy my advances? That's the real issue. If you have a reason of any substance—a husband somewhere, a mortal fear of intercourse, something besides your silly conviction earls don't marry housekeepers— then I will consider desisting." He punctuated his comment with a soft kiss to her neck.

"Keep your lips off me, please." Anna straightened away from him but didn't move off the couch. "I cannot think. I do not even know right from wrong when you start with your kisses and your wandering hands. You don't mean to do it, but you leave me helpless and lost and… You have no clue what I mean, do you?"

"In truth," the earl said, urging her head back down to his shoulder, "I do. You would be astonished, Anna, at how surprised I am at the way matters have progressed between us, and I am not often surprised."

"Well, then," Anna huffed, "all the more reason to give up this courting you seem so bent on."

"Can't say I agree with you." His lips grazed her temple again, completely without conscious thought on his part. "And you have yet to name me a single reason why you could not wed me. Have you taken holy orders?"

"I have not."

"Have you a mortal fear of copulating with me?"

She buried her nose against his shoulder and mumbled something.

"I will take that for a no. Are you married?"

"I am not." And because he heard what he wanted to hear and insisted on hearing, the earl missed the slight hesitance in her answer.

"So why, Anna?" He bit her earlobe gently. "Those were my teeth, not my lips, mind you. We've gone only so far as lovers, and already you must know we would bring each other pleasure upon pleasure. So why do you play this game?"

"It isn't a game. There are matters I hold in confidence, matters I will not discuss with you or anyone, that prevent me from committing to you as a wife should commit."

"Ah." The earl was listening now and heard the

resolution with which she spoke. "I will not pry a confidence from you, but I will make every effort to convince you to confide in me, Anna. When a man marries, his wife's goods become his, but so too, should her burdens."

"I've given you my reason." She lifted her head to regard him closely. "You will leave me in peace now? You will give up this notion of courting me?"

"Knowing you are burdened with confidences only makes me that much more convinced we should be wed. I'd take on your troubles, you know."

"You are a good man," Anna said, touching his cheek, her expression both solemn and sad, "but you cannot be my husband, and I cannot be your wife."

"I will content myself with being your suitor, as we agreed, though now, Anna Seaton, I will also be encouraging your trust, as well." He kissed her palm to emphasize his words. "One last question, Anna." The earl kept hold of her hand. "If you were free of these obligations that you hold in confidence, would you consider my suit then?"

He was encouraged she couldn't give him an immediate no, encouraged she'd offered him the smallest crumb of a confidence, encouraged they'd been more intimate with each other than ever before—encouraged, but also… concerned.

"I'd consider it," she allowed. "That is not the same as accepting it."

"I understand." He smiled at her. "Even a duke mustn't take his duchess for granted."

Anna fell asleep in the secure circle of his arms, her weight resting against him, his lips at her temple. As he carried her to her bedroom, the earl reflected that for a woman who insisted there be no next time, Anna had certainly been reluctant to bring an end to things this time.

It boded well, he thought, kissing her forehead as he tucked her in. All he needed to do now was gain her confidence and meet these obligations she was so determined to carry alone. She was a housekeeper, for pity's sake, how complicated could her obligations be?

❧

Anna awoke the next morning with a lingering sense of sweetness, of stolen pleasures not quite regretted, and—most incongruous of all—of hope. Hope that somehow, she might find a way to extricate herself from the situation with Westhaven that didn't leave them enemies. Westhaven was doing exactly as he said he would: He was giving her pleasure, pleasure beyond her wildest imaginings, pleasure she could keep for herself in memory long after her dealings with him were over, and she would give a great deal to see that those memories were not tainted with a bitter parting.

And under that hope there beat against the cage of reason and duty the wings of another hope, one she didn't even acknowledge: The hope that somehow, she might not have to leave him, not at the end of the summer, not any time soon. She could not marry him, she accepted that, but to leave him might prove equally impossible, and what options did that give her?

Anna was practical by nature, so she forced herself to leave those questions for another time, got out of bed, dressed, and went about her day. Memories of the night preoccupied her, though, and she forgot to don one of her homely lace caps.

She also forgot to chide Morgan for the wisps of hay sticking to her skirts, and she almost forgot to put extra sugar in the earl's first glass of lemonade. She wasn't looking forward to seeing him again, and yet she yearned for the sight of him.

The man and his ideas about courting were botheration personified.

"Post for ye, Missus." John Footman handed her a slim, worn missive posted from a remote inn on the Yorkshire dales, and Anna felt all the joy and potential in the day collapse into a single, hard lump of dread.

"Thank you, John." Anna nodded, her expression calm as she made her way to her private sitting room. She rarely closed the door, feeling the space was one of few places the servants could congregate with privacy, particularly as Mr. Stenson would never set a sanctimonious toe on her carpet.

But she closed the door before reading her missive. Closed it and locked it then sat down on the sofa and stared into the cold grate, trying to collect her courage.

Finding the exercise pointless, she carefully slit the seal on the envelope and read the brief contents:

*Beware, as your location may be known.*

Just that one cautionary sentence, thank God. Anna read it several times then tore both letter and envelope into tiny pieces, wrapped them into a sheet of foolscap, and put them onto the hearth grate to burn later that evening.

Beware as your location may be known.

A warning, but understandably vague. Her location may be known; it may not be. Her location—Southern England? London? Mayfair? Westhaven's household?—may be known. She pondered the possibilities and decided to assume that her location meant she'd been traced to London, at least, which meant her adoption of the profession of housekeeper might also be known and that Morgan was in service with her, as well.

All in all, it amounted to looming disaster and ended, utterly, any foolish fantasies about dallying with the earl for the rest of the summer. Unlocking the door, Anna assembled her writing supplies and penned three inquiries to the employment agencies she'd noted when she and Morgan had passed through Manchester. Bath was worth a try, she decided, and maybe Bristol, as well. A port town had possibilities inland locations did not.

Without volition, her mind had shifted into the calculating, rational, unsentimental habits of a woman covering her tracks. If it hurt her to leave Nanny Fran, to uproot Morgan again, to part from the earl, well, she told herself, the fate trying to find her would hurt more and for a much longer time.

She assessed the room, mentally inventorying the things she'd brought with her, the few things she'd acquired while in London. Nothing could be left behind that might give her away, but little could be taken with them when they left.

She'd done this twice before—prepared, packed, and executed an escape, for that's how she had to think of it. Morgan would have to be warned, and she wasn't going to like this turn of events one bit. Anna didn't blame her, for here, in the earl's house, Morgan wasn't treated like a mute beast. The other servants were protective of her, and Anna had a sneaking suspicion Lord Valentine felt the same way.

It was no way to live, but Anna had cudgeled her brain, and there seemed to be no alternative. When they ran out of hiding places in England, then the Americas were a possibility, but Anna hated to think of going so far from home.

"Beg pardon, Missus?" John Footman was at her door, smiling, which told her it wasn't a summons from the earl, thank God. "Lunch be served, unless you'd like a tray?"

"I'll be along, John." Anna smiled up at him. "Just give me a minute."

She completed her correspondence and tucked it into her reticule. It wouldn't do for the rest of the household to know she was corresponding with employment agencies, much less in what cities. It wouldn't do for them to know she was upset, wouldn't do for them to know she'd soon be leaving, with or without the character Westhaven had promised her.

She got through lunch, feeling frozen inside and frantic at the same time. In the few months she'd held her position, she'd come to treasure the house itself, taking pride in its care and appearance. She treasured the staff, as well—with the exception of Stenson, but even he was dedicated to faithful execution of his duties. They were good people, their lives lived without substantial duplicity or deception. Such a one as she wasn't destined to fit in with them for long.

"Morgan?" Anna murmured as they rose from lunch, "will you join me for a moment?"

Morgan nodded. Anna slipped her arm through Morgan's and led her out to the back gardens, the only place where privacy might be assured. When they were out on the shaded terrace, Anna turned to face Morgan directly.

"I've had a letter from Grandmama," Anna said slowly but distinctly. "She warns us we may have been traced to London. We need to move on, Morgan, and soon."

Morgan's expression, at first joyous to think they'd heard from their grandmother, then wary, knowing it could be bad news, finally became thunderous. She scowled mightily and shook her head.

"I don't want to leave either," Anna said, holding the younger woman's eyes. "I truly would not if there were any choice, but there is no choice, and you know it."

Morgan glared at her and shook a fist.

"Fight," she mouthed. "Tell the truth."

"Fight with what?" Anna shot back. "Tell the truth to whom? The courts? The courts are run by old men, Morgan, and the law gives us no protection. And stuck out on the dales, we wouldn't be able to get to the courts, and well you know it."

"Not yet," Morgan mouthed, still glaring daggers. "Not so soon again."

"It's been months," Anna said on a sigh, "and of course we can't go immediately. I need a character from his lordship, and I have to find positions for us elsewhere."

"Go without me."

"I will not go without you," Anna said, shaking her head. "That would be foolish in the extreme."

"Split up," Morgan persisted. "They need only one of us."

Anna stared at Morgan in shock. The last sentence had been not just lipped but almost whispered, so close was it to audible speech.

"I won't let that one be you," Anna said, hugging her and deciding against making a fuss over Morgan's use of words. "And we'll fight if we have to."

"Tell Lord Val," Morgan suggested, less audibly. "Tell the earl."

"Lord Val and the earl cannot be trusted. They are men, too"—Anna shook her head—"in case you hadn't noticed."

"I noticed." Morgan's glare was temporarily leavened by a slight smile. "Handsome men."

"Morgan Elizabeth James"—Anna smiled back—"shame on you. They might be handsome men, but they can't change the laws, nor can we ask them to break the law."

"Hate this," Morgan said, laying her head on Anna's shoulder. She raised her face long enough for her sister to see the next words. "I miss Grandmother."

"I do, too." Anna hugged her close. "We will see her again, I promise."

Morgan just shook her head and stepped back, her expression resigned. This whole mad scheme had been undertaken more than two years ago, "just until we can think of something else." Well, it was two years, three positions, and many miles later, and nothing else was being thought of. In those years when a gently bred young girl—even one who appeared unable to hear or speak—should be thinking of beaus and ball gowns, Morgan was sweeping grates, lugging buckets of coal, and changing bed linens.

Anna watched her go, her heart heavy with Morgan's disappointment but also with her own. Two years was a long time never to see home or hearth, always to look over your shoulder for those meaning you harm. It was never supposed to go on this long, but as Anna contemplated her remaining years on earth, all she could see was more running and hiding and leaving behind the things—and people—that really mattered.

# Ten

"YOUR HOUSEKEEPER IS KEEPING SECRETS."

Dev threw himself down on the library's sofa, yanked off his boots, and stretched out to his considerable length with a sigh. "And she's a damned pretty housekeeper to have served as your nurse."

"Nurses must be ugly?" Westhaven tossed down his pen. Dev was a different sort of housemate than Val. Dev didn't disappear into the music room for hours at a time, letting the entire household know where he was without being bothersome about it. Dev wandered at will, as apt to be in the library with a book or in the kitchen flirting with Cook and Nanny Fran. He'd seen to moving his riding horses into the mews but still had plenty of time for poking his nose into his brother's business.

"Nurses must be ugly." Dev closed his eyes. "Mistresses must be pretty. Housekeepers are not supposed to be pretty, but then we have your Mrs. Seaton."

"Hands off."

"My hands off?" Dev raised his head and eyed Westhaven. "My hands off your housekeeper?"

"Yes, Dev. Hands off, and this is not a request."

"Getting into the ducal spirit, are you?" Dev closed his eyes again and folded his hands on his chest. "Well, no need to issue a decree. I'll behave, as she is a female employed by a Windham household."

"Devlin St. Just." Westhaven's boots hit the floor with a thump. "Weren't you swiving your house-keeper *while* she was engaged to some clueless simian in Windsor?"

"Very likely." Dev nodded peacefully, eyes closed. "And I put away that toy when honor required it."

"What sort of honor is this? I comprehend what is expected of a gentleman, generally, but must have missed the part about how we go on when swiving housekeepers."

"You were going on quite enthusiastically," Dev said, opening one eye, "when I came down here last night to find a book."

"I see."

"On the sofa," Dev added, "if that pinpoints my interruption of your orgy."

"It wasn't an orgy."

"You were what?" Dev frowned. "Trying to keep her warm? Counting her teeth with your tongue? Teaching her how to sit the trot riding astride? Looked to me for all the world like you were rogering the daylights out of dear Mrs. Seaton."

"I wasn't," Westhaven spat, getting up and pacing to the hearth. "The next thing to it, but not quite the act itself."

"I believe you," Dev said, "and that makes it all better. Even though it looked like rogering and sounded like rogering and probably tasted like it, too."

"Dev…"

"Gayle…" Dev got up and put a hand on his brother's shoulder. "I am the last person to begrudge you your pleasures, but if I can walk in on you, and I've only been underfoot a day, then anybody else can, too."

Westhaven nodded, conceding the point.

"I don't care that you and Mrs. Seaton are providing each other some slap-and-tickle, but if you're so far gone you forget to lock the door, then I am concerned."

"I didn't…" Westhaven scrubbed a hand over his face. "I did forget to lock the door, and we haven't made a habit out of what you saw. I don't intend to make a habit of it, but if I do, I will lock the door."

"Good plan." Dev nodded, grinning. "I have to approve of the woman on general principles, you know, if she has you spouting such inanities and dropping your pants for all the world to see."

"I thought in my own library at nigh midnight I could have privacy," Westhaven groused.

Dev's expression became serious. "You cannot assume you have privacy anywhere. The duke owns half your staff and can buy the other half, for one thing. For another, you are considered a most eligible bachelor. If I were you, I would assume I had no privacy whatsoever, not even in your own home."

"You're right." Westhaven blew out a breath. "I know you're right, but I don't like it. We will be careful."

"*You* be careful," Dev admonished. "Earlier today,

I was minding my own business up on the balcony that opens off my bedroom, and I saw your housekeeper in earnest discussion with the deaf maid. Mrs. Seaton was warning the maid you and Val are men who can't be trusted nor asked to break the law. I thought you should know."

"I appreciate your telling me, but I am loathe to react out of hand to words taken out of context. In some villages, there are laws against waving one's cane in public, and laws against drinking spirits on the Sabbath."

"Are you sure the maid can't speak?" Dev pressed. "Do you really know what became of Mr. Seaton and where the banns were cried? Just who were Mrs. Seaton's references?"

"You raise valid questions, but you cannot question that Mrs. Seaton does a splendid job of keeping this house."

"Absolutely splendid," Dev agreed, "and she trysts with you in the library."

"Are you telling me I shouldn't marry her now?" Westhaven tried for humor but found the question was partly serious.

"You might well end up having to marry her, if last night is any indication," Dev shot back. "Just make damned sure you know exactly who it is you're trysting with before the duke gets wind of same."

Knowing he wouldn't get any more work done after that discussion, Westhaven left the library in search of his housekeeper. He couldn't be precisely sure she was avoiding him—again—but he'd yet to see her that day. He found her in her private sitting room and closed the door behind him before she even rose to offer him a curtsy.

"I wish you wouldn't do that," he said, wrapping his arms around her. She stiffened immediately.

"I wish you wouldn't do *that*," she retorted, turning away her face when he tried to kiss her.

"You don't want me holding you?" he asked, kissing her cheek anyway.

"I don't want you closing the door, taking liberties, and *bothering* me," she said through clenched teeth. He dropped his arms and eyed her curiously.

"What is it?"

"What is what?" She crossed her arms over her chest.

"You were willing enough to be bothered last night, Anna Seaton, and it is perfectly acceptable that your employer might want to have a word or two with you privately. Dev said he saw you and Morgan in heated discussion after lunch. Is something troubling you? Those confidences you referred to last night, perhaps?"

"I should not have trusted you with even that much of a disclosure," Anna said, uncrossing her arms. "You know I intend to seek another position, my lord. I wonder if you've written out that character you promised me?"

"I have. Because Val has yet to return, it remains in my desk. You gave me your word we would have the rest of the summer, Anna. Are you dishonoring that promise so soon?"

She turned away from him, which was answer enough for Westhaven.

"I am still here."

"Anna…" He stole up behind her and wrapped his arms around her waist. "I am not your enemy."

She nodded once, then turned in his arms and buried her face against his throat.

"I'm just… upset."

"A lady's prerogative," he murmured, stroking her back. "The heat has everyone out of sorts, and while I was allowed to sit on my lordly backside for a week, claiming illness, you were expected to be up at all hours."

She didn't contradict him, but she did take a deep breath and step back.

"I did not intend to upset you." The earl offered her a smile, and she returned it just as the door swung open.

"I beg your pardon, my lord." Stenson drew himself up to his unimpressive height, shot a disdainful glance at Anna, and pulled the door shut again.

"Oh, God." Anna dropped down onto her sofa. "It needed only that."

The earl frowned at her in puzzlement. "I wasn't even touching you. There was a good two feet between us, and Stenson was the one in the wrong. He should have knocked."

"He never does," Anna sighed, "and we were not touching, but we looked at one another as something other than housekeeper and employer."

"Because I *smiled* at you?"

"And I smiled back. It was not a housekeeper's smile for her employer."

"Don't suppose it was, but it was still just a smile."

"You need a butler, Westhaven." Anna rose and advanced on him.

"Any footman can answer the damned door. Why do I need another mouth to feed?"

"Because, a butler will outrank that toadying little buffoon, will be loyal to you rather than the duke's coin, and will keep the rest of the male servants toeing the line, as well."

"You have a point."

"Or you could just get rid of Stenson," she went on, "or have your brother perpetually travel around the countryside with Stenson in tow."

"I suppose if Stenson is back, then Val can't be far behind," Westhaven observed.

"I have missed him," Anna said. She looked a trifle disconcerted to have made the admission but let it stand.

"I have, too." Westhaven nodded. "I miss his music, his irreverence, his humor… How is Dev settling in?"

Anna crossed the room and opened the door before answering his question.

"Well enough, I suppose," she replied, busying her hands with an arrangement of daylilies. "He doesn't sleep much, though, and doesn't seem to have much of a routine."

"He'll settle in," the earl said. "You will let me know when Lord Valentine returns?"

"No need for that." Val stepped into the room. "I am back and glad to be back. It is too damned hot to travel, and Stenson was unwilling to travel at night. Not a very servile servant, if you ask me, though he does a wicked job with a muddy boot."

"You." Westhaven pulled his brother into a hug. "No more haring off for you, sir. Nobody knows how to go on without your music in the house or your deviltry to keep up morale."

"I will wander no more," Val said, stepping back, "at least until the heat breaks. I came, though, in search of Miss Morgan."

"She might be in the kitchen," Anna said. "More likely she's reading in the barn. With dinner pushed back these days, she has some free time early in the evening."

"Val?" The earl stayed his brother's departure with a hand on his arm. "You should know, in your absence, I've asked Dev to bunk in with us. He was without his domestic help, and we have the room."

"Devlin, here?" Val's grin was spontaneous. "Oh ye gods and little fishes, that was a splendid idea, Westhaven. If we're to be stuck in Town with this heat, at least let us have good company and Mrs. Seaton's conscientious care while we're here."

He sailed out of the room, leaving Anna and the earl smiling in his wake.

"Good to have him back safe and sound," Westhaven said.

"Three for dinner on the terrace, then?" she asked, every inch a housekeeper.

"Three, and I wanted to speak with you about a practical matter."

"Dinner is very practical.

"Dinner is… yes, well." He glanced at the door. "I have commissioned a fair amount of furniture for Willow Bend, but the place needs drapes, carpets, and so forth. I'd like you to see to it."

"You want me to order those things? Shouldn't your mother or perhaps one of your sisters take that on?"

"Her Grace is bouncing between Town and Morelands and preparing for the summer's house parties. My sisters have not the expertise, nor do I have the patience for working with them on a project of this nature."

"But, my lord, one of them will eventually be living there. My tastes cannot possibly coincide with those of a woman I've never met."

"Not possibly." The earl smiled. "As yours will be better."

"You should not say such things." Anna's frown became a scowl. "It isn't gentlemanly."

"It's brotherly and the truth. Even I know salmon and purple don't go together, but that's the kind of scheme my sisters would consider 'daring,' or some such. And they would pester me endlessly, while you, as I know from firsthand experience, can turn a house into a home with very little guidance from its owner."

"I will take this on," Anna said, chin going up. "Be it on your head if the place turns out looking like one of Prinny's bad starts. What sort of furniture have you commissioned?"

"Why don't we finish this discussion in the library?" the earl asked. "I can make you lists, draw you some sketches, and argue with you without every single servant and both brothers hearing me."

"Give me a few minutes to talk with Cook, and I will join you."

"Twenty minutes, then." The earl took his leave, going up to his bedroom, where he'd no doubt Stenson was attempting to address more than a week's worth of others making shift with his responsibilities.

"Mr. Stenson?" The earl strode into the room without knocking—and why would he?—and caught the fellow actually sniffing the cravat discarded over the edge of the vanity mirror. "Whatever are you doing in my quarters?"

"I am your valet, my lord." Stenson bowed low. "Of course I must needs be in your quarters."

"You will stay out of here and busy yourself with Lord Val and Colonel St. Just instead."

"*Mr. St. Just?*" Stenson might as well have said: *That bastard?!* But Dev would have great good fun putting Stenson in his place, so Westhaven added a few more cautions about the bad form exhibited by the lower orders when they couldn't be bothered to knock on closed doors, and took his leave.

When he returned to the library, he did not immediately begin to list the furniture he'd ordered for Willow Bend. He instead wrote out an order to have all the interior locks above stairs changed and only two sets of keys made—one for him and his brothers, one for his housekeeper.

Sniffing his cravat, for God's sake. What on earth could Stenson have been about?

The question faded as Westhaven spent two hours arguing good-naturedly with his housekeeper over matters pertaining to Willow Bend. That was followed by an equally enjoyable dinner with both of his brothers, during which he realized he hadn't dined with them together since Victor had died months before.

"Will you two help me with my horses?" Dev pressed when they were down to their chocolates and brandy.

"If you insist." Val held his snifter under his nose. "Though coming up from Brighton has left me honestly saddle sore."

"I'll be happy to pitch in, as Pericles can use light duty in this heat, but if I'm to be up early"— Westhaven rose—"then I'd best seek my bed. You gentlemen have my thanks for keeping Mr. Stenson busy, though I don't think he was exactly pleased with the reassignment."

"My shirts will be pleased," Dev said. "It's mighty awkward having to always wear one's jacket and waistcoat because one's seams are all in jeopardy."

"And I found every mud puddle between here and Brighton just to make sure Mr. Stenson was gainfully occupied."

"I am blessed in my brothers," Westhaven said, leaving them with a smile.

"So tell me the truth," Dev said, pushing the decanter at his youngest brother. "You are willing to ride with us because you think it would be good for Westhaven. Just like his housekeeper has been good for him."

Val smiled and turned his glass around on the linen tablecloth. "It will be good for all of us, being together, living here, even if it's only for a little while. I find, though, that I've sat too long here in the evening breezes." He got to his feet and quirked an eyebrow at his oldest brother. "Shall we stroll in the moonlight?"

"Brother"—Dev grinned—"I have heard rumors about you."

"No doubt," Val said easily as they moved off. "They are nothing compared to what one hears about you."

"And that gossip is usually true," Dev said with no modesty whatsoever as they neared the mews. "Now why are we out here stumbling around in the night?"

Val turned and regarded his brother in the moonlight. "So I can remind you not to make disparaging remarks about Mrs. Seaton or her situation with Westhaven where anybody could overhear you. You know what the duke tried to do with the last mistress?"

"I'd heard about Elise. Then you are aware of a situation between Westhaven and Mrs. Seaton?"

"He's considering marrying her," Val said. "Or I think he is. They're certainly interested in each other."

"They're a bit more than interested," Dev said, rubbing his chin. "They were all but working on the succession when I came upon them in the library last night."

"Ye gods. I came upon them in her sitting room this afternoon, door open, all hands in view, but the way they look at each other... puts one in mind of besotted sheep."

"His Grace will be in alt," Dev said on a sigh.

"His Grace," Val retorted, "had best not get wind of it, unless you want Westhaven to immediately lose all interest."

"Gayle wouldn't be that stupid, but he would be that stubborn." Dev tossed a companionable arm around Val's shoulders. "This will be entertaining as hell, don't you think? I'm not sure Westhaven's wooing is entirely well received, and he has to go about it in stealth, winning the lady without alerting the duke. And we have front-row seats."

"Lucky us," Val rejoined. "Doesn't working on the succession comport with welcoming a man's suit?"

Dev's grin became devilish. "That, my boy, is a common misunderstanding among the besotted male sheep of this world. And the female sheep? They like us befuddled, you know…"

❧

"It's a speaking tube," Val explained. Morgan quirked an eyebrow at him, and he smiled reassuringly. "A lot of invalids take the sea air in Brighton," he went on, "so the medical community is much in evidence there. I discussed your loss of hearing with a physician or two, and I've brought it up with Fairly, as well. He'd like to examine you, though he isn't a specialist in the field of deafness."

Morgan tried to keep her emotions from her eyes, but it was difficult, when her eyes were so used to conveying what words could not. She was more than a little infatuated with this man, with his kindness and generosity of spirit, his acceptance of her disability, his care for his brothers and sisters. He was what a brother should be—decent, selfless, thoughtful, and good-humored.

"Will you let me try it?" he asked, holding up the tube. It was shaped like an old-style drinking horn, conical and twisted. He gently turned her by the shoulders and pushed her hair aside. Morgan felt the small end of the tube being anchored at her ear.

"Hello, Morgan. Can you hear me?"

She whirled on him, jaw gaping.

"I can hear you," she whispered, incredulous. "I

can hear your words. Say more." She turned and waited for him to position the speaking tube again.

"Let's try this with the piano," Val suggested, and she heard his words, or much more of them than she'd heard before. She couldn't see his mouth when he used the speaking tube, so she must be hearing him. It felt like a tickling in her ear and like so much more.

"I remember this."

"You remember how to speak," Val said into the tube. "I thought you might. But come, let me play for you."

He grabbed her by the hand, and she followed, Sir Walter Scott forgotten in the hay as they ran to the house. He led her straight to the music room, shut the door, and sat her down on what she'd come to think of as her stool. It was higher, like the stools in the ale houses, and let her lay her head directly on the piano's closed case. Val took the tube and put it wide end down on the piano. He leaned down as if to put his ear to the narrow end of the tube.

"Try it like that."

Morgan perched on the stool and carefully positioned the tube at her ear. Val moved to the piano bench and began a soft, lyrical Beethoven slow movement, meeting Morgan's eyes several measures into the piece.

"Can you hear?"

She nodded, eyes shining.

"Then hear this," he said, launching into a rollicking, joyous final movement by the same composer. Morgan laughed, a rusty, rough sound of mirth and pleasure and joy, causing Val to play with greater enthusiasm. She settled in on the stool, horn to her ear, eyes closed, and prepared to be swept away.

She'd been wrong. She wasn't infatuated with Val Windham; she was in awe of him. He'd brought her music and the all-but-forgotten sensation of a human voice sounding in her ear. All it had taken was a simple metal tube and a kind thought.

❦

"Good God almighty." Dev glanced across the library at Westhaven. "What's gotten into the prodigy?"

Westhaven looked up from his correspondence and focused on the chords crashing and thundering through the house.

"He's happy," Westhaven said, smiling. "He's happier than I've heard him since Victor died. Maybe happier than I've ever heard him... He tends to stay away from Herr Beethoven, but if I'm not mistaken, that's who it is. My God..."

He put down his letters and just listened. Val could improvise melodies so tender and lilting they brought tears. He could be the consummate chamber musician, his keyboard evoking grace, humor, and elegance. He knew every drinking song and Christmas carol, all the hymns, and folk tunes. This, however, was heady repertoire, full of emotion and substance.

*And he plays the hell out of it*, Westhaven thought, amazed. He knew his brother was talented and dedicated, but in those moments, he realized the man was *brilliant*. More gifted than any Windham had ever been at anything, transcendently gifted.

"Jesus Christ, he's good," Dev said. "Better than good. My God…"

"If His Grace could hear this," Westhaven said, "he'd never say another disparaging thing about our youngest brother."

"Hush." Dev's brow knit. "Let's just listen."

And they did, as Val played on and on, one piece following another in a recital of exuberant joy. In the kitchen, dinner preparations stopped. In the garden, the weeding took a hiatus. In the stables, grooms paused to lean on their pitchforks and marvel. Gradually, the music shifted to quieter beauty and more tender joy. As the evening sun slanted across the back gardens, the piano at last fell silent, but the whole household had been blasted with Val's joy.

In the music room, watching Morgan smile up at him, Val had a queer feeling in his chest. He wondered if it was something like what doctors experienced when they could save a life or safely bring one into the world, a joy and a humility so vast they could not be contained in one human body.

"Thank you," Morgan whispered, smile radiant. "Thank you, thank you."

She threw her arms around him and hugged him tight, and he hugged her back. There were some moments when words were superfluous, and holding her slight frame against him, Val could only thank God for the whim that had made him pick up the tube. He let her go and saw she was holding out the tube to him.

"You keep it," he said, but she shook her head.

"I cannot," she said clearly.

"Then let's leave it in here," Val suggested. "You can at least use it when we speak or when you want to hear me play." He put it on top of the piano, puzzled and not a little hurt by her unwillingness to keep the thing. He'd first thought to get her one when he'd seen a pair of old beldames strolling in Brighton, their speaking tubes on chains around their necks like lorgnettes.

Morgan nodded solemnly but put the tube inside the piano bench, out of sight.

"You don't want anyone to know?" Val guessed.

"Not yet," she replied, staring at the closed lid of the bench. "I heard once before," she said, her voice dropping back to a whisper so he had to lean in close to hear her. "We crossed the Penines, and something changed, in here." She pointed to her left ear. "But the next morning, I woke up, and it had changed back. Can we try the tube again tomorrow?"

"We can." Val smiled, comprehension dawning. "Your ear opened up because of the altitude. When you descended, it closed up again."

Morgan looked puzzled and turned her face away.

"Even if I can't hear tomorrow"—she hunched her shoulders against that terrible possibility—"thank you, Lord Valentine, for today. I will never forget your kindness."

"It was most assuredly my pleasure." He beamed at her. "Will you let Lord Fairly take a peek at you?"

"Look only," she said, her shoulders hunching more tightly still. "No treatments. And you will come with me?"

"I will. Westhaven trusts the man, and that should tell you worlds."

"It has to be soon," Morgan said, biting her lip.

"I'll track him down in the next few days. He's almost always at home these days, and I run tame around his pianos."

Morgan nodded and took her leave of him, her joy in the day colored by her recall of Anna's plans. It had been almost a week since Anna had gotten Grandmama's letter, and a perfectly pleasant if hot week, too. Morgan knew the earl had something to do with Anna's lighter moods. Oh, Anna still fretted— Anna was born to fret—but she also occasionally hummed, and she hugged Morgan when no one was about, and she smiled—when she wasn't staring off into space, looking worried.

Good Lord. Morgan stopped in her tracks. What was she going to tell Anna? When was she going to tell Anna? Not for a day or two, Morgan knew, as improvement could be deceptive. Her hearing sometimes got better during really bad storms, only to disappear when the weather moved. Worse than the loss of hearing, though, was the loss of speech.

She'd never realized how the two were related until she couldn't hear. She lost her ability to gauge the volume of her voice and found she was whispering—or worse, shouting—when she thought her tone was conversational. Eventually, she'd just given up, until she was afraid to attempt speech again, the patterns not even feeling familiar to her lips, teeth, and tongue anymore.

But that could all change, she thought. If the speaking tube still worked tomorrow, it could all change.

❧

The week had gone so well, Anna thought as she
rose from her bed. It was another beautiful—if sweltering—summer day, and she'd enjoyed her efforts
to complete the Willow Bend interiors. The earl had
chosen surprisingly pretty and comfortable furniture,
suited to a country home, and to a country home that
wouldn't be simply a gentleman's retreat from the city.

He'd had few suggestions regarding the decorative
schemes, predictably. "Avoid purple, if you please,"
or "no flights of Egyptian fancy. My sisters are
imaginative enough as it is." He liked simple, cheerful,
comfortable arrangements, which suited Anna just
fine. They were easy to assemble, clean, and maintain,
and better still, easy to live in.

And if she felt a pang of envy that some other woman,
one dear to Westhaven, was going to be doing the
living at Willow Bend, she smothered it. She smothered
her anxieties regarding her grandmother's warning and
set to bargaining with herself fiercely instead: I'll work
on the Willow Bend interiors until the letters arrive
from the agencies. I'll enjoy the earl's attentions until I
have to leave. I'll leave Morgan in peace until I know
for certain when and where we're going...

Her life, it seemed, had degenerated into a series of
unenforceable bargains made with herself, while the
business of the household moved along heedlessly.

The Windham males had taken to hacking in the
park early in the morning, with Pericles sometimes
escorting two of the younger stock or taking a day to
enjoy his stall and hay. The men came back hungry
and usually in high spirits.

When Devlin St. Just had moved in, he'd brought

an ability to tease with him, and it was infectious. With only the earl and Lord Val in residence, it was as if their shared grief had pushed out all but the driest humor. With Dev underfoot, bad puns, jokes, ribbing, and sly innuendo cropped up among all three brothers. To Anna, the irreverent humor was the conversational equivalent of the occasional bouquet in the house. It pleased the eye and brought visual warmth and pleasure to the odd corner or bare table.

Nonetheless, Colonel St. Just watched her with a calculating gleam foreign to either the earl or Lord Val. St. Just was a bastard and half Irish. Either burden would have been a strike against him, but his papa was a duke, and so he was received.

Received, Anna thought, but not welcomed. That difference put a harder edge on St. Just than on either of his brothers. In his own way, he was an outsider, and so Anna wanted to feel some sympathy for him. But his green eyes held such a measure of distance when they looked at her, all she felt was… wary.

Still, he was supportive of the earl, proud of Val's music, and well liked by the staff. He always cleaned his plate, flirted shamelessly with Nanny Fran, and occasionally sang to Cook in a lilting, lyrical baritone. He was, in a word, charming, even to Morgan, who usually left the room as quickly as she could when he started his blather.

"Hullo, my dear." The earl strolled into Anna's sitting room and glanced back at the door as if he wanted to close it.

"Good morning." Anna rose, smiling despite herself, because here was the handsomest of the Windham brothers, the heir, and he wanted to marry *her*. "What brings you to my sitting room on this lovely day?"

"We have household matters to discuss." His smile dimmed. "May I sit?"

"Shall I fetch the tea tray?" Anna frowned and realized he wanted to settle in, which would not do, for many reasons.

"No, thank you." The earl took the middle of the settee, extended an arm across the back, and crossed one ankle over the other knee. "How are you coming with the Willow Bend project?"

"I've ordered a great deal in the way of draperies, rugs, mirrors, smaller items of furniture, such as night tables, footstools, and so forth," Anna replied, grateful for a simple topic. "It is going to cost you a pretty penny, I'm warning you, but the results should be very pleasing."

"Pleasing is good. When will it be ready?"

"Much has already been delivered. The rest should arrive in the next few days. I understood there was some urgency about this project."

"There is. I want it done before fall, when I'm likely to be dragooned into the shires by my dear papa for some hunting."

"If you don't want to go hunting, you'd best arrange something with your brothers, so when Papa issues his summons, you are otherwise occupied."

"I'll get right on it."

"And have you gotten right on finding us a butler? Stenson is more in need of stern guidance than ever."

The earl burst out laughing at that image and shook his head as he rose.

"Send me some candidates," he said. "Their

most important qualification must be their ability to withstand the duke's inveigling. I should be on hand Monday and Wednesday next week, though I have appointments back-to-back on Tuesday. I'll expect you to accompany me to Willow Bend on Thursday."

"Me?" Anna rose, as well, memories assaulting her: The earl drinking champagne from the bottle on the library floor, his hand slipping over her bare buttocks in the dark of night, the single rose he'd brought her... "I don't believe that's wise."

"Of course it's wise," the earl said. "How else am I to know which table goes in what room, and which drapes to hang where?"

"I can write it out," Anna suggested, "or go when you're not there."

"I am the owner, Anna." He peered down at her in consternation. "What if I take issue with your decisions? Are we to trundle out there on alternate days until all our quibbling is resolved?"

She admitted the silliness of that but not out loud.

"You aren't afraid, are you?" He cocked his head, frowning. "It isn't likely we'll be stuck in a second monsoon, but we can take the coach if you'd feel better about it."

"Let's see what the weather portends." Anna did want to see the place put to rights. "Who will be doing all of the stepping and fetching?"

"The property is now swarming with locals ready to do the earl's bidding for a bit of the earl's coin. Much of the work should be done before we arrive, but I want your eye on the finished product."

"Very well, then. Thursday."

"And I've been meaning to ask you why you always fall silent when St. Just is in the room." He sidled a little closer and waited for her reply.

"The colonel doesn't particularly care for me. It's merely his tacitly stated and perfectly legitimate opinion."

"He likes you." The earl dipped his head and kissed her cheek. "It might be he doesn't trust you. More likely, he simply envies me, because I saw you first."

Anna's eyebrows shot up in astonishment, but the earl was gone in an instant, no doubt drawn into the breakfast parlor by the scent of bacon, scones, omelets, and—more especially—by the sound of his brothers' laughter.

# Eleven

"Good morning, Your Grace."

Anna swept the deep, deferential curtsy required in the presence of a lady of high rank. "Would you like to wait in the formal parlor, the breakfast parlor, the family parlor, or the library?"

"It's such a pleasant morning," the duchess said. "Why not in the gardens?" Anna found herself returning her smile, as the gardens were the better choice. After several days of increasingly miserable weather, the humidity had dropped in the night, making the morning air delightful.

"Can I bring you some iced lemonade?" Anna asked when she'd seen the earl's mother ensconced on a shady bench. "The earl and his brothers usually return from their morning ride about this time and go directly in to breakfast."

"His brothers?" The duchess paused in the arrangements of her skirts and blinked once. "Can you spare a few minutes to sit with me, Mrs. Seaton?"

"Of course." Anna assumed a seat on the same bench as the duchess. There was a subtle, pleasant

scent to the woman, a gracious but simple hint of
rose with a note of spice. It didn't fit with what Anna
thought a duchess should smell like; it was much less
formal, prettier, more sweet and loving.

"Westhaven's brothers join him regularly for breakfast? I was aware Lord Valentine was a guest here, but
you include St. Just in this breakfast club?"

"I do," Anna said, feeling cornered. Would the earl
want his mother knowing St. Just lived here?

"Is St. Just another guest in the earl's home?" the
duchess asked, frowning slightly at the roses. She was
a pretty woman, even when she frowned: willowy,
hair going from golden to flax, and green eyes slightly
canted in a face graced with elegant bones.

"I would be more comfortable, Your Grace, did
you put that question to your sons," Anna said. A
small, surprised silence followed her comment, and the
duchess's frown became a smile.

"You are protective of him," she observed. "Or of
them. That is admirable and a trait we share. Can you
tell me, Mrs. Seaton, how Westhaven is going on?"

Anna considered the question and decided she
could answer it, honestly if somewhat vaguely.

"He is a very, very busy man," Anna said. "The
business of the duchy is complicated and demands
much of his time, but for the most part, I think he
enjoys getting matters under control."

"His Grace did not always see to the details as
conscientiously as he should. Westhaven does much
better in this regard." As understatements went, that
one was worthy of a duchess, Anna thought, and the
duchess was loyal to her duke, which was no surprise.

"And how is Westhaven's health?"

"He enjoys good health," Anna said, thinking that was honest at least in the present tense. "He has an active man's appetite, much to Cook's delight."

"And is he treating you well, Mrs. Seaton?" The duchess turned guileless eyes on Anna, but the question was sincere.

"He is a very good employer," Anna said, feeling an abrupt, inconvenient, and wholly out-of-character wish that she had someone to talk to. The duchess was as pretty and gracious as an older woman could be, but she struck Anna as first, last, and always, a woman who had borne eight children, taken in two of her husband's by-blows, and buried two of her sons. She was a mother, a *mama*, and Anna sorely, sorely missed her mother. It had taken this conversation to remind her of it, and the realization brought an unwelcome lump to her throat.

The duchess patted Anna's hand. "A good employer can still be a selfish, inconsiderate, clueless *man*, Mrs. Seaton. I love my sons, but they will wear their muddy boots in the public rooms, flirt with the maids, and argue with their father in view of the servants. They are, in short, human, and sometimes trying as a result."

"It is no trial to work for Lord Westhaven," Anna said. "He pays honest coin for an honest day's wage and is both reasonable and kind."

"Your Grace?" Westhaven smiled as he strolled from the mews. "What a pleasure to see you." He bent to kiss his mother's cheek and used the gesture to wink at Anna surreptitiously. "Have you been haranguing Mrs. Seaton about how to fold the linens?"

"I've been trying without success to grill her about whether you finish your pudding these days." The duchess stood and took her son's proffered arm. The earl smiled at Anna and winged his other elbow at her. "Mrs. Seaton?" Anna accepted the gallantry rather than make a fuss.

"I can see you are indeed faring well, Westhaven. You dropped too much weight this spring; gauntness did not become you."

"My staff is taking good care of me. You will be pleased to know both Dev and Val are enjoying my hospitality, as well. They'll be along shortly, but were arguing about a horse when I left the stables."

"I heard no shouting," the duchess remarked. "It cannot be a very serious argument."

"Dev wants Val to take on some work with one of his horses. Val is demurring," the earl explained. "Or letting Dev work for it. How are His Grace and my dear sisters?"

"The girls are glad to be at Morelands, with the heat being so oppressive. They might come back for Fairly's ball, however."

"About which you can regale us at breakfast," Westhaven said. "You will join us. I won't hear otherwise."

"I would be delighted." The duchess smiled at her son, a smile of such warmth and loving regard Anna had to look away. Westhaven's expression mirrored his mother's, and Anna knew the earl had no greater ally than Her Grace, at least in all matters that did not pit him against the duke.

"My lord, Your Grace." Anna slipped her arm from

the earl's. "If you'll excuse me, I'll notify the kitchen we have a guest."

"Please don't put them to any bother, Mrs. Seaton," the duchess said. "The company of my sons is treat enough on any day." The earl offered Anna a slight bow, and Anna knew the gesture wasn't lost on his mother.

"She dotes on you," the duchess commented when Anna had retreated.

"She dotes on all three of us. We have all the comforts a conscientious housekeeper can imagine for us, and then some. Do you know, she keeps marzipan in the pantry for me, chocolates for Val, and candied violets for Dev? We have flowers in every room, the linens are all scented with lavender or rosemary, the house stays cool even in this heat, and I cannot comprehend how she accomplishes this."

Her Grace paused on the back steps. "She did all this before you'd brought your brothers to stay with you, didn't she?"

"She did. I just notice it more now."

"Grief can turn us inward," the duchess said quietly. "I was concerned for you, Westhaven. I know His Grace left the finances in a muddle, but it seems as if cleaning up after your father was all you made time for this spring."

"The finances are still not untangled, Your Grace. We were not faring very well when I was given the reins."

"Are we in difficulties?" the duchess asked carefully.

"No, but we nearly would have been. In some ways, Victor's mourning period saved us some very timely entertaining expenses. A house party at Morelands is nothing compared to one of your balls, Mother."

"You call me Mother when you scold me, Westhaven, but this ball will be underwritten by Fairly and his in-laws, so you needn't frown at me."

"My apologies." They turned at the sound of his brothers' voices coming up the garden paths.

"What ho!" Dev called, grinning. "What light through yonder rose bush shines? Good morning, Your Grace." He bowed low over her hand then stepped back as Val sidled in to kiss the duchess's cheek.

"Mother." Val smiled down at her. "You will join us for breakfast so these two mind their manners around their baby brother?"

"I will join you for breakfast to feast my eyes on the greatest display of young male pulchritude to be had in all of London."

"She flatters," Westhaven said, "before interrogating, no doubt."

The duchess floated into the house, one hand tucked by Westhaven's side, the other wrapped on Val's arm. Dev watched them go, smiling at the tableau before turning back to the rose bushes along the far wall, where Anna was clipping a bouquet.

He propped a booted foot against the low stone wall bordering the bed. "How badly did she interrogate you?"

"Good morning, Colonel St. Just." Anna bobbed a curtsy and put her shears into the wicker basket sitting on the wall. "The duchess was all that was gracious." *Unlike present company.* "If you'll excuse me?"

"I will not," St. Just replied. He emphasized his response by putting a hand on Anna's arm. She met his eyes, looked pointedly down at his hand, and back up at his face, arching a brow in question.

"You need not like me," Anna said, "but you will respect me."

"Or what, Anna Seaton?" He leaned in, giving Anna a hint of his aftershave, a minty scent with a blend of meadow flowers. Anna went still, knowing if she made a fuss, the earl would appear, likely with his mother at his side.

"You are not a bully, Colonel, whatever else may trouble you."

He stepped back, frowning.

"You aggravate me, Mrs. Seaton," he said at length. "I want to assure myself you are a scheming, selfish, vapid little tramp with airs above your station, but the assurance just won't ring true."

Anna flashed him a look of consternation. "Why on earth would you attempt to make such a nasty prejudgment? You yourself have no doubt been subject to just the same sort of close mindedness."

"Now, see?" St. Just almost smiled. "That's what I mean. You don't bother to deny the labels, you just hand them back to me in a neat, tidy little package of subtle castigation. Perhaps I'm only wishing you were venal, so I might poach on my brother's preserves with moral impunity."

"You would not poach on your brother's preserves," Anna said, beginning to see how much of the man was a particularly well-aimed type of bluster. "You are not as wicked as you want the world to think, sir."

"Happens"—he did smile—"I am not, but it also happens you are not just the simple, devoted housekeeper you would have the world think you are, either."

"My past is my own business. Now have you business with me, Colonel, or are you being gratuitously unpleasant?"

"Business," he said shortly. "You have rightly surmised I brood and paw and snort at times for show, Mrs. Seaton. It keeps His Grace from getting ideas, for one thing. But make no mistake on this point: I will defend my brother's interests without exception or scruple. If I find you are playing him false in any sense or trifling with him, I will become your worst enemy."

Anna smiled at him thinly. "Do you think he'd appreciate these threats you make to his housekeeper?"

"He might understand them," St. Just said. "For the other message I have to convey to you is that to the extent you matter to my brother, you matter to me. If he decides he values you in his life, then I will also defend *you* without exception or scruple."

"What is it you are saying?"

"You are a woman with troubles, Anna Seaton. You have no past anyone in this household knows of, you have no people you'll admit to, you have the airs and graces of a well-born lady, but you labor for your bread instead. I've seen you conferring with Morgan, and I know you have something to hide."

Anna raised her chin and speared him with a look. "Everybody has something to hide."

"You have a choice, Anna," St. Just said, her given name falling from his lips with surprising gentleness. "You either trust the earl to resolve your troubles, or you leave him in peace. He's too good a man to be exploited by somebody under his own roof. He's had that at the hands of his own father, and I won't stand for it from you."

Anna hefted her basket and flashed St. Just a cold smile. "Like the duke, you'll wade in, bully and intimidate, and jump to conclusions regarding Westhaven's life, telling yourself all the while you do it because you love him, when in fact, you haven't the first notion how to really go about caring for the man. Very impressive—if one wants proof of your patrimony."

She bobbed him a curtsy with fine irony and walked off, her skirts twitching with her irritation.

As he pasted the requisite smile on his face and went in to breakfast, St. Just reflected he hadn't been wrong: Anna Seaton had secrets; she'd all but acknowledged it.

But his approach had been wrong. A woman who attached Westhaven's interest was going to have backbone to spare. He should not have threatened; he should not have, to use her word, bullied. Well, that could be remedied just as soon as he got through breakfast with Her Grace.

❧

"You are quiet," the earl remarked as they tooled along toward Willow Bend.

"If I am quiet enough, I can fool myself into thinking I am still abed, dreaming on my nice cool sheets." Dreaming of him, most nights.

"Am I working you too hard?" the earl asked, glancing over.

"You are not. The heat can disturb one's rest."

"Are my brothers behaving? Dev is tidy, but Val can be a slob."

"Lord Val's only crime is that he commandeers Morgan for a couple of hours each afternoon and lets her join him in the music room while he works on his repertoire."

"You can trust Val to be a gentleman with her."

"And can I trust you to be a gentleman?"

"You can trust me," the earl replied, "to stop when you tell me to, to never intentionally hurt you, to listen before I judge, and to tell you the truth as far as I know it. Will that do?" It was all he was going to give her, but Anna reflected on how much more he offered than other men in her life were willing to.

"It will do." It would have to.

He turned the conversation to the practicalities of the situation at Willow Bend. There was a temporary crew of day laborers on hand from the local village, and they'd been busily moving furniture, hanging drapes, unpacking the crates of linens and flatware. The scene was very different from their previous visit to the place, with wagons, people, and noise everywhere.

A young boy emerged from the stables to take Pericles, and the earl escorted Anna to the front door.

"I want you to see it the way my sister might," he said, "not as the servants and tradesmen do. So…" He opened the front door, and led her through. "Welcome to Willow Bend, Mrs. Seaton."

She appreciated the public nature of the greeting and appreciated even more that there was a public on hand to witness it. Carpenters, glaziers, laborers, and apprentices were bustling to and fro; hammers banged, the occasional yell sounded above stairs, and boys were scurrying everywhere with tools and supplies.

"Yer lordship!" A stocky man of medium height made his way to their side.

"Mr. Albertson, our pleasure. Mrs. Seaton, my foreman here, Allen Albertson. Mr. Albertson, Mrs. Seaton is the lady in charge of putting the finishing touches on all your work."

"Ma'am." Albertson smiled and tugged his forelock. "You been finishing the daylights out of this place, if I do say so. Where shall we start, milord?"

"Ma'am?" The earl turned to her, his deference bringing an inconvenient blush to her cheeks.

"The kitchen," Anna said. "It's the first room you'll want functional and a very important room to people both upstairs and below."

"To the kitchen, Mr. Albertson." Westhaven waved a hand and offered Anna his arm.

Room by room, floor by floor, they toured the house. Shelves that had been bare now held neat rows of cups and glasses, or stacks of dishes, toweling, table linen, and candles. Anna asked that the spice rack be moved closer to the work table and suggested a bench be added along the inside kitchen wall. She had a bench put into the back hallway, as well, and a pegged board nailed to the wall for jackets, capes, and coats.

"You need a boot scrape, too," she pointed out, "since this is the entrance closest to the stables and gardens."

"You will make a note, Mr. Albertson?" the earl prompted.

"Aye." Albertson nodded, rolling his eyes good-naturedly to show what he thought of feminine notions.

They went on through the house as the morning got under way, finding a set of drapes needing to be switched, some tables that had ended up in the wrong parlors, and a pair of carpets that should have gone in opposite bedrooms. In the music room, she had the harp covered and the piano's lid closed.

"You may leave us now, Mr. Albertson," Westhaven said as they approached the last bedroom. "I take it the men will soon break for their nooning?"

"They will. It be getting too hot to do the heavy work, but we'll be back when it cools. Ma'am." He bowed and took his leave, bellowing for the water dipper before he'd gained the stairs.

"He may lack a certain subtlety," the earl said, "but he's honest, and he's getting the job done."

"And a lovely job it is," Anna said. "The place is looking wonderful."

"I wanted to save this for last," the earl said, opening the door to the final bedroom. It was the room where they'd passed the night, and Anna felt her heart stutter as the earl ushered her over the threshold.

"The Earl of Westhaven Memorial Chicken Pox Ward," Anna quipped, trying desperately for a light tone.

"Among other things. How do you like it?"

She'd intended this to be a masculine room, decorating it in subdued greens with blue accents and choosing more substantial incidental furniture with fewer frills and fripperies. The canopy on the bed had been replaced with dark green velvet, the bed spread dyed to match. The drapes were a lighter version of the same shade, and all of it complemented the dark wood of the bed frame and the colorful Persian carpets scattered on the hardwood floors.

"You are quiet," Westhaven said. "I hoped you would be pleased with the differences."

"I'm pleased." Anna smiled at him. "This is not a room for the lady of the house."

"It is not, of course," the earl agreed. "We saw those rooms earlier. I wanted this to be a room worthy of the memories I hold of it."

"Westhaven…" Anna sighed. "You were being so good."

"I was, and I'm glad you appreciate the effort, but I've left you in peace for days now, Anna, and you didn't come here without expecting me to make some advances."

"I came here," Anna said, sitting down in an upholstered rocker, "to comply with your request to see the house set to rights. I've done that, so we can return to Town now."

"And make Pericles travel in the worst heat of the day."

She glared at him and rose. "Do not put the welfare of your horse above my reputation, *yet again*. Dear Pericles can walk us back to Town for all I care, but our work here is finished."

"Our work, perhaps." The earl regarded her levelly. "Not our dealings. Come." He took her hand and led her to window seat. She didn't resist when he pulled her down beside him and kept her hand trapped in his.

"Talk to me, Anna," he said, wrapping his second hand around the back of hers. "You've become inscrutable, and I have enough sisters to know this is not a good thing."

"You would leave me no privacy." But when the earl stretched out his legs, his thigh casually resting against hers, she did not move away.

"You have more privacy than anyone else in my household," the earl chided. "You answer only to me, have the run of the property, and have the only private sitting room on four floors besides my own. And"—he kissed her knuckles—"you are stalling."

She laid her head on his shoulder, closed her eyes, and felt him nuzzling at her temple.

"Sweetheart," he murmured, "tell me what's troubling you. Dev says you've shadows in your eyes, and I have to agree."

"Him." Anna's head came off his shoulder.

"Has he offended? Pinched Nanny Fran one too many times? Offended Cook?"

"He has offended me," Anna said on a sigh. "Or he would, if I could stay mad at him, but he's just protective of you."

"The duke used that same excuse to nearly unravel my niece's entire family. He was protecting me when he bribed Elise, and he was protecting someone every time he crossed the lines his duchess would not approve of."

"I pointed out the parallel to St. Just when he warned me not to trifle with you."

"And here I've been pleasuring myself nigh cross-eyed because you won't trifle with me," the earl said. Anna smiled at his rejoinder despite herself. When she glanced over, he obligingly crossed his eyes.

"What else did St. Just have to say?" the earl prompted when the moment of levity had passed.

"If you value me, he will, as well. I don't know what that meant, Westhaven. He is a difficult man to read."

"He was welcoming you to the family, and all without a word to me."

"If that is his welcome, one shudders to consider his threats."

"He says you are a lady with secrets. I could not gainsay him."

"I was a lady once," Anna said, not meeting his eyes. "I am in service now."

"And you choose to remain in service rather than accept my suit. It is very lowering to think my kisses, my wealth, I myself, am less appealing to you than bouquets needing water or silver in need of polish."

"You mustn't think that!" Anna lifted her eyes to his, horrified at the honest self-doubt she'd heard in his voice. "You must believe me when I say the failing is mine; any woman would be pleased to have your attentions."

"Any woman?" The earl's smile was self-deprecating. "Guinevere Allen was none too flattered."

"She was enamored of her viscount, and he of her," Anna argued, coming to her feet. "I cannot allow you to think like this. You can have your pick of the last three years' batch of debutantes, and you know it."

"Oh, lucky me." The earl rose, as well. "I can mince about with some child on my arm, one who fears her wedding night and dreads the thought of my attentions. And all the while, she will be hamstrung by my father's machinations, to say nothing of the parents who staked her out in the ballroom like some sacrificial lamb. No man worth his salt wants a wife on those terms. What?" He returned to her side. "I cannot tell if you are horrified, stupefied, or maybe, just perhaps, impressed."

"You understand," Anna said, peering up at him. "You understand what it's like to be that sacrificial lamb."

"I do." He nodded. "I also understand, Anna Seaton, if I cannot have more of you, this instant, I will not answer for the consequences." He brushed his lips over hers. "The workmen are gone, and they won't be back until the heat of the day has cooled. We have this time, Anna, and I would like to use it."

"I will not lie with you." Anna shook her head. "It would be... dishonest."

"I will not lie with you then, either." He kissed her again, more lingeringly. "But I would pleasure us both. Don't for the love of God argue with me, Anna." His arms slipped around her waist. "You need pleasuring almost as badly as I do, and there's nothing to stop us."

"There's me to stop us," she said, but she was kissing him back between her protests.

"Stop me later, then," the earl suggested, shrugging out of his waistcoat while his lips cruised her neck. "Preferably much later." He kissed her more deeply, but to her eternal consternation she was less committed to her protests than he was to his seduction.

For days she'd told herself physical pleasures were fleeting and an undesirable entanglement in her circumstances. She'd told herself she couldn't miss something she'd shared with the earl on only a handful of occasions—a few kisses, some caresses, unimaginable pleasure and intimacy.

But she'd missed *him* like the land misses spring and the flowers miss the sun. She'd missed him like a soldier misses home on the night before battle and the night after. She'd missed him so...

"That's it," the earl coaxed when Anna's arms went around his waist. "No more words, Anna. Unless it's to tell me how to please you."

He kissed her long and deeply, stilling her protests, stealing her will and making it his. She *did* want to share these pleasures with him, with him and no one else, ever. She did *not* want to leave him, and yet leave him she would.

She rose up to press her body more closely to his, and he gathered her more tightly in his arms. All of her reserve and self-control went flying out the window, and in their place was *need*. Need for him, for closeness with him.

"Your clothes," Anna breathed, arching against him.

"Yours," he whispered back. Deftly, he began to undo the buttons down the back of her dress, even as she continued to drink in his kisses. He pushed the cap sleeves of her dress off her shoulders and bent his head to worship her neck with his lips.

"I love that," she said. "The way you touch me there."

"And here," he murmured, shifting lower, "you taste like sunshine, and sweetness, and female."

She was trying to get his shirt out of his waistband but couldn't kiss him and make her hands work at the same time. Gasping, she stepped back.

She eyed him in frustration. "This isn't working. Please take your clothes off. Now, Westhaven."

He smiled an *I thought you would never ask* smile and pulled his shirt over his head, letting her watch. He arched an eyebrow, his hand going to the fall of his trousers, and Anna nodded, holding his gaze the whole time. With deliberate movements, he got out of his boots, stockings, and breeches, standing before her naked, aroused, and unselfconscious.

"Oh, dear…" Anna's eyes went wide as she surveyed him. "You are *very* interested."

He stalked toward her, his erection curving up against his taut belly. "While you are very overdressed. Clothes off, Anna. All of them."

She nodded, knowing it would represent new territory for them. She had never been naked before him, not in the broad light of day.

"Lock the door," she said, swallowing. His smile became feral as he complied with her command. He'd *told* her to strip for him; she deliberately used the imperative on him, as well.

"Quit dithering, love." His tone was gentler, amused but only so patient. Slowly, Anna let the bodice of her dress fall forward then shoved it below her hips. She stepped out of the dress and stood in the middle of its billows, like Venus rising. While Westhaven watched from just a few feet away, she bent to undo her boots and stockings then let her chemise join the dress on the floor.

"Better," he said, holding out a hand to her. "Much, much better."

She took a step toward him then hesitated. He

closed the remaining distance and caught her against him, letting her press her face to his throat.

"Shy?" he asked, amusement back in his voice.

"We are… very undressed," Anna said as a blush rose up her chest and suffused her face. "This is new."

The earl bent his head to kiss her, then slid his hand down to cup her derriere. Before she could react with even another blush, he lifted her and tossed her onto the middle of the bed.

"Stay right there, shyness be damned," he said to her as she rose up to brace her elbows behind her. "You look adorably dazed, thoroughly kissed, and much in need of my company, as you, my dear, need to be relieved of a certain ignorance. Not your innocence, as no man can divest you of that, but your ignorance. I fault Mr. Seaton for not seeing to this."

"My ignorance?" she said, watching him climb onto the bed. "Westhaven…"

"That's talking, Anna," he chided. "You are only to talk if it's to tell me what pleases you."

"It pleases me not at all," she said sternly, "to be handled like a… oof!" He straddled her and gently pushed her onto her back. "What are you about?"

"Hush, sweetheart." He nuzzled her neck, crouching over her. "It's too hot for lecturing. We must conserve our strength."

The bed, Anna realized, took some of the urgency from him. When he could loom over her this way, passively rest his erection against her stomach and know she wasn't going to squirm away, he was easier to deal with. The pace of his kisses slowed, and the quiet of the house settled around them.

"Someday," he said, grazing his nose down her sternum, "you will want it fast and almost rough. You'll want me to shut up, and you won't care if we tear our clothes or leave the door unlocked or make a racket."

"Can you promise me such a day?" Anna arched her back, trying to get closer to him.

"I can promise you as many of those days as you want." He flicked his tongue over her nipple and rested his cheek on the swell of her breast. "I can promise you nights when we get no sleep but rise with more energy than had we slept soundly. I can promise you long afternoons spent in sensual abandon, when we both have places we must be, things we must do, but we let them all go hang." He turned his face and took her nipple into his mouth, and the pleasure he brought her was almost unbearable.

"Yes," Anna breathed, not sure if she'd spoken aloud or simply felt the word in every part of her body. The earl drew more strongly on her and used his fingers to tease the other nipple. He paused and raised himself enough to meet her gaze.

"Take your time, Anna. We have hours if you want them, and my appetite for you is without limit."

"I don't know what you mean," she said, letting her hands stroke through his hair. "Take my time?"

"Our time," he said, closing his eyes. He bent his head to her breasts again and spent long minutes using his mouth to arouse and please her. Her breasts were wonderfully sensitive, and she unabashedly reveled in the nudity that allowed him unfettered access to them.

"Westhaven..." Anna arched restlessly some minutes later. "It's too much."

"It's not enough," he said, easing a hand down over her stomach. He kept his movements deliberate, as if reminding her tacitly they had all the time in the world. Slowly, he caressed her midriff, occasionally letting his fingers tease at her nipples or drift down to tease at the curls above her sex.

"You are losing flesh," he said, leaning over to kiss her breast. "You will please stop this, as I require you to be sturdy."

"I always drop some weight in the summer," Anna said, realizing he was in a different mood entirely from when he tossed her onto the bed. "You are over your chicken pox." She ran a hand over his abdomen, marveling at how perfectly his skin had healed.

"I had good care"—the earl smiled up at her—"and I've been conserving my strength." His hand dipped lower, into her curls, and Anna felt her frustration spike. Well, turnabout was fair play, so she sent her own hand drifting down to explore his erection.

"How long can you stay like this?" She circled him with her fingers and sleeved his length.

"Many men are in a state of near perpetual arousal for much of their adolescence," he said, closing his eyes. "Myself included. It got better at university, when I could actually do something besides pleasure myself several times a day. Hold me tighter, love. Like that." He sighed, gave up, and rolled to his back.

Anna smiled, pleased with herself for getting the better of him. She pushed up and sat cross-legged at his hip then resumed her exploration.

"Are all men as well endowed as you?" she asked, her free hand slipping up to brush over his nipples.

"I am the most well-endowed man on earth," he said, eyes still closed. "You are to be envied among all women; you'll be bowlegged when we become lovers in fact."

"Be serious," she chided, tugging at him gently.

"Serious..." he breathed. "God, that feels good... It's hard to say really who is well endowed and who isn't, as one seldom sees another fellow aroused. We peek, certainly, but I've seen very few cocks other than my own ready to do the deed."

"You've seen other men in this state?"

"Most men wake up in this state," he informed her. "Slow down, sweetheart, or I won't be able to maintain it much longer." She slowed her hand, fractionally, but leaned over and swirled her tongue over his nipple.

"Anna." His hand came up to cradle the back of her head and to contradict the warning in his tone.

"Hmm?" She began to suckle him, and he groaned, his hips moving to complement the stroke of her hand.

"I will get even."

"Shall I stop?" She stilled her hand and brushed his hair back from his forehead. His eyes opened, and she was relieved to see humor in his expression.

"I'm going to use my mouth on you, Anna, and you will scream for me and forget your own name, so much will you like it."

She frowned at that. He'd been very explicit about this threat before. Thinking about it had kept her awake more than one night.

She met his gaze soberly. "What if I want to use my mouth on you?"

"Come here." He wrestled her down to his side, wrapped his arms around her, and tucked her close. "When you are with me like this, there is nothing you can ask of me, nothing you can want or do or think that will earn my censure. I would love to feel your mouth on my cock; I would love to take you in any position you can think of. If you wanted to tie me up, blindfold me, paint my cock blue, I would not deny you."

"Why?"

"I trust you," he said, and his words left her stunned.

"You shouldn't," she replied, her voice small. She felt the impact of her honesty go through him and wondered if she'd destroyed his regard for her in those two little words.

"Why shouldn't I?" His question came slowly, in the same tempo as his hand moving over her body.

"Because I will disappoint you, and then you will feel ashamed and angry, and so will I," she said against his neck. She shifted to straddle him and felt his arms go around her when she curled down onto his chest.

"You will disappoint me in bed?" he asked, his tone tentative.

"Probably there, too," she replied, pressing her nose to his sternum.

"You still think you're leaving me," the earl concluded, his hands stroking along her spine.

"I know I am," she said more firmly, teething his nipple for emphasis. There, she'd said it; she'd been as honest as she could be.

"Because you will not marry me, and so you must

take your virtuous self off when you've endured the requisite dose of my importuning."

Anna rose up and surveyed him balefully. "I did not say I enjoyed an entirely consistent position, nor one that makes sense in all circumstances, but I can't marry you."

"Cannot or will not?" the earl asked, catching her eye and holding it.

"Cannot. Absolutely cannot. Ever."

But she also could not stop toying with his nipples.

"If you could choose, Anna"—he reached down and tugged gently on one of her nipples in retaliation—"what would you choose? This duty that confidentially holds you, or the alternative?"

"You." She leaned up and kissed him. "Were I free to do so, I'd choose *you*."

Not marriage, not freedom, not the title, not security. She would choose him. Her kiss, when she brushed her lips over his again, was different, sweet, wistful, but also the kiss of a woman who felt deeply about the man with her.

She would choose *him*. She could tell him that—give him that.

Anna peered up at him. "Earlier, you said—"

"I say a lot of things." He smiled at her, and to Anna, the expression was tender, a little like the way he looked at Her Grace.

"You said…" She looked abruptly away, flummoxed to find she was still capable of shyness when she was naked, straddling his rigid cock. "You said you would love to feel my mouth on your… on you."

"I did." His hands went still. "I would."

"How does one do this?" she asked, a blush rising over her for him to see. But to her relief he didn't tease, he didn't remark on it, he just waited until she was facing him again.

"However you please," he said levelly, "and only if you please."

"Show me. I want to do this with you."

"Get comfortable," he said, shifting over to one side of the bed. "And stop whenever you aren't comfortable. Take your time, and do what pleases you."

"What if I hurt you?" Anna shifted to rest her cheek low on his abdomen and took him in her hand.

"You can't, short of biting me and drawing blood, but even that can have a certain erotic appeal."

His hand settled on her hair, and she took a moment to inhale the scents of clean sheets, clean man, and anticipation. She licked delicately at his erection, as if she were trying to decide what flavor he was. When his hand sifted through her hair to caress her nape, she relaxed and put her focus on the task. Tentatively, she licked him all over, little teasing swipes of her tongue, like a mama cat patiently grooming a kitten. Inside her own body, she lit fires with that tongue, his permission to indulge her curiosity as incendiary as the naked length of him in the bed.

And then she slipped her mouth over him, and brush fires instantly converged into a wildfire. She experimented, taking him deep into her mouth then more shallowly. Without a word, his hips began to move, slowly, as if he didn't want to startle her. She was content to spend long minutes learning how to coordinate her movements with his, to let the fires rage and warm places in her gone cold longer than she'd realized. When her fingers wrapped around his wet length, he expelled a soft, pleased groan, as if passion was as much a relief to him as it was to her.

"Not much more, Anna," he cautioned hoarsely. "I'll spend…"

Well, that was the point, wasn't it? When he was thrusting smoothly through her hand into her mouth, and his breathing was coming in short, deep breaths, she closed her lips around him and drew firmly.

"Oh, God… Anna… No…" His thrusts grew stronger, despite his words. His hand cradled the back of her head, holding her close; his cock actually pulsed in her mouth, and Anna wasn't about to show him mercy.

"No…" he whispered again, even while his body shouted to the contrary for long, ecstatic moments. "Jesus…" He hissed, eyes closed, head thrown back, hips moving in convulsive shudders of pleasure. "Jesus, God… Anna…"

He went quiet but not quite still, his hand moving slowly over her scalp.

"And you say," he whispered, "I should not trust you." She let him slip from her mouth, and felt tears welling. He should not trust her, but he just had, profoundly. Even in her inexperience, she could divine that much.

"Come here." He leaned up and tugged her to lie along his side. "I can't believe you did that. I can't believe I did that. A man doesn't spend in a woman's mouth. It isn't gentlemanly."

"But it is gentlemanly to spend on her stomach?"

Anna asked in puzzlement. "Or to spend in her body, getting a bastard on her?"

"What was it the great philosopher once said?" He kissed her nose. "The position is not entirely consistent, nor does it make sense under all circumstances?"

Anna continued to frown. "Do you mean you yourself do not spend in a woman's mouth, or that it's like pissing in a well, a civil wrong?"

"Good heavens, you did have a brother, didn't you? It isn't quite like that. It's like eating the dessert set aside for company, or stealing the crown jewels and seeing another blamed. It's just… It's too good," he said. "Too selfish."

"Of me?" Anna asked, still confused. "I'm sorry, but I didn't want to stop, and you said I should stop only when I pleased."

"Love," he sighed, "you could not have pleased me more profoundly if you'd told me Val had sired legitimate twin boys. I have never experienced such generosity, never, and as soon as I recover my wits, I am going to get very, very even indeed."

That was enough to settle her down and put a period to her questions. She closed her eyes and drowsed on his shoulder while he drifted into sleep, his hand still tangled possessively in her hair.

❧

When Anna awoke, she felt replete with the same sense of sweetness she'd had after her encounter with Westhaven in the library. He was wrapped around her, her back spooned to his chest, a sweet breeze wafting in from the open window.

His hand closed gently around her breast, though his breathing did not change. Anna closed her eyes and let the pleasure of that single, soft caress drift through her body. He did it again, and she sighed audibly. A few moments later, his thumb brushed over her nipple, then again.

Take your time, he'd said.

As the earl's hands began to wander—up and down her back, over her buttocks, back to her breasts—she thought over their last encounter in this very bed. She'd lain still, feigning sleep then, too.

What a waste of a night, she thought on a sigh.

"You are awake," the earl murmured, his lips closing over her earlobe.

"I am," Anna said as Westhaven's mouth sent slow ripples of awareness through her body. "But without motivation to get up and seize the remainder of the day."

"There will be no getting up," he remonstrated, his hand sliding between her legs. "And the only thing you'll be seizing is me or the pleasure I owe you."

Anna tried to peer over her shoulder at him.

"You owe me nothing."

"Ah, but I do," he said, nudging her onto her stomach. "And a gentleman always pays his debts."

Anna didn't typically sleep on her stomach and found the position mildly disconcerting. She couldn't see him, could feel only his hand stroking down her back, over her buttocks, back up again.

"Relax, Anna." He kissed her nape. "This will take a while. Let your legs fall open, and just enjoy."

She closed her eyes and felt the caress of his hand dancing over her like the breeze, but better. He knew where to touch, how much pressure to use, when to tease, and when to gratify. His fingers explored her sex from behind then drifted away to trace the long muscles on either side of her spine. He caressed her buttocks with slow, almost pensive attention to the tension in the muscles there then pressed another series of kisses to her nape and shoulders.

She shouldn't let him, she thought... Whole afternoons, but not for them. This was their afternoon, their only afternoon, and then she'd be gone, betraying all the trust he showed her, taking his respect for her and tossing it back in his face.

"On to your back, sweetheart," Westhaven whispered in her ear. When she lazily complied, he started all over again, the same stroking and studying and teasing, but this time his attention wandered from her breasts to her face, to her sex, to her neck and shoulders, and back her breasts.

"Spread your legs for me," he coaxed, but when Anna did, he remained content to tease at her breasts with his fingers. Only gradually did he let his hand drift down in slow, smooth sweeps, then to rest over her sex. He turned his body, and though she didn't open her eyes, Anna felt him crouching over her, his mouth settling contentedly over a nipple.

He was tormenting her, she thought sluggishly, creating such a blend of languor and arousal she couldn't fight either. Why would she want to? His mouth drew on her, and she sifted her fingers through his hair, emotion tangling with the erotic lassitude he created. Precious, she thought. These moments, this man, these sensations... all precious.

He paused and moved lower, resting his face against her abdomen before levering up and reaching for a spare pillow.

"Hips up," he directed, tucking the pillow under her. "You'll see why soon enough." And then he was nuzzling at her belly, nipping at the underside of her breast, and stroking the insides of her thighs.

"Your job," he said, moving yet lower still, "is simply to enjoy. You can tell me to stop, but I might have trouble hearing you, as I intend to be enjoying myself, as well." His words floated into Anna's awareness and floated right back out again. She was nearly asleep, so relaxed had she become.

But not quite asleep, as the earl's caresses had also created a low, buzzing arousal throughout her body. Her breasts wanted his mouth and his fingers, her buttocks wanted that same hand, and her sex wanted all of him. If he'd asked, she'd have consented to join with him, so finely drawn was she between arousal, regret, and lassitude.

He moved to kiss her spread thighs, and Anna knew a fleeting self-consciousness. He was going to *look at her*, to see in the broad light of day the parts of her she hadn't seen herself.

"You are beautiful," he said, as if reading her mind, "and luscious."

The next sensation, as his mouth settled over her, was indescribable. It took the sweet, tender, languorous arousal of all his previous caresses and let it congeal where he drew on her. He was gentle at first, just hinting at what pleasures he could bring her. He'd suckle at her for a moment then use his tongue to lap at her folds, to paint her sex with pleasure.

But then he was back, applying just a little more pressure, and a soft groan escaped Anna's throat.

"Move if you want to," he urged, wrapping an arm around her thigh to anchor her. "Move against me, and you'll feel better."

Tentatively, she rocked her hips, a long, slow roll of her body that eased her ache and made it worse. She moved again, setting up a rhythm, working with him to craft her pleasure. It went on like that, minute after minute of bliss edged with longing, then longing coalescing into need.

"Westhaven?" If a man didn't come in a woman's mouth, was a woman permitted to find her pleasure with a man's mouth? She wanted to ask him, but her mind was too far gone with pleasure.

"Touch your breasts, sweetheart," he murmured. "You'll feel better. Like this." He reached up one long arm and gently pinched at her nipple. He fished for her hand, closed it around her own nipple, and used his fingers to close her grasp on herself.

It wasn't the same as his caresses, but he kept his hand resting over hers, and so there was part of him in the sensations she evoked. When her own hand went still, the better for her to focus on his busy mouth, he closed his fingers again in gentle reminder.

"Westhaven," Anna rasped, *stop*, she wanted to say, but the word would not come to her lips. The feelings he aroused, the physical sensations... they were building, an inexorable welling of pleasure was advancing toward her, but—God help her—not fast enough.

"This will help," he said, and Anna felt him ease a finger shallowly into her body. He was careful, tentative, unwilling to advance beyond a certain point, but it helped focus her frustration. She clamped her muscles around that finger and felt him pause.

"You lovely, naughty girl," he whispered, adding a second finger—but not deep enough. He shifted the angle of his shoulders and took her in his mouth again.

"Please, Westhaven, please…"

She rocked up against his mouth, wanting, wanting, wanting until she would have begged had speech not been beyond her. She begged with her body, with her hands in his hair, with the soft whimpers that escaped her.

Her body began to hum with impending pleasure, to rise and vibrate and sing with it, until it burst through her, finally—fast enough, hard enough, deep enough, and with his mouth and hands and will, he made it last long enough, pushing her onward ruthlessly when she would have accepted just a taste of pleasure, until she was moaning and undulating helplessly against his mouth.

"Westhaven." She ruffled his hair and said it again, her voice soft with the surfeit of pleasure he'd brought her.

"I'm here," he murmured, his face against her belly.

"Cover me," she said, and he reached for the sheets.

"No." She tugged at his scalp. "You, cover me. Please."

It was an odd request, but he rose up on all fours, crouched over her, and lowered his chest to hers.

"All of you," she said, eyes closed, hands drifting over his shoulders and back.

So he settled between her legs, giving her his weight, his erection resting snugly on her belly. When she sighed in contentment, he tucked her crown under his chin and matched his breathing to hers.

"Thank you," she whispered. "For all of it, but this, too. Thank you."

# Twelve

"I CAN HEAR YOU THINKING," WESTHAVEN RUMBLED above her moments later.

"What you did," Anna said, too closely wrapped for him to see her face. "Is that…?"

"Is it what?" he smiled, in charity with all of creation. "Legal? Yes, unlike some other intimate pleasures. Is it biblical, absolutely not. Is it what?"

"Is it something you did with your mistress?"

"Ye gods, Anna." He levered up on his arms and frowned down at her. "What is this fascination you have with a woman you've never met?"

"Not with her." Anna met his gaze, her face crimson. "With you. Is that something men like to do—or you like to do?" A slightly different and more acceptable question, he decided, snuggling back down.

"As a young man," he said, brushing her hair off her forehead, "it's something you want to experience, as it's wicked and forbidden and said to delight those women willing to allow it. But no, I've not offered this to another. There is a whole invisible community of women whose job it is to educate university boys and I put them through their paces and they put me through mine, but not in this regard."

"So you enjoyed it?"

"What I enjoyed," he said, smiling at her, "was bringing you pleasure and learning your responses and feeling close to you when you let yourself go. Some women, Anna, go their whole lives without experiencing passion the way you do. You are lovely, and so, yes, I most assuredly enjoyed doing that with you."

She was blessedly silent while Westhaven anticipated her next outrageous, blushing question.

"I enjoy it, too," she said, "having you find your pleasure in my mouth. It is… intimate."

"There is trust involved," he replied, thinking about it for the first time in years. "On both sides." She nodded under him and closed her eyes.

You do trust me, he wanted to point out. Maybe not completely, but you do. He wanted her to admit it, to him, if not to herself, but wasn't willing to breach that intimacy she'd alluded to. Rather than start a lecture, Westhaven began kissing her, his mood still slow and relaxed.

"Would you like me to…?" she began. He stopped the question by covering her mouth with his then drew back.

"I'll do the work, such as it is," he said. "You relax. We don't want to make you sore."

He rocked against her, their bodies snugged tightly together. She was learning the way his body moved when it sought pleasure and subtly undulated with him. When she tilted her hips just a little, sealing them even more closely together, he buried his face against her neck.

In a very few moments, he felt his pleasure welling up, a thick, hot current radiating up his spine and out through his extremities. He didn't fight it, didn't hold back, but pulsed against her hard for a half-dozen thrusts, and then went still on a long, fraught sigh against her neck.

"God, Anna." He lifted himself off of her. "You utterly undo me." He walked naked across the room to his jacket, extracted a handkerchief, and used the water in the pitcher on the nightstand to wet it. He swabbed at himself thoroughly, rinsed the handkerchief in the basin, and wrung it out. He then sat at her hip, washed his seed off her body, and raised his gaze to hers.

"I am fond of you," he said, "and maybe more than that. If you are in trouble, Anna, I wish you'd let me help you."

"You can't help," she said, her expression unreadable.

He said nothing but climbed into bed beside her and lay back, his hands laced under his head. He should not have made that admission—fond of her, for God's sake—what woman wants to hear that? He was fond of Elise, fond of Rose's pony, George. It was as good as saying he did not love her, which he feared might not be true.

That is to say... He shied off that fence and turned his mind to Anna's virtual admission she was in trouble. That was progress, he decided. From bearing confidences, to being in trouble. Dev had been right, and it meant Westhaven had to take a little more seriously Anna's threats to leave him. What kind of trouble would a young, pretty, gently reared housekeeper have?

She had a brother, he recalled. It was a brother's job to protect a sister, so where was that worthy soul now that Anna needed him? But even a brother had no rights where a husband was concerned.

"Please assure me," he said, glancing over at her, "you have no living husband."

"I have no living husband," Anna recited. But this time, the earl was paying attention, and he raised a skeptical eyebrow.

"That is the truth," Anna remonstrated. "We are merely fornicating, not committing adultery."

He cracked a dry smile. "My dear, we are not even fornicating."

"Not yet." She offered him the same smile back.

"Are you a convicted felon?" he asked, puzzling over it.

"I am not charged with anything that I know of," Anna said, "but you can cease the interrogation, Westhaven. I am fond of you, too."

She sat up, hugging her knees, and Westhaven had the sense she was fighting back tears. Surely there was no more damning testament to a man's seductions than that they left a woman in tears? He reached out and stroked his hand over her elegant spine.

"You are fond of me, but you are leaving me anyway." She nodded once, her back to him, and he felt her heart breaking. With gentle force, he dragged her back into his arms and held her while she cried.

❧

When the hamper had been repacked, Anna stood

beside the earl in the stables, waiting for Pericles to be
harnessed to the gig.

"Penny for them," the earl said softly. He was
standing just a hair too close to her, but there was
nobody save the young stable hand to see, and much
to Westhaven's pleasure, Anna let herself drift back
against him.

"It is lovely here," Anna said. "You are to be
commended for taking such care with a sister's welfare."

He heard the wistful, almost despairing note in
her voice, and knew with absolute conviction Anna
Seaton's brother had somehow disappointed her or
played her false. His mind turned back to those ideas,
the ones he'd been formulating earlier about how to
uncover Anna's troubles and assist her with them.

"I love my sisters. As any brother should love a sister."

"They don't all—brothers, that is," Anna said, stepping away from him. "Some of them love their gold
more or their drink or their flashy Town habits. Being
a sister is sometimes not much more of a bargain than
being a wife."

"You simply have to choose the right brother"—
Westhaven smiled at her gently—"or the right
husband. I have enjoyed our time here, Anna. I hope
you did, as well."

"Even when I cried," she said, a world of resignation
in her tone, "I was glad to be here with you, Westhaven.
Believe that, if you believe nothing else of me."

He handed her into the gig, puzzling over that
comment. They were halfway back to Town, Anna
tucked shamelessly close to him even in the heat,
before his brain woke from its stupor.

What she had meant was: Even when I cried *because I must leave you*, I was glad to be here with you… Believe that if you believe nothing else of me *when I find the courage to finally go*.

The hot, lovely day suddenly became ominous, and where Anna wasn't touching him, he was chilled.

❧

Morgan stood beside Val when they'd left Viscount Fairly's townhouse and *listened*. Fairly had worked a miracle, gently and thoroughly cleaning her ears, explaining that she had scar tissue complicating the natural process and her hearing would always be impaired. She thought he was daft, as she heard everything.

"It's loud," she said wonderingly. "But sweet, too. Like your music. The sounds all go together to say something."

"Let's walk home through the park," Val suggested, offering his arm. "You can hear birds singing, hear the water in the Serpentine, hear the children playing… I never realized how happy the park sounds."

"There's so much…" Morgan took a deep breath and fell in step beside him. "I would never go anywhere I didn't know well, because I could not stop to ask directions. I was confined to those places Anna would take me or that someone else would escort me to. I could not get lost; I could not need assistance."

"That has changed. You may get lost several times a day, just to hear people give you directions. Are your ears hurting?"

"They are…" Morgan frowned. "Not hurting from the viscount's treatment but throbbing, it feels like, with sounds. I'm pleased beyond telling to hear your voice, Lord Valentine."

"Val," he said easily. "I'd like to hear you say my name."

"Valentine Windham." Morgan smiled at him. "Musician and friend to hard-of-hearing chambermaids."

"Did you ask Fairly if the cure is temporary?"

"It is. If I don't look after my ears, they can get into the same state, particularly if I let quacks poke at me and bring me more infections and bleeding and scarring. He gave me an ear syringe and his card, should I have questions. However did you meet such a man?"

"Mutual friends," Val said. "The circumstances were not particularly sanguine."

"This involves your papa's meddling?"

"Nanny Fran's been talking again." Val rolled his eyes.

"She talks all the time. I got much faster at figuring out what is spoken by watching the speaker's lips around her, and when people don't think you can hear, they often say things you ought not to overhear."

"What sorts of things?" Val asked, noticing Morgan's voice was already increasing in range of pitch, taking on the intonations and inflections of a woman who could hear.

"Footmen are a bawdy lot," Morgan said. "Nanny Fran and Cook are just as bad."

"Has anyone been talking out of turn to His Grace?"

"Not that I know of." Morgan frowned. "Mostly, the staff are very loyal to the earl, as he provided employment when His Grace was letting junior staff go, to hear them tell it. And I can." Morgan sighed and hung a little on his arm. "I can hear them tell it. I will be on my knees for a long time tonight and every night. I wonder if I will sing again someday?"

"You like to sing?"

"Love to." Morgan beamed at him. "I used to sing with my mother, and sometimes Anna would join us, but she was an adolescent just as my voice was becoming reliable, and singing was not her greatest talent."

"So you are related to her?" Val asked, but Morgan's hand dropped from his arm. "Morgan," he chided, "Anna brought you into the household with her, she has admitted to Westhaven she knew you when you could hear, and Dev has seen the two of you tête-à-tête over something serious."

Too late, Morgan realized the trap speaking had sprung on her. Deaf and mute, she could not be questioned; she could not be held accountable for any particular knowledge or intelligence.

Val peered down at her as they approached the park. "Dev says Anna has secrets, and I fear he is right. They are your secrets, too, aren't they?"

"It's complicated and not entirely my business to tell," she said, speaking slowly. "This is part of the reason you must not tell anyone I can hear."

"I do not like lying, Morgan. Particularly not to my brother, regarding people in his employ."

"The earl hired me knowing I could not hear or speak," Morgan pointed out. "He is not cheated when you keep this confidence for me. And if it comforts you to know it, I am not even going to tell Anna I can hear."

"You think she would begrudge you your *hearing*?"

"No." Morgan shook her head then grinned. "I can hear that, when I shake my head." She did it again then her smile faded. "Back to Anna and me... For the past two years, Anna is all that connected me with a world I had long since stopped hearing. I owe her more than you know, and yet, having me to look after has also meant she's had to look after herself. Were I not in such great need, Anna might have given up. She might have taken some options for herself that were not at all desirable. In any case, I do not want to disclose I can hear, not until I know it's going to last."

"That much I can understand," Val said. "How long do you think it will take to convince yourself you are back among the hearing?"

"Oh, *listen!*" Morgan stopped, grinning from ear to ear. "It's geese, and they are *honking*. What a wonderful, silly, undignified sound. And there are children, and they are *screaming* with glee. Oh, Valentine..."

The way she'd said his name, with wonder, and joy and gratitude, it lit the places inside him that had been going dark since his closest brother had died. The music rumbling through him when he watched her hearing the sound of childish laughter was not polite, graceful, or ornamental. It was great, bounding swoops and leaps of joy, and unstoppable, unending gratitude.

Brothers slowly wasted of terrible diseases; they died in asinine duels in provincial taverns; and sometimes, a gifted pianist's hand hurt unbearably, but Morgan could also *hear* when the children laughed.

He sat beside her for a long time in the sunshine and fresh air, just listening to the park and the city and to life.

❦

"Gentlemen." Westhaven addressed his brothers as they ambled back from a morning ride. "I need your help."

Val and Dev exchanged a look of quiet surprise.

"You have it," Dev said.

"Anything you need," Val added. "Anything. Anywhere, anytime."

Westhaven busied himself fiddling with the reins of the rangy chestnut gelding Dev had put him on. He might have expected ribbing from his brothers or teasing or idle curiosity, but their unconditional response caught him off guard.

Dev smiled at him, a smile more tender than humorous. "We love you, and we know you are all that stands between us and His Grace. Say on."

"Good to know one's sentiments are reciprocated," Westhaven said, eyeing the sky casually.

"I suspect whatever you need help with," Val chimed in, "we are discussing it here because you do not want to be overheard at home?"

"Perceptive of you," Westhaven said. "The matter at hand is Mrs. Seaton. She is not, as Dev has suggested, exactly what she appears to be. She tells me there is no spouse trying to hunt her down, nor is she wanted on criminal charges, but she is carrying some burden and will not enlighten me as to its nature. She claims the matter is confidential, and it necessitates her departure from my employ in the near future."

Dev quirked an eyebrow. "We are to find out for you what plagues her and make it go away."

"Not so fast." Westhaven smiled at his darkest brother, the one most likely to solve a problem with his fists or his knife. "Before we go eavesdropping in doorways, I thought we might first combine our knowledge of the situation."

When the brothers returned to the townhouse, they took their lemonade—cold tea for Val—into the library, and closed and locked the door. After about an hour's discussion, they boiled down their objective knowledge to a few facts, most of those gleaned from the agency that had recommended her:

Anna Seaton had come down from the North about two years ago and was on her third post has housekeeper. She'd worked first for an old Hebrew, then briefly for a wealthy merchant before joining the earl's household almost six months ago. At each location, Morgan became part of the household staff, as well. Anna admitted to having a brother and a sister, but being orphaned, had been raised by her grandfather, the florist.

"He had to be one hell of a successful florist," Dev observed. "Didn't you say Anna could speak several languages? Tutors, particularly for females, cost money."

"She plays the piano, too," Westhaven recalled. "That means more money, both to own the instrument and to afford the instruction."

"I wonder," Val said slowly, "if Morgan is not this sister Anna has mentioned to you."

"I suppose she could be." Westhaven frowned. "They do not look particularly alike, but then neither do many sisters."

"They have the same laugh," Val said, surprising his brothers. "What? Morgan can laugh—she isn't simple."

"We know, but it's an odd thing to notice," Westhaven said, noting his youngest brother was more than a little defensive of the chambermaid. "You're reminding me, though, Anna said her parents were killed when their buggy overturned and slid down an embankment. They were on an errand to look at a pony for her younger sister. Then you tell me Morgan lost her hearing after a buggy accident left her pinned in cold water. I think you've put the puzzle pieces together correctly, Val."

Dev drew a finger around the rim of his glass. "We need to send someone north who can find us a very wealthy elderly florist, perhaps two years deceased, perhaps still extant, with three grandchildren, whose son died in a buggy accident that cost one grandchild her hearing. How many of those can there be?"

"Don't rule out a title," Val said quietly.

"A title?" Westhaven winced, hating to think he might have been cavorting with some duke's daughter. That hit a little too close to home.

"Anna once teased me about my… public mannerism," Val said.

"You mean"—Dev grinned—"your mincing and lisping?"

"And so on." Val nodded and waved a hand. "She said something like: You are no more a mincing fop than I am an earl's granddaughter. I remembered it, because Her Grace is an earl's granddaughter."

"We can keep it in mind," Westhaven said, "intuition being at least half of what we have to go on. Anything else?"

"Yes." Dev rose from the sofa and stretched. "Suppose we find out who our housekeeper really is, find she's suspected of some wrongdoing, put the accusations to rest, and so forth. Are we going to all this effort just to keep you in marzipan for the foreseeable future? There are easier ways to do that."

Westhaven pushed away from his desk. "We are doing this because the duke will soon be asking the same questions, and his methods will not be discreet nor careful nor at all delicate."

"And ours will be?" Val asked, coming to his feet, as well.

"Utterly. We must be, or there's no point to the effort. If anybody finds out we are poking around in Anna Seaton's past, then they could easily insinuate themselves into her present, and that I cannot allow."

"Very well." Dev scratched his ribs and nodded. "We find the elderly florist, et cetera, and do it without making a sound."

"Not a peep," Val agreed just as his stomach rumbled thunderously. "Not a peep once I get some breakfast."

"We can all use breakfast." Westhaven smiled. "We'll talk more about this later, but only when our privacy is assured." He unlocked the door and departed for the breakfast parlor, leaving his two brothers to exchange a look of consternation.

"So." Val looked to his elder sibling hopefully. "We're going about this stealthy investigation of a housekeeper's personal business, why?"

"Noticed he dodged that one, didn't you?" Dev rubbed his chin. "Smart lad. I would hazard a guess, though, we are abetting our brother's ride to the rescue of the fair damsel because for once, he's delegating the tedious work to someone else and keeping the fun part for himself."

"He picked an odd time to turn up human."

"I didn't think the housekeeper was to your taste." Dev grinned and slung an arm around Val's shoulders. "Thought you were more enamored of the quiet housemaid who—though is she *deaf*—sits in the music room by the hour—*watching* you play?"

"Let's get some breakfast," Val groused, digging an elbow into his brother's ribs to shove him away. Smart lad, indeed. Bad enough to have to dodge the duke's spies among the help, but he'd have to warn Morgan that Dev wasn't going to miss a trick either.

❧

Since their trip out to Willow Bend more than a week ago, Anna had felt the earl watching her the way one man might size up another in preparation for a duel or a high-stakes card game. He studied her but made no more mention of trips to the country or marriage. He kept his hands to himself, but his eyes were on her if they were in the same room.

She tried to tell herself it was better this way, with Westhaven keeping his distance and the household rolling along in its pleasant routine. The three brothers usually went out for an early ride then breakfasted together. Thereafter, the earl would closet himself with Tolliver for most of the morning, while Val repaired to his piano and Dev spent time in the stables or at the auctions. Occasionally, all three would be home for lunch, but more often, it was dinner before they joined each other again.

And occasionally, Anna had noticed, they would join in the library for a brandy before dinner, some three-handed cribbage after dinner, or just to talk. And when they did, the door was both closed and locked.

Since the earl hadn't even thought to lock the door when he was naked with her, Anna wondered what could be holding their interest that demanded such privacy. Something they did not want the duke to learn of, no doubt.

Still, it hurt, a little, not be in Westhaven's confidence—not to be in his arms.

But life went on. The agency from Manchester had written they did not place candidates from London unless or until said candidates were removing to the local environs. Bath had at least two openings, but they were for the households of older single gentlemen who enjoyed "lively" social calendars. Anna knew one by reputation to be a lecherous roué and assumed the other was just as objectionable. She waited in the daily hope of more encouraging news from the remaining possibilities and was thus pleased when John Footman brought her a letter.

One glance at the envelope, however, told her the news was not good. Another epistle from rural Yorkshire could not bode well.

*I am most concerned for you. A man has been about asking pointed questions, and I am sure he was followed when he returned south. Use greatest caution.*

A man asking questions… Dear God, she had caused this. With her reticence and mention of confidences and unwillingness to yield details to his bloody lordship, the Earl of Westhaven. He was resorting to his father's tactics and causing more trouble—more *peril*—than he could possibly imagine. The fear Anna lived with day and night boiled over into rage and indignation at his high-handedness. She barreled out of her sitting room, the letter still in her hand, and almost ran into Devlin St. Just.

"Where is he?" she hissed.

"Westhaven?" St. Just took a step back but kept his hands on her upper arms. "Is there something I can help you with?" His gaze traveled over her warily, no doubt taking in the absence of a cap and the utter determination in her eyes.

"You?" Anna loaded the word with incredulity and scorn. "With your strutting and sneering and threats? You've helped more than enough. *Where is he?*"

"The library." He dropped his hands, and stepped back as Anna stormed away.

"She upset with you?" Val asked as he sauntered out of the kitchen, cookies in hand.

"I did not get off on the proper foot with her, which is my fault," Dev said, "but it's Westhaven who had better start praying."

"Front-row seats, eh?" Val handed him a cookie, and they stole up the stairs in Anna's wake.

❧

"A moment of your time, my lord." Anna kept her voice steady, but her eyes were a different matter. One glance, and the earl knew a storm was brewing.

He rose from his desk. "Tolliver, if you would excuse us?" Taking in Anna's appearance, Tolliver departed with only a brief sympathetic glance at the earl.

"Won't you have a seat?" the earl offered, his tones cordial as he went to close and lock the door.

"I most assuredly will not have a seat," Anna spat back, "and you can unlock that door, Gayle Tristan Montmorency Windham."

An odd thrill went through him at the sound of his name on her lips, one that made it difficult to appropriately marshal his negotiating face. He had the presence of mind to keep the door locked, however, and instead turned to assess her.

She was toweringly, beautifully, stunningly angry. Enraged, and with him.

"What have I done to offend?"

"You..." Anna advanced on him, a piece of paper fisted in her hand. "You are having me investigated. And thanks to you, *my lord*, what might have been a well-planned move to a comparable position will now be a headlong and poorly thought out flight. I cannot believe you would do this to me, behind my back, without saying a word to me."

"What does your letter say?" the earl asked, puzzled. Yes, he wanted to have her investigated but had yet to identify a sufficiently discreet means of doing so.

"It says there is a man asking questions about me back home." Anna waved the letter, keeping her voice low. "And he was followed south when he returned to Town."

"He was not employed by me," the earl said simply, still frowning in thought. "Though I am fairly certain I know who did retain him."

"You did not do this?" Anna asked, spine stiff.

"I am in the process of trying to identify means appropriate to assist you. I am aware, however, your circumstances involve confidences and have thus been unwilling to proceed until utmost discretion can be assured."

He watched the emotions storm through her eyes: Rage that he would admit to wanting to investigate her, shock that he would be honest, and finally, relief, that his better sense had prevailed.

"His Grace," Anna said, the fight going out of her suddenly. "Your thrice damned, interfering ass of a father, abetted by the toad."

"I will dismiss Stenson before sunset," Westhaven assured her. "I will confront my father, as well. Just one request, Anna."

She met his gaze squarely, still upset but apparently willing to shift the focus of her rage.

"Be here when I return," he said, holding her gaze. She huffed out a breath, nodded once, and dropped her eyes.

"Be here." He walked up to her and put his arms around her. She went willingly, to his relief, and held on to him tightly. "Do not pack, do not warn Morgan, do not pawn the silver, do not panic. Be here and try, just try, to find some ability to trust me."

When he was sure she'd calmed down, Westhaven whipped open the library door to find both his brothers lounging against the wall, munching cookies.

"You lot, look after Anna and Morgan. Don't hold the meals for me." He stalked off, bellowing for Pericles, leaving Anna standing shakily between Dev and Val.

"You are no fun," Dev said, passing Anna a cookie. "We couldn't hear a thing, and we were sure you were going to tear a strip off the earl. Nobody tears a strip off Westhaven, not Her Grace, not His Grace, not even Pericles."

"Rose could," Val speculated, handing his drink to Anna. "Come along." He put an arm around Anna's shoulders. "We'll teach you how to cheat at cribbage, and you can tell us what we missed."

"I already know how to cheat at cribbage," Anna said dumbly, staring at the drink and cookie in her hands.

"Teach that in housekeeper school now, do they?" Dev closed the library door behind them. "Well, then we'll teach you some naughty rugby songs instead. She's going to cry, Val. Best get your hankie at the ready."

"I am not going to cry," Anna said, shoulders stiff. But then she took a funny gulpy breath and two monogrammed handkerchiefs were thrust in her direction. She turned her face into Val's muscular shoulder and bawled while Dev rescued the drink and cookies.

❧

"Mother." Westhaven bowed over Her Grace's hand. "I should have listened to you more closely."

"A mother delights in hearing those sentiments from her children, regardless of the provocation," Her Grace responded, "though I am at a loss to divine your reference."

"You tried to tell me at breakfast the other week." Westhaven ran a hand through his hair. "His Grace is off on another wild start, isn't he?"

"Frequently," the duchess said. "But I wasn't warning you of anything in particular, just the need to exercise discretion with your staff and your personal activities."

"My housekeeper, you mean." Westhaven arched an eyebrow at her. "Somehow, the old bastard got wind of Anna Seaton and set his dogs on her."

"Westhaven." The duchess's regard turned chilly. "You will not refer to your father in such terms."

"Right." Westhaven shuttered his expression. "That would insult my half brother, who is an honorable man."

"Westhaven!" The duchess's expression grew alarmed rather than insulted.

"Forgive me, Mother." He bowed. "My argument is with my father."

"Well," the duke announced himself and paused for dramatic effect in the doorway of the private parlor. "No need to look further. You can have at me now."

"You are having Anna Seaton investigated," the earl said, "and it could well cost her her safety."

"Then marry her," the duke shot back. "A husband can protect a wife, particularly if he's wealthy, titled, smart, and well connected. Your mother has assured me she does not object to the match."

"You don't deny this? Do you have any idea the damage you do with your dirty tricks, sly maneuvers, and stupid manipulations? That woman is terrified, nigh paralyzed with fear for herself and her younger relation, and you go stomping about in her life as if you are God Almighty come to earth for the purpose of directing everybody else's personal life."

The duke paced into the room, color rising in his face.

"That is mighty brave talk for a man who can't see fit to take a damned wife after almost ten years of looking. What in God's name is wrong with you, Westhaven? I know you cater to women, and I know you are carrying on with this Seaton woman. She's comely, convenient, and of child-bearing age. I should have thought to have her investigated, I tell you, so I might find some way to coerce her to the altar."

"You already tried coercion," Westhaven shot back, "and it's only because Gwen Allen is a decent human being her relations haven't ruined us completely in retaliation for your failed schemes. I am ashamed to be your son and worse than ashamed to be your heir. You embarrass me, and I wish to hell I could disinherit you, because if I don't find you a damned broodmare, I've every expectation you will disinherit me."

"Gayle!" His mother was on her feet, her expression horror-stricken. "Please, for the love of God, apologize. His Grace did not have Mrs. Seaton investigated."

"Esther…" His Grace tried to get words out, but his wife had eyes only for her enraged son.

"He most certainly did," Westhaven bit out. "Up to his old tricks, just as he was with Gwen and with Elise and with God knows how many hapless debutantes and scheming widows. I am sick to death of it, Mother, and this is the last straw."

"Esther," His Grace tried again.

"Hush, Percy," the duchess said miserably, still staring at her son. "His Grace did not have your Mrs. Seaton investigated." She paused and dropped Westhaven's gaze. "I did."

"Esther," the duke gasped as he dropped like a stone onto a sofa. "For the love of God, help me."

❧

"He was working for some London toff," Eustace Cheevers informed his employer. "His name was Benjamin Hazlit, and he does a lot of quiet work for the Quality down in Town. He never discloses his employers by name, but it's somebody high up."

"Titled?" the Earl of Helmsley asked, mouth tight.

"Most like." Cheevers nodded. "Folk down south distinguish between themselves more. A fellow who works for the titles wouldn't want work from the cits or the squires or the nabobs. Hazlit's offices are top of the trees, his cattle prime, and his tailor only the best. I'd say a title, yes."

"That pretty much narrows it to Mayfair, doesn't it?" The earl's tone was condescending, as if any damned fool might reach such a conclusion.

"Not necessarily," Cheevers said. "There's a regular infestation of money and titles in Mayfair itself, but the surrounds are not so shabby, and there are other decent neighborhoods with quieter money."

An earl worthy of the title would have spent some time in Town, Cheevers thought, keeping his expression completely deferential. But this young sprig—well, this not quite middle-aged sprig—had obviously never acquired his Town bronze. Pockets to let, Cheevers thought with an inward sigh. The word around York was to get paid in advance if Helmsley offered you his custom.

It hadn't been like that when the old earl was alive.

The estate had been radiant with flowers, the women happy, and the bills always paid. Now, most of the gardeners had been let go, and the walls had bleached spots where valuable paintings had once hung. The drive was unkempt, the fences sagging, the fountains dry, and nobody had seen the dowager countess going about since she'd suffered an apoplexy more than two years ago. Where the granddaughters had got off to was anybody's guess.

"So that's the extent of what you've learned?" Helmsley rose, his tone disdainful. "You can tell me the man's name and that he's a professional investigator with wealthy clients? Nothing more."

"It's in the file." Cheevers stood. "You will have his address, the names of those with whom he spoke, what they told him, and so forth. I don't gather he learned much of significance, as people tend to be leery of Town fribbles up here."

"That they do." Helmsley nodded, his expression turning crafty. Cheevers considered the earl and wondered what the man was plotting, as it boded ill for someone. Helmsley had the look of man who could have been handsome. He had height, patrician features, and thick dark hair showing only the barest hint of gray. Cheevers, expert at summing people up, put Helmsley in his early thirties. The man looked older, however, as the signs of excessive fondness for both the grape and rich foods were beginning to show.

Helmsley's nose was becoming bulbous and striated with spider veins. His middle was soft, his reactions slow. Most telling of all, Cheevers, thought, there was a mean, haunted look in the man's gray eyes that labeled him as a cheat and a bully.

Good riddance, Cheevers concluded as he showed himself out. There were some accounts that even the thriftiest Yorkshireman's son was happy to close.

# Thirteen

"WELL?"

Wilberforce Hammond James, ninth Earl of Helmsley, carefully composed his features before turning to face the man who'd thrust open the interior door to the study. He did not face a pretty sight. Hedley Arbuthnot, Baron Stull, was nearly as round as he was tall, and he wasn't exactly short.

Worse, he was untidy. His cravat showed evidence of the chicken he'd consumed at lunch, the wine with which he'd washed down the chicken, and the snuff with which he'd settled his understandably rebellious stomach. That stomach, Helmsley knew, was worked incessantly.

But Stull, who was at least ten years Helmsley's senior, had two qualities that appealed, despite his appearance, lack of couth, and tendency to flatulence. First, he was free with his coin when in pursuit of his own ends, and second, he was as determined as a bulldog.

"Well, what?" Helmsley flicked an imaginary speck of lint from his sleeve.

"Where are the girls?"

"Mayfair," Helmsley said, praying it was true.

"Best get packing then," Stull said, sniffing like a canine catching the scent of prey. "To Mayfair it is."

∼

"He's been gone for hours."

Anna stopped pacing and pinned her gaze on Dev, whom she'd accurately assessed as the more soft-hearted brother. Val was sensitive and perceptive but had learned as his sisters' favored escort to keep some perspective around emotional women.

"He said we weren't to hold meals for him," Dev reasoned. "Meals, Anna, plural. Not just luncheon. He might have gone to talk with His Grace's investigator or taken Pericles for a romp."

"He romped Pericles this morning, when it was cooler," Anna pointed out. "I liked you better when you weren't trying to turn me up sweet."

"I'll go to the mansion and find out what's what," Val said. "When His Grace and Westhaven go at it, they are usually loud, ugly, and to the point. Anna's right—it shouldn't be taking this long."

He shot Dev a sympathetic glance but knew his brother would not have offered to investigate. Dev did not show up at the ducal mansion uninvited or unexpected, and Val wasn't about to ask him to break that tradition now.

The library door opened, and Westhaven strode in, surprising all three occupants.

"What's wrong?" Dev asked. "Don't tell me His Grace got the better of you."

"Well, he did," Westhaven said, going straight for the whiskey decanter, pouring one drink, knocking it back, and pouring another.

"Westhaven?" Val asked cautiously. But it was to Anna the earl spoke.

"For once," he said, "His Grace was blameless. You were investigated by a man named Benjamin Hazlit, who is legendarily thorough and legendarily discreet. He was on the Moreland payroll, but at my mother's request, not the duke's. I did not become aware of this until I had shouted dear Papa down with every obscene expression of my petty, selfish frustrations with him. I ranted, I raved, I shouted, and I told him…"

A pin could have dropped while Westhaven stared at his drink.

"I told him I was ashamed to be his son and heir."

"Ye gods." Val went to the brandy decanter. "About time somebody set him straight." He handed drinks all around but saw Dev was staring at Westhaven with a frown.

"The old windbag got the last word somehow, though, didn't he?" Dev guessed while Anna waited in silent dread.

"I sincerely hope," Westhaven said, pinning Anna with a troubled look, "it isn't quite his last word. Just as Her Grace was explaining that Hazlit was her agent, the duke suffered a heart seizure." The silence became thoughtful as all three brothers considered their father's mortality, and thus their own, while Anna considered the earl.

"He's still alive?" she said, drawing three pairs of eyes.

"He was demanding his personal physicians at full

bellow when I left," Westhaven said. "I've sent Pugh and Hamilton to him and left very strict orders he is not to be bled, no matter how he rants and blusters."

"Are you sure it was real?" Dev asked. "I would not put chicanery past him."

"Neither would I," Val said, eyes on Westhaven's face.

"I am sure it was real though I am not sure how serious it was. I am sure *he* thought he was dying, and of course, he still might die."

"He will die," Val corrected. "We all will. What makes you think he wasn't faking?"

"I've seen him morose, playful, raging, and—with Her Grace—even tender," Westhaven said, "but in thirty years of memory, I cannot recall our father ever looking *afraid* before today. It was unnerving, I can tell you.

"I recall his rows with Bart," the earl went on, shoving back to sit on his desk. "I used to think Bart was half-mad to let the old man get to him so. Why didn't he just let it roll off him, I'd wonder. I've realized though, that there is a kind of assurance to be had when you take on His Grace, and he doesn't back down, doesn't give quarter, doesn't flinch or admit he's wrong, no matter what."

"He's consistent," Dev admitted. "Consistently exasperating."

"But he's always the duke," Westhaven said. "You never catch him breaking role, or doubting himself or his God-given right to be as he is."

Val took a thoughtful swallow of his whiskey. "If the duke falls, then what?"

"Long live the duke," Anna said, holding Westhaven's

eyes for a moment. "I am going to have dinner brought in here on trays. I am sure you will all be going to check on your father afterward. You might want to take Nanny Fran with you, as she's a skilled nurse and would be a comfort to Her Grace."

Westhaven just nodded, seeming relieved she'd deal with the practicalities.

The evening unfolded as Anna predicted, with all three brothers off to the ducal mansion to see His Grace—to watch Westhaven argue with the duke over the choice of physicians—and to offer the duchess their support.

Val elected to stay at the mansion, agreeing to send word if there was any change in the duke's condition, while Dev went off to inform their half-sister, Maggie, of the duke's heart seizure. When Westhaven returned to his townhouse, it was late enough that Anna had dismissed the footman at the front door and waited there herself for Westhaven to return.

She was dressed in only her night rail, wrapper, and slippers when she met him, and heedless of any prying eyes or listening ears she wrapped her arms around him as soon as he was near enough to grab.

"He looks like hell, Anna," Westhaven said, burying his face against her neck. "He finally looks old, and worse, Mother looks old, too. The girls are terrified."

"And you are a little scared, too," Anna guessed, drawing back. "Give me your hat and gloves, Westhaven, and I will fix you a tray. You did not eat worth mentioning at dinner, and Her Grace warned me you go off your feed when you have concerns."

"What else did Her Grace warn you about?" the

earl asked, letting Anna divest him of hat and gloves. She didn't stop there but went on to remove his jacket and his cravat, and then undo his cuff links and roll back his shirtsleeves.

"It is too hot to go about in your finery," Anna said, "and too late."

He'd stood there in the foyer like a tired little boy, and let her fuss with his clothing. She piled his clothing over one arm, laced her fingers through his, and towed him unresisting into the peaceful confines of his home.

∽

The warmth of Anna's hand in his felt like the first good news Westhaven had heard all day.

"My grandfather died just a couple of years ago," Anna said as she led him through the darkened house. "I was so lucky to have him that long, and he was the dearest man. But he suffered some wasting disease, and in the end, it was a relief to see him go, but he held on and held on for my grandmother."

"I can see His Grace doing the same thing," the earl said, squeezing Anna's fingers slightly.

"I recall that sense of dread," Anna continued, "dread that every time Grandpapa dozed off, he was actually dead. He looked dead, sometimes, or I thought he did until I actually saw him pass. Three weeks after he left us, my grandmother had an apoplexy and became quite invalided herself."

"She suffered a serious blow," the earl said as they gained the kitchen.

"We all had," Anna said, sitting him down at

the work table. "I recall the way the whole house-hold seemed strained, waiting but still hoping. We were... lost."

He watched her moving around the kitchen to fetch his lemonade, watched her pour a scandalous amount of sugar into it then assemble him a tray. Something in the practical competence of her move-ments reassured him, made him feel less *lost*. In the ducal household, his mother and sisters, the servants, the physicians, *everybody*, looked to him for guidance.

And he'd provided it, ordering the straw spread on the street, even though the mansion sat so far back from the square the noise was unlikely to disturb his father. The need was for the staff to do something—anything—to feel like they were contributing to the duke's welfare and comfort.

So Westhaven had issued orders, commandeering a sick room in the ducal chambers, sending word down to Morelands, setting Nanny Fran to inventorying the medical supplies, directing his sisters to pen notes to the family's closest acquaintances and extended family, and putting Her Grace to extracting a list from the duke of the cronies he wanted notified and the terms of the notice. He'd conferred with the doctors, asked them to correspond with Fairly on the case, made sure Dev was off to inform Maggie, and finally, when there were no more anxious faces looking to him for direction, let himself come home.

And it was home, he thought, not because he owned the building or paid the people who worked there, nor even because he dwelled here with his brothers.

It was home because Anna was here, waiting for

him. Waiting to care for him, not expecting him—
hell, not really even allowing him—to care for her,
solve her problems, and tell her how to go on.

*I love you*, he thought, watching her pull a daisy
from the bouquet in the middle of the table and put it
in a bud vase on his tray. When she brought the tray to
the table and set it down, he put his arms around her
waist and pressed his face to her abdomen.

"I used to look at your scalp wound this way,"
Anna mused, trailing her finger through his hair to
look for a scar. "I am lucky I did not kill you."

"My head is too hard," he said, sitting back. "I am
supposed to eat this?"

"I will wallop you again if you don't," Anna said
firmly, folding her arms. "And I'll tattle to Pericles, who
seems to have some sort of moral authority over you."

"Sit with me," he said, trying to muster a smile at
her words.

She settled in beside him, and he felt more at peace.

"What do the physicians say?" Anna asked, laying
her head on his shoulder.

"Odd," the earl said, picking up a sandwich.
"Nobody has asked me that, not even Her Grace."

"She probably knows, even if she doesn't admit it to
herself, just how serious this is. My grandparents were
like that, joined somehow at the level of instinct."

"They loved each other," the earl said, munching
thoughtfully. Were he and Anna joined at the level
of instinct? He thought so, or she wouldn't be
sitting here with him, feeding him, and offering him
company when his own family did not.

"They surely did," Anna said. "My grandfather

grew his flowers for *her*. For me and Morgan, too, but mostly for his bride."

"Morgan is your sister," the earl concluded as his sandwich disappeared. Beside him, Anna went still.

"I know you are related," he said, sipping his lemonade then offering it to Anna. "You care for her, and she is much more than a cousin to you."

"You know this how?"

"I know you," he said simply. "And we live under the same roof. It's hard to hide such a closeness. You were willing to murder me for her safety."

"She is my sister."

"Val guessed it," the earl said, biting into an apple slice. "He's a little in love with her, I think."

"With Morgan?" Anna frowned. "An infatuation, perhaps. I am guessing she symbolizes something for him, something to do with his music or his choices in life. I know she adores him for his kindness, but I trust them."

"He plays Herr Beethoven like a man, not a boy."

"You would be better able to decipher that than I." Anna accepted the apple slice he passed her. "His playing to me has lately become passionate, and brilliant as a consequence."

"That's well said," the earl responded, munching thoughtfully.

"You've dodged my question about the physicians," Anna said, rubbing her hand across his lower back.

"They can't tell us anything for sure. The duke's symptoms—the sensation of a horse sitting on his chest, inability to breath freely, pain in the left side of his neck and down his left arm—are classic signs of a heart seizure. But the pains were very fleeting, and His Grace is a very active fellow. He has not felt particularly fatigued, is not in pain as we speak, and hasn't had any previous episodes of chest pain. He may make a full recovery and live another twenty years. The next weeks will be critical in terms of ensuring he gets rest and only very moderate exercise."

"But they also implied he may die tonight. Do you believe he's had no similar incidents, or has he been keeping up appearances for your mother?"

"Dev asked the same thing, and we decided if there had been earlier warnings, Her Grace might be the only one to detect it."

"And she would say nothing, except possibly to His Grace when they had privacy, which they will have little of."

"I can see they have some." The earl glanced over at her. "You learned this from your grandparents?"

"My grandmother. From time to time she shooed everybody away from the sick room and had Grandpapa to herself. It gave us all a break and gave them some time to be together."

"And to say good-bye." The earl sipped his drink again then handed the glass to Anna. "God, Anna, when I think of the things I said to my father today."

"You can apologize," Anna said simply. "It's more than he's ever been willing to do when it's time to mend a fence. And he has bullied his way through many fences."

The earl chuckled at her tart tone, despite his fears and guilt and fatigue. "You are a ruthlessly practical woman, Anna Seaton."

"Eat your marzipan," she ordered. "I've learned to

be practical, and you've no one to talk sense to you tonight save me. A man of the duke's age is lucky to be alive, much less alive and getting up to all the mischief he does. You did not cause his heart seizure, Westhaven. Do not even try to argue with me on this." She leaned over and kissed his cheek then handed him a piece of candy. "Eat."

He obeyed, realizing the food, drink, and conversation had restored him more than he would have thought possible.

"The next week," he said around a mouthful of almond paste, "will be trying."

"Your entire existence as the duke's heir has been trying."

"It has," he agreed, fingering his glass. "But I'm getting things turned around, Anna. The cash flow will soon be reliable and healthy, the estate managers are getting better organized, the girls and Mama and even His Grace are learning to deal with budgets and allowances. By the end of summer, I won't have to spend so much time with Tolliver. I wanted my father to see that."

"You wanted him to offer some gesture of thanks, or perhaps you wanted to be able to brag on yourself a bit and see if he at least notices all your efforts."

"I suppose." He picked up the second piece of marzipan and studied it. "Is that such a sorry thing, for a grown man still to want his papa to approve of him?"

"The sorry thing is that there would be any doubt in your mind that he does." She kissed his cheek again, a gesture that felt comforting and natural to him, then rose and began tidying up the kitchen.

"In all of today's tumult, I'll bet you forgot to fire Stenson and also forgot that our new butler started."

"Sterling." The earl nodded. "I did forget. Have we counted the silver to make sure my choice was worthy? And yes, I have yet to speak to Stenson."

"Send him back to the mansion, then," Anna suggested. "Lord Val is there, and Colonel St. Just's smalls are all mended."

"He's probably told you to call him by name." Anna and Dev might never be the best of friends, but in her tone there was none of the latent prickliness Dev had engendered earlier.

"He is much like your papa," Anna said, pausing as she picked up the earl's tray. "Gruff and sometimes unable to communicate his motivations, but tender-hearted and fierce."

"A good description. He was a grown man, though, before he could even speak clearly among strangers."

"Lord Val told me of the stutter," Anna said, coming back to the table with a clean rag. She bent over to wipe down the table, and Westhaven seized her hand in a gentle, implacable grip.

"Anna?" She straightened slowly and met his gaze. "Spend the night with me."

❧

Anna detected an odd light in Westhaven's eyes, combining daring and ferocity, but behind that, a stark vulnerability, as well. "Spend the night with me," he'd said. Simple, straightforward words with a wealth of complicated meanings.

She closed her eyes, trying to brace herself against

his request and against her own raging desire to grant
it. *Not now*, she thought desperately. Not now, when
they hadn't even discussed that investigator and the
urgent need for her to flee.

"I will behave," the earl said, dropping her wrist.
"I'm too damned tired to really... Well, maybe not too
tired, but too..." He fell silent and frowned. "It is an
unreasonable request and poorly timed. Forget I asked."

Anna opened her eyes and saw he was no longer
looking at her. He rose and stretched, then glanced
over at her where she stood immobilized, the rag still
in her hand.

"I've offended you," he said. "I just want... Will
you be here in the morning?"

He hadn't wanted to put that question into words,
Anna knew. Hadn't wanted to ask her to be with him
in the morning.

"I will be here," Anna said, unable to listen to her
common sense screaming to the contrary. "In your
bed, if you want me there."

He just nodded and took the rag from her, wiping
up the table while Anna finished putting away
the dishes she'd washed. To her, the moment was
resoundingly domestic and somehow right for them.
He wasn't pretentious with her, wasn't always the earl.
Sometimes, like now, he was just Gayle Windham, a
thoroughly, completely lovable and worthy man.

He waited until Anna had finished tidying up, took
a candle from the table, and held out his arm to her.
The gesture was courtly and oddly reminiscent of
Anna's grandparents. *Oh, to grow old with him...* Anna
thought, wrapping her hand around his forearm.

When they gained his room, the sense of domestic peace came with them. Anna finished undressing him; he tucked her into his bed then set about using the wash water kept in ample supply by his hearth. The balcony doors were open, and a refreshing breeze wafted through the room. She watched his ablutions, finding him simply beautiful in the light of the single candle. It wasn't even an erotic appreciation but something more possessive than that. He was beautifully built, of course, but the pensive expression on his face was beautiful to her, too.

*He is the way he is because he cares, and maybe in this, he and his father can finally find some common ground.*

When he wrung out the wet cloth and straightened, Anna flipped back the lavender-scented sheets. "Come to bed."

"Your night rail, madam?" He held out a hand. "It is too hot for all that extra, Anna, and I promise I will not bother you."

"So you've said," she replied, pulling the night-gown over her head and handing it to him. "Did you lock the door?"

"Ye gods." He padded through the dark and took care of the lock, blew out the candle, then climbed in beside her.

"I cannot remember the last time I spent the night with anyone other than a cat in my bed, save for our night at Willow Bend." Anna settled on the mattress as she spoke.

"I could say the same thing." The earl punched his pillow. "It would have different significance. Sorry." He was apologizing for yanking inadvertently on her pillow, but Anna let the apology cover his teasing, as well.

Anna folded her hands on her stomach as they both stretched out on their backs. "What awaits you tomorrow?"

"I'll meet with His Grace," the earl said. "Deliver Stenson his orders, probably call on Maggie, and try to toss enough work at Tolliver so we don't get behind."

Anna reached for his hand, prying it off his own stomach and lacing her fingers through it. "You should send a note around first thing to your brothers and go for your regular ride."

"Instead of seeing if my father is still alive?" The earl's frown was evident even in the darkness, but Anna was more aware that his fingers were closed around hers tightly.

"If he passes in the night you will receive word immediately. Lord Val will see to it. You enjoy your rides tremendously," she went on. "Some days, I think it's the only time you permit yourself to do what you please and not what you ought. And Pericles will not be around forever."

"Using my horse's welfare, Anna?"

"And your brothers need to see that though the duke may be failing, the earl is not; nor is the earl spending every waking minute in anticipation of his father's demise. The earl is too sturdy to capitulate to anxiety like that and too well inured to his responsibilities. Death befalls us, and while it is sad, the duke has lived a very long and good life. Though he will be mourned, his passing will be in the natural order of things, as will the earl's, when the time comes."

He sighed and considered her point.

*I love you,* he thought, *because you are honest with me and because you are willing to speak the truth to me when others might seek to curry favor instead. I love you because you are in this bed with me, not trying to conceive the much-awaited next generation of Windhams, but just holding my hand.*

"I'll go riding."

"Good." Anna rolled toward him, and in the dark he felt her moving on the mattress. She kissed his forehead and sighed. "Now go to sleep, Gayle Tristan Montmorency Windham. I will be here when you waken. I promise."

She wrestled him then into the position she deemed best suited to his slumbers, leaving him lying in her arms, his face resting against her shoulder. She stroked his back in the same easy rhythm he often gave her, and Anna soon heard his breathing even out.

*I will be here when you waken,* she thought, *but for how much longer, I do not know.*

The investigator sent north had precipitated the need the leave, and now, when the duke lay so ill, any temptation to confide in the earl was put to rest. He needed to be looking to his own and not to the troubles brought to him by his housekeeper.

Anna wrapped her arms around the future Duke of Moreland and sent up a heartfelt prayer for his happiness and her own safety.

❧

The days and nights that followed saw shifts in the routine of the earl's household. His morning ride with his brothers, a casual habit earlier, became standard. Stenson's departure brought a sense of relief to everyone, and Sterling, a quiet older gentleman recommended by no less than the Duke of Quimbey, brought order among the footmen.

And the nights...

The earl rose each morning, well rested and ready to face the day, because Anna shared his bed. The need for her hovered in regions Westhaven could not articulate. There was desire in it, but not enough that he initiated any seduction. The simple comfort of her presence was far more precious than any fleeting pleasure might be.

And he had the sense Anna was granting him the boon of her nightly company only because she was more determined than ever to go, and go soon. His Grace had enjoyed four days of continued freedom from chest pains, and the ducal household was beginning to admit to some cautious relief.

Watching Anna sleep, Westhaven frowned as he realized that when the duke was deemed safe from immediate danger, then Anna would likely go.

He would not allow that. *Could not.* Mentally, he kicked himself for not making the time to meet with Hazlit earlier in the week. He'd meet with him today, he vowed, if he had to pursue the man on foot through Seven Dials to see it done.

"You're awake." Anna smiled at him, and he smiled back. Such a simple thing, to start the day with a shared smile. He leaned over and kissed her.

"No fair." Anna shoved the sheets aside. "You've used the tooth powder already." She heaved off the bed, shrugged into her wrapper, and made for the privacy screen in the corner.

She was not too fussy, his Anna. She emerged and made use of his tooth powder and toothbrush, then caught sight of herself in the dressing mirror.

"I look like I was dragged through the proverbial hedge backward. How can you not be overcome with laughter at my appearance?" In the mirror, he assessed her reflection: Her braid was coming un-raveled and she had a wrinkle across her cheek from the pillow seam.

"You look very dear. Come back to bed."

"It is almost light out, your lordship." Anna eyed him balefully. "I am surprised you slept this late."

"Dev has to take his horses back to Surrey today, and Val made for a late night at Fairly's piano. No morning ride for poor Pericles, I'm afraid. Come back to bed, Anna."

There was something… implacable in his voice, and in the gray shadows of the room, Anna felt as if she were suddenly facing a life-defining moment. She could get in that bed, and this time—this time, finally—they would make love. She knew it as surely as a woman knows the scent of her lover, as surely as a mother knows the cry of her child.

Or she could smile, shake her head, and set about tidying herself up for the day.

Slowly, she unbelted her wrapper and walked naked back toward the bed.

"Your courses?" the earl asked as he watched her. "When will they fall?"

"In a few days," she said, not surprised at the

intimacy of the question. In some ways, the past days had seen them become more intimate than lovers. They shared his toothbrush; he brushed out her hair. She helped him dress, and he was her lady's maid. At the beginning and end of each day, they held quiet conversations, holding hands in bed or holding each other.

And moment by moment, Anna stored up the memories. This man, this very wealthy, powerful, handsome, and singular man was hers to love for the next very little while. It was a privilege beyond any she could have imagined, and now he wanted to make these last few memories with her, as well.

She might have been able to deny herself, she thought, but she could no longer deny *him*.

"You still think to leave me, Anna," he said as she settled on the bed, "and I am telling you quite honestly, I will fight you with every weapon I can find, honorable or not. I don't want you to go."

It was the first time he'd said that out loud, but Anna sensed it was the essence of what he was trying to communicate by bringing her back to his bed.

"I don't want you to go," he said again more fiercely.

"I'm here," Anna said, meeting his eyes. "Right now I am here with you in this bed."

He nodded, his gaze becoming hooded. "Where you will stay until I have pleasured you within an inch of your sanity." She smiled up at him for that piece of arrogance and brushed his hair back from his forehead.

"Likewise, I'm sure."

He smiled, a wolfish smile that nonetheless held an element of relief. "No rushing," he warned.

"No promises," she countered, scooting her way under him. "And no more lectures." She wrapped her legs around his flanks and levered up to kiss him. He growled, wrapped his arms around her, and rolled with her across the bed.

"I'm going to fuck you silly," he warned, positioning her on top of him.

"I'm going to let you." Anna smiled down at him. "But not just yet." She tried to scramble away from him, but he caught her by the ankles, slapped her bottom twice audibly, and dragged her back to him, grousing the whole time about troublesome women and naughty housekeepers. This side of him—the playful, exuberant, mating male—fascinated and delighted her.

And she wasn't averse to his hand on her buttocks, either, particularly not when he was so considerately rubbing the sting from her flesh.

"Shall I spank you when you're naughty?" she asked when he had her caged beneath his body.

"Please," he murmured, dipping his head to kiss her. "Spank me as hard and as often as you dare, for with you, I want to be very, very naughty."

The talking was finished, she surmised, as his tongue began to forage at her mouth and his hand covered her naked breast. He was bent not on seduction, so much as arousal and possession. *You are mine*, his hands seemed to say. *I am yours*, his kisses echoed. *All mine*, the insistent press of his cock against her belly declared.

*I am yours*, Anna thought, wrapping her legs around him and bringing her sex to stroke over his erection. And for today, for these moments, *you are mine*.

"Easy," he breathed, his hand going still just as his fingers closed over her nipple.

"No promises," Anna retorted. "I will rush if I please, sir." She glided her fingertips over his nipples and pressed hard with her hips.

"Jesus God, Anna," the earl whispered. "I want to be careful with you... but you..."

But she wanted him too desperately to appreciate his care. Heat was building below the pit of her stomach, in the place where worry and loneliness could make her feel so empty and desperate. It was the heat of desire, desire for him, and desire to give herself to him. He was bringing her fullness in places that had gone too long wanting and lonely.

"I need you inside me," she pleaded softly, framing his face with her hands. "Later you can be careful, I promise. Now, just please... I need you."

"Do not hurry me, Anna. I won't answer for the consequences if you do." But to her great relief, he brought the tip of his cock to the entrance of her sex and began to use it to nuzzle through her folds. He was content to explore that pleasure, lazily rooting and thrusting with little apparent focus, sometimes coming close to his goal, sometimes—deliberately, Anna thought—angling himself to one side, too high, the other side...

"You... are tormenting me."

"Then guide me, Anna," he coaxed. "Show me where you want me."

She was wet—he'd made sure of it—and he was wet as a result, as well. Anna's fingers closed around his shaft and drew him directly to her. She didn't withdraw her touch until he'd advanced enough to understand where she'd put him, snugged against her but not quite penetrating.

"You let me do this part," he cautioned, levering up on his forearms to hold her eyes. "I mean it, Anna. I'm not a small man, and you're... Oh, Jesus." The last word was said on a near groan as he pressed forward just the smallest increment. "God Almighty," he breathed as he lowered his face to her neck. "You are so blessedly fucking..."

*He is joining his body to mine*, Anna thought in wonder. Oh, it felt strange and wonderful and too damned slow by half.

"Westhaven." She arched her hips tentatively, only to have him go still.

"No," he ground out. "You damned let me, for once in your stubborn life, take care of you, Anna. Just... let me."

She liked his cursing and his foul language and the way he was so stern with her, but mostly, she liked the feel of him inching carefully into her body.

And then she didn't quite like it as much.

"Hold onto me," Westhaven urged. "Hold onto me but relax, Anna. I won't move until I feel you relax. Kiss me." He dipped his head and planted slow, easy kisses on her cheeks, her jaw, her eyelids. When her breathing was steady and she was kissing him back, he let a hand drift to her breast, there to knead and fondle and stroke, until Anna heard herself sigh and felt her whole body going boneless in response. Gradually he pressed his cock forward.

And again met resistance.

He slid a hand under Anna's buttocks, braced her,

and without warning, gave a single hard thrust. She winced and stiffened beneath him but made no sound.

"It will go easier now," he assured her, moving much more gently. "Tell me if I'm hurting you."

He had hurt her, Anna thought, but only for a surprising twinge of a moment. It felt better now, and the more deeply he moved into her body, the better she felt.

"I like this," she said, pleased and breathless and bothered. "Don't stop, Westhaven. I do like this."

"Move with me now, Anna. The difficult part is over, and it's all pleasure from here. Fuck me silly..." he teased, but there was a desperate note beneath the tenderness in his tone even as his thrusts became more purposeful.

Anna tried to match the undulation of her hips to his, and that forced him to slow down, to give her time to catch his rhythm. But what he gave up in speed, he made up for in intensity.

"That's it," he whispered a few moments later. "Move like that, and... Anna. *God*."

She was a quick study, able to move with him and send her hand wandering up his side to find his nipple, as well. Her thumb feathered across his puckered flesh in the same deliberate rhythm as he made with his cock, then she applied more pressure, actually rubbing him in a small, gratifyingly erotic circle.

"Anna..." He slipped his own hand more firmly around her buttocks. "Slow down... You've got to let... Ah, Christ. Don't stop, love."

"You either." She traced her tongue over his other nipple. "For the love of God, don't you dare stop."

She tried to quicken their rhythm, but he held firm to the more deliberate pace.

"Westhaven, please…" she wailed softly. "*Gayle…*"

His name, spoken in that hot, pleading tone, had the effect she'd hoped. He let the tempo increase until she was shaking and keening beneath him in the throes of her pleasure. Still he didn't stop but bent his head, took her nipple into his mouth, and drew strongly on her. She flailed her hips desperately against him, whispering his name over and over against his chest, her legs locked around his flanks.

He lifted his head, anchored a hand under her buttocks, and Anna felt a wet heat spreading deep in her body as his thrusts slowed and deepened. Westhaven groaned softly in her ear then went quiet above her.

"You," Westhaven rasped long moments later. "Sweet, ever-loving, merciful, abiding Christ."

He made it to his feet, carefully extricating his softening cock from Anna's body. She winced at the sensation of him leaving but made no verbal protest, merely watching him with luminous eyes in the soft predawn shadows. He used the wash water then brought the damp cloth to the bed.

"Spread your legs for me." She complied, unable to deny him in that moment any intimacy he wanted. Dear God, the things he had made her feel… The cloth was cool and soothing, and yet knowing he wielded it made it arousing, too.

"Take your time," she murmured. "No need to rush."

"Naughty." He smiled approvingly. "But you'll likely be sore, so no more marzipan for you this morning."

"And you won't be sore?"

"As to that"—he tossed the wet cloth over the rim of the basin—"I very well might be. You have much to answer for."

"Much."

"Anna?" The earl climbed over her, bracing himself on his forearms, and regarded her very seriously. "Weren't you going to tell me?"

"Do you need to hear the words?" She met his eyes, feeling sadness crowd out contentment.

"The words?" Guardedness crept up on the tenderness in his eyes.

"Oh, very well," Anna sighed, brushing fingers through the lock of hair on his forehead. "Of course I love you." She leaned up and wrapped her arms and legs around him. "I love you desperately. I would not still be here if I didn't. I would not be leaving you if I didn't. I love you, Gayle Windham. And I probably always will. There... now are we both thoroughly mortified?"

"I am not mortified," he whispered, burying his face against her neck. "I am... awed. Beyond words. You honor me, Anna Seaton. You honor me unbelievably."

He should say more, he knew, but his heart was pounding again, and she could probably feel that, so tightly was he clutching her to him. He should say that he loved her, for he certainly did, but he could not speak, could not contain with words the emotions rioting through him.

"Westhaven?" Anna stroked his back, her tone wary. "Are you well?"

"No," he said, feeling—merciful God—tears thicken in his throat as he held her even tighter. "I am not exactly well. I am…fucked silly."

And he meant it in every possible way.

❧

"I tell you that was her," Stull hissed. "I know my girls, Helmsley, and that's my little Morgan."

"It has been more than two years since you've seen your little Morgan," Helmsley said with as much patience as he could muster. "Women change in those years, change radically. Besides, it can't be her. That girl was laughing and shouting and talking with her swain so the whole park could hear her. Morgan can't do any of those things."

"It's *her*," Stull insisted. "I bet you if we follow her and that callow buffoon on her arm, we will find my Anna, as well."

"You are more than welcome to go haring off in this heat after a girl who obviously is not my sister, though I will grant you a certain resemblance. Morgan's hair was not so light, though, and I do not think Morgan was as tall as that girl."

"You said it yourself," Stull shot back, "women between the ages of fifteen and eighteen will change, delightfully so to my way of thinking."

"So go on. If you're so convinced that's Morgan, trot along. Confirm your hunch."

Stull gave him the mean look a grossly fat boy will often show when taunted then sighed.

"It is too hot," Stull conceded. "If she's in the area, she'll be back here. The park is the only decent air to be had in this miserable city. I'm parched—what say we find us a flagon or two of summer ale and perhaps the wenches that happily serve it?"

"A pint or two sounds just the thing," Helmsley said, knowing Stull, true to his two consistent virtues, would pay for it. "And perhaps we can find someone to watch for your girls in the park. I still have their miniatures."

"Good idea. Put the common man to work and let us do the thinking. What was the name of that inn where we saw the one with the big...?" He cupped his hands over his chest and wiggled his eyebrows.

"The Happy Pig," Helmsley sighed. It would be The Happy Pig. "I'm sure we can find a couple of sharp eyes there, maybe more than a couple."

～

For Anna, the week was passing too quickly. In her mind, the duke's health would be resolved in those seven days, giving him either a cheerful or a grim prognosis. Westhaven was gone during most of the days, spending time with his parents and sisters, tending to business, dashing out to Willow Bend, or riding in the mornings with his brothers.

But the nights... it had been two nights and three mornings since they'd become lovers in fact, and Anna had all she could do to stumble around the house, appearing to tend to her duties. She was swamped with Gayle Windham, her senses overwhelmed with memories of his tenderness, passion, humor, and generosity in bed. He insisted she find her pleasure, early and often. He talked to her before, during, and after their lovemaking. He teased and comforted and aroused and asked no questions other than what pleased her and what did not.

It all pleased her. She sighed, frowning at the flowers she was trying to arrange in the library's raised fireplace. Normally, she could arrange a bouquet to her satisfaction without thought, the patterns simply working themselves out. This morning, the daisies and irises were being contrary, and the thought of Westhaven's hand clamped on her buttocks was only part of the problem.

She heard the door open and assumed Morgan was bringing in fresh water, so she didn't turn.

"Now this is a fetching sight. I don't suppose the buttons of your bodice are going to get stuck in the screen?" Anna sat back on her heels and looked up at Westhaven looming over her. He stretched down a hand and hauled her up, bringing her flush against his body.

"Hello, sweetheart." He smiled then brushed a kiss to her cheek. "Miss me?"

She leaned into him and wrapped her arms around his waist.

"How is your father?" she asked as she always did.

"Improving, I'd say." But her unwillingness to return his sentiments bothered him, and that showed in his eyes. "I met with Hazlit," the earl said, letting Anna walk out of his embrace.

"You did?"

"I got nowhere." Westhaven sat down on the sofa and tugged off his boots. "He is an interesting man—very dark, almost swarthy. It is rumored his grandmother was a Jewess, rumored he is in line for some Scottish title, rumored he is filthy rich." He sat back and stacked his boots beside the sofa. "I'll tell you what is true: That man has the presentation of a cool demeanor down to a science, Anna. He gave away exactly nothing but told me to call again in a few days, thank you very much. He will call on Her Grace and hear from her in person that I am to be trusted with her confidences."

"Her Grace hasn't given you the substance of his investigation?" *I don't have a few more days to tarry*, Anna silently wailed.

"He does not write down his findings," the earl explained, "and he made the appointment to call on Her Grace, and then my father fell ill. He will reschedule the appointment, and Mother will receive him immediately."

"You could simply join that appointment."

"And give the appearance that I am coercing my mother?" the earl countered. "I wish it were simpler, but that man will not be bullied."

"One wonders how such an odd character would winkle secrets out of my dour Yorkshiremen."

"So you are from Yorkshire," the earl replied just as Anna's hand flew to her lips. "Anna..." His voice was tired, and his eyes were infinitely sad and patient.

"I'm sorry." Anna felt tears welling and turned away. "I always get like this when my courses are looming."

"Come here." The earl extended a hand, and Anna's feet moved without her willing it, until she was sitting beside him, his arm around her shoulders. For a long, thoughtful moment he merely held her and stroked her back. "I will meet with Hazlit in a day or two, Anna. What he knows will soon be known to me; I'd rather hear it from you."

She nodded but said nothing, trying to pick through which parts of her story she could bear to tell and how to separate them from the rest. She shifted to the rocking chair, and he let her go, which was good, as she'd be better able to think if they weren't touching.

"I can tell you some of it," she said slowly. "Not all."

"I will fetch us some lemonade while you organize your thoughts. I want to hear whatever you want to tell me, Anna."

When he came back with the drinks, Anna was rocking slowly, her expression composed.

"You're beautiful, you know." The earl handed her a glass. "I put some sugar in it, but not as much as I put in mine." He locked the door then resumed his seat on the sofa and regarded the woman he loved, the woman who could not trust him.

Since their first encounter several days ago, Anna had not repeated her declaration of love, and he had not raised the topic of her virginity. The moment had never been right, and he wasn't sure explanations mattered. Many unmarried housekeepers were addressed as Mrs., and the single abiding fact was that she'd chosen to give him her virginity. *Him.*

"So what can you tell me?" he asked, sitting back and regarding her. She was beautiful but also tired. He was keeping her up nights, and he knew she wasn't sleeping well in his bed. In sleep, she clung to him, shifting her position so she was spooned around him or he around her.

In sleep, he thought a little forlornly, she trusted him.

"When my grandfather died and my grandmother fell ill," Anna began, staring at her drink as she rocked, "things at home became difficult. Grandpapa was a very good and shrewd manager, and funds were left that would have been adequate, were they properly managed. My brother was not a good manager."

Westhaven waited, trying to hear her words and not simply be distracted by the lovely sound of her voice.

"My grandmother encouraged me to take Morgan and flee, at least until Grandmother could meet with the solicitors and figure out a way to get my brother under control. But she was very frail after her apoplexy."

"You came south, then?" The earl frowned in thought, considering two gently bred and very young women traveling without escort far, far from home. Morgan in particular would have been little more than a child and much in need of assistance when away from familiar surroundings.

"We came south." Anna nodded. "My grandmother was able to provide me with some references written by her old acquaintances, people who knew me as a child, and I registered with the employment agencies here under an assumed name."

"Is Anna Seaton your real name?"

"Mostly. I am Anna, and my sister is Morgan."

He let that go, glad at least he was wasn't calling her by a false name when passion held him in its thrall. "You found employment."

"I took the job no one else wanted, keeping house

for an old Hebrew gentleman. He was my own personal miracle, that bone the Almighty throws you to suggest you are not entirely forgotten in the supposedly merciful scheme of things."

"The old Hebrew gentleman was decent to you?" the earl asked, more relieved than he could say to realize whatever price Anna had paid for her decisions, she'd kept her virtue until such time as she chose to share it with him.

"Mr. Glickmann knew immediately Morgan and I were, as he put, in flight. He had scars, Westhaven, from his own experiences with prejudice and mean-spiritedness. He'd been tossed into jail on flimsy pretexts, hounded from one village to another, beaten… He knew what it meant, to live always looking over your shoulder, always worrying, and he gave us the benefit of his experience. He told me the rules for surviving under those circumstances, and those rules have saved us."

"And is one of those rules to trust no one?"

"It might as well be. I trusted him, though, and if he'd only lived longer, then perhaps he might have been able to help us further. But his life had been hard, and his health was frail. Still, he gave us both glowing characters and left us each the kind of modest bequest a trusted servant might expect. That money has been sent from heaven, just as his characters were."

She fell silent, and Westhaven considered her story thus far. Difficult, he tried to tell himself, and sad, but hardly tragic. Still, the what ifs beat at him: What if the job nobody wanted had been working for a philandering lecher? What if they'd been snatched up and befriended by an abbess upon their arrival to London? What if Morgan's deafness had meant no jobs presented themselves?

"Go on," Westhaven said, more to cut off his own lurid imagination than because he wanted to hear more.

"From Glickmann's," Anna continued, "I got employment in the home of a wealthy merchant, but his oldest son was not to be trusted, so I cast around and found your position. The woman the agency picked for the position was at the last minute unable to serve, as she was sorely afflicted with influenza. Rather than make you wait while they interviewed other more suitable candidates, they sent me over, despite my lack of experience and standing."

"Thank God they did," the earl muttered. Anna's fate was hanging by threads and coincidences, with social prejudice, influenza, and pluck standing between her and tragedy.

"What of your brother?" he asked, rolling back his cuffs. "I gather he is part of the problem rather than part of the solution?"

"He is," Anna said, the tart rejoinder confirming the earl's suspicions.

"And you aren't going to tell me the rest of it?"

"I cannot. Grandmother has bound me to silence, not wanting to see the family name dragged through scandal." The earl stifled the urge to roll his eyes and go on a loud rant about the folly of sacrificing one's name for the sake of family pride.

"Anna." He sat forward. "You have no idea—none at all—how lucky you are not to be serving men in doorways for a penny a poke, you and Morgan both, as the pox slowly killed you. Sending you south was rank foolishness, and I can only consider your grand-mother devised this scheme because she considered the situation desperate."

"It was," Anna said, "and I do know, Westhaven. I have seen those women, their skirts hiked over their backs, their eyes dead, their lives already done while some jolly fellow bends them over to have a go before toddling home after his last pint."

If she'd been close enough to see that much, Westhaven thought... Ye gods.

"Let me hold you," he said, rising and tugging her to her feet. "When you are ready, I will hear the rest of it, Anna. You are safe with me now, and that's all that matters."

She went into his arms willingly, but he could feel the resistance in her, the doubt, the unwilling-ness to trust. He led her up the stairs, her hand in his, determined to bind her to him with passion if nothing else.

Each time they were together, he introduced her to new pleasures, new touches, new ways to move. Tonight, he put her on her hands and knees and had her grip the headboard as he sank into her deeply from behind. She met him thrust for thrust, and when her pleasure had her convulsing hard around his cock, he couldn't hold back any longer. And like a stallion, he let his spent weight cover her, resting along her back, his cheek pressed to her spine.

"Down," he panted, easing one of her feet back several inches to explain himself. Anna straightened her knees and slipped to her stomach as his cock slid wetly from her body. He followed her, blanketing her back with his greater weight.

"Are you all right?" He kissed her cheek and paused to suckle her earlobe.

"I am boneless," Anna murmured. "I like this, though."

"What this?" He nuzzled at her neck.

"The way you like to cuddle afterward."

"I am a rarity in that regard," he assured her. "I know of only one other person in this entire bed so prone to shameless displays of affection." His moved his hips partly off her but shifted only a little to the side to kiss her nape.

"You trust me," he said, biting her neck gently.

When she said nothing, he got off the bed to use the basin and water. He washed his hands and his genitals then came back and stood frowning at her for a long moment.

"You do trust me, but only in this," he said again. "You would let me take you in any position, anywhere I pleased, as often as I pleased."

Anna rolled to her back and hiked up on her elbows, wariness in her expression. "You have never given me reason not to trust you in this bed. I am safe with you."

"You don't believe that. You might believe you are safe from me, from the violence and selfishness that can make any man a rutting boar, but you do not believe you are safe with me."

There was such defeat in his tone, such resignation, Anna was almost glad this would be their last night together. In the morning, he'd ride off to meet with his brothers, and she'd gather up her sister and her belongings and board a coach for Manchester. She'd lie in his arms for this one final night, hold him close, breathe in his scent, and love him. But it would be their last night, and this time tomorrow, she'd be far, far away.

It was that simple to do and that impossible to bear.

# *Fourteen*

"MY LORD! MY LORD, YOU MUST WAKE UP!"

Shouts at the bedroom door had Westhaven struggling up from sleep as Anna shook him hard by his shoulder.

"Gayle," she hissed. "Gayle Tristan Montmorency Windham!" She had her fist cocked back to smack him when he caught her hand and kissed her knuckles.

"Please! You must wake up!" Sterling sounded near tears, but the earl only heaved a sigh, knowing he was going to hear himself addressed as "Your Grace" from that moment on for the rest of his life.

"Under the covers," he said to Anna quietly as he reached for his dressing gown. A small part of him was grateful he at least wasn't going to be alone when he got the news of his father's death.

"Yes, Sterling." He opened the door, his composure admirable—worthy of a duke.

"A message, my lord"—Sterling bowed—"from Lord Amery. The messenger says there's a fire at your new property."

*Not His Grace*, the earl thought with soaring relief. Not His Grace, not yet.

But there was a fire at Willow Bend.

"Have Pericles hitched to the gig," the earl said. "Pack a hamper and plenty of water. Send word to my brothers—Val should be at the mansion; Dev will be at Maggie's. Under no circumstances are Their Graces to get wind of this, Sterling." He hoped Dev was at Maggie's, but he might also still be at his stud farm or holed up with old cavalry comrades. He glanced at Douglas's note.

*The Willow Bend stables are ablaze as I write; no loss of life thus far. Will remain on site until the situation is contained. Amery.*

A thousand questions fluttered through Westhaven's head: How did the fire start, how did Amery come upon it, was the house safe, and why the hell was this happening now…?

"What is it?" Anna had risen from the bed, put on her wrapper, and padded over to him silently.

"There's a fire at Willow Bend. Just the stables, according to a note from Amery. I'm going out there."

"I'll go with you."

He sat on the bed and drew her to stand between his legs. "That won't be necessary."

"Fires mean people can get hurt. I can help, and I don't want you to go alone."

He didn't want to go alone, either. He had good memories of her at Willow Bend, and she had a point. Unless he brought medical supplies with him, there were none on hand at Willow Bend adequate to deal with the burns and other mishaps that could come with fighting a fire.

"Please," she said, wrapping her arms around him. "I want to go."

He leaned into her embrace, pressing his face to the soft, comforting fullness of her breast for just a moment. He was torn, knowing he should spare her this but also feeling a vague unease about leaving her side for any extended period.

Mistrust, it seemed, could go both ways.

"Dress quickly," he said, patting her bottom. "Bring a change of clothes. Fires are filthy business."

She nodded and darted for the door, pausing only long enough to make sure the corridor was empty before slipping into the darkness beyond. In her absence, Westhaven heard a clock chime twelve times.

∞

"At least we now know for sure where they are," Helmsley said over their rashers of morning bacon.

"We do." Stull smacked his greasy lips. "But who could have imagined the earl would snatch up his housekeeper to go to the scene of a fire?"

"She may be more than just his housekeeper," Helmsley said. Stull looked up sharply, his expression reminiscent of a dog whose bowl of slops was threatened.

"She damned well better not be, Helmsley," the baron with a snort. "I'll not pay for used goods, and if she's strayed, then she'll be made to wish she hadn't."

Helmsley kept his peace, wishing not for the first time he'd had some choice before embarking on this whole miserable scheme with Stull. But really, what choice had he had? A man needed coin, and a gentleman had few means of obtaining same.

Their time in London had been productive, however. It had been Cheevers's suggestion to check the employment agencies, and with others set to watching in the park, Helmsley had taken his sisters' miniatures and made the rounds. The third agency had recognized Anna's portrait immediately, as her case was memorable: Young, not particularly experienced but obviously very genteel, they'd been able to place her in the household of a ducal heir, no less, and she had worked out there *beautifully*.

Not too beautifully, Helmsley hoped, as Stull could be very nasty when thwarted. In the brief glimpses Helmsley caught of his sister the previous night, Anna had seemed comfortable with the earl but not overly familiar. He hoped for her sake that was the extent of the earl's interest in his housekeeper.

And Morgan, he realized, must have been stashed somewhere else, perhaps absorbing all of Anna's wages with her upkeep. The agency had been forthcoming—for a price—with the information that his lordship was again in the market for a housekeeper, this time for a newly acquired property in Surrey.

Stull's plan had been to draw the earl out to Willow Bend then hie into the city and snatch the housekeeper from under his nose. With Anna in their grasp, it would have been short work to extract Morgan's location from her. It was, like most of Stull's endeavors, clumsily done—and now they had the King's man nosing about, looking for arsonists, which was no small worry.

Arson, even if only the stables burned, was a hanging felony, though they'd be tried in the Lords and probably get transported instead. Helmsley wondered for the millionth time why *his* sisters had to be so stubborn, wily, and unnatural, but it seemed he'd soon be rid of the pair of them.

Stull, greedy shoat, wanted them both, and Helmsley had agreed it would be better for the sisters that way—and easier for him, than if he had to live with either of them when this debacle was complete. And deaf as she was, Morgan's options were limited at best, earl's granddaughter or not.

Stull patted his lips with his napkin, chugged his ale, and belched contentedly. "What say we check in with those fellows watching the park, and perhaps find one of their confreres who might keep an eye on this Westhaven's townhouse, eh? Sooner or later, a housekeeper must go to market, run her little errands, or have her half-day. We can snatch my Anna then, and the earl will be none the wiser."

"A capital idea," Helmsley agreed, rising. It had actually been his idea, proffered as an alternative to torching the earl's country retreat, but Stull was not the most receptive to another's notions once he'd got the bit between his teeth.

Stull rubbed his hands together. "And then we can have a lie down through the worst heat of the day, before turning ourselves loose on the evening entertainments, what?"

"Splendid notion." Helmsley dredged up a smile. In London, the better brothels kept out the likes of Stull and himself. Titled though they were, Helmsley had never taken his seat, and Stull had probably voted exactly twice since coming into his title. They were not... Connected. They were instead caricatures of the sophisticated lordlings on the town, having neither savoir faire nor physical appeal.

With any luck, they would soon be in possession of both of his sisters and on their way back north. Helmsley's pockets would be heavily lined with Stull's gold and his conscience numbed by as much alcohol as a man could consume and remain alive.

❧

"I tell ye, guv, the bird ain't there." The dirty little man spat his words, disdaining his betters with each syllable.

"She has to be there." Helmsley threw up his hands in exasperation. "You set men to watching both the front and back of the house?"

"Lads, not men," the man replied. "Lads be cheaper, more reliable, and not so fond of their ale, nor as apt to wander off when they's bored."

"And in four days," Helmsley went on, "your... boys haven't left the place unattended once?"

"Not fer a bleedin' minute. No bird, at least not the one in yer little paintin'. Maids and laundresses and such, but no lady bird like you showed us. Now where's me blunt, guv?"

"Stull!" Helmsley bellowed, and the baron lumbered out of his room into their shared sitting room. "The man wants his blunt."

Stull frowned, disappeared, and reappeared, a velvet bag in hand. Too late, Helmsley realized the cretin they'd hired to manage surveillance of Westhaven's townhouse was eyeing the velvet bag shrewdly.

"Your coin." Stull counted out the payment carefully and dropped it into the man's hand from a height
of several inches above his palm. "Now be off with
you. She's there, and we know it. Your job is to tell
us when she leaves the house."

"Not so fast," their hireling sneered. "You pay us
for the next four days, too, guv. Unless you want me
sorry self gracin' yer 'umble abode again."

Slowly, Stull counted out another fistful of coins.

"My thanks." The man smiled a gap-toothed grin.
"If we see the bird, we'll send a boy."

He took his leave, and Stull shrugged, much to
Helmsley's relief.

"We'll find her," Stull said. "She's got a decent
job, probably making enough to look after Morgan,
for which we must give my Anna credit, and when
she pokes her nose out of that earl's townhouse, we'll
snatch her up and be gone. I'm for a little stroll down
to the Pig, Helmsley. You can come along and put in
a good word for me with Wee Betty?"

Helmsley smiled thinly and reached for his hat and
gloves. He was of the mind that Anna had once again
given them the slip, just as she had in Liverpool a
few weeks after leaving Yorkshire. He was damned,
*damned*, if he'd spend another two years haring all over
England, drinking bad ale and screwing dirty serving
maids in Stull's wake.

Anna had given her word, in writing, and Helmsley
was going to see she kept it—or died trying. Either
way, the result was the same for him: His troubles
would be over, and so would hers.

# Fifteen

"I TELL YOU, IT'S TIME TO GO HOME," HELMSLEY SAID for the fourth time.

"Not when we're so close," Stull argued in a whispered hiss. "The lads in the park saw that girl again, the one who looks like Morgan, and they trailed her to Mayfair, just a few streets over from the earl's home. I'm telling you, we've found them both."

"Morgan is deaf and mute," Helmsley shot back. "No deaf mute is going to be coddled in the great homes of Mayfair, not in any capacity. Even the footmen have to be handsome as lords, for chrissakes."

Stull glared at him sullenly. "I am beginning to think you don't want me to find your sisters. You'd rather have them wandering the slums of London with no protection whatsoever, when their every need will be met in my care. What kind of brother are you, Helmsley, to abandon the chase now, when they're almost in our grasp at last?"

He was an awful brother, of course. The question was ludicrous coming from Stull. But he wasn't a stupid brother, particularly, and if he was ever to get out of debt, he needed to find Anna and Morgan, hand them over to Stull, and let them make shift as best they could. They were damnably resourceful; their haring all over the realm for two years on little more than pin money proved that much, at least.

But did he really want to be there when Anna realized what he'd done? When Morgan dissolved into tears? When they realized the extent of his betrayal?

"What aren't you telling me, Helmsley?" Stull's look became belligerent. "You threw in with me when the old man died, and don't think you can turn about now. I'll go crying to the magistrate so fast the Lords won't be able to protect you."

Lie down with dogs, Grandpapa used to say, and you wake up with fleas.

"I'm not like you, Stull." Helmsley tossed himself down in a chair, affecting a manner of dejection. "I have been nothing but a burden and an expense to you on this trip. One has one's pride." He managed just the right ashamed, glancing connection with Stull's eyes and saw the baron's ponderous mind catching the scent.

"You found those fellows to watch the park and the earl's house," Helmsley went on. "You thought of drawing Westhaven out to the country with that fire, you provide all the blunt for the whole scheme, while I merely stand by and watch."

"I could spare you for a bit," Stull said. "If you want to head back north, I can manage things here and send word when I have the girls. Might be better that way."

His porcine eyes narrowed as he circled back to his earlier thought.

"You aren't thinking of peaching on me to the magistrate, Helmsley? You're the one who's pissed away your grandpapa's fortune and your sister's dowries. Don't think I won't be recalling that if you turn on me now."

"I know better, Stull." Helmsley shook his head. "You know my dirty business, and I know yours, and we both know where our best interests are served."

"Well said." Stull nodded, chins jiggling. "Now, what say we nip downstairs and grab a bite for luncheon? You can't leave today, old man. Too deuced hot, and you must make your farewells this evening to that bit of French muslin we came across last night."

"I can spend tonight in Town," Helmsley agreed. "I'll go north first thing in the morning and leave this matter entirely in your capable hands."

"Best thing." Stull nodded. "I'll send word when I have the girls."

❧

"The prodigals return." Dev smiled as Anna and the earl trundled in the back door from the townhouse gardens. "Westhaven." He extended his hand to his brother, only to be pulled into a brief hug. Over Westhaven's shoulder, Dev shot a puzzled look at Anna, who merely smiled and shook her head.

"Good to be back," Westhaven said. "My thanks for keeping an eye on things here, and Amery and his neighboring relations send their felicitations."

"By that you mean, Greymoor recalled I outbid him for the little mare he wanted for his countess and has decided to let bygones be bygones."

"He sent his felicitations," the earl repeated, "as does Heathgate, who as magistrate provided us most gracious hospitality these past days while the fire was being investigated. Have we anything to eat?"

"I can see to that," Anna said. "Why don't you wash off the dust of the road, and I'll have your luncheon served on the terrace."

"Join us?" the earl said, laying a hand on her arm.

Her eyes met his, and she saw he would not argue, but he was *asking*. She nodded and made for the kitchen, trying to muster a scold for giving in to his foolishness. At Willowdale, she'd been a guest of the Marquis and Marchioness of Heathgate, as Heathgate served as the local magistrate. There she'd been treated as a guest and as the earl's respected... what? Friend? His fiancée? His... nothing. Certainly not his house-keeper. Anna had allowed the fiction out of manners and out of a sense it was the last chapter in her dealings with Westhaven, an unreal series of days that allowed them a great deal of freedom in each other's company.

And at night, he'd stolen into her room, slipped into her bed, and held her in his arms while they talked until they both fell asleep. He'd told her stories of growing up among a herd of the duke's offspring on the rambling acres of Morelands, of his last parting from his brother Bart, and his suspicions regarding a second ducal grandchild.

She told him what it was like to grow up secure in her grandparents' love, surrounded by acres of flowers and hot houses and armies of gardeners. But mostly, Anna had listened. She listened to his voice, deep, masculine, and beautiful in the darkness. She listened to his hands, to the patterns of tenderness and possession they traced on her bare skin. She listened to his body, becoming as familiar to her as her own, and to the way he used it to express both affection and protectiveness. She listened to his mind, to the discipline with which he used it to provide for all whom he cared for.

She listened to his heart and heard it silently—and unsuccessfully—plead with her for her trust.

✧

"And there be our bird," the dirty little man cackled to an even dirtier little boy.

"So you'll tell the fat swell we seen her?" the child asked, eyeing the pretty lady with the flower basket.

"I will, but happen not today, me lad. He pays good, and we're due for another installment when I call on him tonight. Too hot to do more than stand about in the shade anyways—might as well get paid fer it, aye?"

"Aye." The child grinned at the soundness of his superior's reasoning and went back to getting paid to watch.

"You tell old Whit if the lady goes out, mind, and be ready for yer shift again tomorrow at first light."

✧

"You use the same employment agency as Her Grace," Hazlit began, his eyes meeting the earl's unflinchingly. "So I started there and eventually found copies of references your housekeeper brought with her two years ago. They all came from older women, ladies of quality now residing in York and its surrounds, so I went north."

"You went north," the earl repeated, needing and dreading to hear what came next.

"On her application," Hazlit went on, "Mrs. Seaton put she was willing to work as a housekeeper or in a flower shop, which caught my eye. It's an odd combination of skills, but it gave me a place to start. I took her sketches and what I knew, and wrote to a colleague of mine in York. Some answers essentially fell into my lap from there."

"What sketches?"

"Mrs. Seaton goes to the park occasionally, the same as most of London in the summer," Hazlit said. He opened a folder and drew forth a charcoal sketch that bore a striking resemblance to Anna Seaton.

"It's quite good," the earl said, frowning. Hazlit had caught not just Anna's appearance but also her sweetness and courage and determination. Still, to think Hazlit had sketched this when Anna was unaware rankled.

"It is your property." A flicker of sympathy graced Hazlit's austere features.

"My thanks." The earl set aside the portrait, and gave Hazlit his full attention. "What answers fell into your lap?"

"Some," Hazlit cautioned, "not all. There are not charges laid against her I could find in York or London, but her brother is looking for her. Her name is Anna Seaton James, she is the oldest daughter of Vaughn Hammond James and Elva James nee Seaton, who both died in a carriage accident when Anna was a young girl. Her sister, Morgan Elizabeth James, was involved in the same accident and indirectly lost her hearing as a result. The heir, Wilberforce Hammond James, was the only son and resides at the family seat, Rosecroft, in Yorkshire, along the Ouse to the north-west of the city."

"Granddaughter to an earl," the earl muttered, frowning. "Why did Anna flee?"

"As best my colleague and I can piece together," Hazlit replied, "the old earl tied up his money carefully, so the heir was unable to fritter away funds needed for the girls and their grandmother. The heir managed to do a deal of frittering, nonetheless, and I took the liberty of buying up a number of his markers."

"Enterprising of you," the earl said, reaching for the stack of papers Hazlit passed to him. "Ye Gods…" He sorted through the IOUs and markers, his eyebrows rising. "This is a not-so-small fortune by Yorkshire standards."

"My guess, and it's only a guess, is that Anna knows of the mishandling of her grandfather's estate perpetrated by the present earl, and she made the mistake of trying to reason with her brother. Then too, the younger sister, Morgan, is very vulnerable to exploitation, and if a man will steal from his sisters, he'll probably do worse without a qualm."

"You manage to imply a host of nasty outcomes, Mr. Hazlit," the earl observed, "though nothing worse than my imagination has concocted. Any advice from this point out?"

"Don't let them out of your sight," Hazlit said. "It is not kidnapping if you are a concerned and titled brother looking for sisters whom you can paint as flighty at best. He can snatch either one, and there will be nothing you or anyone else could do about it. Nothing."

"Can he marry them off?"

"Of course. For Morgan, in particular, that would be simple, as she was arguably impaired by her deafness, and marriage is considered to be in a woman's best interests."

"Considered by men," the earl replied with a thin smile. "Well, thank you, Hazlit. I will convince the ladies to remain glued to my side, and all will be well."

Hazlit stood, accepting the hand proffered by the earl. "Better yet, marry the woman to someone you can trust to look out for her and to manage Helmsley. The situation could resolve itself quite easily."

"You are not married, Mr. Hazlit, are you?"

"I do not at this time enjoy the wedded state," Hazlit said, his smile surprisingly boyish. "I do enjoy the unwedded state."

"Thus sayeth we all," the earl said, escorting Hazlit to the front door. "Those of us in expectation of titles sometimes particularly enjoy the unwedded state—while we can." Something briefly shone in Hazlit's dark eyes—regret? Sympathy?—it was gone before the earl could analyze it.

"Good day, my lord," Hazlit said, his eyes drifting to the huge bouquet on the table, "and good luck keeping your valuables safe."

The earl retreated to his study, penned a note asking Val to return to the townhouse at his earliest convenience, and another thanking Heathgate for the recent hospitality. For all Hazlit had been informative, though, Westhaven had the sense there were still answers only Anna could provide.

So he sat for a long time, sipping his sweetened lemonade, contemplating the bouquet in the fireplace, and considering how exactly he could keep Anna Seaton—Anna *James*—safe when her valise was packed and sitting on her bed, just as it had been the night they'd been called out to Willow Bend.

⁓

When darkness was beginning to fall, Westhaven was pleased to see both his brothers would be joining him for dinner. Val, with music books, wardrobe, and horse in tow, had rejoined the earl's household, claiming the duke was bloody well enough recovered to drive anybody to Bedlam.

Dev was clearly trying to contain his questions about the fire out in Surrey, but when the meal was consumed, sweets and all, the earl asked his brothers to take an after-dinner stroll with him to the stables. Once there, away from the house and its balconies, he explained what Hazlit had told him and enlisted his brothers' support in seeing to it Anna and Morgan were kept safe.

"But you can't keep them under surveillance every minute," Dev protested. "They are intelligent women, and they will soon know we're up to something."

"I'll talk to Anna tonight," the earl said. "She has to be made to see reason, or I'll bundle her off to Morelands myself, there to be confined until she'll marry me."

Val exchanged a look with Dev. "So the ducal

blood will out, and you're taking the Roman example of seizing and carrying off your bride."

Westhaven sighed. "I am no more willing to force a marriage on Anna than she would be willing to take her vows on those terms. I would live down to her worst expectations were I to even attempt it."

"Glad you comprehend that much," Dev said. "Best of luck convincing her she needs bodyguards. Morgan, at least, can't argue with us."

"Don't bet on it," Val said, his expression preoccupied. "I have missed my piano though, so I'll leave you, Westhaven, to reason with Anna, while I bare my soul to my art."

"Damn." Dev watched his youngest brother depart and smiled at the earl. "And here I've been baring everything else to the wenches at the Pleasure House. Which of us, do you suppose, has it right?"

"Neither." The earl smiled. "When it comes down to it, I'm having to admit in the things that matter most, it's the duke who has gotten closest to the mark."

Devlin cast him a curious glance then ambled off to tuck in his horses. Westhaven was alone in the darkened alley when he heard the barest thread of a whisper summoning him farther into the shadows.

⌘

"This is short notice, your lordship." Hazlit studied the Earl of Westhaven by the light of the candles in the man's library. It was a handsome room, and Hazlit had noted at their earlier meeting the whole house appeared well cared for. The bouquets were fresh, the wood work polished, the windows sparkling, and not a speck of dust to be seen.

"I apologize for the lateness of the hour, Hazlit," the earl said. "May I offer you a drink?"

"You may." Hazlit accepted the offer, in part because the quality of the drink served told him about a man's character, but also because he had the sense the earl was offering not in an attempt to manipulate but out of sheer good breeding.

"Whiskey or brandy?"

"Whatever you're having," Hazlit replied. "I assume we meet to discuss the same matter?"

"We do," the earl said, handing Hazlit a generous tot of whiskey. "To your health."

"Yours." Hazlit sipped cautiously then paused. "Lovely, but I don't recognize it."

"It's a private label." The earl smiled. "Heathgate owns the distillery and calls this his bribing vintage."

Hazlit nodded. He *had* sampled this vintage before but not often, and it wasn't something he'd admit about one client to another. "My compliments. Now, how can I assist you?"

"Shall we sit?" The earl gestured to the long, comfortable-looking leather sofa, and Hazlit sank into one corner. The earl took up a rocking chair, his drink in hand. "I have become aware my house is being watched, front and back. I had a very interesting discussion last night when I went to bid my horse good night. I was accosted by an urchin loyal to David Worthington, Viscount Fairly, who was picketed in my mews unbeknownst to me."

Hazlit merely nodded, his eyes locked on the earl.

"More significantly," the earl went on, "I was informed my house is also being watched by the minions of one Whit, who is in the employ of two gentlemen from the North, one of whom is obese." The earl paused to sip his drink. "I recently purchased a modest property a short distance from Town, Willow Bend by name. The stables there were burned last week, and other buildings were soaked with lamp oil. By chance, acquaintances happened to see the stables burning and summoned help before the rest of the property could be set ablaze.

"Fortunately, the place was not yet occupied, and only the stables were lost. I hired a runner, who was able to deduce that two men, well dressed, one quite portly, bought a quantity of lamp oil the day before my stables burned, from the last likely source before one leaves Town for the Surrey countryside."

"You suspect these men were sent after Mrs. Seaton," Hazlit suggested.

The earl met Hazlit's eyes. "I suspect one of them of being her brother, the earl. Is he reported to be portly?"

"He is not." Hazlit fished in a pocket of his coat, and brought out a small pad of a paper. "Have you a pen?"

The earl got up and went to his desk, setting out ink, pen, sand, and knife on the blotter. Hazlit brought his drink to the desk, assumed the earl's wingback chair, and with the earl looking over his shoulder, sketched a figure of a man.

"Helmsley," Hazlit said tersely, tearing off the sheet and starting another sketch, this one of the man's face. While Hazlit sketched, the earl studied the little ink drawing.

"Helmsley has bulk to him," Hazlit said as he worked. "He's close to six feet, and bad living is going to ensure middle age is a short interlude before the man's shoulders are stooped, his gut sagging, and his face lined. There."

Hazlit tore off the second drawing. "He bears a slight resemblance to your housekeeper around the eyes and perhaps in the texture and color of the hair."

"He does." The earl frowned. "He's older than Anna?"

"He is. He is not your portly man, though. He qualifies as well fed but not obese."

"Can you take this picture to the man who sold the lamp oil?" the earl suggested, picking up the second drawing. "And maybe get a description of the other fellow?"

"I can. I can also go back north and ask around regarding the portly man."

"That will take some time." The earl leaned against the arm of the sofa. "I hardly need tell you to spare no expense." He appeared lost in thought, and Hazlit waited. "Do you think Anna's grandmother is well enough to travel?"

"She hasn't been seen much off the estate since her husband died," Hazlit replied. "That does not suggest good health, but it might also mean she's a virtual prisoner."

The earl looked up sharply, and Hazlit had the sense his casual comment snapped something into place in the earl's mind.

"If we cannot establish Anna's brother is here in London," the earl said slowly, "then I want you to go north and figure out just where the hell he is. I believe he is the primary threat to Anna's welfare, and his leverage is that he holds her grandmother's welfare in his hands."

"And the fat man?" Hazlit rose. "We know he's in Town and that he's probably lying in wait for Mrs. Seaton."

"But waiting for what?" the earl mused. "For the brother to come to Town and have the legal right to reclaim his sisters, perhaps?"

"Good question," Hazlit agreed. "Let me take the sketches with me, and maybe by tomorrow, I can have some answers for you."

"My thanks," the earl said, showing his guest to the front door.

Westhaven sat in the library for long moments, sipping cold tea and staring at the first sketch. When Anna came in, he slid the drawing into a drawer then rose to meet her.

"You are up late," she observed, going into his arms. He kissed her cheek, and Anna squealed. "And your lips are cold."

"So warm them up," he teased, kissing her cheek again. "I've been swilling cold tea and whiskey and putting off having an argument with you."

"What are we going to argue about?" Anna asked, pulling back enough to regard him warily.

"Your safety," he said, tugging her by the wrist to the sofa. "I want to ask you, one more time, to let me help you, Anna. I have the sense if you don't let me assist you now, it might soon be too late."

"Why now?" she asked, searching his eyes.

"You have your character," he pointed out. "Val

told me you asked him for it, and he gave it to you, as well as one for Morgan."

"A character is of no use to me if it isn't in my possession."

"Anna," he chided, his thumb rubbing over her wrist, "you could have told me."

"That was not our arrangement. Why can you not simply accept I must solve my own problems? Why must you take this on, too?"

He looped his arm over her shoulders and pulled her against him. "Aren't you the one telling me I should lean on my family a little more? Let my brothers help with business matters? Set my mother and sisters some tasks?"

"Yes." She buried her nose against his shoulder. "But I am not the heir to the Duke of Moreland. I am a simple housekeeper, and my problems are my own."

"I've tried," he said, kissing her temple. "I've tried and tried and tried to win your trust, Anna, but I can't make you trust me."

"No," she said, "you cannot."

"You leave me no choice. I will take steps on my own tomorrow to safeguard you and your sister, as well."

She just nodded, leaving him to wonder what it was she didn't say. His other alternative was to wash his hands of her, and that he could not do. "Come up to bed with me?"

"Of course," she said and let him draw her to her feet.

He said nothing, not with words, not as they undressed each other, not as they settled into one another's arms on his big, soft bed. But when communications were offered by touch, by sigh and kiss and

caress, he told her loved her and would lay down his
life to keep her safe.

She told him she loved him, that she would always
treasure the memories she held of him, that she would
never love another.

And she told him good-bye.

~

The next day started out in a familiar pattern, with
the earl riding in the park with his brothers and
Anna joining Cook on the weekly marketing. The
women took two footmen as was their usual custom.
Unbeknownst to Anna, the earl had taken both men
aside and acquainted them with the need to serve as
bodyguards and not just porters.

When the earl and his brothers were safely away
from the mews, he wasted no time informing them of
recent developments.

"So as long as this Whit is content to bilk his
employers and draw out his surveillance contract," the
earl concluded, "we have some time, but it becomes
more imperative than ever that Anna not be left alone."

"Where is she now?" Dev asked, frowning at his
horse's neck.

"At market, with a footman on each arm, both
ordered not to let her out of their sight."

"Let's ride home by way of the market," Dev
suggested. "I have an odd feeling."

Val and the earl exchanged an ominous look.
Whether it was Dev's Irish granny, his own instincts,
or mere superstition, when Dev got a hunch, it was
folly to ignore it.

They trotted through the streets, the morning crowds thinned by the heat. The market was bustling, however, with all manner of produce and household sundries for sale as women, children, and the occasional man strolled from vendor to vendor.

"Split up," the earl directed, handing his reins to a boy and flipping the child a coin. "Walk him."

Val and Dev moved off through the crowd, even as the back of the earl's neck began to prickle. What if Fairly's guardian urchin was wrong, and Whit had gotten tired of watching in the heat? What if Anna had chosen today to slip out of his life? What if the fat man was a procurer, and Anna was already on her way to some foul crib on the Continent?

A disturbance in the crowd to his left had the earl pushing his way through the throng. In the center of a circle of gawking onlookers, Anna stood, her wrist in the grasp of a large, seriously overweight man. Westhaven took one step back then set his fingers to his lips to emit a shrill whistle.

"Come quietly, Anna," the fat man crooned. "I'll be good to you, and you won't have to live like a menial anymore. Now don't make me summon the beadle, my girl."

Anna merely stood there, resistance in every line of her posture.

"We can collect little Morgan," the man went on, happy with his plans, "and be back to York in a week's time. You'll enjoy seeing your granny again, won't you?"

The mention of Morgan's name brought a martial light into Anna's eye, and she looked up, fire in her gaze, until she saw Westhaven. She sent him a heart-rending look, one it took him an instant to decipher: *Protect my sister.*

"Morgan isn't with me," Anna said, her tone resolute. "You get me or nothing, Stull. And I'll come quietly if we leave this minute for York, otherwise…"

"Otherwise," Stull sneered, jerking her arm, "nothing. You are well and truly caught, Anna James, and we'll find your sister, too. Otherwise, indeed."

The earl stepped out of the crowd and twisted the fat man's hand off Anna's wrist. "Otherwise, bugger off, sir."

Stull rubbed his wrist, eyeing the earl truculently. "I don't know what she's told you, good fellow"—he tried for an avuncular tone—"or what she's promised you, but I will thank you to take your hands off my wife and leave us to return peaceably to our home in Yorkshire."

The earl snorted and wrapped an arm around Anna's shoulders. "You are no more her husband than I am the King. You have accosted a woman for no reason and treated her abominably. This woman is in my employ and under my protection. You will leave her in peace."

"Leave her in peace?!" Stull screeched. "Leave her in peace when I've traveled the length and breadth of this country seeking just to bring her home? And she's dragged her poor, addled sister with her, from one sorry scheme to another, when I have a betrothal contract signed and duly witnessed. It's no wonder I don't have her sued for breach of promise, b'gad."

The earl let him bellow on until Dev and Val

were in position on either side of the ranting Stull, a constable frowning at Val's elbow.

"Sir," the earl cut in, his voice cold enough to freeze the ears off of anybody with any sense. "You have produced no such contract, and you are not family to the lady. I do not deal with intermediaries, and I do not deal with arsonists." He nodded to Dev and Val, each of whom seized Stull by one beefy arm. "I want this man arrested for arson, Constable, and held without bond. The lady might also want to bring charges for assault, but we can sort that out when you have him in custody."

"Along with ye, then," the constable ordered Stull. "His lordship's word carries *weight* with me, and that puts you under arrest, sir. Come peaceable, and we won't have to apply the King's justice to your fat backside."

The crowd laughed as Dev and Val obligingly escorted their charge in the constable's wake. The earl was left with Anna in his arms and more questions than ever.

"Come." He led Anna to his horse and tossed her up, then climbed up behind her. He was on Dev's big young gelding, and the horse stood like a statue until Westhaven gave the command to walk on. Anna was silent and the earl himself in no mood to hold a difficult discussion on the back of a horse. He kept an arm around her waist while she leaned quietly against his chest until they were in the mews.

When the grooms led the horse away, Westhaven tugged Anna by the wrist across the alley and through the back gardens, pausing only when Morgan came into sight, a basket over her arm.

"Morgan!" Anna dropped the earl's hand and rushed to wrap her arms around her sister. "Oh, thank God you're safe."

Morgan shot a quizzical look over Anna's shoulder at the earl.

"We ran into Stull in the market," the earl explained, watching the sisters hugging each other. "He was of a mind to take his betrothed north without further ado. I was not of a mind to allow it."

"Thank God," Morgan said quietly but clearly. Anna stepped back and blinked.

"Morgan?" She eyed her sister closely. "Did you just say 'thank God?'"

"I did." Morgan met her sister's gaze. "I did."

"You can hear and speak," the earl observed, puzzled. "How long have you feigned deafness?"

"When you went out to Willow Bend, Anna." Morgan's eyes pleaded for understanding. "Lord Val took me to see Lord Fairly. He's a physician—a real physician, and he was able to help. I've not wanted to tell you, for fear it wouldn't last, but it's been days, and oh, the things I've heard... the wonderful, beautiful things I've heard."

"I am so happy for you." Anna pulled her close again. "So damned happy for you, Morgan. Talk to me, please, talk to me until my ears fall off."

"I love you," Morgan said. "I've wanted to say that—just that—for years. I love you, and you are the best sister a deaf girl ever had."

"I love you, too," Anna said, tears threatening, "and this is the best gift a deaf girl's sister ever had."

"Well, come along you two." The earl put a sister under each arm. "As pleasing as this development is, there is still a great deal of trouble brewing." As both sisters were in tears, it clearly fell to him to exercise some rational process, otherwise the lump in his own throat might have to be acknowledged.

He ushered them into his study, poured lemonade all around, and considered the situation as Anna and Morgan beamed at each other like idiots.

"Don't forget your sugar," Anna said, turning her smile on him. "Oh, Westhaven, my sister can hear! This makes it all worthwhile, you know? If Morgan and I hadn't fled York, she might never have seen this physician. And if you can hear and speak…"

"I cannot be so easily declared incompetent," Morgan finished, grinning.

"Unless…" Anna's smile dimmed, and she glanced hesitantly at the earl. "Unless Stull and Helmsley convince the authorities you were feigning your disability, and that would be truly peculiar."

The earl frowned mightily. "Rather than speculate on that matter, what can you tell me about this betrothal contract Stull ranted about. Is it real?"

"It is," Anna said, holding his gaze, her smile fading to a grimace. "It is very real. There are two contracts, in fact. One obligates me to marry him in exchange for sums he will pay to my brother; the other obligates Morgan to marry him in the event I do not, for the same consideration."

"So your brother has sold you to that hog." It made sense enough. "And you were unwilling to go join him in his wallow."

"Morgan was to have come with me," Anna added, "or I with her. Whichever sister he married, he agreed to provide a home for the other sister, as well. Even if I married him, I could not have kept Morgan safe from him."

"He is depraved, then?"

"I would not have rejected a suitor out of hand," Anna said, her chin coming up, "just for an unfortunate fondness for his victuals. Stull makes the beasts appear honorable, though."

"And you know this how?"

"Grandmother hired on a twelve-year-old scullery maid," Anna said wearily. "The girl was nigh torn asunder trying to bear Stull's bastard. The baby did not live, but the mother did—barely. She was not"—Anna glanced at Morgan—"mature for her years, and she had no family. Stull preyed on her then tossed her aside."

"Who is he? He comports himself like a man of consequence, at least in his own mind."

"Hedley Arbuthnot, eighth Baron Stull," Anna said. "My betrothed."

"Don't be so sure about that." The earl looked at her, frowning. "I want to see these contracts, as in the first place, I don't think a conditional betrothal is enforceable, and in the second, there is the question of duress." And a host of other legal questions, such as whether Helmsley had executed the contracts on behalf of his sisters, and if Morgan was a minor when he did. Or did he sign on behalf of Anna, who was not a minor, and thus bind himself rather than her?

And where in the tangle of questions did the matter of guardianship of the ladies' funds come into it?

The earl looked at Morgan. "You are going to let my brother escort you to the ducal mansion. Stull does not know where you are and does not know you have regained your ability to speak and hear. It is to our advantage to keep it that way."

"You"—the earl turned an implacable glare on Anna—"are going to go unpack your damned valise and meet me back here, and no running off. Your word, or I will alert the entire staff to your plans, and you will be watched from here to Jericho unless I am with you."

"You have my word," she said quietly, rising to go, but turning at the last to give Morgan one more hug.

She left a ringing silence behind her, in which the earl helped himself to the whiskey decanter, pouring a hefty tot into his lemonade.

"So what hasn't she told me?" The earl turned and met Morgan's gaze.

"I don't know what she has told you."

"Precious bloody little." The earl took a swallow of his cocktail. "That she was keeping confidences and could not allow me to assist her. Christ."

"She was. My grandmother made us both promise our situation would not become known outside the three of us. Anna and I have both kept our word in that regard, until now."

The earl ran a hand through his hair. "How could this come about? That Anna could be obligated to marry a loathsome excuse for a bore—or boar?"

"It was cleverly done." Morgan sighed and stood, crossing her arms as she regarded the back gardens through the French doors. "Helmsley sent Grandmother and me off to visit a friend of hers, then took Anna aside and told her if she didn't sign the damned contract, he'd have me declared incompetent.

In a similar fashion, he told me if I didn't sign the contract, then he'd put a pillow over Grandmother's face. Anna doesn't know about that part, and I don't think he'd do it..."

"But he could. What a rotter, this brother of yours. And lousy at cards, I take it?"

"Very. We were in hock up to our eyeballs two years ago."

"So he probably told your grandmother some Banbury tale, as well," the earl said, staring at his drink. "What do you think would make Anna happy now?"

"To be home," Morgan said. "To know Grandmother is safe, to see Grandpapa's gardens again, to know I am safe. To stop running and looking over her shoulder and pretending to be something we're not."

"And you, Morgan?" The earl shifted to stand beside her. "What do you want?"

"I want Anna to be happy," Morgan said, swallowing and blinking. "She was so... So pretty and happy and loving when Grandpapa was alive. And the past two years, she's been reduced to drudgery just so I would be safe. She deserves to be happy, to be free and safe and..." She was crying, unable to get out the rest of whatever she wanted to say. The earl put down his drink, fished in his pocket for his handkerchief, and pulled Morgan into his arms.

"She deserves all that," he agreed, patting her shoulder. "She'll have it, too, Morgan. I promise you she'll have what she wants."

When Val and Dev joined him in the library less than an hour later, Anna was still unpacking while Morgan was busy packing. The earl explained what he knew of the situation, pleased to hear the magistrate had agreed to delay Stull's bond hearing for another two days.

"That gives us time to get Morgan to Their Graces," the earl said, glancing at Val. "Unless you object?"

"It wouldn't be my place to object," Val said, his lips pursed, "but I happen to concur. Morgan can use some pampering, and Her Grace feels miserable for having set Hazlit on their trail. This will allow expiation of Her Grace's sins, and distract His Grace, as well."

"Creates a bit of a problem for you," Dev pointed out.

"How so?" Val frowned.

"How are you going to continue to convince our sire you are a mincing fop, when every time Morgan walks by, you practically trip over your tongue?"

"My tongue, Dev, not my cock. If you could comprehend the courage it takes to be deaf and mute in a society that thinks it is neither, you would be tripping at the sight of her, as well."

Dev spared a look at the earl, who kept his expression carefully neutral.

"You will both escort Morgan to Their Graces later this afternoon," Westhaven said. "For now, I'd like you to remain here, keeping an eye on Anna."

"You don't trust her?" Dev asked, censorship in his tone.

"She gave her word not to run, but I am not convinced Stull was the only threat to her. Her own brother got her involved in this scheme with Stull, and he's the one who benefits should Stull get his hands on Anna. Where is Helmsley, and what is his part in this?"

"Good question," Dev allowed. "Go call on Their Graces, then, and leave the ladies in our capable hands."

Val nodded. "His Grace will be flattered into a full recovery to think you'd entrust a damsel in distress to his household."

The earl nodded, knowing it was a good point. Still, he was sending Morgan to the duke and duchess because their home was safe, a near fortress, with servants who knew better than to allow strangers near the property or the family members. And it was nearby, which made getting Morgan there simple. Then, too, Anna saw the wisdom of it, making it one less issue he had to argue and bully her through.

He found Anna in her sitting room, sipping tea, the evil valise nowhere in sight.

"I'm off to Moreland House," the earl informed her, "to ask Their Graces to provide Morgan sanctuary. I will ask on your behalf, as well, if it's what you want."

"Do you want me to go with her?" Anna asked, her gaze searching his.

"I do not," he said. "It's one thing to ask my father and mother to keep Morgan safe, when Stull isn't even sure she's in London. It's another to ask them to keep you safe, when I am on hand to do so and have already engaged the enemy, so to speak."

"Stull isn't your enemy," Anna said, dropping her gaze. "If it hadn't been him, my brother would have found somebody else."

"I am not so convinced of that, Anna." The earl lowered himself into a rocking chair. "The society in York is provincial compared to what we have here in London. My guess is that there were likely few willing to collude with your brother in defrauding your grandfather's estate, shackling you and Morgan to men you found repugnant and impoverishing your sickly grandmother into the bargain."

"That is blunt speech," she said at length.

"I am angry, Anna." The earl rose again. "I fear diplomacy is beyond me."

"Are you angry with me?"

"Oh, I want to be," he assured her, his gaze raking her up and down. "I want to be furious, to turn you over my knee and paddle you until my hand hurts, to shake you and rant and treat the household to a tantrum worthy of His Grace."

"I am sorry." Anna's gaze dropped to the carpet.

"I am not angry with you," the earl said gravely, "but your brother and his crony will have much to answer for."

"You are disappointed in me."

"I am *concerned* for you," the earl said tiredly. "So concerned I am willing to seek the aid of His Grace, and to pull every string and call in every favor the old man can spare me. Just one thing, Anna?"

She met his gaze, looking as though she was prepared to hear the worst: Pack your things, get out of my sight, give me back those glowing characters.

"Be here when I get back," the earl said with deadly calm. "And expect to have a long talk with me when this is sorted out."

She nodded.

He waited to see if she had anything else to add, any arguments, conditions, or demurrals, but for once, his

Anna apparently had the sense not to fight him. He turned on his heel and left before she could second guess herself.

# *Sixteen*

"I HAVE COME TO SEEK ASSISTANCE," WESTHAVEN SAID, meeting his father's gaze squarely. The duke was enjoying his early afternoon tea on the back terrace of the mansion, and looking to his son like a man in a great good health.

"Seems to be the season for it," the duke groused. "Your dear mother will hardly let me chew my meat without assistance. You'd best have a seat, man, lest she catch me craning my neck to see you."

"She means well," the earl said, his father's response bringing a slight smile to his lips.

The duke rolled his eyes. "And how many times, Westhaven, has she attempted to placate your irritation with me, using that same phrase? Tea?"

"More than a few," the earl allowed. "She doesn't want to lose you, though, and so you must be patient with her. And yes, a spot of tea wouldn't go amiss."

"Patient!" the duke said with a snort. He poured his son a cup and added a helping of sugar. "That woman knows just how far she can push me, with her Percy this and dear heart that. But you didn't come here to listen to me resent your mother's best intentions. What sort of assistance do you need?"

"I'm not sure," Westhaven said, accepting the cup of tea, "but it involves a woman, or two women."

"Well, thank the lord for small favors." The duke smiled. "Say on, lad. It's never as bad as you think it is, and there are very few contretemps you could get into I haven't been in myself."

At his father's words, a constriction weighting Westhaven's chest lifted, leaving him able to breathe and strangely willing to enlist his father's support. He briefly outlined the situation with Anna and Morgan, and his desire to keep Morgan's whereabouts unknown.

"Of course she's welcome." The duke frowned. "Helmsley's granddaughter? I think he was married to that... oh, Bellefonte's sister or aunt or cousin. Your mother will know. Bring her over; the girls will flutter and carry on and have a grand time."

"She can't leave the property," Westhaven cautioned. "Unless it's to go out to Morelands in a closed carriage."

"I am not to leave Town until your quacks allow it," the duke reported. "There's to be no removing to the country just yet for these old bones, thank you very much."

"How are you feeling?" the earl asked, the question somehow different from all the other times he'd asked it.

"Mortality," the duke said, "is a daunting business, at first. You think it will be awful to die, to miss all the future holds for your loved ones, for your little parliamentary schemes. I see now, however, that there will come a time when death will be a relief, and it must have been so for your brother Victor. At some point, it isn't just death; it's peace."

Shocked at both the honesty and the depth of his father's response, Westhaven listened as he hadn't listened to his father in years.

"My strength is returning," the duke said, "and I will live to pester you yet a while longer, I hope, but when I was so weak and certain my days were over, I realized there are worse things than dying. Worse things than not securing the bloody succession, worse things than not getting the Lords to pass every damned bill I want to see enacted."

"What manner of worse things?"

"I could never have known your mother," the duke said simply. "I could linger as an invalid for years, as Victor did. I could have sent us all to the poor house and left you an even bigger mess to clean up. I guess"—the duke smiled slightly—"I am realizing what I have to be grateful for. Don't worry…" The smile became a grin. "This humble attitude won't last, and you needn't look like I've had a personal discussion with St. Peter. But when one is forbidden to do more than simply lie in bed, one gets to thinking."

"I suppose one does." The earl sat back, almost wishing his father had suffered a heart seizure earlier in life.

"Now, about your Mrs. Seaton," the duke went on. "You are right; the betrothal contracts are critical but so are the terms of the guardianship provisions in the old man's will. In the alternative, there could be a separate guardianship document, one that includes the trusteeship of the girl's money, and you have to get your hands on that, as well."

"Not likely," the earl pointed out. "It was probably drawn up in York and remains in Helmsley's hands."

"But he will have to bring at least the guardianship papers with him if he's to retrieve his sisters. You say they are both over the age of eighteen, but the trust document might give him control of their money until they marry, turn five and twenty, or even thirty."

"I can ask Anna about that, but I have to ask you about something else."

The duke waited, stirring his tea while Westhaven considered how to put his question. "Hazlit has pointed out I could protect Anna by simply marrying her. Would you and Her Grace receive her?"

In a display of tact that would have made the duchess proud and quite honestly impressed Westhaven, the duke leaned over and topped off both tea cups.

"I put this question to your mother," the duke admitted, "as my own judgment, according to my sons, is not necessarily to be trusted. I will tell you what Her Grace said, because I think it is the best answer: We trust you to choose wisely, and if Anna Seaton is your choice, we will be delighted to welcome her into the family. Your mother, after all, was not my father's choice and no more highly born than your Anna."

"So you would accept her."

"We would, but Gayle?"

His father had not referred to him by name since Bart's death, and Westhaven found he had to look away.

"You are a decent fellow," the duke went on,

"too decent, I sometimes think. I know, I know." He waved a hand. "I am all too willing to cut corners, to take a dodgy course, to use my consequence at any turn, but you are the opposite. You would not shirk a responsibility if God Almighty gave you leave to do so. I am telling you, in the absence of the Almighty's availability: Do not marry her out of pity or duty or a misguided sense you want a woman in debt to you before you marry her. Marry her because you can't see the rest of your life without her and you know she feels the same way."

"You are telling me to marry for love," Westhaven concluded, bemused and touched.

"I am, and you will please tell your mother I said so, for I am much in need of her good graces these days, and this will qualify as perhaps the only good advice I've ever given you."

"The only good advice?" Westhaven countered. "Wasn't it you who told me to let Dev pick out my horses for me? You who said Val shouldn't be allowed to join up to keep an eye on Bart? You who suggested the canal project?"

"Even a blind hog finds an acorn now and then," the duke quipped. "Or so my brother Tony reminds me."

"I will get my hands on those contracts." The earl rose. "And the guardianship and trust documents, as well, if you'll keep Morgan safe."

"Consider it done." The duke said, rising. "Look in on your mama before you go."

"I will," Westhaven said, stepping closer and hugging his father briefly. To his surprise, the duke hugged him right back.

"My regards to St. Just." The duke smiled winsomely. "Tell him not to be a stranger."

"He'll come over with Val this evening," Westhaven said, "but I will pass along your felicitations."

The duke watched his heir disappear into the house, not surprised when a few minutes later the duchess came out to join him.

"You should be napping," his wife chided. "Westhaven was behaving peculiarly."

"Oh?" The duke slipped an arm around his wife's waist. "How so?"

"He walked in, kissed my cheek, and said, 'His Grace has advised me to marry for love,' then left. Not like him at all." The duchess frowned. "Are you feeling well, Percy?"

"Keeps his word, that boy." The duke smiled. "I am feeling better, Esther, and we did a good job with Westhaven. Knows his duty, he does, and will make a fine duke."

Her Grace kissed his cheek. "More to the point, he makes a fine son, and he will make an even better papa."

❧

"From this point on," the earl said, "you are my guest, the granddaughter and sister of an earl, and every inch a lady."

"A lady would not be staying under your roof unchaperoned."

"Of course not, but your circumstances require allowances to be made. Morgan is safe at the mansion, and you will be safe with me."

Anna rose from the library sofa. "And what if you

cannot keep me safe? What if the betrothal contract is genuine? What if when I break that contract, the damned baron has the right to marry Morgan?"

"I can tell you straight out Morgan's contract is not valid," the earl replied. "She signed it herself, and as a minor, she cannot make binding contracts except for necessaries. Even if a spouse is considered a necessary, she can legally repudiate the contract upon her majority. The family solicitors are busily drafting just such a repudiation, though it would be helpful to see the contract she signed."

"You are absolutely sure of this?"

"I am absolutely sure of this," the earl rejoined. "I spend hours each day up to my elbows in the small print of all manner of contracts, Anna, and I read law at university, since that is one profession open to younger sons. Morgan cannot be forced to marry Stull."

"Thank you." Anna sat back down, the fight going out of her. "Thank you so much for that."

"You are welcome."

At least, Anna thought, he wasn't telling her he wanted to paddle her black and blue, and he wasn't tossing her out on her ear—not yet. But he'd learned what manner of woman she was, one who would sign a contract she didn't mean to fulfill; one who would flee familial duty; one who would lie, hide, and flee again to avoid security and respectability for both herself and her sister.

The earl took up the rocker opposite the sofa. "There is yet more we need to discuss."

Their talk, Anna recalled. He'd warned her they

would be having a lengthy discussion; there was no time like the present.

"I am listening."

"This is going to come out wrong," the earl sighed, "but I think it's time you gave up and married me."

"*Gave up and married you?*" Anna repeated in a choked whisper. This was one outcome she had not foreseen, and in its way, it was worse than any of the others. "Whatever do you mean?"

"If I marry you," the earl went on in reasonable tones, "then the worst Stull can do is sue for breach of promise. As he was willing to pay for the privilege of marrying you, I am not sure there are even damages for him to claim. It is the only way, however, to prevent him or some successor in your brother's schemes from marrying you in another trumped-up circumstance."

"And if he sues, it ensures you are embroiled in scandal."

"The Windham family is of sufficient consequence Stull's paltry accusations won't be but a nine days' wonder. Marry me, Anna, and your troubles will be over."

Anna chewed her fingernail and regarded the man rocking so contentedly opposite her. Marry him, and her troubles would be over...

Marry him, she thought bitterly, and her troubles would just be starting. He'd never said he loved her, never asked for her brother and his nasty friend to descend like this. She wasn't raised to be a duchess, and polite society would never let him forget he'd married, quite, quite down.

"I am flattered," Anna said, staring at her hands

in her lap, "but can we not wait to see how matters resolve themselves?"

"You are turning me down," Westhaven said. "Stubborn, stubborn, stubborn." He rose and smiled down at her. "But then, if you weren't so stubborn, you'd be married to Stull by now, and that isn't an eventuality to be considered even in theory. I've put you in the largest guest room, and you are dead on your feet. Let me light you up to your bed, Anna."

She hadn't realized he'd had her things moved, and so accepted his arm in a daze. She was tired—bone weary and emotionally wrung out. The day had been too eventful, bringing with it both joy, relief, and loss.

"You are my guest," the earl said when he'd lit the candles in her bedroom. "I will wish you sweet dreams and promise you again to see this entire matter sorted out. You will consider my proposal and perhaps have an answer for me in the morning."

He bowed—*bowed!*—and withdrew, leaving Anna to sit on the bed, staring unseeing at the hearth.

Since he'd learned she was betrothed to another, the earl had not touched her, not as a lover. He'd offered his arm, his hospitality, and his name in marriage, but he had not been able to touch her as a lover.

It spoke volumes, Anna thought as she drifted off. He was a dutiful man and he needed an heir and he was sexually attracted enough to her, despite her deceit, that he could get a child or two on her. She owed him more than that, though, and so her last thoughts as she found sleep were of how she could spare him the very thing he dreaded most: A wife chosen out of duty.

❧

Several doors down the hall, the earl lay naked on his bed, cursing his solitude, his houseguest, and his own lack of charm. *Give up and marry me?* What manner of proposal was that? He was tempted to get up, stomp down the hall, and drag her back to his bed, but desire on his part was not the same thing as capitulation on hers.

"Well, Papa," he muttered into the night, "I cannot see the rest of my life without her, but alas, I am certain the sentiment is not reciprocated."

A soft knock on his door had his heart leaping in hopes Anna was seeking him out. He tossed on his dressing gown and opened the door to find Dev standing there, smiling slightly.

"Saw the light under your door and thought you might want to know Stull is again at liberty."

"I thought we had at least a few days to catch our breath."

"The magistrate had to leave Town and moved up his hearings," Dev reported. "Somebody came along and made bail for the dear baron."

"Come in." The earl stepped back and busied himself lighting a few more candles. "Do we know who might have bailed him out?"

"One Riley Whitford," Dev said. "Better known as old Whit, late of Seven Dials and any other stew or slum where vice runs tame."

"You know the man?" the earl asked, settling on the sofa in his sitting room.

"He was involved in a race-fixing scheme just about the time I left for the Peninsula." Dev ambled into the room as he spoke. "Clever man, always knows how to put somebody between him and the consequences of his actions."

"He was the one managing the surveillance of my house." The earl scowled. "Stop pacing, if you please, and sit quietly like the gentleman Her Grace believes you to be."

"How she can be so deluded?" Dev rolled his eyes, looking very much like a dark version of His Grace. But he sat in a wing chair and angled it to face his brother. "What will you do with Anna?"

"I've proposed and proposed and proposed." The earl sighed, surprising himself and apparently his brother with his candor. "She'll have none of that, though the last time, she put me off rather than turn me down flat."

"Things are a little unsettled," Dev pointed out dryly.

"And marriage would settle them," the earl shot back. "Married to me, there wouldn't be any more nonsense from her brother, not for her or Morgan. Her grandmother would be safe, and Stull would be nothing but a bad, greasy memory."

"He is enough to give any female the shudders, though maybe Anna has the right of it."

"What can you possibly mean?" The earl stood up and paced to the French doors.

"You and she are in unusual circumstances," Dev began. "You are protective of her and probably not thinking very clearly about her. She is not a duke's daughter, as you might be expected to marry, not even a marquis's sister. She's beneath you socially and likely undowered and not even as young as a proper mate to you should be."

"Young?" the earl expostulated. "You mean I can get her to drop only five foals instead of ten?"

"You have a duty to the succession," Dev said, his words having more impact for being quietly spoken. "Anna understands this."

"Rot the fucking succession," Westhaven retorted. "I have His Grace's permission to marry for love, indeed, his exhortation to marry only for love."

"Are you saying you love her?" Dev asked, his voice still quiet.

"*Of course I love her*," the earl all but roared. "Why else would I be taking such pains for her safety? Why else would I be offering her marriage more times than I can count? Why else would I have gone to His Grace for help? Why else would I be arguing with you at an hour when most people are either asleep or enjoying other bedtime activities?"

Dev rose and offered his brother a look of sympathy. "If you love her, then your course is very easy to establish."

"Oh it is, is it?" The earl glared at his brother.

"If you love her," Dev said, "you give her what she wants of you, no matter how difficult or irrational it may seem to you. You do not behave as His Grace has, thinking that love entitles him to know better than his grown children what will make them happy or what will be in their best interests."

Westhaven sat down abruptly, the wind gone from his sails between one heartbeat and the next.

"You are implying I could bully her."

"You know you could, Gayle. She is grateful to you, lonely, not a little enamored of you, and without support."

"You are a mean man, Devlin St. Just." The earl sighed. "Cruel, in fact."

"I would not see you make a match you or Anna regret. And you deserve the truth."

"That's what Anna has said. You give me much to think about, and none of it very cheering."

"Well, think of it this way." Dev smiled as he turned for the door. "If you marry her now, you can regret it at great leisure. If you don't marry her now, then you can regret that as long as you can stand it then marry her later."

"Point taken. Good night, St. Just. You will ride in the morning?"

"Wouldn't miss it." Dev smiled and withdrew, leaving his brother frowning at the door.

Dev was right, damn him to hell and back. In Westhaven's shoes, His Grace would have married Anna, worn her down, argued, seduced, and argued some more until the woman bowed to his wishes. It was tempting to do just that—to swive Anna silly, maybe even get her pregnant, lavish her with care and attention, and send Stull packing.

But her brother had tried to take her choices from her, and His Grace had made many efforts to take the earl's choices from him. It was not a respectful way to treat a loved one.

So… He'd solve her problems, provide her sanctuary, and let her go, if that was what she wanted.

But he'd resent like hell that honor—honor and love—required it of him.

❧

"I trust you slept well?" the earl inquired politely over breakfast.

"I did." Anna lied with equal good manners. "And you?"

"I did not," the earl said, patting his lips with his napkin. "Though riding this morning has put me more to rights. I regret you will not be able to leave the house today."

"I won't?" Anna blinked at him over her teacup. He was very much the earl this morning, no trace of humor or affection in his eyes or his voice.

"Stull has made bail," Westhaven explained. "I do not put it past him to make another attempt to abduct you."

"I see." Anna put down her tea cup, her toast and jam threatening to make an untimely reappearance.

The earl laid a hand on her arm, and she closed her eyes, savoring the comfort of that simple touch. "You are safe here, and he can't force you to do anything, in any case. You won't go beyond the back gardens, though, will you?"

"I will not," Anna said. "But what happens next? I can't simply wait here in this house until he gives up. He won't—not ever. It's been two years, and he's spent considerable coin tracking me down."

"I've had him arrested on charges of arson," the earl reminded her. "He is likely not permitted to leave London itself, or he will violate the terms of his bond, baron or no baron. You can have him arrested for assault, though if he does have a betrothal contract, that likely won't fly very far."

"He has one," Anna rejoined. "I was trying to recall

its particulars last night as I fell asleep, but it was more than two years ago that I signed it, and my brother did not want me to read the document itself."

"I cannot wait to meet this brother of yours. My sisters and my mother know better than to sign anything—anything—without reading each word."

"You are a good brother. And they are good sisters."

The earl looked up from buttering his toast. "You would have been a good sister to Morgan by allowing Stull to marry her?"

"No"—Anna shook her head—"but I am hardly a good sister to Helmsley for having refused to marry the man myself."

The earl put down his toast and knife. "You had two choices, as I see it, Anna: You could have married Stull, in which case he was essentially free to take his pleasure of you or Morgan, or to use Morgan to control you. In the alternative, you could have married Stull and left Morgan in your brother's care, in which case he'd just be auctioning her off behind Stull's back. Those options are unthinkable."

He went back to buttering his toast, his voice cool and controlled. "You created a third option, and it was the best you could do under the circumstances."

"It was," Anna said, grateful for his summary. But then, why did he still appear so remote?

"Until you met me," the earl went on. "You had a fourth option, then."

"I could have broken my word to my grandmother." Anna rose. "And taken a chance you would not laugh at me and return me to Stull's loving embrace, errant, contractually bound fiancées not something your average earl is willing to champion at the drop of a hat."

He remained sitting. "I deserve better than that."

"Yes," she said, near tears, "you most assuredly do, and if we marry…"

She whirled and left the room, her sentence unfinished and her host unable to extrapolate her meaning. If they married… what?

"I see we're starting our day in a fine temper." Dev sauntered in.

"Shut up." The earl passed him the teapot. "And do not attempt any more advice so early in the day, Dev. I do not like to see Anna upset."

"Neither do I." St. Just poured himself a cup of tea and frowned at the earl. "I don't like to see you upset either. What is the plan for the day?"

"I have to meet with Tolliver, of course, and I asked Hazlit to stop by, as well. I've sent for a dressmaker to see to Anna, and expect that will keep us out of each other's way for the day. What of you?"

"I am going to visit with some old army friends," Dev said, getting to work on a mountain of scrambled eggs. "I should be back by midday and will make it a point to join Anna for lunch."

"My thanks." The earl rose, feeling none too pleased with the day before him. "Tell her…"

Dev shook his head. "Tell her yourself."

❧

The morning was interminable, with no Anna tapping softly at the door with a little lemonade or marzipan for him, no water for his bouquets, no anything but work and more work. He sent Tolliver off well before luncheon but was pleased to find Benjamin Hazlit had chosen that hour to call.

"Join me for luncheon," the earl suggested. "My kitchen is not fancy, particularly in this heat, but we know how to keep starvation at bay."

"I will accept that generous offer," Hazlit said. "My breakfast was ages ago and not very substantial." The earl rang for luncheon on a tray, sending up a small prayer of thanks he'd have a valid excuse for not joining Anna and Dev on the back terrace. When lunch came, it showed that Anna was not behaving herself exclusively as a guest: There was a single daisy in a bud vase on each tray, and the marzipan was wrapped in linen, a little bouquet of violets serving as the bow.

"Your kitchen isn't fancy," Hazlit remarked, "but somebody dotes on their earl."

"Or on their lunch trays," the earl said. He quickly brought Hazlit up to date regarding Baron Stull's allegations of a betrothal, and the need to secret Morgan with Their Graces.

"Good move," Hazlit said. "Divide and conquer, so to speak. When I got your note, I did some poking around regarding Stull."

"Oh?" The earl paused in the demolition of his chicken sandwich.

"He's a bad actor," Hazlit said. "Been making a nuisance of himself in the lower-class brothels, trying to procure young girls, and using thugs to spy on your house."

*My poor Anna.*

Hazlit went on to advise the earl Stull had been identified as the purchaser of a large quantity of lamp oil, "right down to the grease stains on his cravat." The tallish gentleman with him, however, had remained in the shadows. Hazlit further suggested there would be another attempt to kidnap Anna.

"Why won't the baron just take his lumps and go home?"

Hazlit's gaze turned thoughtful. "So far, the evidence for arson is all circumstantial. The charges won't stick. He has a betrothal contract he thinks is valid, and he has Helmsley over a barrel, so to speak, financially. He wants Anna, and he wants her badly. You haven't described him as a man who is bright enough to cut his losses and find some silly cow who will bear him children and indulge his peccadilloes."

"And she would have to be a cow," the earl muttered, grimacing. "I hate just sitting here, waiting for those idiots to make the next move."

"And they hate just sitting there"—Hazlit reached for a piece of marzipan—"doing nothing. You should probably prepare yourself for some kind of legal maneuvering."

"What kind of maneuvering?"

"Charges of kidnapping or alienation of affections, breach of promise against Anna, demands of marriage from Helmsley."

"Demands that I marry her?" The earl scowled thunderously. "In God's name why?"

"If Helmsley sees you are a fatter pigeon than Stull, he'll rattle that sword."

"Christ." The earl got up and paced to the window.

Anna and Dev were on the terrace, and she was smiling at something he'd said. Dev's smile was flirtatious and a little wistful—charmingly so, damn the scoundrel.

"We can hope it's a moot question," Hazlit said, rising to his feet. "If Stull attempts to remove her from your property, then you bring the kidnapping charges, and that will be the end of it. Unless she's married to the man, she can testify against him in any court in the land."

"What was the extent of the old earl's estate?" the earl asked, staring out the windows. Hazlit named a figure, a very large and impressive figure.

The earl continued to watch as Dev and Anna laughed their way through lunch. "If Helmsley has gambled that away, then he is guilty of misfeasance?"

"He most assuredly is," Hazlit replied, coming to stand where he, too, could look out at the back terrace.

"So I need to prove Helmsley guilty of misfeasance," the earl said, "and foil the baron's attempts at kidnapping, and then Anna should be safe but penniless."

"Not penniless. There is a trust fund that simply cannot be raided, not by God Almighty or the archangel Gabriel, as it is set aside for Anna's exclusive use. Her grandmother has seen to it the money was wisely invested."

"That is some good news." The earl turned finally, as Dev was escorting Anna back into the house. "Do you know how much she has left?" Hazlit named another figure, one that would keep even a genteel lady comfortably for a very long time.

The earl turned, watching as Hazlit gathered up his effects. "If nothing else, I appreciate my family more, my siblings and my parents, for this glimpse into Anna's circumstances."

"You are a fortunate man," Hazlit said. "In your family, in any case. I'm off to loiter away the afternoon at the Pig. I'll report when something warrants your attention."

"I will await your communication," the earl said, seeing his guest to the door. "But patience is not my greatest strength."

The earl had no sooner returned to the library than Dev appeared, Anna in tow.

"So who was that?" Dev asked.

"Who was who?"

"That handsome devil who eyed us out the window, the one who stood right beside you," Dev shot back.

"Benjamin Hazlit. Our private investigator." The earl turned his gaze to Anna. "He thinks you should marry me."

"Let him marry you. I think I should join a convent."

"Now that," Dev said, "would be an inexcusable waste."

"I quite agree." The earl smiled thinly. "Hazlit says we wait now and expect either the baron to try to abduct you again or your brother to bring kidnapping charges."

Anna sat down in a heap. "As a man cannot kidnap his wife, we have another brilliant reason to marry me to you."

"Sound reasoning," the earl said. "I gather you are not impressed."

"I am not impressed." Anna rose abruptly. "And

what do you mean, Westhaven, by summoning a dressmaker here?"

"I meant you to have some dresses," the earl said. "Dresses that are not gray or brown or brownish gray or grayish brown. I meant for you to enjoy, at least, the fashions available to you here in London and to spend some time in a pursuit common to ladies of good breeding. I meant to offer you diversion. What did you think I meant?"

"Oh." Anna sat back down.

"I believe I will check on my horses and maybe take one out for a hack," Dev said and headed for the door.

"In this heat?" the earl asked, incredulous. Dev was nothing if not solicitous of his horses.

"A very short hack," Dev conceded over his shoulder, leaving Anna and the earl alone in the library.

~

*Why are you ignoring me?* Anna silently wailed. But she knew why: Westhaven was treating her as a guest, and not as a guest with whom he was in love.

In all her dealings with him, Anna realized, she had worried for him. Worried he would suffer disappointment in her, worried his consequence would suffer for associating with her, worried she wasn't at all what he needed in a duchess. In hindsight, she saw she should have saved a little worry for herself—worry that her heart would break and she would be left to pick up the pieces without any clue as to how to go about it.

Westhaven was frowning at her. "Anna, are you perhaps in need of a nap?"

"Like a cranky child? Yes, I suppose I am. Are you?"

He smiled at that, a slow, wicked, tempting grin that heartened Anna immeasurably.

*I missed you last night*, but she didn't say it. Couldn't say it, with his frown replacing that grin.

"Did you know," the earl said, "you're a wealthy woman?"

"I am *what*?" Anna shot back to her feet. "Your jest is in poor taste, Westhaven."

"You *are* tired." The earl shifted to sit in his rocker. "Sit down, Anna, and let us discuss your situation."

"My situation?" Anna sat as bid, not liking the serious light in his eye.

"You are wealthy," the earl repeated. He described her trust fund and her grandmother's stewardship of it. "You can do any damned thing you please, Anna James, and in terms of your finances, you needn't marry anybody."

"But why wasn't I allowed to use my own money?" Anna wailed. "For two years, I've not had more than pin money to spare, and you tell me there are thousands of pounds with my name on them?"

"There are, just waiting for you to claim them."

"Why wouldn't my grandmother have told me of this?"

"She might not have known at the time of your departure exactly what funds were available for what purpose," the earl suggested gently. "She was unwell when you came south, and solicitors can be notoriously closemouthed. Or she might not have wanted to risk Helmsley getting wind if she tried to communicate with you. You must ask her."

"I knew we had dowries," Anna said, shaking her head. "Of course my brother would not tell me I had my own money. Damn him."

"Yes," Westhaven agreed, pulling her to her feet. "Damn him to the coldest circle of hell, and Baron Lardbucket with him. You still look like you need a nap."

"I do need a nap," Anna sighed and looked down at his hand linked with hers. There was something she needed much more than a nap, but the earl was apparently not of like mind. Well, damn him, too.

"I'll leave you, then," Anna said, chin up, tears threatening.

"You will see me at dinner," the earl warned her. "And Dev and Val, as well."

She nodded, and he let her go.

Now what in blazes, the earl wondered, could make a sane woman cry upon learning she was financially very well off indeed?

For his part, the knowledge was more than justification for tears. When Anna thought herself penniless and facing lawsuits, she hadn't accepted his offer of marriage. How much more hopeless would his situation be when she had the coin to manage without him entirely?

❧

Anna presented herself freshly scrubbed for dinner, but she'd slept most of the afternoon away first. She had not joined all three brothers for a meal previously and found them to be formidably charming, the earl less overtly so than Val and Dev.

"So what will you do with your wealth?" Dev asked. "The only suitable answer is: Buy a horse."

"She could buy your stud farm," Val remarked, "and then some."

"I will look after my grandmother and my sister," Anna said. "Nothing else much matters, but I would like to live somewhere we can grow some flowers."

"Will you move back north?" Val asked, his smile faltering.

"I don't know. All of my grandmother's friends are there; my best memories are there."

"But some difficult memories, too," the earl suggested, topping up her wine glass.

"Some very difficult memories. I've always thought it made more sense to grow flowers in a more hospitable climate, but the need for them is perhaps greater in the North."

"Will you grow them commercially?" Dev asked.

"I simply don't know," Anna said, her gaze meeting the earl's. "Until things are resolved, and until I have a chance to sort matters through with Grandmama and Morgan, there is little point in speculating. Shall I leave you gentleman to your port and cigars?"

"I never learned the habit of smoking," the earl said, his brothers concurring. "Would you perhaps rather join us in a nightcap, Anna?"

"Thank you, no." Anna stood, bringing all three men to their feet. "While your company is lovely, my eyes are heavy."

"I'll light you up," the earl offered, crooking his arm at her. Anna accepted it, taking guilty pleasure in even that small touch. When they were safely out of earshot, the earl paused and frowned at her. "You aren't coming down with something, are you?"

"I am just tired."

"You have every right to be." He patted her hand, and Anna wanted to scream. She held her tongue though, until they'd gained her bedroom.

"Is this how it's to be, Westhaven?" She crossed her arms and regarded him as he lit her candles.

"I beg your pardon?" He went on, carefully lighting a candelabra on her mantle.

"I am suddenly a sister to you?" Anna began to pace. "Or a stranger? A houseguest to whom you are merely polite?"

"You are not a sister to me." The earl turned to face her, the planes of his face harsh in the muted light. "But you are under my protection, Anna, as a guest. You are also a woman who has repeatedly told me my honorable intentions are not welcome. I will not offer you dishonorable intentions."

"Why not?" she shot back, wishing her dignity was equal to the task of keeping her mouth shut. "You certainly were willing to before."

"I was courting you," he said, "and there were lapses, I admit. But our circumstances are not the same now."

"Because my grandfather was an earl?"

"It makes a difference, Anna." Westhaven eyed her levelly. "Or it should. More to the point, you are likely to be the victim of another attempted kidnapping in the near future, and your brother is guilty of misfeasance, at the very least."

"You can't prove that," Anna said. But more than

fatigue, what she felt was the weight of the earl's withdrawal.

He walked over to her, hesitated then reached up to brush a lock of hair back behind her ear. "You are tired, your life is in turmoil, and while I could importune you now, it would hardly be gentlemanly. I have trespassed against you badly enough as it is and would not compound my errors now."

"And would it be ungentlemanly," Anna said, turning her back to him, "to simply hold me?"

He walked around to the front of her, his eyes unreadable.

"Get into your nightclothes," he said. "I'm going to fetch you some chamomile tea, and then we'll get you settled."

Anna just stood in the middle of her room for long minutes after he'd left, her heart breaking with the certain knowledge she was being *humored* by a man who no longer desired her. She desired him, to be sure, but desire and willingness to destroy a good man's future were two different things.

Still, it hurt terribly that while she missed him, missed him with a throbbing, bodily ache, he was not similarly afflicted. She had disappointed him then refused his very gentlemanly offers and now he was done with her, all but the wrapping up and slaying her dragons part.

"You are ready for bed," the earl said, carrying a tray with him when he rejoined her. "Your hair is still up. Shall I braid it for you?"

She let him, let him soothe her with his kindness and his familiar touch and his beautiful, mellow baritone describing his conversation with his father and the various details of his day. He lay down beside her on the bed, rubbing her back as she lay on her side. She drifted off to sleep, the feel of his hand on her back and his breath on her neck reassuring her in ways she could not name.

When she woke the next morning, it was later than she'd ever slept before, and there was no trace of the earl's late-night visit.

Anna slept a great deal in the days that followed. Her appetite was off, and she cried easily, something that put three grown men on particularly good behavior. She cried at Val's music, at notes Morgan sent her, at the way the odd-colored cat would sit in the window of the music room and listen to Beethoven. She cried when her flower arrangements wouldn't work out, and she cried when Westhaven held her at night.

She cried so much Westhaven remarked upon it to his father.

"Probably breeding." The duke shrugged. "If she wasn't one to cry before but she's crying buckets now, best beware. Does she toss up her accounts?"

"She doesn't," the earl said, "but she doesn't eat much, at least not at meals."

"Is she sore to the touch?" The duke waved a hand at his chest. "Using the chamber pot every five minutes?"

"I wouldn't know." The earl felt himself blushing, but he could easily find out.

"Your dear mother was a crier. Not a particularly sentimental woman, for all her softheartedness, but I knew we were in anticipation of another happy event when she took to napping and crying."

"I see." The earl smiled. There were depths to his parents' intimacy he'd not yet glimpsed, he realized. Sweet depths, rich in caring and humor.

"Mayhap you do." The duke's answering smile faded. "And your mother was most affectionate when breeding, as well, not that she isn't always, but she was particularly in need of cuddling and cosseting, much to my delight. If this woman is carrying your child, Westhaven, it puts matters in a different light."

"It does."

"I'm not proud to have sired two bastards"—the duke frowned—"though in my day, these things were considered part of the ordinary course. Times aren't so tolerant now."

"They aren't," Westhaven agreed, sitting down as the weight of possible fatherhood began to sink in. "I would not wish bastardy on any child of mine."

"Good of you." The duke smiled thinly. "The child's mother is the one you'll have to convince. Best not fret about it now, though. Things sometimes work themselves out despite our efforts."

The earl barely heard him, so taken was he with the idea of creating a child with Anna. It felt *right*: in his bones it felt right and good. She would be a wonderful mother, and she would make him an at least tolerable father.

Papa.

The word took on rich significance, and the earl turned to regard his own sire.

"Weren't you ever afraid?" he asked. "Ten children, three different women, and you a duke?"

"I wasn't much of a duke." The old man snorted. "Not at first. But children have a way of putting a fellow on the right path rather sooner than he'd find it himself. Children and their mothers. But to answer your question, I was fairly oblivious, at first, but then Devlin was born, and Maggie, and I began to sense my own childhood was coming to a close. I was not sanguine at this prospect, Westhaven. Many of our class regard perpetual childhood as our God-given right. Fortunately, I met your mother, and she showed me just how much I had to be fearful of."

"But you kept having children. Fatherhood couldn't have been all that daunting if you embraced it so frequently."

"Silly boy." The duke beamed. "It was your mother I was embracing. Still do, though it probably horrifies you to hear of it."

"No." Westhaven smiled. "It rather doesn't."

The duke's smile faded. "More to the point, you don't have a choice with children, Westhaven. You bring them into this world, and you are honor bound to do the best you can. If you are fortunate, they have another parent on hand to help out when you are inclined to be an ass, but if not, you muddle on anyway. Look at Gwen Hollister—or Allen, I suppose. She muddled on, and Rose is a wonderful child."

"She is. Very. You might consider telling her mother that sometime."

He shifted the conversation, to regale his father with an account of his time spent with Rose. It seemed like ages ago that His Grace had come thundering into the sick room at Welbourne, but listening to his father recount more stories of Victor and his brothers, Westhaven had the strong sense the duke was healing from more than just his heart seizure.

Westhaven took his leave of his father, so lost in thought he had little recollection of his journey home. Pericles knew the way, of course, but ambling along in the heat, the earl was preoccupied with the prospect of fatherhood. When he gained his library, he sat down with a calendar and began counting days.

He'd retrieved Nanny Fran from the duke's household, and he wasn't above putting the old woman up to some discreet monitoring of Anna's health. By his calculations, he had not been intimate with Anna when she should have been fertile, but women were mysterious, and he'd taken no precautions to prevent conception.

It hit him like a freight wagon that in that single act, he'd probably taken away as many of Anna's options as her brother and Stull combined, and he'd never once considered behaving any differently. He sat alone in his library for a long time, thinking about Anna and what it meant to love her were she carrying his child.

❧

At the same time, Anna was sitting on the little bed in the room she'd used when she held the title housekeeper, thinking what an odd loss it was to not be even that anymore to the earl. She had found it heartening that she could earn her own keep. Looking after the earl and his brothers had been particularly pleasurable, as they took well to being tended to.

She, however, did not take well to being tended to. Not lately. For the past several nights, the earl had served as her lady's maid, taking down her hair, bringing her a cup of tea, and spending the end of the day in quiet conversation with her. All the while, even on those nights when he rubbed her back and cuddled her close on the bed, she felt him withdrawing to a greater and greater emotional distance.

He wasn't physically skittish with her, but rather very careful. Anna wanted to think he was almost cherishing, but there was no evidence of desire in his touch. And she bundled into him closely enough the evidence would have been impossible to hide. She clung to him for those times when he offered her comfort but felt all too keenly the comfort he was no longer interested in offering, as well.

She was losing him, which proved to her once and for all that her decision to leave—her many, many decisions to leave—were the better course for them both.

Better, perhaps, but by no means easier.

❧

"I am being followed," Helmsley said, taking a long swallow of ale. Ale, for God's sake, the peasant drink.

"You are a well-dressed gentleman on the streets when few are about," Stull said. "No doubt you attract attention, as I do myself. I want to know why you're back in dear old London town, where you don't fit in and you do depend on my coin."

Helmsley rolled his eyes. "Because I am being followed. Big, dark chap, rough-looking, like a drover returning north without his flock."

"And what would a drover be doing staying at the better inns, when they have their own establishments for that purpose?" Stull replied, draining his own tankard.

"You take my point." Helmsley nodded, glad he didn't have to explain everything. "I thought you should know."

"You thought I should know." Stull frowned. "But you've been gone nigh a week, which means you probably made it halfway to York before turning about and deciding to tell me."

Helmsley studied his ale. "I had a delay on the way out of Town. Horse tossed a shoe, then it was too late to travel. He came up lame the next day, and rather than buy another horse, I had to wait for him to come right."

"And you waited for how long before realizing you had company?"

"A few days," the earl improvised. "I was traveling slowly to spare the horse."

"Of course you were." Stull scowled. "You're up to something, Helmsley, and you'd best not be up to crossing me."

"I am up to nothing." Helmsley sighed dramatically. "Except imposing further on your hospitality. Now, why haven't we collected my sisters yet?"

Stull banged his empty tankard in a demand for more ale and launched into a convoluted tale of arrests, accusations, and indignities. From his ramblings, the earl concluded Stull had yet to locate Morgan but tried at least once to abduct Anna almost literally from the Earl of Westhaven's arms.

"So where does this leave us?" Helmsley asked.

He had been followed, but he'd also been struck with an idea: Dead, Anna was worth more to him than alive. The difficulty was, she had to die—or at least appear to die—before she wed Stull, or all her lovely money would fall into the hands of the baron. The thought that the baron might procure a special license and start his connubial bliss with Anna before Helmsley even saw her again had sent Helmsley right back down the road.

Of course, he should offer Anna the option of faking her own death and disappearing with a tidy sum, but working in concert with Stull for the past two years had left a bad taste in Helmsley's mouth. Partners in crime were tedious and a liability.

Once Anna had been dealt with, Morgan could be used to appease Stull. It would then be easy to arrange an accident for Stull—ingested poison seemed the appropriate remedy—and then as Stull's widow, Morgan would inherit a goodly portion of the baron's wealth, as well.

A tidy, altogether pleasing plan, Helmsley congratulated himself, but one that would require his presence in London, where the gaming was better, criminals for hire abounded, and Stull could be closely monitored.

"So how do you propose we retrieve dear Anna?" Helmsley asked. "I gather snatching her from the market did not go as planned."

"Hah," Stull snorted then paused for a moment to leer at the young serving maid. "That damned Westhaven got to throwing his weight around and had me arrested for arson. The charges will be dropped, of course, and it gives me the perfect excuse to malinger in Town. The plan remains simply to snatch the girl. She's helpless when it comes to her flowers, and I have it on good authority she's out in the back gardens several times a day. We'll just seize our moment and seize your sister."

"Simple as that?"

"Simple as that." The baron nodded. "Trying to nab her in the market, I admit, was poorly thought out. Too many people around. This time, however, I'm prepared."

"What does that mean?" Helmsley made his tone casual.

"If that damned earl makes a ruckus"—Stull wiped his lips on his handkerchief—"I'll wave the betrothal contract at him. And for good measure, I'll wave your guardianship papers, as well."

"Hadn't thought of that," Helmsley said slowly, though of course he had. "Why not simply send a solicitor 'round to the earl with the documents? If he's a gentleman, as you say, he should send Anna along smartly, and Morgan with her, assuming she's nearby?"

"You don't understand your peers, Helmsley." Stull leaned forward. "I'll wave that document around, but I'm not turning the earl's solicitors loose on it. The Quality don't engage in trade, and anything that smacks of business befuddles 'em to the point where they must bring in the lawyers. That will take weeks, at least, and I am damned tired of waiting for my bride."

"I'm sure you are," Helmsley said, as he was damned tired of waiting for Stull to pay off his debts. He also silently allowed as how any solicitor of suitable talent to serve a future duke would likely find holes the size of bull elephants in the contracts. "Your plan sounds worthy to me, so what are we waiting for?"

The baron smiled, an ugly grimace of an expression. "We are waiting for Anna to go pick her bedamned flowers."

# Seventeen

"Why the frown?" Val asked, helping himself to the lemonade provided for the earl and Mr. Tolliver each morning.

"Note from Hazlit." The earl handed the missive to his brother, Tolliver having been excused for the day. "He began the journey north to track down Helmsley, and lo, the fellow was not more than a day's ride from Town, supposedly waiting for his horse to come sound. He rode right back into Town and connected with Stull at the Pig."

"So you have your miscreants reunited." Val scanned the note. "I wonder what the foray north was about in the first place?"

"Who knows?" The earl sipped at his drink. "They don't strike me as a particularly cunning pair."

"Maybe not cunning," Val conceded, "but ruthless. They were going to torch an entire property, for reasons we still don't know. That's a hanging offense, Westhaven, and so far, they've gotten away with it."

"The charges are pending, and I suspect if we catch

one of them, the other will be implicated in very short order."

Val sat on the arm of the sofa. "Stull hasn't implicated Helmsley yet."

"The arson charges are not likely to stick," the earl said, "though they do create leverage."

"Or unpredictability," Val suggested.

"Possibly." The earl noted that Val was being contrary, which wasn't like him. "How is Miss Morgan?"

"Thriving," Val said glumly. "She's blooming, Westhaven. When I call upon her, she is giggling, laughing, and carrying on at a great rate with our sisters, the duke, the duchess..."

"The footmen?" the earl guessed.

"The butler, the grooms, the gardeners," Val went on, nodding. "She charms everybody."

"It could be worse." The earl got up and went to the window, from which he could see Anna taking cuttings for her bouquets. "You could have proposed to her, oh, say a half-dozen times and been turned down each time. Quite lowering, the third and fourth rejections. One gets used to it after that. Or tries to."

"Gads." Val's eyebrows shot up. "I hadn't realized it had reached that stage. What on earth is wrong with the woman?"

"Nothing. She simply believes we would not suit, so I leave her in relative peace."

"Except you tuck her in each night?"

"I do." The earl's eyes stayed fixed on the garden. "She is fond of me; she permits it. She is quite alone, Val, so I try not to take advantage of the liberties I'm granted. I comprehend, though, when a woman doesn't even try to kiss me, that I have lost a substantial part of my allure in her eyes."

"And have you talked to her about this?"

"I have." The earl smiled faintly. "She confronted me quite clearly and asked how we were to go on. She wants comforting but nothing more. I can provide that."

Comforting and cosseting and cuddling.

"You are a better man than I am." Val smiled in sympathy.

"Not better." The earl shook his head. "Just... What the *hell* is going on out there?!"

A pair of beefy-looking thugs had climbed over the garden wall and thrown a sack over Anna's head. She was still struggling mightily when the earl, both brothers, and two footmen pounded onto the scene and wrestled Anna from her attackers.

"Oh, no you don't," St. Just snarled as he hauled the larger man off the wall. "You stay right here, my man, and await the King's justice. You, too, Shorty." He cocked a pistol and leveled a deadly look at the two intruders.

Baron Stull let himself in through the gate. "I say, none of that now. Westhaven, call off your man."

"Stull." Westhaven grimaced. "You are trespassing. Leave, unless you'd like the constable to take you up now rather than when these worthies implicate you in kidnapping."

"I ain't kidnapping," Stull huffed. "You want proof this lady is my fiancée, well here it is." He thrust a beribboned document at the earl, who merely lifted an eyebrow. On cue, Val stepped forward, retrieved the document, and handed it to a footman.

"Take it to His Grace," the earl ordered. "Tell him I want the validity of the thing reviewed, and it's urgent."

"Now see here." The Earl of Helmsley sauntered in through the gate, and Westhaven felt Anna go tense. "There will be no need for that. Anna, come along. Tell the man I'm your brother and the guardian appointed by our grandpapa to see to you and our sister. Grandmama has been missing you both."

"You are not and never were my guardian," Anna said. "I was of age when Grandpapa died, and while you may control some of my funds, you never had legal control of me."

"Seems the lady isn't going to be going with you," the earl said. "So you may leave, for now."

"Now, my lord." Helmsley shook his head. "Let's not be hasty. I, too, brought proof of my claims with me. Perhaps Anna would like to read for herself what provision Grandpapa made?" With his left hand, he held out a second document, rolled and tied with a ribbon. As Anna took a step forward to snatch the document from his hand, the earl noticed Helmsley's right hand was hidden in the folds of his coat.

"Anna, don't!"

But his warning was too late. As Anna reached for the document, Helmsley reached for her, wrapping her tightly against his body, a gun held to her temple.

"That's enough!" Helmsley jerked her hard against him, the document having fallen to the cobblestones. "Stull, come along. We've got your bride, and it's time we're going. Westhaven, you are free to call the magistrate, but we'll be long gone, and when it comes down to it, your word against ours will not get you very far in criminal proceedings, particularly as a woman cannot testify against her spouse." He wrenched Anna back a step, then another, keeping Anna between him and the earl.

A shot was fired, followed instantly by a second shot. Anna sagged against her brother but was snatched into Westhaven's arms.

"I'm hit." Helmsley's hand went to his side, gun clattering to the cobblestones beside the document. "You bastard!" Helmsley shouted at St. Just in consternation. "You just *shot* me!"

"I did." St. Just approached him, pistol still in hand. "As I most assuredly am a bastard, in every sense of the word, I suggest you do not give me an excuse to discharge my second barrel just to shut you up. Defense of a loved one, you know? Deadly force is countenanced by every court in the land on those grounds."

"Val…" the earl's voice was urgent. "Get Garner or Hamilton. Get me a damned physician. Anna's bleeding."

"Go." Dev nodded at Val. "John Footman and I will handle these four until the constable gets here."

❧

Anna was weaving on her feet, the earl's arm around her waist holding her up until she felt him swing her up against his chest. The earl was bellowing for Nanny Fran, and pain was radiating out from Anna's shoulder, pain and a liquid, sticky warmth she vaguely recognized as her own blood.

"Hurts," she got out. "Blazes."

"I know," the earl said, his voice low, urgent. "I know it hurts, sweetheart, but we'll get you patched up. Just hang on."

Sweetheart, Anna thought. Now he calls me sweetheart, and that hurt, too.

"I'll be fine," she assured him, though the pain was gaining momentum. "Just don't…"

"Don't what?" He laid her on the sofa in the library and sat at her hip while Nanny Fran bustled in behind him.

"Don't go," Anna said, blinking against the pain. "Quacks."

"I won't leave you to the quacks." The earl almost smiled, accepting a pair of scissors from Nanny Fran. "Hold still, Anna, so we can have a look at the damage."

"Talk." Anna swallowed as even the earl's hands deftly tugging and cutting at the fabric of her dress made the pain worse.

"What shall I talk about?" His voice wasn't quite steady, and Anna could feel the blood welling from her shoulder and soaking her dress even as he cut the fabric away from her wound.

"Anything," she said. "Don't want to faint."

Her eyes fluttered closed, and she heard the earl start swearing.

❧

"Clean cloths," Westhaven said to Nanny, who passed him a folded linen square over his shoulder. "Anna, I'm going to put pressure directly onto the wound, and it will be uncomfortable."

She nodded, her face pale, her eyes closed. He

folded the cloth over her shoulder and pressed, gently at first but then more firmly. She winced but said nothing, so he held the pressure steady until the cloth was soaked then added a second cloth on top of the first.

"Have we carbolic and basilicum?" the earl asked.

"We do," Nanny Fran replied. "And brandy by the bottle." She held her silence for long tense moments before peering over Westhaven's shoulder again. "Ain't bleeding so much," she observed with grudging approval. "Best take a look."

"Not yet," the earl said, "not until the bleeding stops. Time enough to clean her up later."

By the time the physician arrived—Dr. Garner—Anna's wound was no longer bleeding, and her shoulder had been gently cleaned up but no dressing applied.

"Capital job," the physician pronounced. "It's a deep graze, right over the top of the shoulder. Few inches off, and it would have been in the neck or the lung. Looks as if the powder's been cleaned adequately. You're a lucky girl, Miss James, but you are going to have to behave for a while."

He put a tidy dressing on the wound and urged rest and red meat for the loss of blood. He prescribed quiet and sparing laudanum if the pain became too difficult. He also pulled the earl aside and lectured sternly about the risk of infection. The doctor's demeanor eased a great deal when the earl described the initial attention given the patient.

"Well done." The doctor nodded. "Fairly will be proud of you, but your patient isn't out of the woods yet. She needs peace and quiet, and not just for the wound. Violent injury takes a toll on the spirit, and even the bravest among us take time to recover."

"And if she's breeding?" the earl asked quietly.

"Hard to say." The physician blew out a slow breath. "She's young and quite sturdy, generally. Not very far along and strikes me as the sensible sort. If I had to lay odds, I'd say the child is unaffected, but procreation is in hands far greater than ours, my lord. All you can do is wait and pray."

"My thanks." Westhaven ushered the doctor to the front door. "And my thanks, as well, for your efforts with my father. I know he hasn't been an easy patient."

"The old lords seldom are." The doctor smiled. "Too used to having their way and too concerned with their dignity."

"I'll try to remember that"—the earl returned the smile—"should I ever be an old lord."

When the doctor was on his way, Stull and Helmsley had been taken into custody, and the household settling down, the earl was surprised to see evening was approaching. He made his way to Anna's sitting room and the small bedroom beyond it.

"I'll sit with her, Nanny," the earl said, helping the older woman to her feet. "Go have a cup of tea; get some fresh air."

"Don't mind if I do." Nanny bustled along. "Cuppa tea's just the thing to settle a body's nerves."

Westhaven frowned at his patient where she reclined on her pillows. "I hate that you're hurt."

"I'm none too pleased about what happened either," Anna said. "But what, exactly, did happen?"

"Your brother attempted to abduct you," the earl

said, taking the seat Nanny had vacated. "St. Just deterred him by means of a bullet, but the gun your brother had trained on you discharged, as well."

"You mean my brother shot me?"

"He did. I cannot say it was intentional."

"How is he faring?" Anna asked, dropping his gaze.

"He's gut shot, Anna," the earl said gently. "We sent him Dr. Hamilton, whom I believe to be competent, but his prognosis is guarded, at best."

"He's wounded and in jail?" Anna said, her voice catching.

"He's enjoying the hospitality of the Crown at a very pleasant little house St. Just owns, with professional nursing care in addition to armed guards. He is a peer, Anna, and will be cared for accordingly."

It was more than Helmsley deserved.

"Anna." The earl's hand traced her hairline gently. "Let me do this."

She met his gaze and frowned, but he wasn't finished. "Let me put matters to rights for you. I will take care of your brother and see to final arrangements if any need be made. If you like, I will notify your grandmother and have her escorted south. We can do this in the ducal traveling coach, in easy stages, I promise."

"Do it, please," Anna said, wiping at her eyes with her left hand. "My thanks."

"Anna." Westhaven shifted to sit at her left hip and leaned down over her. He carefully cradled her cheek with his left hand and tucked her face against his neck. "It's all right to cry, sweetheart."

She wiggled her left arm out from between them

and circled his neck, pulling him close, and then turned her face into his warmth and wept. Unable to move much beyond that, her tears streamed from her eyes into her hair and onto the earl's cheek. He held her and stroked her wet cheeks with his thumb, letting her cry until his own chest began to ache for her.

Westhaven levered up enough to meet her gaze. "You must allow me to manage what I can for you now. All I want is to see you healed, the sooner the better."

"For now, have you a handkerchief, perhaps?"

"I do." He produced the requisite handkerchief and wiped at her cheeks himself before tucking it into her left hand. "And I am willing to read you Caesar, beat you at cribbage, discuss interior decoration with you, or speed your recovery by any means you please."

"I am to be served my own medicine," Anna said ruefully.

"Or perhaps you'd like to be served something to eat? Maybe just some toast with a little butter or jam, or some soup?"

"Toast and butter, and some cold tea."

"It will be my pleasure." The earl rose and left her. And Anna felt his absence keenly. Nanny Fran was dear, but she muttered and fussed and did very little to actually ensure the patient was comfortable. The earl returned, bearing a tray with cold tea, buttered toast, a single piece of marzipan, and a daisy in a bud vase.

"You brought me a flower." Anna smiled, the first genuine smile she'd felt in ages.

"I have been trained by an expert." The earl smiled back. He stayed with her while she ate then beat her at cribbage. When night fell, he asked Val to play for her, the slow, sweet lullabies that would induce a healing sleep. When she woke in the night, he got her to the chamber pot and back into bed and held her left hand until she drifted off. Nanny Fran shooed him out the next morning, but by early afternoon he was back.

When Dr. Garner reappeared to check the wound, the earl stayed in the room, learning how to replace the dressing and how to identify the signs of proper healing. For three more days, he was by her side, until Anna was pronounced well enough to sit in the gardens and move about a little under her own power.

On the fifth day, the duchess came to call with Morgan. While Anna and Morgan chatted volubly in the back gardens, the duchess took her son aside and pointed out some difficult truths.

Anna was the acknowledged granddaughter of an earl, and the danger of infection was diminishing with each day.

Morgan missed her sister.

The earl's offers of marriage had been rejected not once but several times.

The earl was running a bachelor establishment, not just for himself but for his two equally unmarried brothers.

*Something was going to have to be done*, the duchess concluded, her preferred *something* obvious to her son.

"Give me a couple more days," the earl reasoned. "Anna is still uncomfortable, and even a short carriage ride will be difficult for her."

"I can understand that," the duchess said, "and she deserves some notice of a change of abode, but, Westhaven, what will she do now?"

"We've discussed it, we'll discuss it some more. Plan on receiving her the day after tomorrow before tea time."

"Morgan will be very pleased." The duchess rose. "You are doing the right thing." The earl nodded, knowing his mother spoke the truth. It was time to let Anna get on with her life and to stop hoarding up memories of her for his own pleasure.

Her convalescence had been pleasant. They'd spent hours together, mostly talking, sometimes reading. The earl worked on his correspondence while Anna slept or while she dozed in the shade of the gardens. They talked about the Rosecroft estate up in Yorkshire and the effect of her brother's lack of heirs; they talked of Morelands and how pretty it was. He apprised her of the rebuilding of the stables at Willow Bend and brought her correspondence from the Marchioness of Heathgate and Gwen Allen, wishing her a speedy recovery.

When those good wishes made her cry, he lent her his handkerchief and his sturdy shoulder and brought her bouquets to cheer her up, and still, they did not talk about what mattered.

❧

"Has my mother put you to rights?" the earl asked. He looked handsome to Anna, in shirtsleeves and waistcoat, his cuffs turned back as he wandered onto the back terrace where she was enjoying the sunshine on a chaise.

"She clucked and fussed and carried on appropriately," Anna said. "I am to make a speedy and uneventful recovery by ducal decree."

"Your grandmother will be here late next week, you know, if all goes well." Westhaven sat on the edge of her chaise, regarding her closely. "You don't look so pale, I'm thinking."

"I don't feel so pale," she assured him. "I've not taken the time to just sit in the sun for more than two years, Westhaven. It's bad for one's ladylike complexion, but in the North, we crave the sun."

"Will you be going back there?"

Anna fingered the cuff of her sleeve. "I do not want to. I want to remember Rosecroft as it was in my grandfather's day, not in the neglect and disrepair my brother allowed."

"You don't ask about him," Westhaven said, taking her hand.

"I assume he is malingering."

"He is not doing well. It's to be expected."

"And Stull?"

"Made bond. But seems content to await trial at the Pig. I did bring trespass charges, just for the hell of it, and assault and conspiracy to assault in your name, as well."

"Will any of it stick?"

The earl smiled, and the expression had a lot of big, white, sharp teeth to it. "It's a curious thing about assault, but it's both a tort and a crime."

"A tort?" Anna frowned.

"A civil wrong for which the law provides a remedy." The earl quoted. "Like, oh, slander, libel, and the like."

"You are saying I can sue him personally, not just bring criminal charges?"

"You already have," the earl informed her. "On the advice of the duke, of course."

"Why would I do such a thing, when lawsuits take forever to resolve, and all I want is to be shut of that man immediately?"

"Civil matters are often settled with money judgments, Anna, and while you might think you have sufficient capital, Morgan might not be of the same mind, nor your grandmother."

"I see." Anna pursed her lips. "I trust your judgment, Westhaven. Proceed as you see fit."

"I will," he said and brought her hand up sandwiched between both of his. "There's something else we need to discuss, Anna."

"There is?" She watched him matching their hands, finger for finger.

"Your grandmother will be scandalized to find you dwelling with three bachelors, and my mother has reminded me Morgan is worried about you."

"Morgan just visited, and my grandmother will hardly be scandalized to find I'm alive and well."

"Anna..." He met her gaze. "I've made arrangements for you to remove to the mansion the day after tomorrow, where you will complete your convalescence under my mother's care."

"Westhaven..." He rose abruptly, and Anna came to her feet more slowly. "Gayle? Is this what you want?"

He looked up at her use of his name, a sad smile breaking through his frown.

"It is what must be, Anna." He kept his hands in his pockets. He did not reach for her. "You are a well-bred young lady, and I am a bachelor of some repute.

If it becomes known you are under my roof without chaperonage, then your future will be bleak."

More bleak, Anna wanted to rail, than when Stull and Helmsley were hounding me across England?

"I will miss you," Anna said, turning her back to him, the better to hide her tears. God above, she'd turned into a watering pot since getting involved with the earl.

"I beg your pardon?" He'd stepped closer, close enough she could catch his scent.

"I will miss you," Anna said, whirling and walking straight into him. She wrapped her arms around his waist and clung, while his arms gently closed around her. "I will miss you and miss you and miss you."

"Oh, love." He stroked the back of her head. "You mustn't cry over this. You'll manage, and so will I, and it's for the best." She nodded but made no move to pull away, and he held her as closely as her wounded shoulder would allow.

&#x224b;

In the library, Val looked up from rummaging for a penknife and frowned at Dev.

"Are you peeking?" Val asked, moving to stand beside his brother at the window.

"Enjoying my front-row seat," Dev replied, scowling. "I do not understand our brother, Valentine. He loves that woman and would give his life for her. But he's letting her go, and she's letting him let her go."

"Could be a flanking maneuver." Val watched as Anna cried her heart out on Westhaven's shoulder. The couple was in profile, though, so when Westhaven bent his head to press his lips to her temple, the expression on his face was visible, as well.

"Come away." Val tugged at Dev's sleeve, and Dev left the window. "We should not have seen that."

"But we did see it," Dev said. "Now what are we going to do about it?"

"We will not meddle," Val said. "We are not the duke, Devlin. I have every confidence Westhaven will let Anna catch her breath and then approach her properly."

"Why wait?" Dev pressed. "They love each other now. And I have my suspicions as to why Anna cries so easily these days. I am years your senior, and I can recall the duchess's last few confinements."

"They love each other," Val said, "clearly they do, but Anna deserves to be approached as the wealthy young lady of quality she is, not as a housekeeper on the run from venal schemes. And I don't want to hear talk of confinements, particularly not when His Grace has ears everywhere."

"Westhaven's honor has gotten the best of his common sense," Dev argued. "Anna doesn't want to be approached later; she wants to be approached now."

"Then why does she keep turning him down?" Val said reasonably. "His efforts to woo her would be an embarrassment, were I not convinced he has the right of it."

"I don't know." Dev rubbed his chin and glanced at the window. "This whole business makes no sense, and I am inclined—odd as it might sound—to hear what His Grace has to suggest."

"I agree." Val sighed, closing the desk drawer with

a bang. "Which only underscores that Westhaven isn't making one damned bit of sense."

❧

In the less than two days that remained to them, the earl and Anna were in each other's pockets constantly. They sat side by side in the back gardens, on the library sofa, or at breakfast. When Dev and Val joined them for meals, they affected a little more decorum, but their eyes conveyed what their hands and bodies could not express. Anna was again sleeping upstairs, and the earl was again joining her at the end of each day.

The earl drew a brush down the length of her dark hair. "I have asked Dev and Val to escort you to Their Graces tomorrow, Anna."

"I see. You are otherwise occupied."

"I will be. I think you will enjoy my mother's hospitality, and my sisters will love you."

"Morgan adores them," Anna said, her smile brittle. "Mourning has left them in want of company, and Morgan is lonely, as well."

"And you, Anna." The earl's hand went still. "Will you be lonely?"

She met his eyes in the mirror above the vanity, and he saw hunger there. A hunger to match his own.

"I am lonely now, Westhaven." She rose and turned. "I am desperately lonely, *for you*." She pressed her lips to his, the first they'd kissed in weeks, and though his arms came around her briefly, he was the first one to step back.

"Anna, we will regret it."

"I will regret it if we don't," she replied, her expression unreadable. "I understand, Westhaven, I must leave tomorrow, and in a way it will be a relief, but…"

"But?" He kept his expression neutral, but his breathing was accelerated from just that brief meeting of lips. And what did she mean, leaving him would be a *relief*?

"But we have this night to bring each other pleasure one last time," she said miserably. "What difference can it make how we spend it?"

He had been asking himself that same question for days and giving himself answers having to do with honor and respect and even love, but those answers wouldn't address the pure pain he saw in Anna's eyes.

"I do not want to take advantage of you," he said. "Not again, Anna."

"Then let me take advantage of you," Anna pleaded softly. "Please, Westhaven. I won't ask again."

She desired him, Westhaven told himself. That much had always been real between them, and she was asking him to indulge his most sincere wish. That it was his most sincere wish didn't mean he should deny her, didn't mean he should assume, with ducal arrogance, he knew better than she what she needed.

"Come." He tugged her by the hand to stand by the bed and slowly undressed her, taking particular care she not have to move her right shoulder and arm. When she was on the bed, resting on her back, he got out of his own clothes and locked the door before joining her.

"We will be careful, Anna." He crouched over her

naked, his erection grazing her belly. "You are injured, and I cannot go about this oblivious to that fact."

"We will be careful," she agreed. Her left hand cradled his jaw and then slid around to his nape to draw him down to her. "We will be very careful."

He remained above her, his weight on his forearms, even as he joined his mouth to hers and then his body to hers.

"Westhaven." Anna undulated up against him. "Please, not slow, not this time."

"Not slow, but careful."

"Not that either, for God's sake."

He laced his fingers through hers where they rested on her pillow and raised himself up just enough to hold her gaze.

"Careful," he reiterated. "Deliberate." He slowly hilted himself in her and withdrew. "Measured." Another thrust. "Steady." Another. "But hot," he whispered, "Hard... deep..."

"Oh, God, *Gayle*..." Her body spasmed around his cock, clutching at him just as hot, hard, and deep as he'd promised her. She buried her face against his shoulder to mute her keening groans of pleasure, and still he drove her on, one careful thrust at a time.

"I am undone," she pronounced, brushing his hair back from his brow. "I am utterly, absolutely undone."

"I am not." The earl smiled down at her, a conqueror's possessive smile. "But how is your shoulder?"

"You can even think to ask? My shoulder is fine, I believe, but as I am floating a small distance above this bed, I will have to let you know when I am reunited with it."

"You are pleased?" he asked, lacing his fingers with hers. "This is what you wanted?"

"This is what I needed," she said softly as he began to move in her again *carefully*. "This is what I sorely, sorely needed."

"Anna... When you leave tomorrow...?"

"Yes?" She closed her eyes, making it harder to read her. He laid his cheek against hers and closed his fingers around hers, needing as much contact as he could have.

"When you leave tomorrow and I am not there, this will be part of it," he said, turning his face to kiss her cheek then resting his cheek against hers again.

"I don't know what you mean."

"I will be thinking of you," he said, "and you will be thinking of me and of this pleasure we shared. It's...good is the only word I can find. Joyous, lovely, beautiful, somehow, even if it can't be more than it is. I wanted you to know how I feel."

"Oh, you." Anna curled up to his chest tears flowing. "Gayle Tristan Montmorency Windham. Shame on you; you have made me cry with your poetry."

He kissed her tears away this time and made her forget her sorrows—almost—with his loving, until she was crying out her pleasure again and again. He let himself join her the last time, his own climax exploding through him, leaving him floating that same small distance above the bed, until sleep began to steal his awareness.

He tended to their ablutions then stood gazing down at Anna where she dozed naked on her left side. It was time to go, he knew, but still, dawn was hours away.

"Don't go." Anna opened her eyes and met his gaze. "We will be parted for a long time, Westhaven. Let us remain joined just a little while longer."

He nodded and climbed into bed, spooning himself around her back and tucking an arm around her waist. This night's work was pure, selfish folly, but he'd treasure the memory, and he hoped she would, as well.

He made love to her one more time—sweetly, slowly, just before dawn, and then he was gone.

∽

Anna slept late the next morning and considered it a mercy, as the earl had told her he was off to Willow Bend for the day. Val and Dev had ridden out, and so she had breakfast to herself. Her shoulder was itchy, and it took her longer to pack than she'd thought it would, but before long, she was being summoned for luncheon on the back patio.

"You look healthy," Dev said. "If I did not know you were sporting the remains of a bullet wound, I would think you in the pink."

"Thank you." Anna smiled. "I slept well last night." For the first time in weeks, she truly had.

"Well"—Val sat down and reached for the iced lemonade pitcher—"I did not sleep well. We need another thunderstorm."

"I wonder." Anna's eyes met Val's. "Does Morgan still dread the thunderstorms?"

"She does," he replied, sitting back. "She figured out that the day your parents died, when she was trapped in the buggy accident, it stormed the entire afternoon. Her associations are still quite troubling, but her ears don't physically hurt." Dev and Anna exchanged a look of surprise, but Val was tucking into his steak.

Dev turned his attention back to his plate. "Anna, are you ready to remove to the ducal mansion?"

"As ready as I'll be," Anna replied, her steak suddenly losing its appeal.

"Would you like me to cut that for you?" Dev asked, nodding at the meat on her plate. "I've pulled a shoulder now and then or landed funny from a frisky horse, and I know the oddest things can be uncomfortable."

"I just haven't entirely regained my appetite," Anna lied, eyeing the steak dubiously. "And I find I am tired, so perhaps you gentleman will excuse me while I catch a nap before we go?"

She was gone before they were on their feet, leaving Dev and Val both frowning.

"We offered to assist him in any way," Dev said, picking up his glass. "I think this goes beyond even fraternal devotion."

"He's doing what he thinks is right," Val responded. "I have had quite enough of my front-row seat, Dev. Tragedy has never been my cup of tea."

"Nor farce mine."

❧

She didn't see him for a week.

The time was spent dozing, trying on the new dresses that had arrived from the dressmaker's, getting to know the duke's daughters, and being reunited with her grandmother. That worthy dame was in much better form than Anna would have guessed, much to her relief.

"It took a good year," Grandmama reported, "but the effects of my apoplexy greatly diminished after that. Still, it did not serve to let Helmsley know I was so much better. He wasn't one to let me off the estate, but I was able to correspond, as you know."

"Thank God for loyal innkeepers."

"And thank God for young earls," Grandmother said. "That traveling coach was the grandest thing, Anna. So when can I meet your young man?"

"He isn't my young man." Anna shook her head, rose, and found something fascinating to stare at out the window. "He was my employer, and he is a gentleman, so he and his brothers came to my aid."

"Fine-looking fellow," Grandmama remarked innocently.

"You've met him?"

"Morgan and I ran into him and his younger brother when she took me to the park yesterday. Couple of handsome devils. In my day, bucks like that would have been brought to heel."

"This isn't your day"—Anna smiled—"but as you are widowed, you shouldn't feel compelled to exercise restraint on my behalf."

"Your dear grandfather gave me permission to remarry, you know." Grandmother peered at a tray of sweets as she spoke. "At the time, I told him I could never love another, and I won't—not in the way I loved him."

"But?" Anna turned curious eyes on her grandmother and waited.

"But he knew me better than I know myself. Life is short, Anna James, but it can be long and short at the same time if you're lonely. I think that was part of your brother's problem."

"What do you mean?" Anna asked, not wanting to point out the premature use of the past tense.

"He was too alone up there in Yorkshire." Grandmother bit into a chocolate. "The only boy, then being raised by an old man, too isolated. There's a reason boys are sent off to school at a young age. Put all those barbarians together, and they somehow civilize each other."

"Westhaven wasn't sent to school until he was fourteen," Anna said. "He is quite civilized, as are his brothers."

"Civilized, handsome, well heeled, titled." Grandmother looked up from the tray of sweets. "What on earth is not to like?"

Anna crossed the room. "What if I said I did like him, and he and I were to settle here, two hundred miles from you and Rosecroft? When would you see your great-grandbabies? When would you make this journey again, as we haven't a ducal carriage for you to travel in?"

"My dear girl." Her grandmother peered up at her. "Yorkshire is cold, bleak, and lonely much of the year. It is a foolish place to try to grow flowers, and were it not the family seat, your grandfather and I would have removed to Devon long ago. Now, have a sweet, as your disposition is in want of same."

She picked out a little piece of marzipan shaped like a melon and smiled encouragingly at her granddaughter. Anna stared at the piece of candy, burst into tears, and ran from the room.

&ca

"Anna." Westhaven took both her hands and bent to kiss her cheek. "How do you fare? You look well, if a bit tired."

"My grandmother is wearing me out," Anna said, her smile strained. "It is good to see you again."

"And you," the earl responded, reluctant to drop her hands. "But I come with sad news."

"My brother?"

The earl nodded, searching her eyes.

"He passed away last night but left you a final gift," the earl said, drawing her to sit beside him on a padded window seat. "He wrote out a confession, implicating Stull and himself in all manner of crimes, including arson, misfeasance, assault, conspiracies to commit same, and more. Stull will either hang or be transported if he doesn't flee, as deathbed confessions are admissible evidence."

"My brother is dead." Anna said the words out loud. "I want to be sad, but no feeling comes."

"He was adamant he wasn't trying to shoot you. Dev spent some time with him, and though your brother considered murdering you for money, he couldn't bring himself to do it. He insisted the gun went off by accident."

"And Dev?" Anna looked troubled. "Will charges be pressed, and is he all right?"

"It is like you to think of St. Just. But Anna, your family's title has gone into abeyance. You might lose Rosecroft."

"Dev served on the Peninsula for nearly eight years," Anna said. "He brought two peers of the realm to justice when they were bent on misbehavior. Let him have Rosecroft. Grandmama has just informed me it's a stupid place to try to grow flowers, but it's pretty and peaceful. Horses might like it."

"Then where will you live? I thought you were going to bow to the wishes of your family and remove to Yorkshire?"

"My family." Anna's lips thinned. "Morgan flirts with everything she sees, and Grandmother is suddenly tired of northern winters. I am related to a couple of tarts."

"Even tarts have to live somewhere."

"Will you sell me Willow Bend?" She looked as surprised by her question as he was, as if it had just popped into her head.

*I'd give it to you*, he wanted to say. But that would be highly improper.

"I will, if you really want it. The stables are done, and the house is ready for somebody to live there."

"I like it," Anna said, "very much in fact, and I like the neighbors there. It's large enough I could put in some greenhouses and an orangery and so on."

"I'll have the solicitors draw up some papers, but Anna?"

"Hmm?"

"You know I would give it to you," he said despite the insult implied.

She waved a hand. "You are too generous, but thank you for the thought. Tell me again St. Just is not brooding. He took a man's life, and even for a soldier, that cannot be an easy thing."

"He will manage, Anna. Val and I will look after him, and he could not let your brother make off with you. The man did contemplate your murder, though we will never know how sincerely."

"Dev knew"—Anna frowned—"and I knew. Helmsley wasn't right. Something in him broke, morally or rationally. It's awful of me, but I am glad he's dead."

"It isn't awful of you. For entirely different reasons, I was glad when Victor died." He wanted to hold her, to offer her at least the comfort of his embrace, but she wasn't seeking it. "Are you up to a turn in the garden?"

"I am." Anna smiled at him, but to him, it was forced, at best an expression of relief rather than pleasure. When they were a safe distance from the house, he paused and regarded her closely.

"You aren't sleeping well," he concluded. And neither was he, of course. "And you look like you've lost weight, Anna. Don't tell me it's the heat."

"You're looking a bit peaked yourself, and you've lost weight, as well."

*I miss you terribly.*

"Are my parents treating you well?" the earl asked, resuming their sedate walk.

"They are lovely, Westhaven, and you knew they would be, or you wouldn't have sent us here. I am particularly fond of your papa."

"You are? That would be the Duke of Moreland?"

"Perhaps, though the duke has not been in evidence much. There's a pleasant older fellow who bears you a resemblance, though. He delights in telling me stories about you and your brothers and sisters. He flirts with my grandmother and my sister, he adores his wife, and he is very, very proud of you."

"I've met him. A recent acquaintance, but charming."

"You should spend more time with him," Anna said. "He is acutely aware that with Bart and Victor, he spent years being critical and competitive, when all he really wants is for his children to be happy."

"Competitive? I hadn't thought of that."

"Well," Anna stopped to sniff at a red rose, closing her eyes to inhale its fragrance. "You should. You have brothers, and it can't be so different from sons."

*Tell me now, Anna*, he silently pleaded as she ran her finger over a rose petal. *Tell me I could have a son, that we could have a son, a daughter, a baby, a future—anything.*

"How soon can I remove to Willow Bend?" she asked, that forced, bright smile on her face again.

"Tomorrow," the earl said, blinking. "I trust you to complete the sales transaction, and the house will fare better occupied. It will please me to think of you there." She stumbled, but his grip on her arm prevented her from falling.

"I have been dependent on the Windhams' kindness long enough," Anna said evenly. "I know Morgan and Grandmama will be glad to settle in somewhere."

"Anna." He paused with her again, knowing they would soon be back at the house, and Anna had every intention of moving out to Surrey, picking up the reins of her life, and riding out of his.

"How are you really?"

The bright, mendacious smile faltered.

"I am coping," she said, staring out across the beds of flowers. "I wake up sometimes and don't know where I am. I think I must see to your lemonade for the day or wonder if you're already in the park on

Pericles, and then I realize I am not your housekeeper anymore. I am not your anything anymore, and the future is this great, yawning, empty unknown I can fill with what? Flowers?"

She offered that smile, but he couldn't bear the sight of it and pulled her against his chest.

"If you need anything," he said, holding her against him, "*anything*, Anna James. You have only to send me word."

She said nothing, clinging to him for one long desperate moment before stepping back and nodding.

"Your word, Anna James," he ordered sternly.

"You have my word," she said, smile tremulous but genuine. "If I am in any difficulties whatsoever, I will call on you."

The sternness went out of him, and he again offered his arm. They progressed in silence, unmindful of the duke watching them from the terrace. When his duchess joined him, he slipped an arm around her waist.

"Esther." He nuzzled her crown. "I find I am fully recovered."

"This is amazing," his wife replied, "as you have neither a medical degree nor powers of divination."

"True." He nuzzled her again. "But two things are restored to me that indicate my health is once again sound."

"And these would be?" the duchess inquired as she watched Westhaven take a polite leave of Miss James.

The duke frowned at his son's retreating back. "The first is a nigh insatiable urge to meddle in that boy's affairs. Devlin and Valentine dragooned me into a shared tea pot, and for once, we three are in agreement over something."

"It's about time."

"You don't mind if I take a small hand in things?" the duke asked warily.

"I am ready to throttle them both." The duchess sighed, leaning into her husband. "And I suspect the girl is breeding and doesn't even know it."

"St. Just is of like mind. He and Val all but asked me what I intend to do about it."

"You will think of something. I have every faith in you, Percy."

"Good to know."

"What was the second piece of evidence confirming your restored health?"

"Come upstairs with me, my love, and I will explain it to you in detail."

❧

"I am here at the request of my duchess," Moreland declared.

"Your Grace will always be welcome," Anna said. "I'm sure Grandmama and Morgan will be sorry they missed you."

"Making the acquaintance of that scamp, Heathgate." The duke shook his head. "I could tell you stories about that one, missy, that would curl your hair. His brother is no better, and I pray you do not allow me to stray onto the topic of Amery."

"He loves your granddaughter," Anna countered, "but have another crème cake, Your Grace, and tell me how your duchess goes on."

"She thrives as always in my loving care," the duke intoned pompously, but then he winked at Anna and reached for a cake. "But you tell her I had three of these, and she will tear a strip off the ducal hide. Seriously, she is doing well, as are the girls. I can't say the same for old Westhaven, though. That boy is a shambles. Were it not for his brothers, I'd move him back to the mansion."

"A shambles?" Anna felt the one crème cake she'd finished beginning to rebel.

"A complete shambles." The duke munched away enthusiastically. "His house is in no order whatsoever. Old Fran is running things any damned way she pleases, and you know that cannot be good for the King's peace. Tolliver has threatened to quit, St. Just is back to his drinking and brooding, and Valentine has taken to hiding from them both in the music room."

"I am distressed to hear it. But what of the earl? How does he fare?"

"Forgets to eat." The duke sighed. "Not a problem he inherited from me. Rides his horse every day, but otherwise, it's business, business, and more business. You'd think the boy's a damned cit the way he must read every paragraph and negotiate every price. Mark my words, the next heart seizure will be his."

"Your Grace," Anna said earnestly, "isn't there something you can do? He respects you, more than you know."

"I've reformed." The duke reached for a fourth crème cake. "I do not meddle. I've learned my lesson; Westhaven needs to learn his. He did seem to manage better when you were on hand, but no matter. He'll muddle along. So"—the duke rose, brushing crumbs from his breeches—"My duchess will want to know, how fare you?"

He leveled a lordly, patrician look at her.

"I am well." Anna rose a little more slowly.

"Not fainting, are you?" The duke glowered at her. "Makes no sense to me at all. The lord plants a babe in a woman's womb then has her wilting all over. I can understand the weeps and the constant napping, but the rest of it… Not the way I'd have arranged it. But the Almighty is content to make do without my advice for the nonce, much like my children."

"I am well," Anna repeated, but a ringing had started in her ears.

The duke leaned over and kissed her forehead.

"Glad to hear it, my dear," he said, patting her arm. "Westhaven would be glad to hear it, too, I expect."

"Westhaven?"

"He's an earl," the duke said, his eyes twinkling. "Handsome fellow, if a bit too serious. Gets that from his mother. Lonely, if you ask me. I think you've met him."

"I have." Anna nodded, realizing she'd walked her guest to the door. "Safe journey home, Your Grace. My regards to the family."

The duke nodded and went smiling on the way to his next destination.

❧

"Not managing well, at all." The duke shook his head. "Your mother was concerned enough to send *me*, Westhaven, and I am barely allowed off the leash these days, as you well know."

"You say she looked pale?"

"Women in her condition might look a little green around the gills at first, but then they bloom, Westhaven. Their hair, their skin, their eyes... She isn't blooming and she's off her feed and she looks too tired."

"I appreciate your telling me this," the earl said, frowning, "but I don't see what I can do. She hasn't asked for my help."

The duke rose, snitching just one more piece of marzipan. "I am not entirely sure she understands her own condition, my boy. Grew up without a mother; probably thinks it's all the strain of losing that worthless brother. You might find she needs blunt speech if your offspring isn't to be a six-months' wonder.

"A six-months' wonder," the duke repeated, "like Bart nearly was. He was an eight-months' wonder instead, which is readily forgivable."

"He was a what?" The earl was still frowning and still pondering the duke's revelations regarding Anna's decline.

"Eight-months' wonder." The duke nodded sagely. "Ask any papa, and he'll tell you a proper baby takes nine and half months to come full term, first babies sometimes longer. Bart was a little early, as Her Grace could not contain her enthusiasm for me."

"Her Grace could not...?" The earl felt his ears turn red as the significance of his father's words sunk in.

"Fine basis for a marriage," the duke went on blithely. "What? You think all ten children were exclusively my fault? You have much to learn, my lad. Much to learn. Now..." The duke paused with his hand on the door. "When will your new housekeeper start?"

"My new housekeeper?"

"Yes, your mother will want to know and to look the woman over. You can't allow old Fran to continue tyrannizing your poor footmen."

"I haven't hired anybody yet."

"Best be about it." The duke glanced around the house disapprovingly. "The place is losing its glow, Westhaven. If you expect to resume your courting maneuvers in the little season, you'll have to take matters in hand, put on a proper face and all that."

"I will at that," the earl agreed, escorting his father to the door. "My thanks for your visit, Your Grace."

The earl was surprised witless when his father pulled him into a hug.

"My pleasure"—the duke beamed—"and your dear mama is probably relieved to be shut of my irresistible self for an hour or two, as well. Mind you don't let that old woman in the kitchen get above herself."

"I'll pass along your compliments." The earl smiled, watching his father trot down the front steps with the energy of a man one-third his age.

"Was that our esteemed sire?" Dev asked, emerging from the back of the house.

"It was. If I'd known you were home, I would have made him wait."

"Oh, no harm done. Did he have anything of merit to impart?"

"Anna is not doing well," the earl said, wondering when he'd lost all discretion.

"Oh?" Dev arched an eyebrow. "Come into the library, little brother, and tell me and the decanter all about it."

"No decanter for me," the earl demurred as he followed Dev through the door, "but some lemonade, perhaps, with lots of sugar."

"So the duke called on Anna and found her in poor spirits?"

"Poor health, more like. Pale, tired, peaked…"

"Like you." Dev stirred sugar into his lemonade.

"I am merely busy. As you have been busy liquidating Fairly's stables."

"And flirting with his fillies." Dev grinned. "They are the sweetest bunch, Westhaven. But did His Grace intimate Anna had that on-the-nest look about her?"

"And what would you know about an on-the-nest look?"

"I breed horses for a living," Dev reminded him. "I can tell when a mare's caught, because she gets this dreamy, inward, secret look in her eye. She's peaceful but pleased with herself, too. I think you are in anticipation of a blessed event, Westhaven."

"I think I am, too," Westhaven said. "Pass me the decanter." Dev silently obliged and watched as his brother poured whiskey into the sweetened lemonade.

"I promised you last week," Dev said slowly, "not to let you get half seas over again for at least ten years."

"Try it." The earl pushed the decanter toward him. "One cocktail does not a binge make."

"Very ducally put," Dev said, accepting the decanter. "How will you ensure my niece or nephew is not a bastard, Westhaven? I am prepared to beat you within an inch of your life, heir or not, if you don't take proper steps."

The earl sipped his drink. "The problem is not that I don't want to take proper steps, as you put it. The problem is that it is Anna's turn to propose to me."

# Eighteen

DEV EYED HIS BROTHER. "I WASN'T AWARE THE LADIES got a turn at the proposing. I thought it was up to us stalwart lads to risk rejection and to do the actual asking."

"We can take first crack," the earl said, his finger tracing the rim of his glass, "but I took first through fifth, and that means it's her turn."

"I'm sure you'll explain this mystery to me, as I hope at some point to put an end to my dreary bachelor existence," Dev murmured, taking a long swallow of his drink.

The earl smiled almost tenderly. "With Anna, I proposed, explaining to her she should marry me because I am titled and wealthy and so on."

"That would be persuasive to most any lady I know, except the lady you want."

"Precisely. So I went on to demonstrate she should marry me because I am, though the term will make you blush, lusty enough to bring her a great deal of pleasure."

"I'd marry you for that reason," Dev rejoined, "or I would if, well... It's a good argument."

"It is, if you are a man, but on Anna, the brilliance

of my logic was lost. So I proposed again and suggested I could make her troubles disappear, then failed utterly to make good on my word."

"Bad luck, that." Dev sipped his drink. "Her troubles are behind her now."

"And she has neither brother nor family seat to show for it," the earl said gently, "though if I haven't thanked you before, Devlin, I am thanking you now for pulling that trigger. Helmsley was a disgrace."

"I was aiming for his hand, though. I grabbed your pistol, and I've never shot with it before. I apologized to Anna and Morgan both, but they just tried to make me feel better."

"I am ordering you to feel better. Anna herself said Helmsley was morally or rationally broken somehow. Could you imagine selling any one of our sisters to Stull?"

"No," Dev said, "and that perspective does put it in a more manageable light. But back to your proposals, as the tale grows fascinating."

"Well, I blundered on," the earl said. "She was to marry me for legal reasons, if all else failed, to prevent kidnapping charges, since I hadn't prevented the kidnapping attempt. She was to marry me to spike Stull's guns and so forth. One has to be impressed at the single-minded focus of my proposals, particularly when juxtaposed with their consistent failure to impress."

"Juxtaposed," Dev mused. "Very ducal word. So you fell on your arse."

"I did, and my sword. Shall we have another drink?"

"One more"—Dev waggled a finger—"and that's it." He did the honors, even remembering to sugar the lemonade heavily first. "This is a delightful summer concoction, though it needs mint or something."

"It needs a taller glass."

"So you are done proposing?" Dev sipped his drink.

"I am. I forgot to propose for the one reason that might have won the prize."

"That being?"

"She loves me." Westhaven smiled wistfully. "She cannot bear to think of the rest of her life without me."

"That reason." Dev nodded sagely. "I will remember that one, as it would not have occurred to me either. Do you think it will occur to Anna?"

"I hope to God it does." The earl took a long pull of his drink. "I cannot make a move at this point unless she invites it."

"Why not? Why not just ride out there, special license in hand, and lay down the law? You haven't tried that approach. You can name it after me, the Devlin St. Just Proposal of Marriage Option Number Seven."

"Dev, I fear you are getting a bit foxed."

"A bit, and I am not even the one trying to drown my sorrows. Am I not the best of brothers?"

"The very best," the earl agreed, his smile carrying a wealth of affection. "But I cannot exercise option number seven, as that option was preempted by the lady's late brother. She did not tolerate attempts to lay down the law."

"He's dead," Dev observed. "Not much appeal to that approach. So what now?"

"Wait. Sooner or later, Anna's condition will become apparent even to her, and then I can only hope she will recall who it was that got her pregnant."

Dev lifted his glass. "Another good reason for having a candle lit when you're swiving one you want to keep. I think our little brother would benefit from such profound wisdom. Where has he got off to?"

As if summoned by magic, Val strode through the door, his expression bleak, his gaze riveted on the decanter.

"There's good news and bad news," Dev said as he slid his drink into Val's hand. "The good news is we are going to be uncles again, God willing. The bad news is that so far, Westhaven's firstborn will be taking after me rather than the legitimate side of the family."

"And this is bad news, how?" Val asked.

Dev grinned. "Is he not the best of little brothers?"

"The very best," the earl agreed, pouring them all another round.

❧

Fortunately for Westhaven, Anna's note did not arrive for another two days. By that point, he, Dev, and Val had sworn not to overimbibe for the next twenty years and endured the hangovers required to make the vow meaningful.

> *Westhaven,*
> *I am bound by my word to seek your assistance should I find myself in difficulties. The matter is not urgent, but I will attend you at Willow Bend at your convenience. My regards to your family, and to St. Just and Lord Valentine most especially.*
> *Anna James*

> *PS You will soon be running out of marzipan.*
> *Mr. Detlow's sweet shop will be expecting your*
> *reorder on Monday next.*

Being a disciplined man, the earl bellowed for
Pericles to be saddled, barked an order to Cook to
see about the marzipan, snatched up the package he'd
been saving for Anna, and was on his way out of
Town at a brisk trot within twenty minutes of reading
her note. A thousand dire possibilities flitted through
his mind as Pericles ground up the miles.

Anna had lost the baby, she had mismanaged her
finances, she had decided not to buy the place, but
rather, to move back north. She'd found some hapless
swain to marry, the neighbors were not treating her
cordially, the house had dry rot or creeping damp, or
the stables had burned down again.

Only as he approached the turn to the lane did he
realize he was being needlessly anxious. Anna had sent
for him about a matter that wasn't urgent, and he was
responding to her summons. Nothing more, nothing
less. He brought his horse down to the walk, but for
some reason, his heart was determined to remain at
a gallop.

"Westhaven?" Anna greeted him from the drive
itself, where she was obviously involved in some
gardening task. Her dress was not brown or gray but
a pretty white, green, and lavender muslin—with a
raised waistline. She had on a floppy straw hat, one
that looked to have seen better days but was fetching
just the same, and her gloves were grubby with honest
Surrey dirt.

"You certainly got here quickly." Anna smiled at him.

He handed off his horse to a groom and cautiously returned the smile. She looked thinner, true, but there were freckles on her nose, and her smile was only a little guarded.

"It is a pleasant day for a ride to the country," Westhaven responded, "and though the matter you cited isn't urgent, delay seldom reduces the size of a difficulty."

"I appreciate your coming here. Can I offer you a drink? Lemonade? Cider?"

"Lemonade," the earl said, glancing around. "You have wasted no time making the place a home."

"I am fortunate," Anna said, following his gaze. "As hot as it has been, we've finally gotten some rain, and I can be about putting in flowers. Heathgate has sent over a number of cuttings, as have Amery and Greymoor."

They would, the scoundrels.

"I've brought along a few, as well," the earl said. "They're probably in the stables as we speak."

"You brought me plants?" Anna's eyes lit up as if he'd brought her the world.

"I had your grandmother send for them from Rosecroft. Just the things that would travel well— some Holland bulbs, irises, that sort of thing."

"You brought me my grandfather's flowers?" Anna stopped and touched his sleeve. "Oh, Westhaven." He glanced at the hand on his sleeve, wanting to say something witty and ducal and perfect.

"I thought you'd feel more at home here with some of his flowers," was all that came to mind.

"Oh, you." Anna hugged him, a simple, friendly

hug, but in that hug, he had the first glimmering hope that things just might come right. She kept his arm, wrapping her hands around it and toddling along so close to his side he could drink in the lovely, flowery scent of her.

"So what is this difficulty, Anna?" he asked as he escorted her to the front terrace.

"We will get to that, but first let us address your thirst, and tell me how your family goes on."

He paused as they reached the front door then realized her grandmother and sister would likely join them inside the house. "Come with me." He took her by the hand and tugged her along until they were beside the stream, the place where they'd first become intimate. She'd had a bench placed in the shade of the willows, so he drew her there and pulled her down beside him.

"I told myself I'd graciously listen to whatever you felt merited my attention," he began, "but, Anna, I have been worried about you, and now, after several weeks of silence, you send me two sentences mentioning some problem. I find I have not the reserves of patience manners require: What is wrong, and how can I help?"

A brief paused ensued, both of them studying their joined hands.

"I am expecting," she said quietly. "Your child, that is. I am… I am going to have a baby." She peeked over at him again, but he kept his eyes front, trying to absorb the reality behind her words.

He was to be a father, a papa, and she was to be the mother of his child.

His *children*, God willing.

"I realize this creates awkwardness," she was prosing on, "but I couldn't not tell you, and I felt I owed it to you to leave the decision regarding the child's legitimacy in your hands."

"I see."

"I don't gather you do," Anna said. "Westhaven, I'd as soon not raise our child as a bastard, so I am asking you to marry me. We do suit, in some ways, but I will understand if you'd rather choose another for your duchess. In fact, I've advised you to do just that on more than one occasion. I will understand."

Another pause while Anna studied their joined hands and Westhaven called upon every ounce of ducal reserve to keep from bellowing his joy to the entire world.

"I must decline," he said slowly, "though I comprehend the great honor you do me, and I would not wish bastardy on our progeny either."

"You *must* decline?" Anna repeated. There was disappointment in her tone, in her eyes. Disappointment and *hurt*, and even in the midst of overwhelming joy, he was sorry for that. There was no surprise, though, and he was even more sorry for that.

"I must decline," the earl repeated, his words coming a little faster than he intended, "because I have it on great good authority one accepts a proposal of marriage only when one cannot imagine the rest of one's life without that person in it, and when one is certain that person loves one and feels similarly in every respect."

Anna frowned at him.

"I love you, Westhaven," she reminded him, "I've told you this."

"You told me on one occasion."

Anna held up a hand. "I see the difficulty. You do not love me. Well, I suppose that's honest."

"I have not been honest," the earl corrected her swiftly, lest she rise and he give in to the need to tackle her bodily right there in the green grass.

"At the risk of differing with a lady, I must stand firm on that one point, but I can correct the oversight now." He slipped off the bench and took her right hand in both of his as he went down on one knee before her.

"I love you," he said, holding her gaze. "I love you, I cannot foresee the rest of my life without you, and I hope you feel similarly. For only if you do feel similarly will I accept your proposal of marriage or allow you to accept mine."

"You love me?"

"For God's sake." He was off his knee in an instant, dusting briskly at his breeches. "Why else would I have tried to keep my bloody paws off you when you were just eight and twenty feet down the hall? Why else would I have gone to my father—Meddling Moreland himself?—to ask for help and advice? Why else would I have let you go, for pity's sake, if I didn't love you until I'm blind and silly and... Jesus, yes, I love you."

"Westhaven." Anna reached out and stroked a hand through his hair. "You are shouting, and you mean this."

"I am not in the habit of lying to the woman whom I hope to make my duchess."

That, he saw, got through to her. Since the day she'd bashed him with her poker, he'd been honest with her. Cranky, gruff, demanding, what have you, but he'd been honest. So he was honest again.

"I love you, Anna." His voice shook with the truth of it. "I love you. I want you for my wife, my duchess, and the mother of all of my children."

She cradled her hand along his jaw, and in her eyes, he saw his own joy mirrored, his incredulity that life could offer him a gift as stunningly perfect as the love they shared, and his bottomless determination to grab that gift with both hands and never let go.

She leaned into him, as if the weight of his honesty were too much. "Oh, you are the most awful man. Of course I will marry you, of course I love you, of course I want to spend the rest of my life with you. But you have made me cry, and I have need of your handkerchief."

"You have need of my arms," he said, laughing and scooping her up against his chest. He pressed his forehead to hers and jostled her a little in his embrace. "Say it, Anna. In the King's English, or no handkerchief for you."

He was smiling at her, grinning like a truant schoolboy on a beautiful day.

"I love you," Anna said. Then more loudly and with a fierce smile, "I love you, I love you, I love you, Gayle Windham, and I would be honored to be your duchess."

"And my wife?" He spun them in a circle, the better to hold her tightly to his chest. "You'll be my wife, and my duchess, and the mother of my children?"

"With greatest joy, I'll be your wife, your duchess, and the mother of all your children. Now please,

please, put me down and kiss me silly. I have missed you so."

"My handkerchief." He set her down on the bench, surrendered his handkerchief with a flourish, and wrapped his arm around her shoulders. "And my heart, not in that order."

And then he bent his head and kissed her silly.

# Epilogue

ANNA WINDHAM, COUNTESS OF WESTHAVEN, WAS enjoying a leisurely measure of those things which pleased her most: peace and quiet at the end of the evening and anticipation of her husband's exclusive company in the great expanse of the marital bed.

"I can wait, Anna." Her husband's voice shook a little with his mendacity, and behind those beautiful green of his eyes, there was both trepidation and heat. "It's been only a few months, and you must be sure." He stood beside the bed, peering down at her where she lay.

"It has been eternities," Anna said, "and for once, your heir appears to have made an early night of it. Come here." She held out her arms, and in a single moment, he was out of his dressing gown and settling his warmth and length over her.

"Husband, I have missed you."

"I'm right here. I will always be here, but we can't rush this. You've had a baby, given me my heir, and you must prom—"

She kissed him into silence then kissed him into kissing her back, but he was made of ducally stern stuff.

"Anna, I'll be careful. We'll take it slowly, but you need to tell—"

She got her legs wrapped around his flanks and began to undulate her damp sex along the glorious length of his rigid erection.

*Take it slowly. What foolishness her husband spouted.*

"We'll be fine," she whispered, lipping at his ear lobe. "Better than fine."

As they sank into the fathomless bliss of intimate reunion, they were fine indeed, and then much, much, *much* better than fine.

# Acknowledgments

It takes a village to transform a first-time author's aspirations into the lovely book you're reading now. At the risk of leaving out a few deserving villagers, I'd like to thank my editor, Deb Werksman, who has been patient and supportive over a long haul, and my agent, Kevan Lyon, who has been forbearing with an author who has more enthusiasm than industry expertise (for now!). The art department, marketing, and copyediting folks all deserve an enthusiastic nod, along with editorial assistants and numerous other contributors.

And first, last and always, I must thank my family, whose emphasis on education and the life of the mind resulted in my having enough imagination to create *The Heir*. Enjoy!

Also by Grace Burrowes:

*The Soldier*

*The Virtuoso*

*Lady Sophie's Christmas Wish*

*Lady Maggie's Secret Scandal*

*Lady Louisa's Christmas Knight*

*The Bridegroom Wore Plaid*

*Lady Eve's Indiscretion*

*Darius*

*Nicholas*

*Ethan*

*Beckman*

*Once Upon a Tartan*

# About the Author

Grace Burrowes is the pen name for a prolific and award-winning author of historical romances. Her manuscripts have finaled or garnered honorable mention in the New Jersey Romance Writers Put Your Heart in a Book contest, the Indiana Romance Writers Indiana Golden Opportunity contest, the Georgia Romance Writers Maggie contest, the Virginia Romance Writers Fool for Love contest, and the Spacecoast Romance Writers Launching a Star contest. She won the historical category in both the Maggie and the Indiana Golden Opportunity contests. She is a practicing attorney specializing in family law and lives in rural Maryland. Grace can be reached through her website, graceburrowes.com, and through her email at graceburrowes@yahoo.com.

THE *Soldier*

DEVLIN ST. JUST, EARL OF ROSECROFT, PREPARED HIS OWN tea and took a cautious sip. "What is your relationship to the child?"

"One might say I am her cousin of sorts, though it isn't common knowledge and I would prefer to keep it that way."

"You don't want the world associating you with the earl's bastard?" her host asked, stirring his tea slowly.

Emmie met his eyes. "More to the point, Bronwyn does not realize we are related and I would prefer to be the one to tell her."

"How does that come about?" The earl regarded her over the rim of his teacup even as he sipped.

"My aunt was kind enough to provide a home for me when my mother died," Emmie said, lips pursed as the recitation was not one she embarked on willingly. "Thus I joined her household here before Bronwyn was born. When the old earl got wind of that, he eventually sent me off to school in Scotland."

"So your aunt brought you here, and you were then sent off to school by the beneficent old earl."

"I was, and thereafter my aunt became the young earl's mistress. I suspect his grandfather sent me off to spare me that fate."

"And Winnie is the late earl's by blow? Your aunt must have been quite youthful."

"She was ten years older than Helmsley but said since his mama died when he was young, she suited him."

"Did you know the late earl?"

"I knew him. When the old earl grew ill about three years ago, I was retrieved from where I was governessing in Scotland, with the plan being that I could help care for him. When his lordship saw I was subjected to unwanted attentions, he established me on a separate property."

"In what capacity?" The earl topped off her teacup, a peculiarly civilized gesture, considering he was leaving her no privacy whatsoever.

"I support myself," Emmie replied, unable to keep a touch of pride from her voice. "I have since I returned to Yorkshire. On the old earl's advice, I never rejoined my aunt's household in the village, hence Winnie doesn't understand we are cousins. I'm not sure it ever registered with Helmsley, either."

"Did it register with Helmsley he had a daughter?"

"Barely." Emmie spat the word, unable to keep the disgust from her tone. "My aunt did well enough with Winnie, though she was careful not to impose the child on her father very often. Helmsley was prone to …poor choices in his companions. One in particular could not be trusted around children and so Winnie was an awkward addition to her father's household after my aunt's death."

"And now she's been appended to your household?"

"She is, she finally is." For the second time that evening Emmie smiled at him, but she teared up as well, ducking her face to hide her mortification.

"Women," the earl muttered. He extracted his handkerchief and passed it to her.

"I beg your pardon." Emmie tried to smile and failed, but took his handkerchief. "It was difficult, watching her grow from toddler to child, and seeing she'd had no one to love her since my aunt died."

"One must concede, you seem to care for the child." The earl regarded her with a frown. "But one must also inquire into what manner of influence you are on her. You aren't supporting yourself as your aunt did, are you?"

"I most assuredly am *not* supporting myself as you so rudely imply." She rose to her feet and tried to stuff his damp hankie back into his hand. "I work for honest coin and will not tolerate your insults."

"Keep it." He smiled at her slightly while his fingers curled her hand around his handkerchief. "I have plenty to spare. And please accept my apologies, Miss Farnum, as your character is of interest to me."

"Whyever is it any of your business how I earn my keep?" She resumed her seat but concentrated on folding his handkerchief into halves and quarters and eighths in her lap rather than meet that piercing green stare of his again.

The earl seemed to find something amusing. "I am interested in your character, Miss Farnum, because you are a friend of Miss Winnie's and she has become my concern."

"About Bronwyn." Emmie rose again and paced away from him. "We must reach some kind of understanding."

"We must?"

"She is my family," Emmie pointed out, then more softly, "my only family. Surely you can understand she should be with me?"

"So why wasn't she?" the earl asked, one dark eyebrow quirked where he sat sipping his tea. Emmie had the thought that if he'd had a tail, he'd be flicking it in a lazy, feline rhythm.

"Why wasn't she what?" Emmie stopped, turned from him, and busied herself straightening up a shelf of books.

"Why wasn't she with you? When I plucked her off that fountain, she was filthy, tired, and hadn't eaten all day."

"I couldn't catch her." Emmie frowned at the books.

"I beg your pardon?" The earl's voice came from her elbow, but she was damned if she'd flinch.

"I said, I could not catch her." Emmie did peek then and realized the earl wasn't just tall, he was also solid with muscle, a big man. Bigger than he looked from across a room, the scoundrel.

"And I could not run her off," the earl mused. "It might comfort you to know, Miss Farnum, I am the oldest of ten and not unused to youngsters."

"You do seem to get on well with her, but I have an advantage, my lord. One you will never be able to compete with."

"An advantage?"

"Yes." Emmie nodded, feeling a little sorry for him, because he really would not be able to argue the point much further. "I am a female, you see. A girl. Well, a grown woman, but I was a girl, as Bronwyn is."

"You are a female." The earl looked her up and down and Emmie felt herself blushing. "Why so you are, but how does this make yours the better guidance?"

"There are certain things, my lord..." Emmie felt her blush deepening, but refused to back down. "Things a lady knows a gentleman will not, things somebody must pass along to a little girl in due course if she's to manage in this life."

"Things." The earl's brow knit. "Things like child-birth, perhaps?"

Emmie swallowed, resenting his bluntness even while she admired him for it. "Well, yes. I doubt you've given birth, my lord."

"Have you?" he countered, peering down at her.

"That is not the point."

"So no advantage to you there, particularly as I have attended a birth or two in my time, and I doubt you've managed that either."

"Why on *earth* would..." Emmie's mouth snapped shut before she could ask the obvious, rude, burning question.

"I was a soldier," he said gently. "And war is very hard on soldiers, but even harder on women and children, Miss Farnum. A woman giving birth in a war zone is generally willing to accept the assistance of whomever is to hand, regardless of standing, gender, or even what uniform he wears."

"So you've a little experience, but you aren't going to tell me you're familiar with the details of a lady's bodily... well, that is to say. Well."

"Her menses?" The earl looked amused again.

"You might have some greater degree of familiarity than I, I will grant that much, but as a man with five sisters, I am far more knowledgeable and sympathetic regarding female lunation than I had ever aspired to be. And surely, these matters you raise—childbirth and courses—they are a ways off for Miss Winnie?"

"Bronwyn," Emmie muttered. Standing so close to him, she could catch the earl's scent and it managed to combine both elegance and barbarism. It was spicy rather than floral, but also fresh, like meadows and breezes and cold, fast running streams.

"She *answers* to Winnie," he said, "and she got away from you."

"She did." Emmie's shoulders slumped as some of the fight went out of her. "She does. I've lost her for hours at a time, at least in the summer, and nobody has any real notion where she gets off to. It wasn't so bad when my aunt first died, but it has gotten worse the older Bronwyn gets. I was terrified…"

"Yes?" The green eyes holding hers steadily bore no judgment, just a patient regard with a teasing hint of compassion.

"I was terrified Helmsley would take her south, or worse, let that cretin Stull get hold of her; but Helmsley was her father, so I'd no right to do anything for her, nor to have any say in how she goes on."

"And had your aunt lived, the law would have given Helmsley no claim on the child, nor any obligation to her either."

"Oh, the law." Emmie waved a dismissive hand. "The law tells us the better course would have been to allow the child to starve while her dear papa gambled away the estate. Do not quote the law to me, my lord, for it only points out what is legal and what is right do not often coincide where the fate of children is concerned."

"Legalities aside then, I am in a better position to assist the child than you are. Just as the old earl gave you an education to allow you to make your way as a governess, I am sufficiently well heeled I can provide every material advantage for Winnie too. If it comes to that, I can prevail upon the Moreland resources for the child as well."

"But I am her cousin," Emmie said, feeling tears well again. "I am her cousin and her only relation."

"Not so, though the reverse might be true. The child's Aunt Anna is now married to my brother, which makes me an uncle-in-law or some such, and I am one of ten, recall. Through marriage, Winnie has a great deal of family."

"But they don't know her," Emmie quietly wailed. "I am Winnie's family. *I am.*"

"Shall we compromise?" he asked, drawing Emmie's arm through his and escorting her to the sofa. "It seems to me we are considering an either/or outcome, with either you or myself having Winnie's exclusive company. Why can't she have us both?"

"You could visit," Emmie said, warming to the idea. Maybe, she allowed, he was an enlightened barbarian. "Or perhaps Winnie might spend time here, as she considers this her home."

"I do not *visit* my responsibilities, Miss Farnum," the earl replied, resuming his seat across from her. "Not when they require regular feeding and bathing and instruction in basic table manners that should have been mastered long ago."

"So how do we compromise?" Emmie ignored the implied criticism by sheer will. "If Winnie lives here with you, how is that a compromise?"

"Simple." The earl smiled at her, a buccaneer's smile if ever she saw one. "You live here too. You've said you have experience governessing; the child needs a governess. You care for her, and hold yourself out as entitled to assist with her upbringing. It seems a perfectly feasible solution to me. You remain as her governess until such time as I find a replacement, one who merits your approval and mine."

"Feasible." Emmie felt her mouth and eyebrows working in a disjointed symphony of expressions, none of which were intended to convey good cheer. "You want me to be a governess to Bronwyn?" She rose, and the earl watched her but remained seated.

"There's a difficulty." She hoped her relief did not show on her face.

"Only one?"

"It is formidable." Emmie eyed *him* up and down. "I am qualified to supervise a child of Bronwyn's age, but I have always been more a friend to her than an authority figure. I am not sure she will listen to me, else I would not find myself fretting so often over her whereabouts."

"Having not had a papa to speak of and having lost her mother, the child has likely become too self-reliant, something that can only be curbed, not entirely eradicated. And while the child may not listen to you, I have every confidence she will listen to me."

"*Every* confidence?" Emmie arched an eyebrow and met his gaze squarely.

"I got her into the house." The earl started counting off on his fingers. "I inculcated basic table manners, I engaged her in civil discussion when she was intent only on repelling boarders, and," he arched an eyebrow right back at her, "I got her into the bathtub, where she was soaped, scrubbed, and shampooed into something resembling a lovely little girl."

"You did." Emmie scowled in thought. "May I inquire how?"

"Nelson at Trafalgar. One can only demonstrate sea battles under appropriate circumstances."

"*You* gave her a bath?" Miss Farnum's eyes went wide.

"Soap and water are not complicated, but the tweeny is hardly likely to comprehend naval strategy. I'll provide the child the right bath toys and my direct involvement shouldn't be necessary from this point out. You do, I assume, have a grasp of naval history?"

"Naval history?" Emmie all but gasped in dismay.

"Well, no matter. I can teach you a few major battles and any self-respecting child will take it from there. So are we agreed?"

"On what?" Emmie felt bewildered and over-whelmed, perhaps as if a cavalry regiment had just appeared charging over the nearest hill and her all unsuspecting in their path.

"You will serve as her temporary governess until we find somebody we both approve to serve in that capacity. I shall compensate you, of course."

"I will not take money for looking after family."

"And how will you support yourself if you do not take money for services rendered?"

"That's the other reason I cannot agree to this scheme." Emmie all but snapped her fingers, so great was her relief. "I cannot let my customers down. If I stop providing goods for any length of time, they'll take their business elsewhere and I'll get a reputation for being unreliable. It won't serve, your lordship. You'll have to think of some other compromise."

"What is your business that your customers would be so fickle?"

Emmie smiled with pride. "I am a baker, my lord. I make all manner of goods, but breads and sweets especially."

"I see. There is no impediment, then."

"Of course there is." Emmie gave him a version of the local art-thee-daft look. "I cannot abandon my business, my lord, else I will have no income when we find a permanent governess for Bronwyn."

"You don't abandon your business," the earl informed her. "You merely see to it here. The kitchens are extensive, there is help on hand, and you were obviously prepared to look after your cousin and your commercial obligations at the same time, so you should be able to do it easily at Rosecroft."

"You would have me turn Rosecroft into a bakery?" Emmie all but squeaked. "This is an old and lovely manor, my lord, not some…"

"Yes?"

"My customers would not be comfortable coming here to pick up their orders. Helmsley was not on good terms with most of his neighbors and you are a stranger."

"Then we'll have your goods delivered. Really, Miss Farnum, the measures are temporary, and I should hope the good folk hereabouts would understand Winnie has lost both father and mother. As her family, we must put her welfare before somebody's tea cakes and crumpets."

She met his eyes, and sighed a sigh of defeat, because he was, damn and blast him, right. Nobody's tea cakes, crumpets, or even daily bread, was as important as Bronwyn's future. And he was also right that Bronwyn did so have family, powerful, wealthy family, who could offer her much more than a cousin eking out a living baking pies in Yorkshire.

"I'll want your apple tart recipe," she said, chin up.

The earl's lips quirked. "Dear lady, why wouldn't I give out such a thing to everybody at whose table I might someday sit? I've never understood the business of hoarding recipes. Now, how quickly can we arrange for you to start?"

He was gracious in victory, Emmie decided. She had to give him that. He'd also gotten Bronwyn into the tub and he had the best apple tart recipe she had ever tasted. The picture wasn't entirely bleak. Moreover, the Rosecroft kitchens might need a thorough scrubbing, but as he led her on a brief tour she saw the ovens were huge, the counter space endless, and the appointments surprisingly modern and well kept.

"My inventory will have to be moved and I will need storage for it as well."

"Details, and ones I'm sure you'll manage easily." The earl put her hand on his arm as they left the kitchen. "As we've lost the light, Miss Farnum, I must conclude the hour has grown late. Will you allow me to call the carriage for you?"

"I am not but a half mile up the lane. It will not serve to bother the stables for so paltry a journey. I walked here, I'll enjoy the walk home."

"As you wish." He led her through the house to the front door, where her frayed gloves and ugly bonnet were waiting on a table. "Shall I carry it for you?" He held the bonnet up by its ribbons, her gloves folded in the crown. "It's not as if you need to protect your complexion at this hour."

"I can carry it." She grabbed for the bonnet, but his blasted eyebrow was arching again.

"I do not comprehend yet all the local nuances of manners and etiquette, Miss Farnum, but I am not about to let a young lady walk home alone in the dark." He angled his free elbow out to her and gestured toward the door held open by the footman.

Barbarian. She wanted to stomp her foot hard—on his—and march off into the darkness. She'd capitulated—albeit grudgingly and perhaps only temporarily—to his idea of sharing responsibility for Bronwyn, she'd put up with his sniping and probing and serving her tea. She'd agreed to move her business activities to his kitchens, but she would not be bullied.

"I know the way, my lord," she said, glaring at him. "There is no need for this display."

"You are going to be responsible for Winnie's first efforts to acquire a sense of decorum and reserve, Miss Farnum." He picked up her hand and deposited it back on his forearm, then led her down the steps. "You must begin as you intend to go on and set a sincere example for the child. She'll spot fraud at fifty paces and even my authority won't be able to salvage your efforts then. A lady graciously accepts appropriate escort."

"Is this how you trained recruits when you were soldiering?" She stomped along beside him, completely oblivious to the beauty of the full moon and the fragrances of the summer night. "You box them in, reason with them, tease, argue, taunt, and twist until you get what you want?"

"You are upset. If I have given offense, I apologize." His voice was even, not the snippy, non-apology of a man humoring a woman's snit. She hauled him through the darkness for another twenty yards or so before she stopped and heaved a sigh.

"I am sorry," Emmie said, dropping his arm. "I suppose I am jealous."

He made no move to recapture her hand, but put his own on the small of her back and guided her steps forward again. "You are jealous of what?"

"Of your ease with Bronwyn. Of the wealth allowing you to provide so easily for her. Of your connections, enabling you to present her a much better future than I could. Of your ability to wave a hand, and order all as you wish it."

"Are we being pursued by bandits, Miss Farnum?" the earl asked, his voice a velvety baritone in the soft, summery darkness.

"We are not."

"Then perhaps we could proceed at less than forced march? It is a beautiful night, the air is lovely, and I've always found darkness soothing when I took the time to appreciate it."

"And from what would the earl of Rosecroft need soothing?" She nearly snorted at the very notion.

"I've felt how you feel," he said simply. "As if another had all I needed and lacked, and he didn't even appreciate what he had."

"You?" She expostulated in disbelief, but walked more slowly and made no objection to his hand lightly touching her back. "What could you possibly want for? You're the firstborn of a duke, titled, wealthy; you've survived battles and you can charm little girls. How could you long for more than that?"

"My brother will succeed Moreland, if the duke ever condescends to expire. This harum scarum earldom is a sop thrown to my younger brother's conscience, and his wife's, I suppose. He and my father had considerable influence with the Regent, and Westhaven's wife may well be carrying the Moreland heir. Anna made the suggestion to see Rosecroft passed along to me and Westhaven would not rest until that plan had been fulfilled."

"How can that be?" Emmie watched their moon shadows float along the ground as they walked. "A duke cannot choose which of his offspring inherits his title."

"He cannot. According to the letters patent it goes to the oldest legitimate son surviving at the time of the duke's death."

"Well, you aren't going to die soon, are you?" She glanced over at his obviously robust frame, puzzled and concerned for some reason to think of him expiring of a pernicious illness.

"No, Miss Farnum, the impediment is not death, but rather the circumstances of my birth." There was a slight, half-beat pause in the darkness, a hitch in her gait he would not have seen, but she suspected he might have felt with his hand on her person.

"Oh."

"Oh, indeed. I have a sister similarly situated, though Maggie and I do not share even the same mother. The duke was a busy fellow, in his youth."

"Busy and selfish. What is it with men, that they must strut and carry on, heedless of the consequences to any save themselves?"

"What is it with women," he replied, humor lacing his tone, "that they must indulge our selfish impulses, without regard to the consequences even to themselves?"

"Point taken." For a barbarian, he reasoned quickly and well, and he was a pleasant enough escort. His scent blended with the night fragrances, and it occurred to her he'd already admitted to being comfortable with darkness.

And in his eyes, in odd moments, she'd seen hints of darkness. He referred casually to serving king and country, and he admitted now to being a ducal bastard. Well, what would that matter? By local standards, he would be much in demand socially, and the squire's daughters would toss themselves at him just as they did at Helmsley once long ago—poor things.

She was so lost in her thoughts she stumbled over a gnarled old tree root and would have gone down but for the earl's arm around her waist.

"Steady on." He eased her up to find her balance but hesitated before dropping his arm. In that instant, Emmie gained a small insight into why women behaved as foolishly as her mother and aunt and countless others had done.

"My thanks," she said, walking more slowly yet. The heat and strength of him had felt good, reassuring in some inconvenient way. For twenty-five years, Emmaline Farnum had negotiated life without much in the way of male protection or affection and she'd been at a loss to understand what, *exactly,* men offered that would make a woman suffer their company, much less their authority.

And she still didn't know, exactly, what that something was, but the earl had it in abundance. Even on his best, barbarian camouflaging behavior, it was readily apparent to her the sooner they found Bronwyn a real governess, the better for them all.

"Why do you still wear black?" the earl asked as he ambled along beside her. "Your aunt died several years ago and one doesn't observe full morning for years for an aunt."

"One doesn't have to, but my aunt was like a mother to me, so I dyed my most presentable wardrobe black and haven't had the coin to replace it since. Then too, wearing black made me less conspicuous to Helmsley and his cronies."

"You did not respect my predecessor. I suppose you don't respect many men, given your mother raised you alone."

Another pause, but again his hand was lightly at her back, steadying her.

"My mother told me my father tried, but he became restless and she could not find it in her heart to force him to stay."

"She did not care for him?"

"She did. I never want to fathom a love like that, a love that puts a loved one aside and says it's for the best."

"Did she know she carried his child when she wished him on his way?"

"No." Emmie sighed, feeling his hand at her back as she did. "She was not... she did not have clear indications of her predicament, early on, and by the time she was convinced the unthinkable had happened, her fellow had shipped out for India."

"Be very, very glad she didn't follow the drum," the earl said, something in his voice taking on the darkness. "It is no life whatsoever for a woman."

"Particularly not when the man ends up dying in battle, and there you are, no man, no means, no home and hearth to retreat to, and babies clinging to your skirts."

"This is an abiding theme with you, isn't it?" The earl's voice was merely curious now, but he was identifying a pattern accurately.

"I have avoided the Rosecroft grounds as much as possible," Emmie said, her steps dragging. "Helmsley was an eloquent reminder of how dishonorable a titled, supposed gentleman can be."

"He was a thoroughly disagreeable cad," the earl agreed. "A more disgusting excuse for a man, much less a gentleman, I have yet to meet, unless it was that porcine embarrassment colluding with him, the Baron Stull."

"So you met Helmsley?"

"I killed him," the earl said easily, taking her hand in his. "Watch your step. We've reached a rough patch."

❧

# A *Duke* TO *Die For*

## BY AMELIA GREY

THE RAKISH FIFTH DUKE OF BLAKEWELL'S UNEXPECTED AND shockingly lovely new ward has just arrived, claiming to carry a curse that has brought each of her previous guardians to an untimely end…

### Praise for Amelia Grey's Regency romances:

"This beguiling romance steals your heart, lifts your spirits and lights up the pages with humor and passion."
—*Romantic Times*

"Each new Amelia Grey tale is a diamond. Ms. Grey… is a master storyteller." —*Affaire de Coeur*

"Readers will be quickly drawn in by the lively pace, the appealing protagonists, and the sexual chemistry that almost visibly shimmers between."
—*Library Journal*

978-1-4022-1767-8 • $6.99 U.S./$7.99 CAN

# A Marquis to Marry

## by Amelia Grey

"A captivating mix of discreet intrigue
and potent passion." —*Booklist*

"A gripping plot, great love scenes, and well-drawn
characters make this book impossible to put down."
—*The Romance Studio*

---

THE MARQUIS OF RACEWORTH IS SHOCKED TO FIND A YOUNG
and beautiful Duchess on his doorstep—especially when she
accuses him of stealing her family's priceless pearls! Susannah,
Duchess of Brookfield, refuses to be intimidated by the
Marquis's commanding presence and chiseled good looks.
And when the pearls disappear, Race and Susannah will have
to work together—and discover they can't live apart...

---

**Praise for *A Duke to Die For*:**

"A lusciously spicy romp." —*Library Journal*

"Deliciously sensual... storyteller extraordinaire Amelia Grey
grabs you by the heart, draws you in, and does not let go."
—*Romance Junkies*

"Intriguing danger, sharp humor, and plenty of simmering
sexual chemistry." —*Booklist*

978-1-4022-1760-9 • $6.99 U.S./$8.99 CAN

# *Lessons in*
# *French*

## BY LAURA KINSALE
*New York Times* bestselling author

> "An exquisite romance and an instant classic."
> —*Elizabeth Hoyt*

### HE'S EXACTLY THE KIND OF TROUBLE SHE CAN'T RESIST...

Trevelyan and Callie were childhood sweethearts with a taste for adventure. Until the fateful day her father drove Trevelyan away in disgrace. Nine long, lonely years later, Trevelyan returns, determined to sweep Callie into one last, fateful adventure, just for the two of them...

"Kinsale's delightful characters and delicious wit enliven this poignant tale...It will charm your heart!"

—*Sabrina Jeffries*

"Laura Kinsale creates magic. Her characters live, breathe, charm, and seduce, and her writing is as delicious and perfectly served as wine in a crystal glass. When you're reading Kinsale, as with all great indulgences, it feels too good to stop."

—*Lisa Kleypas*

978-1-4022-3701-0 • $7.99 U.S./$8.99 CAN

# SEIZE THE FIRE

by Laura Kinsale

*New York Times* bestselling author

"Magic and beauty flow from Laura Kinsale's pen."
—*Romantic Times*

AN UNLIKELY PRINCESS SHIPWRECKED
WITH A WAR HERO WHO'S GOT HELL TO PAY

Her Serene Highness Olympia of Oriens—plump, demure, and idealistic—longs to return to her tiny, embattled land and lead her people to justice and freedom. Famous hero Captain Sheridan Drake, destitute and tormented by nightmares of the carnage he's seen, means only to rob and abandon her. What is Olympia to do with the tortured man behind the hero's façade? And how will they cope when their very survival depends on each other?

"One of the best writers in the history of the romance genre." —*All About Romance*

978-1-4022-4683-8 • $9.99 U.S./$11.99 CAN

# MIDSUMMER MOON

### BY LAURA KINSALE
*New York Times* bestselling author

"The acknowledged master."
—*Albany Times-Union*

#### IF HE REALLY LOVED HER,
#### WOULDN'T HE HELP HER REALIZE HER DREAM?

When inventor Merlin Lambourne is endangered by Napoleon's advancing forces, Lord Ransom Falconer, in service of his government, comes to her rescue and falls under the spell of her beauty and absent-minded brilliance. But he is horrified by her dream of building a flying machine—and not only because he is determined to keep her safe.

"Laura Kinsale writes the kind of works that live in your heart." —Elizabeth Grayson

"A true storyteller, Laura Kinsale has managed to break all the rules of standard romance writing and come away shining." —*San Diego Union-Tribune*

978-1-4022-4689-0 • $9.99 U.S./$11.99 CAN